continued . . .

Kris Longknife
INTREPID

"[Kris Longknife] will remind readers of David Weber's Honor Harrington with her strength and intelligence. Mike Shepherd provides an exciting military science fiction thriller."
—*Genre Go Round Reviews*

"A good read for fans of the series and of military science fiction."
—*RT Book Reviews*

Kris Longknife
AUDACIOUS

"Mike Shepherd is a fantastic storyteller who excels at writing military science fiction. His protagonist is a strong-willed, independent thinker who does what she thinks is best for humanity . . . There is plenty of action and tension . . . This is a thoroughly enjoyable reading experience for science fiction fans."
—*Midwest Book Review*

" 'I'm a woman of very few words, but lots of action': So said Mae West, but it might just as well have been Lieutenant Kris Longknife, princess of the one hundred worlds of Wardhaven. Kris can kick, shoot, and punch her way out of any dangerous situation, and she can do it while wearing stilettos and a tight cocktail dress. She's all business, with a Hells Angel handshake and a 'get out of my face' attitude. But her hair always looks good."
—*Sci Fi Weekly*

"The [fifth] book in this fast-paced, exciting military SF series continues the saga of a strong heroine who knows how to kick serious ass and make an impression on friends and enemies alike. Mike Shepherd has a great ear for dialogue and talent for injecting dry humor into things at just the right moment . . . The characters are engaging, and the plot is full of twists and peppered liberally with sharply described action . . . Military SF fans are bound to get a kick out of the series as a whole, and fans will be glad to see Kris hasn't lost any of her edge."
—*SF Site*

More praise for the Kris Longknife novels

"A whopping good read . . . fast-paced, exciting, nicely detailed, with some innovative touches."

—Elizabeth Moon, Nebula Award–winning author of
Echoes of Betrayal

"Shepherd's grasp of timing and intrigue remains solid, and Kris's latest challenge makes for an engaging space opera, seasoned with political machination and the thrills of mysterious ancient technology, that promises to reveal some interesting things about the future Kris inhabits." —*Booklist*

"Everyone who has read Kris Longknife will hope for further adventures starring this brave, independent, and intrepid heroine. Mike Shepherd has written an action-packed, exciting space opera that starts at light speed and just keeps getting better. This is outer-space military science fiction at its adventurous best." —*Midwest Book Review*

"I'm looking forward to her next adventure."

—*The Weekly Press* (Philadelphia)

"Fans of the Honor Harrington escapades will welcome the adventures of another strong female in outer space starring in a thrill-a-page military space opera. The heroine's dry wit, ability to know what she is good at [as well as] her faults, [all] while keeping her regal DNA in perspective, especially during a crisis, endear her to readers. The audience will root for the determined, courageous, and endearing heroine as she displays intelligence and leadership during lethal confrontations."

—*Alternative Worlds*

"[Shepherd] has a good sense of pace . . . Very neatly handled, and served with a twist of wry." —*Bewildering Stories*

"If you're looking for an entertaining space opera with some colorful characters, this is your book. Shepherd grew up Navy, and he does an excellent job of showing the complex demands and duties of an officer. I look forward to the next in the series."

—*Books 'n' Bytes*

Kris Longknife
FURIOUS

Mike Shepherd

ACE BOOKS, NEW YORK

THE BERKLEY PUBLISHING GROUP
Published by the Penguin Group
Penguin Group (USA) Inc.
375 Hudson Street, New York, New York 10014, USA
Penguin Group (Canada), 90 Eglinton Avenue East, Suite 700, Toronto, Ontario M4P 2Y3, Canada
(a division of Pearson Penguin Canada Inc.) • Penguin Books Ltd., 80 Strand, London WC2R 0RL,
England • Penguin Group Ireland, 25 St. Stephen's Green, Dublin 2, Ireland (a division of Penguin
Books Ltd.) • Penguin Group (Australia), 250 Camberwell Road, Camberwell, Victoria 3124, Australia
(a division of Pearson Australia Group Pty. Ltd.) • Penguin Books India Pvt. Ltd., 11 Community
Centre, Panchsheel Park, New Delhi—110 017, India • Penguin Group (NZ), 67 Apollo Drive,
Rosedale, Auckland 0632, New Zealand (a division of Pearson New Zealand Ltd.) • Penguin Books
(South Africa) (Pty.) Ltd., 24 Sturdee Avenue, Rosebank, Johannesburg 2196, South Africa

Penguin Books Ltd., Registered Offices: 80 Strand, London WC2R 0RL, England

This is a work of fiction. Names, characters, places, and incidents either are the product of the author's
imagination or are used fictitiously, and any resemblance to actual persons, living or dead, business
establishments, events, or locales is entirely coincidental. The publisher does not have any control over
and does not assume any responsibility for author or third-party websites or their content.

KRIS LONGKNIFE: FURIOUS

An Ace Book / published by arrangement with the author

PUBLISHING HISTORY
Ace mass-market edition / November 2012

Copyright © 2012 by Mike Moscoe.
Cover art by Scott Grimando.
Cover design by Annette Fiore DeFex.
Interior text design by Kristin del Rosario.

ISBN: 978-1-937007-39-3

ACE
Ace Books are published by The Berkley Publishing Group,
a division of Penguin Group (USA) Inc.,
375 Hudson Street, New York, New York 10014.
ACE and the "A" design are trademarks of Penguin Group (USA) Inc.

PRINTED IN THE UNITED STATES OF AMERICA

10 9 8 7 6 5 4 3 2 1

1

Princess Kristine Longknife studied herself in the mirror above the bar. She didn't look any different. Her Navy blues still sported the two and a half stripes of a lieutenant commander. Why did she *feel* so different?

She sat in her usual chair at the far end of the bar. The next eight chairs were empty, by mutual consent of both her and the small crowd at the other end. A few misinformed men had entered her space.

One look from Kris, and they fled.

At the other end of the bar, quiet chatter rose and fell. An occasional joke brought forth bleary laughter. A deathly hush resided at Kris's end.

The emphasis was on death.

Kris lifted her nightly liter of Scotch and swirled the liquid around, studying it in the faint light. This faithful soldier was about half-gone.

Kris poured herself another shot of the fiery liquid. There was no tremble in her hands. No sign at all that she had polished off the first half of her nightly allotment in the three hours since she had come off duty.

She downed the shot without tasting it. Some people waxed

lyrical about the warmth of good Scottish whiskey as it passed from lips to stomach.

Kris hated the stuff.

To her it tasted more like something for cleaning paint-encrusted brushes, something you'd punish yourself by imbibing.

"Punish." There was that word again. It seemed to come up a lot in Kris's thoughts.

"Punish," as in they're dead, and you're alive, and you ought to be punished for that state of affairs.

Kris poured herself more poison and drank it down. The last time she had crawled into a bottle, after little Eddy died, and she survived the kidnapping, the liquor at least did its job. It wrapped her in cotton candy and made the days easy to forget and deadened the terrors of the nights.

Now her nightly self-medication did nothing to tame the nightmares.

Well, she'd managed to show up at the squadron with nothing worse than a dull headache from the night before. And no, so far, she hadn't let herself partake of the hair of the dog that bit her the night before. The fast patrol boats were puny, but any warship, no matter how tiny, could easily turn and kill a handler who did not treat her with respect.

Kris had killed enough already. She would not add more to her list of slaughtered subordinates.

Kris poured another shot and eyed it like she might some hostile alien cruiser. She'd had quite a few of them in the crosshairs of her 24-inch pulse lasers. Those she knew how to handle.

It was what you did after you'd won the fight that had Kris defeated.

She reached for her punishment.

"Auntie Kris, please come home," left Kris clenching an empty fist.

A glance in the mirror above her head showed a thirteen-year-old girl in a tee that shimmered through the faces of some popular band. Her swirling floor-length skirt showed every color of the rainbow, and sparkled as well.

Kris closed her eyes against the glare; teenagers were going to go blind before they reached twenty if all those riotous colors stayed in fashion. The Navy officer turned to face her latest truant officer. "You can't come in here. You're under age."

Cara, one of the few survivors of Kris's company, gave her a short teen shrug . . . *whatever* . . . and shot the barkeep a quick, easy grin. He went on doing what he was doing at the other end of the bar, and Cara flounced over to sit next to Kris.

"It doesn't seem that anything is really illegal on Madigan's Rainbow so long as it doesn't mess with one of the shareholders."

The thirteen-year-old had gotten that right. The hired help could do just about anything on this benighted planet. Anything but upset one of the old farts who owned a share in the place. Inconvenience one of them, and you'd be on the next ship out.

Maybe inside with oxygen to breathe if you didn't piss them off too much. Otherwise, maybe outside with not so much to breathe.

"You know, the day after I arrived, I tried to buy a share in this . . . place," Kris settled for. Cussing in front of a thirteen-year-old girl seemed undignified. Besides, considering Cara's background on New Eden, she likely knew far worse than Kris had picked up in her sheltered upbringing and years in the Navy.

"You did?" Cara answered, wide-eyed. "What happened?"

Warming to a conversation with someone who would let Kris ramble where she chose, the princess and major shareholder in Nuu Enterprises went on.

"I plunked down a credit chit worth two shares, dared them to say I wasn't rich enough to buy into their little hideaway."

"Wow," was Cara's innocent reaction.

"Then the planet manager let me in on a little secret. You don't just have to have money; you got to be liked."

"Oh," Cara said. Even a teenager from New Eden knew the reputation Longknifes had in human space.

"Yep, any shareholder could veto any new applicant."

"What happened?" was more a space holder than a question.

"An hour after the general manager sent out my application,

she had a list of vetoes that was longer than her stockholders list."

"How'd that happen?" Now there was honest puzzlement, rare in a teenager.

"Some people vetoed me twice. Didn't want to risk their first veto getting lost on the net."

"Oh," Cara said. "I see."

"Yeah," Kris said, downing the drink she'd poured before Cara arrived. "I may have billions of good Wardhaven dollars in my portfolio, but I'm just a scat-lugging hireling on Madigan's Rainbow."

Kris considered that as she poured her next drink. After surveying the smooth flow of liquid from bottle to shot glass, she made a command decision.

"Barkeep, a drink for my short friend here."

"I'm not that much shorter than you," Cara snorted under her breath. And she spoke the truth. Her last growth spurt, fueled by good food on the *Wasp*, was carrying her close to Kris's own six feet.

Further discussions of altitude and attitude was cut short by the bartender's curt, "What will you have?"

"A Shirley Temple," Cara beamed proudly, "with three cherries."

The bartender set to work at his end of the bar.

"Where'd you learn about a Shirley Temple?" Kris demanded after downing her own poison and refilling her glass.

"Auntie Abby told me to order one if you insisted I drink something."

Unlike "Auntie Kris," Abby really was Cara's aunt, and only living relative in human space. Not that following a Longknife around both in and out of human space made it all that easy to stay a *living* person, relative or otherwise.

Abby was nominally Kris's maid. She was also a whole lot more, some of which helped Kris stay alive.

Sometimes.

Barely.

At the moment, no one could help Kris stay alive but Kris. Maybe.

"So," Kris said, belting down another shot, "why'd Abby send you to get me?"

"Because she already had one black eye and doesn't want another," had the kind of innocent truth that one mumbled under one's breath, not expecting a teenager to pick up on it and pass it along.

It was also true.

Last night, Kris had objected to being dragged off to bed before her liter was a truly dead soldier. Surprises of surprises, Kris had caught Abby off guard and landed a good one. Shocked, whether at what she'd done or that Abby had actually dropped her guard for a second, Kris went docilely to bed.

And had to suffer through today with more attention and less of a headache.

Sending a kid, and a girl at that. Abby was really playing dirty.

Kris managed to get three more shots in while Cara polished off her drink and openly relished the taste of each bright red cherry.

Last cherry gone, Cara hopped off her chair and grinned at Kris. "Time to go."

"Why?" Kris answered belligerently.

"I got a surprise for you."

"What kind of surprise?"

"If I told you, it wouldn't be a surprise," had the kind of logic even a three-year-old could understand. A three-year-old or a drunk.

Kris was neither. At least the lack of the trembles seemed to say so. After weighing her options only slightly less carefully than Kris weighed starting a war between the entire human race and some really nasty aliens, Kris decided to follow Cara.

The young woman led: out of the bar, out of the hotel, and out into the streets of Elysian Fields. It was late, and the streetlights had already been dimmed. It was an obvious encouragement to all the worker bees that management expected you to be early to bed and early to rise.

Few here held out any hope of being healthy, wealthy, or wise. You either made it before you got here, or you did what you were told and were grateful for the chance.

There were a few exceptions to that policy. Do something that really won the approval of management, and you might be rewarded with a significant bounty.

Kris suspected that catching one Kris Longknife in an escape attempt had a very high bounty on it. No one had told her, but the looks she got, the questions she was asked whenever she varied one millimeter from her normal schedule fairly shouted a bounty with a lot of zeros and commas. Kris might be wanted for crimes against humanity on 150 planets, but she wasn't dumb, or any less observant than she'd been when she got herself into this mess.

Tonight, as they made their way back to Kris's nearly palatial quarters . . . after all, she *was* a Longknife and she *did* command FastPatRon 127, the main defense Madigan's Rainbow had against smugglers and the odd alien scow that might wander by . . . Cara gabbed up a blue streak. She talked about how this or that reminded her of that place or the other on New Eden.

Kris hadn't spent that much time on New Eden before the government invited her to go elsewhere in a hurry. But Elysian Fields did not look at all like Eden's main city. New Eden was run-down and shabby, in need of urban renewal or at least several new coats of paint. Fields was washed and scrubbed, planted and flowering . . . or else.

Kris let the teenager babble while walking a straight line to prove she could.

Then Cara took a turn that Kris normally didn't take on her walk home. It wasn't a turn that would make her miss Kris's quarters, it was just that Kris had fallen into a habit of always taking the more scenic route. The one next to the park. It left her in easy reach of a bush if the Scotch suddenly demanded to vacate the premises.

Cara turned away from the park and onto a road lined with four-to-eight-story walk-ups.

Pickled brain or no, Kris checked for her service-issue automatic. It was in its usual place in the small of her back. This could just be a new kid in town taking a shortcut through a bad part of town.

Officially, Fields had no "bad" part of town. Still, there were places that fell well below the medium income. Some of the old

codgers living here had reputations. There were whispered stories of how they'd made their billions without benefit of law and
in ways the courts would have frowned upon if they'd come to
their attention. Kris had picked up hints that things were not
always as calm as they seemed among the owners.

There had to be someplace on the planet where one could
procure that which wasn't displayed in the gleaming windows
of the stores.

Cara made another turn, still talking like a magpie. The
alcoholic buzz was gone. Kris was on full alert. Cara was now
walking away from their quarters.

Inconspicuously, Kris's eyes roved, looking for a friendly
cop, who would most solicitously tell Kris she was not going
the way she should and ask why.

Or a thug looking for a big payday and finding a spectacular one. Just the value of the raw components of the computer
at Kris's neck would make the thief a billionaire.

Not that Nelly had said a word to Kris in over three weeks.

There was, of course, always the risk of an assassin. Kris
had dodged plenty of them. Some genius had cut her security
detail here to zero . . . well, Abby . . . insisting that Madigan's
Rainbow was a totally benign planet.

Like there would ever be one where Kris was concerned.

There was a reason Kris was wanted on 150 planets. And
a lot of people going through worse stages of grief than she
was would gladly see her dead.

Fear blew a cold wind through Kris's brain, driving the
final wisps of whiskey's self-induced fog before it. Still yap-
ping, Cara stooped to check her shoe. "I got this huge rock in
it," she insisted.

Kris ground her teeth. They had stopped in front of a nar-
row alley. The smell of garbage and urine assailed the air.
More proof that these Elysian fields had an ugly underbelly.
Kris peered into the dark of the alley but could see nothing.

Cara stood up and huffed "I'm glad that's taken care of."

THE DECEPTION IS GOING FINE, Nelly said, speaking in
Kris's head for the first time in almost a month. NOW GET
YOUR DRUNK ASS UP THAT ALLEY, YOUR STUPID HIGHNESS.

2

Kris fled up the alley, stumbling over trash and garbage, bouncing first off the right wall, then the left. A door opened, showing little light. The shadow of an arm reached out and grabbed for Kris's shoulder.

GET INSIDE, Nelly screamed in Kris's skull.

Kris let herself be guided in the door.

"Gee, that was fun!" Cara said, hardly out of breath.

Kris, more out of shape than she wanted to admit, still gasped out, "What's going on here?" as she produced her automatic. She held it low, not pointed at anyone or anything in particular.

But at everything in general.

"Put the gun away," an all-too-familiar and wonderful voice said even as the lighting went from near nonexistent to just painfully dim.

"Penny!" Kris managed not to shout. "What are you doing here?"

"Trying to stay invisible," said the Navy lieutenant, intelligence officer, and daughter of a cop. She aimed Kris at a cheap dining-room table with four mismatched and even shabbier chairs. Abby, Kris's erstwhile maid, was already in one. Cara slipped easily into another. Penny settled Kris in the one facing Abby before taking the last chair.

Kris took a moment to survey her surroundings. The room was tiny, cluttered with dirty dishes, leftover Chinese food cartons, and other junk. Several cockroaches scuttled from the brighter light. This was not Kris's Tac Center on the *Wasp*. Still, with the present company, it felt more like home than anyplace Kris had been for way too long.

"And invisible we will stay," Nelly said from around Kris's neck. Kris's personal computer had been often upgraded since it was given to her before first grade. After the latest upgrades, she'd taken to arguing with Kris more often than not. And now she told atrocious jokes. The alien chip Kris had volunteered to have planted in Nelly's self-organizing matrix for examination might have had something to do with the present state of affairs.

It didn't matter. The last month, while Nelly had given Kris the silent treatment, had been its own special kind of hell.

"I've fed old feed, properly revised, so that our watching dogs will not notice the loop," Nelly went on. "It shows Kris and Cara taking a side trip into the park to violate a bush. Kris is now collapsed in her own vomit, and Cara is crying for her to get up, while making sure Our Princess doesn't suffocate. That should keep the boys at the station house delighted for some time."

"Did you have to make me that disgusting?" Kris grumbled.

"I would have made it worse," Abby snapped, rubbing gingerly at her eye.

"I'm sorry about that," Kris said. "I never thought I could lay a hand on you."

"And you wouldn't have," Abby said, "if I hadn't let you. This shiner was just the excuse I needed to let the security cameras in our quarters show me sulking in my bath while I sent poor Cara to beard the beast tonight."

"We've got security cameras in our bathrooms!" Kris squeaked.

"Goes to show how much you needed me," Nelly said.

"All of us are under a tight security lockdown," Penny said.

Kris might have befogged her brain an hour ago, but that didn't mean she'd miss important information now. "You aren't supposed to be here," she said to Penny.

"My assumption is that if I'm caught, my folks will not get a body to bury."

Kris leaned back in her chair. "It's that bad?"

"Baby ducks," Abby said, "consider yourself to have gotten off easy. I was told in no uncertain terms that if I did anything but help you look pretty and presentable, Cara and I would end up dead, very dead. Haven't you noticed how good I've been lately?"

"I noticed you showed up with only three self-propelled steamer trunks," Kris said. Until Kris got the *Wasp* for her home away from home, she and her team had gauged how much trouble they were in by the number of steamer trunks following Abby through customs. It wasn't unusual for her to leave Kris's quarters with three or four and have as many as a dozen following her an hour later.

What she produced from them was always amazing and usually critical to keeping Kris and company alive.

Now Abby chuckled. "You had your royal head so far up your ass, I didn't think you noticed."

"Did most of your tricks get confiscated?" Kris asked

"Most, but not all. Nowhere close to all. What surprised me is that none of them even tried to get their meat hooks into Nelly or any of her kids."

"I had something to do with that," Nelly said, seeming to clear her nonexistent throat. "There wasn't a lot on Wardhaven about me and the kids. What there was, I made disappear. It's easy to run boneheads around in circles if they don't know what I've got up my sleeves."

"Smart move," Penny said, stroking Mimzy at her own collar. There weren't just four sharp minds met around this table, but eight.

"Where's Jack?" Kris asked, choking on the question.

Penny shook her head. "He didn't play cool. When they put you on that fast boat to Wardhaven with no security, Jack went ballistic. No common sense at all. What got into that man?"

"We kissed," Kris said softly, letting the memory of Jack's soft caress warm her.

"Oh," Penny said. "That explains it."

The four women sat silently for a moment, savoring that revelation.

"Yes," Kris whispered. "For a few seconds there on the pier at High Chance, we were making up for lost time." Internally, Kris winced at her choice of words. A bride of three days when widowed fighting under Kris's command, Penny of all people did not need to hear of lost time.

But Penny only nodded before going on. "Jack was pretty adamant that he had to follow you. You weren't safe without him. Admiral Santiago did her best to calm things down. Did she see the way it was between you two?"

"Yeah," Kris admitted.

"Now I understand Jack's problem," Penny said. "Dumb me. I should have put two and two together, but I never thought you two would ever find the time for something more serious than arguing over your next stupid or suicidal move."

"Me neither," Kris muttered. "But when you're being chased across the galaxy, by really nasty and mad aliens, sometimes you think about what's really important."

The three others gave that thought the sardonic chuckle it deserved. They'd all been with Kris on the *Wasp*, making high-speed jumps into the unknown. Dodging some pretty upset and vengeful aliens. Not knowing if they'd have the fuel to slow down. Or the wits to find their way home.

"Where is Jack now?" Kris asked.

"He's detailed to security on HellFrozeOver," Penny said.

"You're kidding," Kris said.

"What's that?" Cara asked.

"A naval station in the Wardhaven system," Nelly said quickly. "It orbits a large gas giant, and the base sends tankers down into it to recover reaction mass, which is then shipped to High Wardhaven for fleet use. There is also a private concern that does the same for commercial use. There are unconfirmed reports that very top secret research is also carried out at the base, but the government refuses to answer questions."

"Wow," Cara said.

"The night I announced that I'd joined the Navy, my father swore he'd see that my entire career was on HellFrozeOver," Kris said. "He's threatened me with it a few other times. Jack must have really pissed them off. Is he in charge of security?"

"Nope," Penny answered. "They don't trust him any farther than they can throw him and a herd of elephants. The commander of that hellhole, with orders to ride close herd on Jack, is a certain Colonel Hancock."

"Old Hard Case himself!" Kris said.

"You know him?" Penny asked.

"I served with him on the Olympic Humanitarian Mission. Another hellhole, only this one rainy and bandit-ridden. I wondered what happened to him after that mission closed down. I thought he'd have the good sense to get the message and retire."

"How many people around you are afflicted with good sense?" Abby asked dryly.

Kris shrugged an admission of the question, if not an answer.

"You got any IOUs with Colonel Hancock?" Penny asked.

Kris shook her head. "He saved my bacon once or twice, and mine and Tommy's neck once when I got us up a flooding creek without a boat, or rather with a boat that suddenly wasn't there." At the questioning glances, Kris shrugged. "There was a problem with Smart Metal that was dumb. Or maybe intended to kill me. Nothing that could stand up in a court of law. You know how that goes."

"Oh don't we," all the women said in three-part harmony.

"So, if any markers were left on the table," Penny concluded, "they're yours, not his."

"Sad but true," Kris admitted.

"Let's face it." Abby said. "Most everyone who's met our girl here is only too glad to see her rear end sashaying out of their lives. I don't know many who want to see that flat chest of hers coming at them."

"Oh, I love your way with words," Kris said with a sigh.

"Well, I know of at least one fellow whose first thoughts are of you," Penny said.

"Who would that poor fool be?" Abby asked.

"A certain cop on New Eden. You remember an Inspector Juan Martinez?"

"Yes, good man," Kris said. "He and his proud caballeros helped save a whole lot of people's necks, including mine, when one of Harry Peterwald's henchmen tried to replace their government with something more sympathetic to Green-feld's imperial goals. What's he up to now?"

"Making sure that someone else doesn't foist a government on New Eden more to their liking than the one the people of New Eden might choose on their own," Penny said.

"And this matters to us how?" Abby drawled.

"I'm getting to it, and it's why I'm risking my neck looking you three up to gab about old times. It seems that somebody intended to rig last month's elections on New Eden. Part of it was sleight of hand, part of it was inciting some unhappy folks to do things that might or might not be in their best interests. Anyway, Juan and some of his police friends got wind of what was happening, and, having been burned once, they were a bit more shy of this crap than the average guy.

"After everything but the crying was over, a reporter, Winston Spencer, drew the assignment to cover the story for Galactic News Network. He and Juan are talking over a drink or two when it comes up that they have both had the misfortune of making your acquaintance. You do know both of them, don't you?" Penny asked.

"I'm acquainted with the reporter," Kris lied. "I don't really know him."

From the looks on Abby's and Penny's faces, she could have saved herself the lie. Neither was buying it.

With a scowl, Penny went on. "So Juan tells Winston more than what made it into the official police reports on the incident."

Abby put her elbows on the table and rested her chin on her spread fingers. "Do tell," she said, the image of a gossip in full harp.

"It seems one of the main movers and shakers of this conspiracy liked to brag to his girlfriends about what a big man he was. He blabbed pretty much the entire scheme, but he added an extra twist. They were going to solve the alien problem as well."

"Alien problem? What's that mean?" Kris asked.

"Juan doesn't know, but what he does know is that the talking dude was found by his girlfriends the next day with his throat slit. That's what sent them to the police."

"But they didn't know what he meant by that," Kris said.

"Nothing. The investigation found only a whole lot of nothing when they tried to follow up on it."

"And you risked coming here why?" Kris asked.

"Because, at the very bottom of the pit, in the dark that couldn't be pulled into the light of any court, Juan and his cops found the fingerprints of your grandpa, Alex Longknife."

Abby whistled.

"Now do you see why I'm risking my neck for this quality time together?" Penny asked, glancing at the squalor around them. "Your rich grandfather who swore never to get involved in politics again is using ugly means to try to take over planets. And his henchmen think this is only a means to an end that might have aliens involved."

Kris pushed herself gingerly away from the table, trying not to put her hands into anything that might have mutated into something deadly, all the time shaking her head at the thought of how much death and mayhem a way-too-scared and way-too-wealthy Longknife could create.

"I don't think this calls for a drink," was all she could think to say.

"I'll drink to that," Nelly said.

3

Kris let her team enjoy Nelly's joke. "You're getting better, girl," she told her personal and not very personable computer.

"I didn't have much to do for the last month," Nelly answered, pointedly.

"Well, the vacation is over. Nelly, how safe are we at the moment?"

"You're stretching your safety margins. Abby needs to get out of that bath, and you need to get out of your vomit. Penny, here, needs to get moving. This hideout is needed by some real thugs, and I can't vouch for the cops not banging down the door much after they get here."

"Can you and your kids keep Penny off the security net?" Kris asked.

"We've done it for a week now."

"You've been here a week?" Kris said.

"I needed a couple of days to connect with Abby, then a few more to set up this meeting. Kris, if you think you've lived in a security bubble before, you have no idea how tight things are around you now."

"Yeah," Kris admitted. She hadn't known, and she hadn't been all that interested in knowing how tight the shackles were on her legs. It didn't seem to matter, there was no way to cut the chains.

And no real reason to try.

Now she had a reason.

Jack needed help to get out of his mess. And, apparently, all human space needed to be saved from one of her relatives.

Oh joy.

With a promise from Nelly to arrange another meeting soon, they slipped away. The light in the room once again became near nonexistent. Penny went first, her clothes ninja black, and, Kris suspected, absorbing her body heat to make her a hole in the night. Abby went next and vanished before her footsteps were lost in the night.

Kris and Cara quickly found themselves back on the street, retracing their path to the road across from the park. Cara put her shoulder under Kris's arms, and the two of them staggered a bit.

YOU'RE BACK ON THE GRID, Nelly warned Kris. The walk back to quarters went quickly, with Kris trying to absorb all that had been dumped on her.

She really was a prisoner here.

Jack was locked away just as tight and had even less of a chance than she did to get out of jail.

Grampa Al, of all people, was dabbling in politics *and* alien affairs!

And none of it got down to the real problem: Kris had started a war with alien hordes, and humanity seemed intent on pretending it hadn't happened.

Back in her quarters, Kris played her part. She dutifully apologized to Abby for her black eye . . . and was ignored by her surly maid. She sputtered through a cold shower, griping the whole time at Abby, then let herself be put to bed.

Only after the lights were turned out did she attempt to contact Nelly.

CAN WE TALK? Kris asked her computer.

IF WE DON'T DO TOO MUCH OF IT. I THINK THEY'RE MONITORING MY ELECTRICAL USE AND YOUR BRAIN ACTIVITY.

CAN THEY DO THAT?

I WOULD. NOW QUIT WASTING TIME.

CAN YOU GET ME OFF THIS PLANET THE SAME WAY YOU GOT PENNY HERE?

NOT LIKELY. WE'LL HAVE TO COME UP WITH SOMETHING ELSE.

ARE YOU WORKING ON IT?

OF COURSE, KRIS. IF WE DIDN'T THINK WE HAD A CHANCE, WE NEVER WOULD HAVE LET PENNY BRING MIMZY DOWN HERE.

Right, of course. Nelly would never needlessly risk one of her kids.

KRIS, I NEED TO DO SOME OTHER STUFF, AND I CAN'T DO IT AND TALK TO YOU. THAT WAS ONE OF THE REASONS I WASN'T TALKING TO YOU. THAT AND YOU BEING A LUSH. I'LL TALK MORE WHEN I HAVE SOMETHING TO SAY. GOOD NIGHT.

On that note, Kris rolled over. And found she could not sleep.

Undulled by alcohol, her mind spun madly through the last five years of her life. Assassination attempts, one after another, flashed before her. And battles—battle after battle with high butcher bills extracted from enemy and friend alike.

Kris tried squeezing her eyes tighter shut. She did everything she could to drive her skull to blankness.

Nothing worked.

Finally, a tiny voice in the back of her head asked, *Do you really want to go back to this? Are you crazy enough to think they're worth saving yet again?*

"No," Kris shot back to herself. "I've never wanted all that. I'm not crazy."

Well, you're sure acting crazy. Look around you. You're safe here. No one's taking potshots at you. No one's asking you to go out and save the world. Hell, Kris, what has saving anything got you but a kick in the gut? Has anyone ever said thank you?

Kris sighed. This other self had a point.

I mean, you don't have to crawl into a bottle, any more than you have to get back onto this damn horse and go charging back out into the bloody slaughter for those ungrateful SOBs. Calm down, girl. Take a deep breath. You can put your time on Madigan's Rainbow to better use. There's no reason why you have to gallop out of here and pull their and Grampa Al's chestnuts out of the fire.

Kris took that deep breath. She was none too sure where this other self of hers was coming from, but she did have some very good points. Yes, Penny and Abby had risked a lot to get her a chance to bust out, but where was she going?

Don't have any idea, do you? that voice pointed out.

But then you usually don't have a clue where you're going and what you'll do when you get there, another side of Kris joined in from somewhere deep in herself. *You don't know, but somehow you pull the right miraculous rabbit out of your hat. That's what you do best. Right?*

Yeah, right, came back at her. *But you know you're running out of rabbits. Even Captain Drago said you were scraping the bottom of your rainbow's pot of gold. How much longer before there's just no more of you left?*

Kris allowed herself another deep breath. Both her selves were dead-on. And if Kris was honest with herself, her stay-here version was way ahead on points.

What was there out there for her but more bloody gambles with her own and a whole lot of other people's lives?

There's Jack. Because he got crosswise with those damn Longknifes, they've got him locked in a corner. He could be stuck there for the rest of his life unless someone like you lends him a hand, came back at Kris.

Kris found herself scowling. Nobody put Jack in a corner. Not while she had a say in it. And besides, she wanted Jack. She needed Jack. She even missed fighting with him. She missed bouncing ideas off him. Missed having him bent over a battle board beside her, the smell of him close. His warmth . . .

Right, his warmth close but never touched. Never touched until she finally did . . . and they carted her away and left him standing there on the dock.

That decided it for Kris. Not for all humanity. Not for Grampa Al. Certainly not for King Ray. But for Jack. Yes. For Jack, Kris would take this ticket out of her quiet little corner of the universe and see what havoc the morrow brought.

Kris rolled over to the other side and went to sleep, perchance to dream of Jack.

4

Next morning, Kris went about her duties as commander of FastPatRon 127 much the same way she had for the last month, but now her eyes saw what she'd ignored.

She was most definitely locked away in Siberia.

Her XO was always at her elbow; she or the leading chief was Kris's constant shadow. Kris couldn't go to the head without company. And her duties involved spending a whole lot of time in meetings and even more at her desk, reviewing paperwork.

Kris had never really commanded a ship. On the *Wasp*, she had Captain Drago to handle all the administrative details. When she'd commanded PF-109, they'd operated by Hooligan Navy standards and left most of the boring stuff to Commander Mandanti on their tender.

Did it really take all these reports to run a dozen small ships?

She'd managed only one jaunt up to the space station to review her twelve fast patrol boats and their crews in person.

Only one.

Clearly, someone had heard of the legendary charisma and leadership of those damn Longknifes and was taking no chances that Kris might actually lead her squadron into something that the powers that be didn't want. Kris had to wonder just how scared they were of her. The fast patrol boats were tiny things, powered by small matter/antimatter reactors. No one in their right mind would risk them in star jumps.

Then again, the Longknife legend didn't credit Kris's relatives with much right-mindedness. And Kris's Navy career to date didn't show much evidence of one for her either.

After a morning full of meetings with people who loved the sound of their own voices and weren't much good at listening, lunch was at the club. With no significant military presence, Madigan's Rainbow had no officer's club, but there was one restaurant that doubled as the place for the top managers of Elysian Fields to see and be seen.

As usual, Kris's lunch turned into a four-martini affair. Her XO saw that Kris's glass was refilled anytime it got close to empty.

DON'T YOU EVEN THINK OF REDUCING YOUR ALCOHOLIC INTAKE, Nelly warned before Kris could do just that.

Kris did manage to leave some slop in the bottom of the fourth.

HIT THE HEAD, Nelly ordered cryptically, as Kris headed back to work.

Kris excused herself from her XO, who suddenly manifested a need for the same stop.

THIRD STALL.

Kris went to it.

FEEL INSIDE THE TOILET-PAPER DISPENSER.

Kris made to get some paper to blow her nose . . . and found a small vial with an easy open lid, something like those used for eye drops.

KEEP IT HIDDEN, BUT PUT A DROP ON YOUR FINGER, AND PUT IT ON THE BACK OF YOUR TONGUE.

Kris did—and was immediately and violently sick.

KEEP THAT HANDY, Nelly said. GOOD-BYE.

A moment later, Kris sheepishly cleaned out her mouth and washed her face under the eyes of her watchdog XO.

"I guess I can't hold my liquor like I used to," Kris said.

"Maybe you ought to check in with the clinic. Any chance you could be pregnant?"

Kris laughed at the thought. "Even Longknifes need a man

for that, and, no, my last assignment was a tad too busy for anything like that."

The XO had made a point of not wanting to know anything about Kris's last mission. So had everyone else Kris ran into.

Everyone.

First night on planet, Kris had wandered into a karaoke bar and hit upon an idea. She signed up for a stint singing.

Once Kris got her hands on the mike, she didn't sing a note, but started laying out for all what she'd seen and done.

At least Kris had tried.

She hadn't gotten three words out before four burly men appeared out of nowhere and grabbed her. A smaller man got his hands on the mike and started singing off-key, while the others hustled her out the back door of the bar.

A calm-looking little guy in a suit smoking something joined them in the dark alley. He finished his smoke while eyeing Kris, then flicked the butt at her.

"Don't *ever* try that again," he said. "Next time, my associate will get to play with you a lot more. A whole lot more." He turned on his heels and left. A minute later, the four guys let go of Kris and seemed to vanish into thin air.

Kris was left shaking. She was shocked that she had been taken so easily. Anger and frustration filled her at what had been done to her. Barely able to stand, she stumbled down the street and into the bar that became her regular.

She found herself drinking as she thought over her problems. Then she found herself just drinking because she had problems.

In the end, she just drank.

Afternoons at the squadron had always been a blur to Kris. After a four-martini lunch, how could it be otherwise? Today, her XO brought her the usual pile of reports she said Kris needed to read.

Today, she read. They were long, detailed reports on ships boarded and health, safety, and drug inspections conducted by her boats. Cargo manifests were carefully reviewed and containers checked with contents verified. New passenger arrivals, their qualifications, and future jobs were all here, as well as who was vouching for them and the duration of their contracts. They were usually for thirty years plus.

Why am I reading all this junk?

Right, she was reading it because her subordinate told her she had to, and she didn't know better. Or have anything better to do.

Kris started to throw the thick printouts across the room.

Then thought better of it.

NELLY, IS THIS ROOM BUGGED?

FOUR VISUAL, FOUR ELECTROMAGNETIC, AND EIGHT AUDIO. DON'T TALK TO ME.

Kris put a dazed look back on her face and continued slowly thumbing through the reports. On the last page of each, she scrawled her signature as illegibly as she could manage. It was all a blur, but that was how Kris thought she'd been doing it.

Fifteen minutes before quitting time, her XO came in to review Kris's work, say some nice things, and take away the stack. It was enough to make Kris vomit without using her little bottle.

"Here's a list of ships coming in over the next couple of days," the XO said, slipping a flimsy onto Kris's desk in place of the pile she removed. "There should be no problem. Our ships will intercept each one of them close to the jump point and escort them to the station."

Kris nodded at the banality. Security was tight here, even she remembered hearing this all before. FastPatRon 127 was Coast Guard and Drug Enforcement, immigration control, and a whole lot of other stuff. What it wasn't was a fighting unit. If anyone ever threw so much as a harsh word in FastPatRon 127's direction, her captains wouldn't know what to do about it.

This was all wrong . . . and it was Kris's job to make it right . . . but no one wanted anything changed.

No wonder she was drinking again.

As her XO left, Kris put on her blues blouse and followed her. It was early, but Kris always left early. Kris gave her commanding subordinate a bleary smile and stumbled off.

"Royal Pain is gone for the day," was the last thing Kris heard as the door closed slowly behind her. Kris wondered who the report was directed to. Nelly could probably tell her but wouldn't. There was no need for Kris to know.

All that mattered was how good they were and if they were better than Nelly.

Kris swallowed a feral grin.

No one was better than Nelly.

At her usual place, her usual stool was empty. Her usual bottle was already open with her usual shot glass in place. Kris imagined that somewhere, someone was running a tab for her and sending a bill to Nelly to pay.

There were too many invisible fingers in this stew.

It had to change.

A silent hour later, Kris had polished off a fifth of her liter, and excused herself to the ladies' room to get rid of it before it did too much damage to her alertness tonight.

Two hours and another pit stop later, Cara showed up. She gaily ordered a Shirley Temple "with three cherries." While the barkeep was busy making it, Kris managed to slip a drop of her "medicine" down her throat.

As the bartender delivered Cara's drink, Kris was explosively sick right there on the bar.

Cara said "Eew" and removed herself a few stools over to enjoy her own nonalcoholic drink. Especially the cherries. Kris made insincere apologies to the barkeep as he cleaned up her mess.

He was very likely one of her keeps. He deserved all she could do to mess with his day.

Only when Cara had most sincerely enjoyed her drink did she offer to take Kris off the bartender's hands. He had several things to say about that, none at all nice.

Kris managed to upchuck her last drink with no help from her little vile of bile.

Cara and Kris staggered forth with only vituperations filling the air behind them.

The trip home was disappointingly dull. Still, Kris managed to spend a good half hour in the park. The stockholders had imported samples of most of the surviving songbirds of Earth. Kris was pretty sure that, if they could have managed it, they would have caged the birds for their sole pleasure. But the birds sang best when free, so as sunset came on, they sang in the park for rich and poor alike.

Kris was painfully reminded of how the world came alive

again for her younger self after Grampa Trouble sobered her up.

How could she have let herself crawl back into the bottle?

Well, she'd had some serious weights dragging her down and some serious help pushing her in. If only Nelly or someone would tell her what was coming down. She hated being treated like a kid again—shuffled from here to there with no idea of why.

When Cara said it was time to go, Kris went.

Abby ordered a shower to clean Kris up, then washed her hair of the stink left behind by throwing up on the bar. A hair wash from Abby was a sensual delight, from the smell of the shampoos she used to the kneading of her hands on Kris's scalp. Kris felt herself coming alive some more.

She still regretted the deaths of all those who'd followed her into hell and failed to come back to things like brilliant sunsets, chirping birds, and tingling shampoos.

They deserved better than they got.

But there was nothing Kris could do to make that up to them. Killing herself, or just living dead, would add or subtract nothing from their fate.

However, finding out what Grampa Al was up to might, just might, keep a whole lot more people from being added to the long list of dead that Longknifes were responsible for.

Kris went to bed with no objections. She occupied her falling asleep with memories of some of the more spectacular fights between her and Jack.

She let herself linger on those few moments when they shared that kiss, and fell asleep dreaming of more kisses to come.

5

"YOU afraid of the dark, claustrophobic, or would you mind suffocating to death?" Abby asked as she woke Kris up in the dark of the night.

The clock on Kris's night table said it was 2:00 A.M.

"I was kind of hoping not to die for a long, long time," Kris muttered.

"Right, I've heard the joke. In some other woman's bed with some other woman's husband. Quick. We don't have much time. Get in this."

This was one of Abby's steamer trunks. Kris had always suspected she could fit her slim, six-foot frame into one of them. Now was her chance to find out.

Only she found herself sharing it with several canisters, cans, boxes and other stuff she couldn't identify in the dark.

As Kris started wedging herself in she asked, "Where are you shipping me?"

"Out of system. You may be in a shipping container open to space for a while. Maybe a long while. Here are some pills. They'll help you sleep. Try not to turn on any lights for the first twenty-four hours."

"How will I know that?" Kris asked. It really was tight in there.

"I'll tell you," Nelly said. "Now hurry up. We can't keep hiding this, and we've got a whole lot more invisibility spells to cast."

Abby closed the trunk and latched down the lid.

Now Kris did discover the meaning of claustrophobia. She felt her panic rising, her pulse quickening. A need for light, space, freedom welled within her.

FOR CHRIST'S SAKE, KRIS, TAKE THE DAMN PILL! Nelly growled in Kris's skull.

Kris took one of the pills, even as she wondered where Nelly was getting these latest additions to her vocabulary.

In a couple of heartbeats, she felt calmer.

Then sleepy.

The thought crossed her mind that she might never wake up. That she might find out real soon what awaited people after life . . . if anything. She wondered if Tommy would be there, his wide, lopsided grin welcoming her as he said, "I told you so."

Even as the steamer trunk began to bump along on its way to who-knew-where, Kris was nodding off to sleep.

6

Kris felt the bright light even with her eyes closed.

So she opened her eyes. And blinked immediately. That light was really bright. Several blinks later, she started to make out a face.

It was smiling, and familiar.

It wasn't Tommy.

"You're dead," Kris said. "Am I?"

"The reports of my death are much exaggerated," came in a familiar drawl.

"Captain Elizabeth Luna, what do you mean you're not dead? I saw your ship blown out of space," Kris's eyes were getting used to the light. That, and someone had finally quit shining it right in her eyes.

"Those bad actors did indeed do severe bodily harm to the old *Archie*," Captain Luna agreed. "They also left a few vacancies in my crew, but, I will point out, not one for a captain."

"I see," Kris said, blinking rapidly.

"My owner had been complaining that the *Archimedes III* wasn't nearly as palatial as his other corporate buddies' yachts, so he wasn't heartbroken to send the insurers a bill for a new boat. They howled, but by the time I got my old bones out of the fancy body-and-fender shop he put me up in on Ward-haven, the new *Archimedes IV* was ready for business. It's never too hard to locate the right scoundrels for a ship like this, and I've been plying the space ways for several months while you were getting into all kinds of troubles."

"That I have," Kris admitted. "Say, is there a head any-where handy? I threw up most of what I drank yesterday, but there are still a few drops that wants to exit the old-fashioned way."

"Sailor, show this woman to our least-fancy head," Captain Luna ordered. So it was that Kris found herself doing her busi-ness in facilities that made the master suite at Nuu House look downright poorly. Quickly done, Kris rejoined her hostess.

"Would you mind telling me how you managed to pull this off? You and Nelly and, oh, hi Penny. I see you made it as well."

"Ms. Pasley has been my right-hand man for oh these last five years," Captain Luna assured Kris.

"Gosh," Kris said, falling into the down-home cadence of the captain. "And I thought she'd been my death-defying side-kick for all those five years."

The topic of the debate joined them in a walk down a curv-ing hallway whose decor would not have been out of place in a royal palace on Earth.

"I got the paperwork to prove my claim," Luna assured Kris.

"So where is Lieutenant Pasley?" Kris asked.

"She never left High Chance," Penny said. "Admiral San-tiago found a place for me on her staff. But I was pretty run-down, after all the running around a certain damn Longknife put me through," Penny said with a sly sideways glance at Kris.

"There was this place, Itsahfine, not much of a planet, but the ancient aliens who built the jump points had left a lot of dusty ruins on it. Once upon a time, Penny and a guy she'd just met thought it would be great to spend a long leave bouncing around the place." Penny's voice took on a faraway quality at the recollection of what she and Tommy had never done because he'd gotten too close to a damn Longknife.

"Anyway, Mimzy spotted a lone woman tourist who had

booked passage and rooms on Itsahfine and was my spitting image. Mimzy did a bit of this and that, and suddenly Lieutenant Pasley is taking sixty days of leave there and Third Officer Pasley is Captain Luna's long-serving hand."

"Will it hold up?" Kris asked.

"Itsahfine is pretty backward. Not much of a grid there to walk off of. It's held up so far. Mimzy swears that she's put in place a subroutine on the woman's credit chit. Whatever she pays for: Hotel, food, what have you will show up on my credit report. Sixty days from now, it will all vanish, and the charges will go back to whom they belong. As I see it, we've got six more of my eight weeks' leave to save humanity. That's not usually too tight a schedule for a Longknife I know to pull off a miracle or twelve."

Luna enjoyed a hearty belly laugh at that.

Kris nodded soberly, tasting the risk her friend was taking. "What about Abby and Cara? And how did you get me on this ship?"

"Getting you on wasn't all that hard," Luna insisted, and opened the door into quarters that made palatial look shabby. "This is the CEO's suite. If you promise not to trash it, it's yours for the trip."

Kris took the measure of the place, as much as she could see from the door. "I'm more worried about me finding my way out of here when the time comes. You got a GPS or something?"

"I'll make sure you don't get lost," Nelly said dryly.

"I figured Nelly would help," Captain Luna quipped. "Otherwise, I would have dumped you in something smaller. I really want you to hide out here for this voyage. Nobody's supposed to be in here. None of the crew will be coming in, and I don't want to wave you around too much."

"Are you afraid someone will turn us in?" Penny asked.

"Not bleeding likely. Several of my crew served with the princess here during that little dustup and all its fun around Wardhaven. Them that weren't there all wish they'd had the honor . . . and survived it in one piece. It's just that what's out of sight is out of mind, and the less said, the better. Come, take a load off your feet. By my reckoning, I'm four or five answers behind your questions."

Kris settled into a chair that would have fit right into any of the sitting rooms of Nuu House. Thick, rich, brocade upholstering didn't keep it from conforming itself to her body. A low hum went through Kris as it gently began massaging her.

"So, Abby and Cara," Kris said. "How are they not getting the short end of this stick?"

"I think I can answer that best," Nelly said. "It's good to be able to put all of me back to work again. Kris, I won't apologize for giving you the silent treatment this last month. You were a pig and all that, but I really had to do it. They had sensors trained on us the whole time. Officially, I was just your average, run-of-the-mill, souped-up personal assistant. That's what I made the records say. But if I started using a lot more electricity, or communicating with your brain and all, the jig would be up. So I lay low, did my planning slowly and in out-of-the-way places, then brought things together when Penny showed up with Mimzy."

"Okay, nonapology not accepted," Kris said with a grin, "but what about Abby and Cara?"

"You, Kris, are locked in your room," Nelly said. "There is a small electronic device that is programmed to call in sick tomorrow and shout through the door at Abby and Cara that you don't want to be disturbed anytime they try to disturb you. With any luck, we'll be on the other side of this jump before anyone decides to knock down the door and see what's really going on in that room."

"And when they do?" Kris said.

"Abby and Cara will have, what do you call it, plausible deniability. The powers that be can think whatever they want, but your maid and niece have a story, and they will stick to it. You've vanished into thin air. By the way, Kris, I've checked into your family history. Vanishing into thin air is something no damn Longknife has ever done before. Congratulations," Nelly finished.

"That . . . sounds . . . workable," Kris said slowly as she measured the plan and found it, well, workable. Putting that worry aside, Kris turned to her next question.

"This may be none of my business, and I may really not want to know how you did it, but, Elizabeth, how did you do this?"

"'Tweren't no problem." The captain beamed. "The CEO I work for had been trying for some time to get his grandmother to retire to someplace where her phone wouldn't reach him. When Penny came to me with the problem of springing you from the perfect prison, I suggested to Leopold that the old girl might love a seaside villa on Madigan's Rainbow if she could take seven or eight of her favorite bridge cronies with her. He liked the idea. Granny proved willing, and off we and Penny went to save the princess.

"That was the easy part. Now, getting you off planet looked to be the hard part until Nelly here suggested a sleight of hands. We'd off-loaded the aging bridge bidders, lock, stock, and a whole lot of barrels. Nelly suggested maybe we off-load one too many crates. What if the fine silver and china from the *Archie IV* got sent dirtside by accident?

"I got to go charging down screaming for my missing treasure, and you just happened to ride back up in its place," Captain Luna finished with a wide grin.

Kris considered the idea and found a flaw. "What happens when they find a box load of fine china and silver with the *Archie*'s address on it?"

"They won't," Captain Luna beamed. "Said items were all made of dumb metal that is, as we speak, dissolving and leaking out of a box from which all identification and addresses are likewise going away. They may find an empty box in the corner of their warehouse, but it's not going to tell them a thing."

"That's good. Really good," Kris said in awe at the chicanery.

"Coming from you, I'll take that as faint praise," the captain said, chortling.

"Where do we go now?" Kris asked.

"I'm told you need to get to New Eden," the yacht skipper said. "I wasn't told why, and that is as far as I can take you. My CEO has a party he wants to throw. I figure the less I know about what comes next, the better off we'll all be."

With that, Luna stood. "My boss has this place rigged so that it can record every breath anyone in here takes, or can, just as completely, record nothing during the slaughter of several innocents. I've got the system turned off. Nelly can vouch for that."

"It is off, and I have the only key, for the moment," Nelly said.

"So, there's a buttery that I had outfitted for the grand dame and her bridge cronies. It should feed you two for the next week or three." Captain Luna paused, eyed Kris, then went on.

"Kris, I can't help but say you look like hell. Whoever's been riding you has done it hard and put you away wet, girl. There's a workout room right off the master bedroom. If you want to hang with those hardworking Marines I usually hear you like, you better look after yourself, girl."

"You say it so eloquently, Captain," Kris said, standing herself.

"That's why I make the big bucks. Now, lock the door once I'm gone. Anyone coming by will knock. Oh, and if we get boarded in system, you know where the air lock is. Don't make me space you myself."

On that note, they parted.

7

Kris was too strung out to sleep, so she and Penny set out to survey the suite. Kris's circumnavigation of the Milky Way had been a major voyage of discovery. Traipsing through the huge rooms of the suite was like some sort of safari. Kris half expected to stumble upon a pack of lions chasing a herd of elephants.

The rich and enormous sitting room had the master suite off to the right and two just-as-massive bedrooms with expansive baths off to the left. The master suite bath included not only a shower for six but also a small swimming pool for twelve, as well as sauna and the usual equipment, much of it in gold. All this furnished a room that took up only slightly less space than the drop bay on the *Wasp*.

A door beside the sauna led to a workout room. Its computer began counseling them the moment they walked in. The electronic trainer had the same opinion of Kris's present physical state as Luna and began listing all the things it could do for Kris.

Kris quickly crossed to the door that led back to the sitting room.

After the verbose exercise room, the space behind the two other bedrooms was a bit of a puzzle. It was a silent and strangely vacant room. There were tables and several utilitarian chairs. And shelves. Lots of shelves.

It was Nelly who figured it out, spotting the hardwired plug-ins and the electronically secure power outlets.

"This would make a perfect computer command center," she observed. "What was done here would stay here until it was ushered out."

"Should we do our planning in here?" Penny asked.

"I don't think we need to," both Nelly and Mimzy said at the same moment.

Nelly went on. "The entire suite is quite self-contained. Your captain friend was not kidding. What goes on in here stays in here. It's just that this particular room is prepared to power and support a major server farm. It could take a data stream from the outside, mash a whole lot of numbers inside, and send them on their way in a most secure manner. You remember when you asked us to do a full analysis and forensic work-up on the St. Petersburg economy? And do it without getting caught?"

Kris allowed that she did.

"This place is set up to do that. Fully loaded, I bet this place could do it every day for a different planet's worth of data, day in and day out. I'd love to command a place like this," Nelly finished with longing in her voice.

"Who knows, maybe you will," Kris said, with no commitment. She'd never considered Nelly as anything but her own computer. Yes, Nelly was great at playing all kinds of dirty tricks on other computer systems, look at what she'd done tonight. The thought of Nelly cracking the whip over a farmful of less flexible but no less powerful computers left Kris . . . strangely uncomfortable.

Penny broke the stretching silence with a challenge to Kris. "Let's see what that workout room can do."

Kris really didn't want to, but it was either let the workout room show what it really could do, try the buttery, or go to bed.

Kris wasn't hungry or sleepy, so PT won.

But Kris didn't have to let it win without some complaining. "What is it with everybody? I don't look that bad to myself in the mirror."

Penny said nothing more but challenged Kris to a game of handball. The room quickly organized itself as a court even as it provided the two young women with suitable clothing, and, at Penny's request, private facilities for each to change.

Penny left Kris flailing and out of breath in the first minute of the game.

"Okay, okay, you win," Kris said, hunched over and struggling to catch her breath. "I'm out of shape. So, what are you going to do about it?"

The trainer computer said it had just the thing for Kris. While Penny worked out on a contraption that looked like the results of mating a ski machine with a bike with a rowing shell using all the jigs and presses that you normally only found in a spaceship-fabrication dock, Kris was offered a box.

It was a big box that opened up for her to sit in comfortably with only her head sticking out. When it closed, strange things started to happen. Initially, it was little more than a pleasant massage, not unlike the chair in the sitting room.

Then it got more physical.

Kris found she could be made to stand, as well as lie down, inside the box, as it went through the business of seeing that every muscle in her body got a workout.

On Chance, Kris had tossed a caber and strained some muscles she hadn't expected to discover until she gave birth to her first child. This box put even those muscles through a workout.

Thirty minutes later, thoroughly wrung out, Kris stumbled into her lavish shower. Much to the shower's disappointment, Kris demanded and got, "Just a simple shower. Nothing fancy. Water. Warm. Soap."

Quickly done and toweled dry by herself—"Thank you very much"—Kris tumbled into a suddenly inviting bed.

"That was a good beginning," the training computer assured her. "You should be up to three-hour-long workout by day after tomorrow."

"Shut up. Lights out," Kris ordered.

As wrung out as she was, Kris expected sleep to be waiting for her. It wasn't.

What kept going over in her mind as she waited for sleep was the thought of Nelly and her command center of obedient and pliant supercomputers. And the trainer with its attitude toward human flesh. All these and God only knew what else that lurked in the future of the human race left Kris wondering if Grampa Al was really the problem she ought to be risking her neck to foil this month.

Given the choice between wasting her night chewing on that problem versus sleeping, Kris chose sleep.

But her last thoughts were of Jack and a prayer that she might meet him in her dreams.

8

Next morning, Kris found a soak in a warm tub essential before stumbling out to breakfast. A breakfast that was another matter.

The buttery turned out to be as obstreperous as the gym. Penny had to resort to physically searching the pantry for honest food. In a pout over Kris's and Penny's refusal to breakfast on pate foie gras or a salmon soufflé, the kitchen closed up.

Nelly, of course, wouldn't let that happen. The pantry doors did open for Penny, but the stove had to be managed personally by Mimzy, or Penny's bacon and eggs would have been left cold or burned to a crisp.

"There is such a thing as programming a computer to be too helpful," Nelly observed. "Maybe I should adjust this one's parameters a bit."

"Let's don't and say we did," Kris said. "Remember, Nelly, this boat belongs to someone else. They've gotten everything the way they want it. We need to leave it the way we found it."

"There is that," Nelly agreed, then couldn't avoid another try. "I could back up the old code and reload it before we leave."

"No!" came from both Kris and Penny.

Kris chose to drink her breakfast; a healthy shake that

assured her of all the vitamins, minerals, protein, and fiber she would need for an active morning.

And Kris's morning was active. Penny saw to it that Kris subjected herself to another session with the infamous trainer.

"Can't we talk about something?" Kris asked, as Penny settled her into the box.

"Nope. I didn't understand half of what Juan said about what your Grampa Al pulled on New Eden. What's there can wait until we get there to be dumped into your lap. What I would like to know is, what is it with your Grandfather Al? What's he think he's doing?"

Kris shrugged as the machine began to beat up on her. No gentle massage to start with today. "I don't remember a lot about Grampa Al. I was only ten when he and father had their blowup after poor Eddy was kidnapped. Father thought the proper response was to get aggressively involved in making Wardhaven safe for everybody. Grampa Al didn't."

Kris paused, to catch her breath and to remember. "I'd never seen grown-ups shout at each other like my father and his father did that evening over supper. I never saw Grampa Al again until I was a boot ensign and discovered how dangerous it was to be one of those damn Longknifes. I think I went to see my grampa with some idea that I could help him. Foolish me."

"How'd the visit go?" Penny asked, sweating in the throes of her own contraption.

"Short," Kris said. "You have no idea how hard it was to make it through all his checkpoints; and then he had nothing to say to me. He did offer me a job, deep inside his secure web. He's offered me jobs several times. Always with the same requirement. Let myself be bricked up inside his fortress."

"But he's coming out of his web, or at least sending agents out to mess with the rest of us," Penny said.

"That's what bothers me. When Grampa Al and my father were arguing about Father's going into politics, Al was dead set against it. 'Get out of the public eye,' he shouted. 'Make money and let it build a wall around us.' But here he is trying to take over Eden. That doesn't sound like the Grampa Al I remember. Yes, I know he's gotten more crazy about his personal safety. Still, you and I know any walls he's built won't stand a second if a monstrous mother ship makes orbit over Wardhaven."

Kris paused for a moment. "But why didn't Al go talk to his own father? King Ray wants folks ready for the aliens. Why doesn't Al work with him?"

Penny shook her head. "And what is our beloved king doing?" she scowled. "First, he locks you up on Madigan's Rainbow, then he starts some sort of PR campaign to test the waters to see if people are willing to do something about maybe defending themselves."

Kris felt like spitting but had neither the air nor the spare liquid.

"Both your grandpa and great-grandpa are alike in one thing," Penny said.

"What's that?"

"Neither one trusts the rest of humanity with the problem it faces. Both are doing what *they* think is right, but both are all too willing to keep the rest of us in the dark."

Kris leaned back to think, while the machine did its thing, sweating the poisons that she'd swallowed so easily in the last months out of her body and soul.

Penny had a point. Longknifes were all too ready to apply their own solution to humanity's problems. Of course, if Kris was honest, humanity's problem was there because of what a certain Kris Longknife had done.

NOT FAIR, KRIS, Nelly said, interrupting Kris's thoughts with some of her own. THOSE ALIENS HAVE BEEN OUT AMONG THE STARS FOR A HUNDRED THOUSAND YEARS OR MORE. HUMANITY HAS BEEN OUT HERE LESS THAN FOUR HUNDRED. WE WERE LUCKY THAT WE NEVER RAN INTO ONE OF THEM BEFORE. THEY WERE UNLUCKY ENOUGH TO RUN INTO YOU AND THOSE THREE HELLBURNER TORPEDOES. THE FIRST MOVES IN THIS WAR HAVE BEEN MADE. THE ONLY RATIONAL QUESTION IS WHAT MOVES DO WE MAKE NEXT? YOUR GRAMPA RAY THINKS WE NEED TO THINK ABOUT IT A WHILE. I DON'T KNOW WHAT YOUR GRAMPA AL THINKS HE CAN DO, BUT I DON'T TRUST EITHER OF THEM. DO YOU?

Mentally, Kris shook her head. I AGREE WITH YOU, NELLY. GRAMPA RAY WANTS TO TAKE TIME HE MAY NOT HAVE. I DON'T KNOW WHAT GRAMPA AL THINKS HE'S DOING, BUT IF

IT'S ANYTHING LIKE WHAT HE'S DONE FOR THE LAST FIFTEEN YEARS, IT WILL INVOLVE TRYING TO BUY HIMSELF SECURITY. I *KNOW* I DON'T LIKE RAY'S SOLUTION, AND I DOUBT I'LL LIKE AL'S SOLUTION ONE WHIT MORE.

Kris concentrated on the work at hand while trying to decide whether she'd burned off enough of her dissolute ways to reward herself with some real food for lunch.

9

Kris and Penny were just sitting down to filet mignon, baked potatoes, and mixed vegetables served by a joyfully appreciated kitchen, when Captain Luna came on the room's speaker.

"I don't want to worry you two, but we've been hailed and ordered to return to High Madigan station."

"Why *forever* for?" Kris said, putting a little of Cara's drama into a question she could not raise any surprise for.

"They ain't telling, and I ain't asking. I told 'em my CEO intends to use this scow for a jaunt with his board of directors. I named a few, and they said they'd get back."

"You think you put the fear of the Almighty in them, or at least of the almighty dollar?" Penny asked.

"I would think so, but one of Kris's mosquito boats has broken away from the incoming freighter it was escorting. It's gone to one-and-a-half-gee deceleration and looks like as soon as it bleeds off all its velocity inward, it's gonna start blasting for us out here. 'Course, if it don't pump its engines any more than one and a half gees, we'll be long gone through the jump before it gets within range of us."

"Nelly, do you know anything about this?" Kris asked.

"Yes, but I didn't want to disturb you and Penny at your lunch."

"Disturb us," Kris said, dryly.

"About thirty minutes ago, five muscle types showed up at your quarters, Kris, demanding admittance inside the house and inside your room. Abby did her best to come down with a bad case of the slows, but they busted down your door about ten minutes ago, if I've got my time lag right for speed-of-light communications."

"Can't a girl take a day of sick leave without everyone having kittens?" Kris asked the ceiling.

"Is there any chance that the skippers of those boats of yours will develop hair on their chest and take off after me seriously?" Captain Luna asked. "I dearly don't want to have to pull up my skirts and make a run for it. Aside from flashing my well-shaped ankles for the boys, it tends to make you look guilty of something."

"I really can't claim any credit for the training of that splinter fleet," Kris said. "They made it clear to me they wanted me pushing paper, not pushing gees. Unless I missed something in one of my drunken stupors, those boats have never cranked themselves up past one and a half gees, and none of them have high-gee stations. For what it's worth, I'm not sure my XO ever read what those boats can do if you put the hammer down."

"Or studied what you did around Wardhaven orbit?" Captain Luna added.

"Dada reports the home wreckers have departed," Nelly reported. "They stared daggers at Cara and Abby, but didn't say a word. Abby says they'll likely be okay."

"I hope so," Kris said. Penny had shared that if things went bad, her folks would not have a body to bury. Abby had said she was threatened with death if she didn't do exactly what was expected. Kris wondered what she would be doing now if those five toughs had put a gun to Cara's head and told Abby to use her computer to get Kris back there, or they'd kill the kid.

Apparently, these government-sponsored terrorists hadn't thought things through. Or they were too new at plumbing the depths of degradation to do it all that well.

Which left Kris feeling guilty that she hadn't taken a full

minute to identify just what torture would make her rethink her flight.

Rethink?

Would she have turned Luna around if they *had* made Cara and Abby's life the price for her freedom?

Kris was glad she didn't have to answer that question.

"Keep me filled in on what happens, Captain. Nelly, I want to know immediately if you receive a new message from Abby. No delay. You understand?"

"You will know the second I do, Kris," Nelly said.

"Captain, could I have a look at your tactical plot?" Kris asked.

Across from the breakfast table, a painting in a heavy golden frame suddenly changed from a vision of a lovely riverbank where several formally dressed men were having a picnic with a handful of voluptuous nude women into a tactical display of the system, then narrowed down to the space between Madigan's Rainbow and the jump Captain Luna had the *Archimedes* headed for.

"Tighten in, Nelly, on just the patrol boat and the *Archie*." The screen did.

"Show me times to intercept and time to jump, assuming no changes in accelerations or decelerations."

"We jump in an hour. That boat never gets to within two hundred thousand klicks. The 18-inch pulse lasers on those tinker toys can't boil water much past thirty thousand klicks. They aren't really accurate much past twenty thousand."

Kris had bitter memories of trying to get her boats well within three thousand klicks if she wanted to do any real damage to a battleship.

"Let me know, Captain, if they call you back," Kris said.

"I'll let you listen in on the call," Luna promised, and rang off.

Kris found her steak had cooled while they'd talked. The kitchen warmed it right there on the plate at the table. Kris ate with one eye on the screen.

Through the meal, the boat held to its sedate one and a half gee.

Kris found herself gnashing her teeth. "What kind of skippers did they hire for my squadron?" she grumbled.

Penny had survived plenty of radical maneuvering under Kris's command. Hard jinxing at high gees and worse. "Just be glad they did crew those boats with those grandmothers in long skirts and bustles. Would you really want to be pursued by the likes of a Kris Longknife?"

Kris chuckled. "Good point."

Kris and Penny did not bus their own table; the kitchen assured them it would clean up. It seemed to think it a joke that anyone in this suite would even think of it. Which left Kris wondering who had programmed that in and why.

Penny was pushing Kris back into the box for another hour's workout when the *Archie* announced to all hands. "Prepare for zero gee as we approach the jump point."

The box was giving Kris a workout, doing something like cross-country skiing, moving her arms and legs in a rhythm against resistance, when Captain Luna nudged the yacht through the jump.

"All hands, prepare for one-point-five gees. This old girl has places to go and sights to see. Let's get a move on."

"Nelly, did you hear anything from Abby and Cara, Mata Hari, or Dada?"

"No message traffic from them, Kris. And yes, I'm worried for them, too."

10

Captain Luna kept the spurs to *Archie*. Her words, not Kris's. Never slowing to below 1.5 gees, they came through the Gamma Jump at New Eden late on the fourth day after leaving Madigan's Rainbow.

They were immediately informed by High Eden that they had orders to search the *Archimedes* for a fugitive as soon as she tied up at the station.

Penny suggested they look for a place to hide.

Kris seriously doubted that hiding was what a Longknife did. Of course, she had no desire to handle things Captain Luna's way . . . walking out the air lock. It took Kris all of five seconds to settle on her own way.

"I didn't come here to look for a place to hide. I want to find out what Grampa Al is up to. I'll meet the inspection party on the quarterdeck."

Penny seemed a bit nonplussed. "I don't think a gussied-up hussy of a boat like this has a quarterdeck."

"I'll meet them at the front door," Kris growled.

"In what you got on?" Penny asked.

She had a point. Kris had come aboard in her usual nightwear. A Wardhaven U shirt and a pair of Marine Corps red-and-gold gym shorts. Sometimes she wore Navy blue gym shorts. Red and gold was just the luck of the draw that night.

Penny and Kris had not found any clothes in the palatial quarters they shared, but on the second day, a collection of dungarees and blue denim shirts had been passed through the door after a knock. That, and panties and bras, which, to Kris's great surprise, actually fit. That apparel was what Penny made reference to.

These were work clothes that the engineering division might wear. Solid working clothes for working people who didn't make contact with the well-heeled passengers who roamed the fancy-dress parts of the ship.

"You thinking we should go aft and mix in with the black gang in Engineering?" Kris asked.

"I'm wondering if that was what Captain Luna had in mind when she got us decked out like this," Kris's intelligence chief said. "After all, I doubt Luna really wants to face a charge of harboring a fugitive."

Kris made a face. Skulking did not fit into any part of the Longknife legend she'd read growing up. Slinking in to blow something up . . . yes. Skulking around to hide your face . . . not so much.

"Let's wait and see what Captain Luna says," Kris decided.

Which meant Kris went another round with the coach in the box. Great fun.

Kris was recovering from an hour in the box and enjoying a delicious dinner when Captain Luna trotted in, followed by the steamer trunk Kris had arrived in. She settled herself at the table. It promptly added a place for her, and an equally scrumptious meal appeared before her.

She dug in hungrily.

With her mouth full, she asked. "So, how you going to handle this inspection?"

"I'm not going out the air lock," Kris said, putting a solid marker down.

The captain made a face as she shoveled in another mouthful. "I didn't expect you would. What's your Plan B?"

"Penny, here, thinks we ought to drop down to Engineering and pass ourselves off as part of your black gang. Or just me. You say Penny's papers are in order."

"Yep, Penny's no problem. As usual, it's you, Princess."

"And you don't have an expert forger on board that could knock me out some papers before we tie up?"

Captain Luna laughed. Then she had to cough something up that went down the wrong way. When she settled back down, she scowled at Kris.

"Me, not have the best forger in fifty light-years? Don't make me laugh. Really, don't. This is good chow. Be a shame to die from it."

Kris folded her arms in front of her. "Okay, then we'll cut to the chase. I prefer Plan C. I meet the inspection party on your quarterdeck or whatever you call that space where folks come aboard."

Captain Luna eyed Kris sideways. "You sure of that?"

"I admit that I'd like to get a good look at the boarding party before I settle on Plan B or C."

"I kind of like the way you handled the last boarding party," Captain Luna said through a grin.

"Which last boarding party?" Kris asked carefully. Her sins were many, and it would be a shame to confuse one with another.

"Those pirates at Port Royal. That was some panic party."

"How do you know about them?" Kris asked with a sigh.

"Everyone knows about them. The video of you running and them chasing and you finishing 'em up with a mop in the face. It's the funniest viral video in human space."

"How'd that get out?" Kris said, eyeing Penny.

"Don't look at me. I'm right along with you in a truly frumpy dress, running for all I'm worth."

"Abby!" Kris breathed. "I thought I'd kept that woman too busy to sell anything to her sources."

Clearly, Kris hadn't.

"Hmm," Penny said, eyeing the overhead. "Cara was bragging to me that she was getting real good at video mash-ups."

"No good deed goes unpunished," Captain Luna chortled, then sobered quickly. "So which of your plans is B and C? You're dressed to hide out in my engineering spaces. Not so good for greeting and impressing a boarding party. Steamer trunk, open."

Behind her, the trunk's two sides slid apart. The yacht skipper left the table, chewing on a big bite, and rummaged through the contents of what had accompanied Kris aboard. Among the air cylinders and minimum life-support food rations was a carefully hung suit: beige, in Berber wool, complete with blouse and two-inch matching heels.

"Princess enough for you, Your Highness," Captain Luna read from a note in Abby's perfect handwriting.

"It will do," Kris said. "When do we match air locks?"

"In half an hour. I really should be getting back to my bridge. Between the knuckleheads in my bridge watch and the illiterate computers the owner dumped on me for the ship, this scow could probably steer itself for a couple of dozen jumps and dockings. Still, a good captain doesn't let her crew know just how superfluous she is."

"I'll remember that when . . . or if . . . I ever get a ship of my own," Kris said.

"You could take worse advice," Luna said, and left Kris to change.

"Are you going to hide out in the crew?" Kris asked Penny as she examined her dress for today.

Penny shook her head. "Where thou goest, I go," she said. "If you think you can handle dressing yourself, I'll duck down to my putative quarters and dress for guests. Or jail. Depending."

"Guests or jail. Yep," Kris agreed.

11

Kris was glad for Penny's company as she waited to see what lay ahead of her that evening. The *Archie* caught a tie-down at High Eden on the first pass, and the station pulled her smartly into dock. The air locks matched; Kris's ears felt the tiny change as the *Archie* adjusted to High Eden's ever-so-slightly-different air pressure.

Then nothing happened.

Nothing happened for ten solid minutes.

"Think we should make a run for it?" Penny asked.

Kris frowned. She was ready for a lot of things. A delay was not one of them. After a moment's reflection, Kris shook her head. "Shot while trying to escape isn't a part of the Long-knife legend, and I, for one, don't intend to add it."

Penny nodded.

They waited a bit more.

Then two men in civilian clothes presented themselves at the pier, police credentials in clear sight.

"You know either of these two jokers?" Captain Luna asked over the net.

"Yeah," Kris said. "The short one is Police Lieutenant Juan Martinez. He and his Fraternal Order of Proud Caballeros helped me quite a bit last time I was here. The other guy is Inspector Johnson of the New Eden Secret Service."

"That's pretty much what they say, except Martinez is now Senior Chief Inspector Martinez."

"He certainly earned the promotion," Kris agreed.

"Do I let them in?"

Kris considered for all of five seconds. These two were not the ones she would have sent to haul herself away in cuffs. Also missing were the search dogs and other apparatus that would have been needed to do a real dust down of a ship the size and complexity of the *Archimedes IV*.

"Have someone bring them to me," Kris said.

"Will do."

Kris turned to Penny, who had returned wearing a pantsuit with enough pockets to stash half a jewelry store in . . . or hide a major electronic suite. "I forgot to ask, is New Eden one of the hundred and fifty planets I'm wanted on for crimes against humanity?"

"Kris," Nelly drawled, "I would have warned you if it was. And you're up to a hundred sixty-three planets. Some have judiciaries that require due process."

"One hundred and sixty-three." Penny whistled. "How many more are still processing?"

"Twelve," Nelly said, "and no, New Eden isn't one of them either. If you ask me, despite the haste with which they rushed you out, you did leave a good impression."

"We'll find out soon enough. Penny, come sit beside me. Suite, can you move two chairs to in front of me?" While Kris clearly occupied the senior chair in the suite, two chairs equal in size and comfort to Penny's moved from beside a couch to where Kris wanted them. They were in front of her, but with plenty of room for people first to stand in her presence.

Kris intended to get all the mileage out of her princess card that she could. The colors of the chairs changed: Kris's to a royal red and gold, Penny's to royal blue and gold. The other two chairs were more sedate earth tones.

NELLY, DID YOU DO THAT?

NOPE. YOU DO REMEMBER WHO OWNS THIS TUB?

RIGHT. REMIND ME WHEN I FINALLY GET A ROYAL YACHT TO ASK LUNA WHERE SHE GOT HER PROGRAMMING.

You bet, Nelly added with open professional respect.

Captain Luna, herself, ushered the police officers in. Penny stood. Kris stayed seated. The skipper almost suppressed her grin as Kris offered Senior Chief Inspector Martinez her hand. He gallantly bowed over it, said, "Your Highness," and kissed it.

Inspector Johnson studiously did not see that, and merely said, "Ms. Longknife."

"Commander, I think, is appropriate," Kris said, motioning the men to their chairs.

Luna whistled, and a third chair headed their way, changing to earth tones as it moved, until a low whistle from the captain switched it to blue and gold to match Penny's. The four settled into their chairs . . . and silence.

Kris wondered how long the hush would last but lacked the time for that kind of fun. She broke it with a question. "I understand you seek a fugitive from the law?"

"Yes," Johnson said, clearly jumping in without the approval of the senior chief inspector, who rewarded his intervention with a sour frown. "Wardhaven has issued an arrest warrant for you. You are a deserter."

"'Deserter'?" Kris said. "I thought you had to be absent without leave for at least thirty days before they started using that nasty word."

"That was my understanding, too," Penny said.

"I can read you the relevant portion of the UCMJ," Nelly added.

"And, if I recall correctly, I signed out for sixty days leave. I know it was approved. I approved it myself," Kris said, with the most winsome smile she could manage.

"As commander of Fast Patrol Squadron 127," Nelly primly pointed out, "Kris has the delegated authority to sign all leave requests. That includes her own."

"That may have slipped someone's notice," Inspector Johnson noted.

"No doubt," Kris agreed.

Senior Chief Inspector Martinez noticed how close Captain Luna was coming to splitting a gut at this military-law comedy, and chose to cough gently. "No doubt the warrant has more to do with certain U.S. officials not wanting a certain princess traipsing around human space and less about the fine points of the law."

"I think you may have hit the nail on the head," Kris said, trying to make the observation sound as vacuous as possible.

"So, gentlemen," Captain Luna said, "I could enjoy this show all night, but I do have this ship, and it does need to be gallivanting around human space, and at the moment, it ain't doing any gallivanting at all."

"Yes," Kris said, standing. "What do we want to do? With me or otherwise?"

"If I had my way," Inspector Johnson said caustically, "I'd chain you to this boat and send you off to wherever it takes you."

"But you aren't going to have your way," Senior Chief Inspector Martinez said.

He offered Kris his arm. "Your Highness, if you will come with me, several very important people wish to meet you. There are certain matters of great import to discuss."

Kris took his arm. "Why, Juan, you never talked that way last time my shadow darkened your door."

"He wasn't a senior chief inspector," Inspector Johnson observed.

"And Her Highness hadn't saved our lovely planet from overthrow and enslavement, right, Alex?"

Inspector Johnson did not honor that question with an answer.

The two Navy officers, the two police types, and two of Abby's steamer trunks exited the *Archimedes IV* with all due decorum and haste. The *Archie* was backing out of dock before Kris and her party had ridden the escalators from the pier to the main deck of the space station.

"I forgot to thank her," Kris said.

"No doubt you can when she sends you a bill," Penny said.

"If that space scoundrel can figure out an address to send it to," Inspector Alex Johnson observed sourly.

12

Like all established planets, New Eden had a space elevator. Kris and company quickly boarded a ferry. Like any large ferry system, it had a VIP lounge.

It also had a special and private section for cops.

Johnson led them past the VIP lounge and into the police holding area. He was kind enough not to lock Kris and Penny in a cell but rather offered them a pair of chairs: cheap, hard, and uncomfortable. The two inspectors settled into similar seats.

"Would either of you like to tell us what's going on?" Kris asked.

"No," said Johnson, jumping in before Martinez could even open his mouth. "The president wants to talk to you. He'll tell you what he wants you to know."

Martinez gave the Secret Service agent a sour look, but nodded. "President Oscar Castillo wants to share his concerns with you. I imagine Alex is right, if a bit abrupt."

Johnson let the complaint roll off his back like water off a peacock's feathers.

"Well"—Kris tried to sound as innocent and chatty as possible—"then this matter of a warrant for my arrest is not really an issue."

"No," Senior Chief Inspector Martinez said.

"Speak for yourself, Juan. We are a signed member of the Union of Societies, and as such, ought to honor arrest warrants from other planets of the union."

Kris didn't know what to take the most umbrage at. That he wanted to arrest her—or that he'd changed Grampa's United Society into something a whole lot less united sounding.

Just how much trouble is Grampa, King Ray to most, having keeping his 173 planets together in one . . . something or other?

Kris decided that changing the subject might well be in order.

"How have things been going since I was last here?"

"Peacefully," Inspector Johnson shot back, not only to forestall a comment by Martinez but also to cut off further conversation.

Senior Chief Inspector Martinez ignored the Secret Service inspector. "It's amazing how few people have died in helicopter accidents. Our death rate by heart attack is actually below the average for a developed planet," he said with a grin.

On Kris's last visit to Eden, both of them had noted the high incidence of those sorts of deaths and attributed them not to natural causes but to infighting among various parties of several persuasions.

It was nice to see that Kris had made a change that was appreciated.

"President Castillo is also a product of your last visit."

"Was he one of the unenfranchised workers?" Kris asked. A large part of New Eden's population had been made up of people brought in to do the menial labor. They and their children had never been given citizenship and the vote. Even Police Lieutenant Martinez was one of the marginalized. Kris was only too happy to be credited with that change.

"No, his family was one of the early arrivals, before the vote got so limited. Still, he and his family had been fighting for change, and you dropped it right in his lap."

Senior Chief Inspector Martinez glanced at Inspector

Johnson, who was studiously looking the other way and ignoring his new superior, as well as Kris.

Then Johnson did turn to Kris. "Don't expect any hugs and kisses. Not after all the trouble you've got us in. Us and the whole human race."

Kris gave the most innocent shrug she could manage. "It seemed like a good idea at the time."

"Now who's bringing up topics we were expressly forbidden to raise?" Martinez said. "Naughty, naughty."

Johnson went back to staring at the bulkhead to Penny's right.

Kris leaned back in her seat and got as comfortable as the chair allowed. It looked to be a long, quiet trip.

Martinez surprised her. "Your *grandmadre* Ruth still comes to teach at our university."

"The kidnapping didn't slow her down, huh?" Penny said.

"Not likely," Martinez said. "Though I do think our kids are not so much fun for her. Their blinders are off. They can see a whole lot more of the world around them. She doesn't have to fight them so much to see the injustice and do something about it."

"Yeah," Johnson growled. "Now we have student protests every Friday, like clockwork."

"It only seems that way to you, Alex," Martinez replied. "If you followed them in *my* media, you'd know that every one of the protests has its own issues and own set of things they want to change."

"You're just bragging because you bought into those scandal sheets when they went public and made a small fortune," the Secret Service agent shot back.

"And you are still bent out of shape that three of your favorite ones have closed. I told you the *Hungry I* has all the cartoons you liked. Just subscribe, *mi hombre*."

"And wade through all those rumors. Never! They're wrong half the time."

"Which is better than being wrong all the time."

Both men were starting to show red at the neck and cheeks. Kris wondered if they were armed and how hard it would be to wrestle them into separate cells.

"Gentlemen, gentleman," she said. "Enough. I see things have changed, and change is hard. Okay. Thank you for the update on your lovely planet. I'll happily ride in silence the rest of the trip."

The men fell quiet, leaving Kris to wonder how it happened that the two of them had been sent to get her. Clearly, New Eden still had several faces. Once more, Kris would have to figure out on the run which was the true one.

The ride down took half an hour. They left the ferry through a different exit from the rest of the paying passengers. Kris found herself being helped into a police SUV, as dark as the night, and the driver took the four of them into traffic without a word.

They'd merged into a crosstown throughway and accelerated into the fast lane at a speed only a cop, or teenager, would risk.

Except Kris noticed a red sports car zip past them as if they were parked.

A moment later, the car slowed down, pulled back next to them and its window came down. Kris spotted a camera in the window and blinked when it flashed.

"Reporters," Inspector Johnson grumbled from where he sat across from Penny. The women had been given the plush backseat of the rig.

Kris gave one of her, "I have to do this," smiles at the car across from them, wondering if the dark windows were allowing any real picture taking.

"Gun!" Kris shouted and ducked as the window beside her blossomed into a constellation of starbursts, and the SUV demonstrated just how heavily armored it was.

Senior Chief Inspector Martinez threw himself at Kris as Johnson began shouting into his wrist, "Tag! Tag! Where the hell are you guys?"

Martinez landed heavy on Kris as the rig went into a high-negative-gee deceleration. Kris heard a distant crash, which she guessed was "you guys" doing some tagging of their own.

It must have been good for the police, because the SUV accelerated smoothly back to an even faster speed, and Martinez climbed off of Kris and returned to his seat with a mumbled apology. Kris wasn't sure whether it was for the attack or the personal contact.

She didn't ask for a clarification.

She did say, "Senior Chief Inspector Martinez, you may recall on that application for a gun carry permit I gave you many moons ago, I listed several attacks on my life. Do we need to add another one, or was that just a routine traffic stop on New Eden?"

Both inspectors had the good humor to smile sardonically at Kris's question.

"I suspect we'll credit this one to you, Your Highness," Martinez said. "I don't think someone wants you to meet our president."

"Who knows I'm on planet?" Kris said. She wasn't exactly shocked. Maybe not even surprised. Still, somebody was moving fast.

And had tentacles in a whole lot of pots that other folks thought were secret.

Outside, they quickly picked up a phalanx of five other equally heavy SUVs. The rest of the drive to wherever they were going was uneventful.

They pulled into the basement of a skyscraper; Kris didn't get a glimpse of its top. Tires squealed as they took turns at high speed.

"This is worse than jinking the *Wasp*," Penny muttered. "And we had high-gee stations on her."

"What's a high-gee station?" Johnson asked.

"Something you ought to have if you're going to drive like this," Kris shot back, as they came to a noisy halt.

Kris unstrapped herself from the backseat with much the same relish as she'd unstrapped herself from the crashed Greenfeld Ground Assault Craft on the planet that never got named. She did it quickly, but by the time she had dismounted, a praetorian guard of heavily armed police had flooded the place, leaving open only the route to an elevator.

Kris headed that way, with Penny and the two inspectors right behind her. Inside, there was only one button to push; Kris waited to see who would push it.

Finally, Johnson did.

The elevator took off like a rocket for orbit. Kris remembered to tighten her leg muscles to keep all the blood from rushing to her feet. It wouldn't do to walk into the new president's presence only to swoon into his lap.

Or maybe that was the idea.

Johnson was saying something about this being an exact replica of an oval office some politician on Earth used to have. Kris nodded. She remembered that office. It was supposed to give the incumbent a major advantage in impressing the visiting team.

Kris prepared to meet impressive with blasé.

The room *was* impressive, and the view out the window was spectacular from like a gazillion stories up. But the man behind the thick oak desk just looked tired as he put down what he been reading and stood as Kris entered.

He did not extend his hand; Kris did not offer hers. Kris approached to within three or four meters of him and halted. The two of them looked each other over for a long moment. Kris was none too sure what he saw. What she saw was a dark, middle-aged man struggling in a job far too large for him.

Maybe for any single human being.

He broke the silence. "So, you're the little girl that started this great big war."

Kris glanced around and shook her head. "I sure don't see any great big war."

That got a snort of laughter from the president. He motioned Kris to a couch and settled into a rocker beside her as the others took places on the couch across from Kris.

"Not what I hear from your great-*grandpadre*. At least half the messages I read from our king concern those space aliens and us maybe being at war with them. I wish he'd get some other bee up his nose. Go chasing after some other hobgoblins. I thought space pirates were quite good enough for the old war horse."

"The space aliens are out there," Kris said.

"But even you said you only found them on the other side of the galaxy. They've never bothered us or the Iteeche. At least they hadn't until you blew one of their mother ships to pieces."

"I didn't exactly blow it to pieces, and it fired on us first," Kris said in her own defense.

"I wish you hadn't gone on that voyage of discovery. We've got quite enough problems to handle without going looking for them."

"I've found that most of my problems find me, whether I look for them or not. Isn't that your experience with the problems you have?"

The president nodded, a tight, sad smile on his face, and a distant look settled in his eyes.

"But you didn't bring me here to talk about my recent unpleasant voyage. I have to sleep with it every night, and if you really wanted to do something about it, you'd have formally charged me. Why am I here?"

"You Longknifes don't beat around the bush."

"With so many trying to kill us, we can't afford the time."

"Hmm, yes. Senior Chief Inspector, do we know anything about that attack?"

"No, Mr. President. The car was stolen. The driver and gunman are dead. They were both small players available for hire. We're trying to trace the money, but it doesn't look like it will be easy."

"It had to be hastily arranged," Kris said. "I've only been here for an hour."

"The ship you rode in on was generally reported to be harboring you," Martinez said. "I've suspected you might be in system for eight hours. Clearly, somebody else did, too."

The president used both hands to rub the closely trimmed white hairs on his head, as if trying to rub away some of the tension in his skull. "Let me know what you find out, as soon as you find it out. Understood?"

"Yes, Mr. President."

"Which brings us back to why you are here," the president said, now fixing his full attention on Kris.

"Yes, it does," Kris agreed.

The president leaned back in his rocker. "Your *grandpadre* Alexander has been notably apolitical for a Longknife."

"Yes. He abandoned politics when I was a child and concentrated on growing the Nuu fortune. From the size of my trust fund, I'd say he's been very successful."

"Yes. Can you think of anything that might reignite his interest in politics?"

"Honestly, sir, I'd never, ever, expect him to do that. I was there at the dinner table when he and my father had it out. I can't think of anything that would bring him out of his imposed security lockdown."

"I do not doubt the truth of what you witnessed, young woman, but I also don't doubt the rather tenuous and nebulous evidence that Senior Chief Inspector Martinez and his cohorts of forensic computer experts have uncovered. Admittedly, I'd hate to have to argue this in court. It would likely put a dozen juries to sleep. Still, I found myself filled with belief when I reviewed the data. And I am filled with dread that a very wealthy Longknife may be going rogue."

"I agree, that would be a nightmare," Kris said.

"So. You will tell your great-*grandpadre* Raymond of this. And give your *grandpadre* Alexander a personal request from me and all hundred and seventy-two other heads of governments in the Union of Societies that this is not acceptable behavior. If he continues to cause us trouble, our taxing authorities may cause him an equal or greater amount of trouble."

"I wasn't planning on going back to Wardhaven," Kris lied. Jack was there. She was going there. How? Now that was the question.

"I really think you should," the president said. "Senior Chief Inspector Martinez, arrange for her travel, by whatever means as may likely result in her actual arrival."

"It will be done, Mr. President."

And on that note, Kris and Penny were ushered out.

13

Which left Kris moving, but with no fewer questions. Where was she going? How would she get there? And what would she do when she arrived?

Senior Chief Inspector Martinez took Kris and Penny back down the elevator. Somehow, Inspector Johnson detached himself and vanished. At the bottom of the elevator, the small army of heavily armed police were gone. So were all the black SUVs.

In their place stood a simple green sedan. On closer observation, Kris corrected her initial impression. The tires were oversize, and when she boarded it, it stayed solid as a tank. When she hit the button, and the window rolled down, the glass was three centimeters thick.

Penny nodded with approval.

Martinez himself took the driver's seat. Then a light gray car, very much the twin of Kris's green one, pulled up. Martinez lowered his window; the other car lowered the passenger-side window. Inspector Johnson asked, "Where are we going?"

"You'll know when we get there," Martinez answered. "Who's driving?"

"Someone I trust. I didn't even give him time to call the wife and explain why he'd be missing dinner."

There was an audible complaint from the driver. Something

along the line of this is the third time this month, and it was only the sixth. "Estella is really getting tired of this."

"That's what you get for being a good cop," both police officers said.

"Poor kid will get no sympathy here," Penny muttered through a grin.

"Follow me," Martinez said, the window came up, and they took off at a proper civilian speed. The gray car followed at a proper civilian interval.

"Where are we going?" Kris asked.

"Officially, you are in one of six SUVs headed for a safe house. A young policewoman, not quite as tall as you, fully armored, is taking your place as target."

"God have mercy on her," Penny prayed.

"I agree. We, however, are headed for my house."

"Your house! Won't that be dangerous for your family?" Kris asked.

"Yes, but my wife's been wanting to meet you, and there's someone else who does, too. So I'm taking you where I figure no one will look for you. Okay?"

"I guess," Kris said.

"So, are you protected?" the senior chief inspector asked.

"She's not even wearing her spider-silk underwear," Penny snorted.

"Things were peaceful on Madigan's Rainbow," Kris offered as an excuse.

"She was drinking again and putting on weight," Penny corrected. "She probably couldn't fit into her silk armor."

Kris gave Penny a nasty look but didn't disagree.

"There are vests under the backseat, Penny. Please get one out for Her Highness."

Penny did and tossed it to Kris. Then Penny pulled out a second one and put it on while Kris did the same with hers.

"There," Kris said. "You both happy?"

"Satisfied," the senior inspector said. "I won't be happy until I see you walking away from me and Eden." The rest of the drive was silent.

Their destination was an adobe brick building with red roof tiles and an attached garage. The door opened automatically;

they drove right in. Kris was able to dismount with no one outside the wiser.

"Johnson will park halfway down the block and keep an eye on us," Martinez said as he opened the door and led Kris into the house through the washroom and kitchen. His wife, a pleasant-looking woman, stood in the living room with two boys beside her.

Kris recognized one of them. "Bronc, you and your mother were supposed to be on your way to Hurtford."

The teenager had the good sense to look embarrassed. "I was, but I didn't want to go," he said.

Martinez took over the explanation. "He vanished a day before he was supposed to leave. With him nowhere to be seen, his mom balked. He turned up, right where I figured he would, back in Five Corners, hanging with a couple of his hacker friends."

The kid gave an expressive shrug as in, "Where else would I be."

"I got his mother a job working for one of the socialites you saved. It was amazing how grateful those folks were, for the first month or so. Problem was, her job's pay was mainly room and board, and there was no room for a teenager, so Carmella and I took him in. He's been going to school with Esteban, and learning like a house afire. Now, don't you kids have home-work or something?"

Carmella took the hint and herded the boys out of the room. Juan waved Kris to the couch and took what clearly was the Papa chair. When he continued, it was in a whisper. "Bronc's schoolwork is only sharpening his computer skills. I'm not sure he's a good influence on Esteban or the rest of his classmates. But it was Bronc and his hacker buddies from the old neighbor-hood, working with Esteban's classmates, who initially turned up the hints that something was wrong as we went into our first election since the one we had to have after your last visit."

The senior chief inspector shrugged. "I didn't know whether to buy them new computers or ground them. So I did both and turned what they'd found over to my police computer-forensic team. By the way, when the Marines marched out on your ship after that past 'unpleasantness,' several of the computers you bought for your own investigation turned up with Bronc's friends. I hope you don't mind."

"If it helped you in your more recent 'unpleasantness,'" Kris said, "they earned their keep. But tell me, without going into all the gory details, what happened here?"

Nelly made one of her polite coughs before interjecting, "I'll dig into all the 'gory details,' as Her Highness so delicately put it. Do you mind if I access what's on Bronc's and Esteban's hard drives?"

"Feel free to talk with them about it as well. I doubt if either one of them is getting any homework done tonight." Kris felt the slight vacancy in her head as she often did when Nelly concentrated her attention elsewhere.

"Would you like a cup of coffee or tea?" coming from Juan told Kris she was in for a long night.

"Tea, if you have any that's not caffeinated."

"I think Estella keeps some herbal tea," he said as he headed for the kitchen, and Kris followed.

"My wife reads minds," Juan said as he spotted the already warm teakettle and packets of tea laid out, ready for them to chose from. "She knows I like something warm in my hand when I have to talk about hot topics."

They both chuckled at that.

Tea in hand, they settled at a friendly dinner table—simple and just right for a family meal. Growing up, Kris's meals had been served in a cold, palatial setting, with nothing warm and friendly about them. When she could, she'd slip away and have supper with the cook and her husband.

These surroundings reminded Kris of those easier meals. Somehow, however, she doubted that the talk around the table tonight would be warm or simple.

"What are you setting me up for?" Kris asked.

"Unpleasant truths," the senior inspector said.

"I've been hit over the head with plenty of them. Hit away."

"The attack tonight bothers me," the police officer said. "I thought we had you locked up behind solid security. Yes, we had two arrest warrants for you, but the president doesn't want to serve either one of them. It will be embarrassing if it becomes common knowledge that we had you in our control and let you go."

"So it wasn't just my safety that was at stake but your government's embarrassment," Kris pointed out.

"Worse. We don't want to get on the bad side of both our king and Wardhaven."

"Hold it. You said you had two arrest warrants. One from my Grampa Ray and one from my father?"

"Yes."

"That doesn't sound right. I know I didn't get much outside news on Madigan's Rainbow, but . . ." Kris tried to think this piece of news through, and gave up. "What's been going on while I was locked away in Siberian ice?"

"It's hard to put it into a few words, Kris, but let's say the Articles of Confederation for the, ah, something or other, is causing a lot of confusion. Lots of legal challenges are working their way to the newly established Supreme Court, but lots of planetary judiciaries are already refusing to accept any legal decisions they don't agree with. You noticed that the president used the term 'Union of Societies.'"

"Yes, he and Inspector Johnson."

"Alex says whatever the powers that be are saying," Juan scoffed. "However, since, as the president told you, your great-*grandpadre* is pretty *simpatico* about raising taxes to mobilize a fleet, there are a whole lot of people suddenly a whole lot less interested in being one of the hundred and seventy-three planets in the U.S. Unless, of course, they can replace King Ray with someone of their choosing."

"It sounds like a mess."

"Or worse."

"Hold it," Kris said, a thought rising to the surface of an otherwise-bubbling-and-confused mind. "If your president is so down on the central government, what was this effort at trying to get a different government on Eden?"

"I have no idea," Juan said. "We are not the worst, Kris. We are kind of in the middle. If I'm reading the takeover correctly . . . and there was a whole lot of confusion about just what they wanted to do . . . they intended to take us out of the Union."

"Grampa Al is taking political action against his father?" Kris had to say the words. Her mind was refusing even to hold on to the idea.

"It sounds crazy, doesn't it?"

"To say the least. And you think the assassination attempt tonight was from my Grampa Al?"

Juan shrugged. "I was prepared for someone who'd lost a loved one in your fleet to maybe take a potshot at you, but that doesn't appear to be the case. Those were hired killers. They obviously didn't act alone. Someone had to leak your itinerary, and someone else had to pay these guys. As much as I hate to say it, this was either the actions of someone who was trying to curry favor with Alexander Longknife after having failed miserably to subvert Eden and used what money and access was left over."

Juan paused here. He took a sip of his tea and looked Kris square in the eye. "Or your *grandpadre* ordered a hit on you."

Juan let the silence stretch before adding. "Do you know your *grandpadre* well?"

Kris shook her head. "No. Once he and father argued about staying in politics, Grampa Al pretty much disappeared from my life."

Kris let the thought roll around in her skull. She'd gotten used to the idea that Henry Smythe-Peterwald XII wanted her dead and would pay a princely sum for her splattered body. She'd come to terms with the idea that the odd-and-sod soldier or Sailor might shoot her or blow her out of space. That's what happened to people who chose the Navy for a profession.

But her own grandfather!

It had to be a mistake. Or bad choices by some underling. Flesh and blood did not turn on flesh and blood.

Then Kris connected a few more dots of her puzzle. "You say *both* my father's Wardhaven government and my great-grandfather's royal government issued a warrant for my arrest?"

"Yes," Juan said.

"Two arrest warrants and one killer for hire. That covers my whole family."

Juan gave Kris an expressive shrug. "It certainly looks like it could be that way."

"And your president wants you to put me on a slow boat or a fast boat to Wardhaven, huh?"

"Yes. I have two choices for you. Both leave tomorrow. One is a small corvette, the *Dainty*, similar to your old *Typhoon*. Only Eden never bought into the Smart Metal stuff, so our accommodations are always small and cramped. The other is a container ship that also has facilities for passengers, folks in a hurry who want to go now, not when the next liner leaves. Which one interests you?"

"What are the benefits of one over the other?" Kris asked.

Juan chewed on his lower lip. "If you take the *Dainty*, you are on Eden sovereign territory and if you are met by a Marshal, either U.S. or Wardhaven, with an arrest warrant at the pier, you can stay on board, or not, your choice."

"You're ready to claim that a U.S. ship is the sovereign territory of the planet it comes from?" Maybe things were worse for King Ray than she thought.

"Yes, our ships have those orders. You have to understand, there is no legal precedent, yet. And it would be more than embarrassing for our president if the first time we took that stand was between you and your family."

"I imagine so." Kris had a strong suspicion that if push came to shove, she'd be shoved out the air lock.

Hopefully onto the dock at High Wardhaven station and not into vacant space, but she wasn't taking bets on which just now.

Kris swallowed hard, and asked, "And what's the other option?"

"The *Yellow Comet* of the Comet lines. Her captain, Sam Tidings, owes you. You rescued his daughter. She was a docent at that charity art auction you attended. The one that got shot up. You and your man, Captain Montoya, fell on top of her and protected her from the auto cannon."

"Yes," Kris said. She remembered the big-breasted Samantha Tidings. Jack had thrown himself on her and hadn't even bounced. Both Kris and Jack had taken a lot of cannon fire. And had been black-and-blue and hurting for quite a while after. Body armor, at least what they'd had at the time, stopped bullets. It left the bullet's energy to be absorbed by the flesh below.

One or two shots were no problem. An auto cannon on full automatic was something else entirely.

"I take it that Tidings's *Yellow Comet* makes no claim to sovereignty?"

"All too true," Juan said, "but the accommodations are much better, and he brags about his chefs."

"Any suggestions how I get aboard unnoticed?"

"I have a few."

14

The next morning was full of surprises.

The steamer trunk Kris had used to board the *Archie* showed up along with the second one, which had mysteriously appeared. Captain Luna had dropped them on the pier after Kris left with her police escort. It had taken a while for them to get through customs; there was a reason Abby rarely let the contents of her trade be examined. It also took several calls to get it sent to Senior Chief Inspector Martinez's home.

Kris suspected she'd better get out fast before more than just her luggage caught up with her.

But the next surprise was delightful.

"Is my great-granddaughter in here somewhere?" came as Estella answered an insistent knock at the door. Senior Inspector Martinez was already on his wrist talking to Inspector Johnson and had a picture of who was at the door before it was answered.

"Gramma Ruth!" Kris shouted. "How'd you know I was here?"

"Young woman, I survived the Iteeche and your grampa Trouble. I can smell a relative if I'm on the same planet with her. Oh, and I keep Bronc supplied with the latest new games and hacker programs. You don't honestly think he would keep his auntie Ruth from knowing that Kris was back in town?"

Kris breathed a sigh of relief. Bronc to Gramma Ruth, or Gramma Trouble, as she seemed to be today, was a risk Kris could accept.

Gramma Ruth held Kris out at arm's length for a look. "You don't seem to be much the worse for letting that scoundrel Ray run you around on his leash."

"The last bit of trouble I did myself," Kris admitted.

"Says you. That man could manipulate the sun out of the sky if he felt the need. You headed back to Wardhaven?"

"I'm a fugitive, Gramma, wanted for crimes against humanity on a hundred and fifty plus planets. Do you really want to know where I'm going next?"

"Maybe not. But if you're headed for Wardhaven, I might be able to arrange for you to see the man you want to see."

"If I *were* going to Wardhaven, I have no idea who I'd want to see. Grampa Ray and Father have issued arrest warrants for me, and I don't think Grampa Al much likes me, either."

"Why would you want to see them? I mean the man you really want to see."

"And who would that be?"

"Jack. The fellow you were making cow eyes at the last time you were here."

"I was not making cow eyes at Jack!"

"Says you. Remember, I'm your Gramma Ruth. I grew up on a farm. I know cow eyes when I see them, girl."

"Gramma, I really need to be getting out of here. If you've found me, people with guns can find me."

"Piffle. I'm a lot smarter than the average person with a gun. And me with a class to teach in fifteen minutes. Young woman, you have got to quit traipsing around the galaxy and sit a spell with your Gramma Ruth. We need to watch the grass grow."

"All I ever grow are weeds, Gramma."

"Says you. Okay, I see that cop eyeing me and his watch. Take care, kiddo," and with a peck on the cheek, the whirlwind known as Gramma Ruth was gone.

"How am I getting on the *Yellow Comet*," Kris asked, "and how soon?"

"In that," Juan said, pointing at the steamer trunk, "and right away. The sooner you get off this planet, the happier I and a whole lot of elephants above me will be."

"That sounds like a deal. Will you or Penny lead my trunk aboard?"

"Penny," Juan said.

The aforementioned intelligence officer came out from the back room, dressed like a wealthy, if nearly hundred-year-old, matron. "What did you say about me, deary? I don't hear so well." She was stooped over and struggling with a cane.

Kris let herself be locked into her trunk.

It was just as dark and claustrophobic as before. Kris located her little box of pills, took one, and trusted Penny to get her to someplace safe in the next two or three hours.

15

"So what do you think of our quarters this time?" Penny asked a groggy Kris as light streamed into her slightly opened steamer trunk.

Kris yawned and stretched. That brought her up against the boundaries of her trunk. She pushed it open wider and stood. Her new quarters were a whole lot smaller than her last. Several of this room would fit quite comfortably into the sitting room on the *Archie*. And this room, and a small bathroom off to one side, were all there was.

Still, it was larger than her stateroom on the *Wasp*.

But then, she hadn't shared that room with Penny.

There was one comfortable-looking chair, a desk with its own station chair, and a bed. Two could likely sleep in it if they didn't mind being too friendly . . . and if one of them didn't roam around the bed at night.

Kris had never shared a bed with anyone in her life.

"Think we could order a cot in?" Kris asked.

"And what would one old maid need with a bed and a cot?" Penny answered with a raised eyebrow.

"You have a point," Kris agreed, and tried, unsuccessfully, to keep from making a face at the prospects before her.

"Your Highness, we *are* on the run, you know," said Penny, her eyes sparkling.

"All too truly," Kris said, pushing her trunk open more and stepping out. Beside her trunk was the other, as yet undiscovered, one. Kris eyed it, wondering at its contents.

There was a knock at the door.

"Who is it?" Penny asked, her voice coming out cranky and creaky.

"Captain Tidings," came back, and the monitor on the door came alive to show a middle-aged man in a gray merchant-marine uniform with four stripes on the sleeve.

"Please come in," Penny said, and the door admitted him.

"I'm glad to see that you both made it on board, Your Highness," the captain said with a smile and an offered hand. "I never had a chance last time you were on Eden to thank you for saving my daughter's life."

Kris shook the offered hand and found herself smiling back. "I did have to leave precipitously."

"Yes. I never did understand that. I know that many of your Marines were injured while saving so very many of us, but I should have thought that you could get care just as well on Eden as on Wardhaven."

So, Kris thought, *once again, what politics ordered was not necessarily what politics confessed to have done.* "We do what we are told," Kris said.

"Well, I'm glad that I can do something for you now. If you wish, I can open the room next door for you. You are our only set of passengers."

"Set?" Kris said.

"Yes. I've officially signed aboard Mrs. Travaford and her traveling companion and medical assistant, Stephanie Ootlaw. Line policy allows me to open up vacant rooms for the comfort of such important passengers as Mrs. Travaford." With that he produced a key pad, tapped a few numbers, and a loud click came from the restroom.

Penny and Kris followed the captain to that necessary facility. It was small, but sported a shower tub that had a small sign asking passengers to limit their showers to no more than five minutes. A second door in the room opened onto a room identical to the one whose measurements Kris had found depressingly limited.

"Two rooms will certainly be better than one," Kris admitted.

"Now about meals. We normally require passengers to come to the mess deck. The ship's crew and officers eat together because there aren't that many of us. I really don't want to have the cook bring your meals to the room. That would be very unusual and create talk. On the occasions we've had a passenger of the status we're affording Mrs. Travaford, their servant has collected the meals."

Kris frowned. "That might be a problem since I'm the one we're trying to keep out of the spotlight."

"Certainly you have a disguise you intend to use on Wardhaven," the captain said. "The first time a camera gets a good picture of you, and they run face recognition, there will be all kinds of problems."

Penny nodded, displaying a grin that ill became one of her advanced age. "Yes, we do have a few tricks up our sleeves. We might as well start applying them during our time aboard and see how well Her Princessness here adapts to them."

"Huh?" ill became Kris, but it was all she got out.

The captain seemed to be enjoying some private joke. He nodded, and excused himself. The belly laugh didn't start until the door closed behind him.

"What was that all about?" Kris asked.

"You'd be laughing, too, if you saw the look on your face."

"So, how are we going to get me past face-recognition software?" Kris grumbled. "Will I have to look as old as you?"

"I don't think Abby had that in mind. But let's see what she has in that other trunk for you."

An hour later, Kris eyed herself in the mirror and didn't recognize herself. She had curves. All kinds of curves. Far more than any woman would ever want.

Her breasts were now double E's or F's. She had trouble just walking in them, and God help her if she ever had to run. However, her extra top hamper was now balanced by a butt that was double something or other.

There was also a wrap around her waist that added volume there as well.

Over it all was a size-twentysomething dress that covered it all with no style at all.

"Oh," Penny added as if as an afterthought, "if you need to, you can pull the foam out of your boobs and your butt and fill them with grenades, spare ammo, explosives, whatever."

Kris studied all the padding. "I could supply an army if I could lug the weight."

"Well," Penny said, fluffing her gray hairs, "I sure couldn't hide anything."

"We could trade places," Kris offered. Or maybe suggested. Strongly suggested.

"You're known throughout space as a tall beanpole. Security will take one glance at this and look elsewhere for you."

Nelly cleared her throat diplomatically. "But that face of hers will be spotted in two milliseconds by any security camera."

"So we change the face," Penny said, and headed back to the trunk to return with a plain brown box.

"You have a lovely nose," she said.

"It's too big," Kris shot back.

"So, we'll make it bigger," Penny said, and produced a bulbous nose that not only went out farther, but also added breadth and width to Kris's own.

"A funny nose will not fool a good computer," Nelly pointed out.

"We'll do more than just mess with her nose," Penny said as she glued up and applied the false proboscis smoothly onto Kris's face.

Done, she delved once more into Abby's box of tricks. "Cheekbones. How do we mess with such lovely cheekbones? Ah, this will do it."

And Kris found her cheeks fleshed out. Her jaws grew jowls, and, with a flourish, Penny added a double chin.

"I look horrible." Kris sighed.

"You sure don't look like yourself," Nelly agreed. "But you need to do something about the forehead."

"I'm coming to that. How about beetle brows." A moment later, Kris's brows had been shaved and a new forehead glued in place.

"I don't look natural. Anyone who looks at me will tell I'm loaded down with plastic junk," Kris growled.

"Okay, try smiling," Penny said.

Kris did. In the mirror she saw something fit to frighten children or curdle milk. "See?"

"Looks just like my aunt Frieda," Penny said. "Lord, how I hated when she came visiting. Everybody has an Aunt Frieda."

"I didn't," Kris insisted.

"Well, everyone but you has an Aunt Frieda, and one look at you will make them want to be anyplace else but where you are."

"Gee, thanks," Kris said, and frowned. Which, in the mirror, gave her back something that looked like it might have crawled out from under a bridge to dine on children's toes.

"Kris," Nelly said. "I've run you through standard security face recognitions. You do not come out anywhere close to your normal profile. I've also run you through the best available commercial recognition programs. Even they give you less than a forty-nine-percent probability of being you, and they are all set in the factory not to report anything below fifty percent to cut down on the false positives. This disguise should get you through security."

"If you say so," Kris said, and tried to saunter across the room. She managed it, but she'd never be able to do it in high heels. Fortunately, companions and aids in Kris's putative job only wore reasonable shoes: solid, low, ugly.

Finally, an upside to this charade—at least her feet would like it.

As if Kris didn't feel hideous enough, Penny added the *pièce de résistance*.

"Roll up your sleeves and close your eyes."

"Why?" Kris asked.

"Do it, then you'll see."

Kris was none too sure about this. She'd been dressed by Abby and Penny before. Just once. They had her walking the worst streets of Turantic as a streetwalker. Only passing Jack off as her trick had kept her from a whole lot of worse fates than death.

Admittedly, she'd be wearing a whole lot more in this disguise; still, Kris strongly suspected that Abby and Penny would be laughing for a long time about what they'd talked her into this time.

Kris rolled the three-quarter-length sleeves of her dress up past the elbows and closed her eyes. She heard the "pssst" of an aerosol can but kept her eyes shut until Penny announced, "You can look."

Kris did.

"I've got freckles! A million of them!"

"Or more," Penny said, glee on her face and in her voice.

Kris took her new self in. "Even Jack would never recognize me."

"And he certainly wouldn't want to kiss you," Penny agreed.

"This is horrible.

"Prison might be worse," Nelly offered.

"Much worse," Penny agreed.

"Will I need an hour to get all this on every time I go out?"

"Nope," Penny said, "this is you. You'll walk in it, sleep in it. Until we decide to take this off, you are the woman you see."

"Do I get to take a bath?" Kris asked in a small voice.

"If the advertising on this box can be trusted, you could swim the English Channel in this and it wouldn't come off, whatever that is."

"We'll see if I can take a bath in it first," Kris said.

"How about you get us some lunch?" Penny said. "I'm starving. Getting you all fancy-dressed worked up an appetite."

Kris frowned, but she went to do her mistress's bidding.

Penny was right about the disguise. Nobody recognized Kris Longknife as she collected two dinners. Also, no one tried to strike up a conversation.

The men and women of the crew took one look at her, and their eyes just kind of slid away to somewhere else. Even the captain's.

Kris had heard other girls in high school complain that ugliness was an invisibility spell all its own. Kris had had other problems at the time and hadn't given their complaints much thought.

She owed them an apology.

Or maybe being someone's servant made you invisible.

Kris smiled to herself. Being someone's ugly servant, now that really put you out of everyone's notice.

16

Throughout the voyage, Kris continued to go unnoticed by most of the crew. The one exception was a junior cook. After she complimented him on the chow, he started giving Kris a few extra tidbits from the kitchen. Maybe it was the junior cook's low status among the Sailors that made him so eager to talk to her. Or the warts on his face. Or maybe he was just a man who appreciated compliments.

Kris's stint as a serving girl gave the Nuu Enterprise's trust-fund baby a whole lot of new things to think about.

When she wasn't thinking about starting a war and losing her last command.

And finding Jack.

What had Gramma Ruth meant when she said she could help Kris find Jack? Get back to Jack? Kris was one jump away from Wardhaven, and she still had no plan for what to do when she got there. No plan other than to put one foot in front of the other and follow her nose.

Even to Kris, that didn't sound like much of a plan.

It only got worse when they docked at High Wardhaven.

"Kris," Nelly said, her voice almost quivering, "I can't attach to the net."

"Can't attach?" Kris said, not expecting the Magnificent Nelly to have a problem on her home turf.

"Yes, Kris. All my certifications have been canceled. Even my secret backup ones. There's a new security wall in place and it won't let me in until I fill out a long list of questions, and they verify them. Kris, I'm toast."

"Me too," Mimzy added from Penny's neck. "I didn't have a whole lot of certificates, but none of mine are working, either."

"Kris, I've tried all my children's certificates," Nelly said. "We are totally locked out of this network."

"Since when?"

"I'm not sure, Kris. I was careful not to access Wardhaven while I wasn't talking to you. I just used the Madigan's Rainbow net there, and not a lot of it. Mimzy?"

"I used the Chance net, but once we started moving, I closed down pretty tight."

"Hold it," Kris said. "Jack's on HellFrozeOver. His Sal must be attached to the Wardhaven net."

"I've already tried it, Kris. The reply I got with his certificates was the same as I got from my own. Kris, they've isolated me and my kids from Wardhaven. I don't know about everywhere else, but here, they've slammed the door in our face, locked it, and thrown away the key."

Kris didn't like the sound of that. "So Sal is just a standalone computer for Jack. No access to anything at all."

"That's horrible," Mimzy said.

"That's all of us now," Penny said.

There was a knock at the door.

The screen immediately showed Captain Tidings. Kris took a second to make sure he was alone . . . she was coming down with a bad case of seriously paranoid after Nelly dropped that bomb . . . and then let him in.

"I have a message for you, Mrs. Travaford," he announced.

"Who from?" Kris didn't think anyone knew what name Penny was traveling under. Suddenly, she was not at all happy that someone did.

"There is no originator on the message," the captain shrugged. "It's also very cryptic. I almost trashed it, but I thought you might be able to make something of it."

He handed it to Kris. The message was brief.

Meet me at My Old Haunt.

                                                                T

"Does that mean anything to you?" Captain Tidings asked.

It might, but Kris was not going to share it with anyone who wasn't walking in her own footsteps.

"I'm not at all sure," Kris said, folding the message to keep it out of sight.

The captain accepted Kris's vagueness, and went on, "I strongly suspect that you don't want to use your own credit chit here."

"Captain, I'm not sure my credit chit still works here." The discovery that Nelly, Mimzy, and Sal were barred from the net gave Kris a strong hunch that her money was no good either. Kris was none too happy to be going down to Wardhaven with no plan. Now she couldn't even go down. She had no way to pay for her and Penny's beanstalk tickets.

"I thought you might find yourselves in that situation. Here are some gift chits. They're sold to encourage people to spend them on just what they cover. Here are several to pay your travel, elevator, bus, even taxi fares. These should let you eat for a while and these last two should cover a hotel room for a few days. These kind of things are popular in the travel industry. If you give people money, they'll spend it just the way they want. Give them some of these, and they've got to take the vacation they need. Great idea."

"It sure is," Kris said, suddenly seeing options opening before her.

"Again, I want to thank you for saving my daughter. She's married now, and I expect to see my first grandchild when this voyage is done. Her mother and I can't thank you enough for all the joy we feel just now."

What could Kris say to such gratitude? "I'm glad Jack and I were there and could do what we did." Even if it had hurt like hell for the next couple of days.

With that, the captain took his leave.

"So, what's the massage mean?" Penny asked, as soon as the door was closed.

"That's what I'm trying to figure out," Kris said, unfolding the message and studying it.

"Could T be General Trouble?" Nelly asked. "Your Grandma Ruth hinted that she'd get him involved."

"She did," Kris agreed slowly, not at all sure she wanted any help that came from that branch of her family tree. The general was Trouble. Trouble to his enemies. Trouble to his troops, and double trouble to his superiors. What he'd been to Kris was a whole lot of trouble.

When Grampa Trouble suggested that she needed a good security team and hinted at Jack, Kris had drafted him into the Marines one very distinctive rank below her. Then Trouble took a very angry Jack out for drinks and showed him the new law that allowed the security chief of a serving member of the royal blood to countermand any order he considered dangerous to his primary's survival.

Her survival, there being no other member of the royal family then on active duty. Then or now.

Kris had thought she had a great way to keep Jack just where she wanted him. Once Jack returned from Trouble's briefing, it was an open question as to just who had who, where.

It had been fun, arguing with Jack over just which of her orders he could countermand. How Kris would love to argue with Jack just now.

Which reminded Kris of an argument she had with Jack. It was right after the Battle of Wardhaven. Election day, to be exact. Kris was so mad at her father that she'd refused to vote for him. She wasn't willing to vote for the opposition, not after the mess they'd gotten Wardhaven into during their brief interregnum, so she'd just not voted. Besides, she'd been rather busy at the time, attending the funerals of all those who had died under her first command, of sorts.

It was Jack who dragged her out of her funk and took her down to a dive on the wrong side of the tracks from the space elevator. There she'd found Grampa Ray and Trouble. Them and a whole lot of folks like them.

Even the barkeep seemed like an old friend of Trouble's.

That was the first time Kris didn't wait for orders but insisted that she be sent out on training duty to teach other planets how to use their fast patrol boats. It had seemed like a good idea at the time. Of course, after two assassination attempts, it had seemed like an even better idea for her to go someplace far, far away.

Which led to another set of problems.

But what was the name of the bar?

"Kris, I've searched my stored archives," Nelly said. "There's no place by the name of My Old Haunt on Wardhaven. Well, there is, but it only opened four years ago. I don't think General Trouble could be talking about that one."

"No, no I don't think he means that. Penny, let's get our game faces on. Thanks to the generosity of Captain Tidings, we are going down the beanstalk."

"And then where?"

"I'll know it when I get there."

17

Putting their game faces on took a bit longer than Kris had expected.

With just the gift chits the captain had given them, it would be very hard for "Mrs. Travaford" to play the role of a wealthy widow out to see human space and spend her late husband's money. The fake jewelry went into Abby's steamer trunk.

There they found just the worn dress needed to bring Penny down five or ten social levels from the wealthy "Mrs. Travaford" to poor pensioner "Mrs. Travaford."

They also found spider-silk bodysuit armor. The new kind, backed up with liquid metal to absorb and spread some of the kinetic and traumatic force of being hit.

To Kris's delight, she slipped right into her armor. When Kris pointed that out to Penny, she made a face at Kris as she continued donning her gear and dress.

After burying herself in the padding of her disguise, Kris found a wig. It turned her hair dowdy and brown but lowered her forehead and was armored as well.

They were going to war. Now Kris felt ready.

No one remarked on them as they left the *Yellow Comet*. The station trolley line ran close by; they quickly caught a ride.

Penny hobbled into the elevator station, making good use

of her cane. Kris shambled along behind her, head down, shoulders hunched over. The steamer trunks rolled along haltingly behind them. Somewhere in the short trip, the luggage went from spotless to banged up and dented.

DID YOU DO THAT NELLY?

I CAN'T GET US ON THE MAIN NET, BUT I CAN HANDLE MY LOCAL ONE, KRIS.

The ferry station was on night routine; two attendants watched a football game. Old Mrs. Travaford inserted her credit chit backward, so Kris stepped forward to help her. The flub drew only a glance from the two watchers. Once they saw that things were back on track, they went back to their game.

Penny and Kris toddled toward the ferry. With each step Kris expected the security alarms to go off. People might be distracted, but automated security cameras never were. Her face and her body were being scanned dozens of times a minute.

There was no sudden flood of security guards. No alarms. No nothing.

They made their way aboard and found an out-of-the-way corner to huddle down in. Just two lonely women traveling with all their worldly goods in the beat-up trunks beside them.

Penny fell asleep as befitted her apparent age. Kris stayed nervously watchful, eyeing anyone who walked by. Her disguise continued to work its magic; no one looked at her twice.

Glad for the uneventful ride, Kris still found herself with a problem as they made their way off the ferry and into the Wardhaven down station. Abby's steamer trunks were far too large for any cab. The answer to that was found off to a side. There were lockable storage bins. No papers required, just swipe your credit chit and take the key. One of the captain's gift chits was accepted.

Load lightened, one old lady and her unremarkable granddaughter were left trying to hail a cab on a dark and rainy night. Five empty cabs splashed by them before one stopped.

"Where you ladies want to go?" the cabby asked as Kris hastened to stake her claim on the car by settling a complaining grandmother in the backseat.

"The Smuggler's Roost," Kris said.

"That dive! You ladies really don't want to go there. You'll never get out of that neighborhood alive at this time of night."

"My son says he will met us there," Mrs. Travaford snapped. "I have not heard from my son in twenty years. He says to meet him there. I will meet him there, young man," Penny told the driver, who was at least ten years older than she.

Kris held back a grin. No question about it—Penny was a quick study.

"That's a really bad neighborhood, ladies."

"That is why I bought my granddaughter a pistol at a pawnshop back home. You have the gun, don't you, Stephanie dear?"

"Yes, Grandmother, but I really think you should have let me fire it a few times. They say you should practice with something as dangerous as a gun."

No one said Kris wasn't a fast study, too.

"We only bought the six bullets that were in it. We can't go wasting them."

"Yes, Grandmother," Kris said, dutifully.

The cabby just shook his head. "Be it upon your heads," he said, and took off into the rain and dark. Kris had been too self-absorbed in her own problems to pay much attention to the ride when Jack brought her there. It had also been a sunny day. Tonight, in the rain, the cabby was right.

This was no place for a little old lady.

Kris was glad she wasn't carrying some cheap six-shooter from a pawnshop. She had her Navy-issue sidearm. Despite the layers of disguise, it was in easy reach.

They pulled up to a shabby building in a block of redbrick buildings that looked even more the worse for wear. If there was a streetlight, it was dead. There was no light but the flickering neon lights of beer signs. Even the bar's own sign, SMUGGLER'S ROOST, was blacked out and faded.

Clearly, people came here because they knew what was here, not because something attracted them.

"You sure you want to get out here?" the cabby asked one last time.

"Yes," Kris said, looking as dubious as the heavy makeup allowed.

"I can wait here for you. I won't even turn on the meter."

"No, no," Mrs. Travaford insisted. "My son said he'd meet us here. I will not leave until I see him."

"Or they throw us out at closing," Kris added under her breath.

Mrs. Travaford shot Kris a dirty look.

The cabby turned to take Kris's gift chit and run it through his net connection. When he handed the card back to Kris, there was a second card with it. "If you need a ride, just put that next to your commlink. It will dial my company. Some of us don't like coming into this part of town at night, but I'll tell the dispatcher to call me. I'll come get you, no matter what."

"Thank you so much," Kris said, and meant it. The driver was dark-skinned, and the hanging from his rearview mirror proclaimed that Allah was merciful. Once again, Kris had run into a Moslem cabby willing to go out of his way to help her.

Kris closed the door, hoping that driver was right. Tonight, let Allah be merciful. Kris could use all the mercy she could beg, borrow, or steal.

She helped Penny hobble into the bar, holding the door open for her. The scene inside was smoky and warm, lit mainly by the colorful beer signs flickering along the walls. There were plenty of empty tables. But several had extra chairs pulled up around them, making for cozy familiarity. One table broke into loud guffaws as they entered.

Few people bothered to take in the newcomers. None of them gave Kris or Penny a second look. The barkeep looked them over, frowned, but quickly went back to filling an order. Having established a basic awareness of the scene, Kris started examining the dark nooks at the corners and the back. All the people in the front were strangers to her.

Great-grampa Trouble was fairly easy to spot. Even in the dim light, his ramrod-straight back was distinctive. Penny spotted him about the same time as Kris and needed no urging to start working her way slowly toward him.

There might be no security cameras here; still, a suddenly spry hundred-year-old might make folks talk, and talk to people Kris didn't want talked to.

Beside Grampa Trouble sat another soldier, distinctive by the haircut even out of uniform. Colonel Hancock hadn't changed a bit. He was eyeing them as they approached. The general turned to follow his gaze and studiously took Kris's measurements. Neither looked away.

A third man sat deep in the shadows of the booth. It was hard to make out his features. but Kris saw enough.

Jack was here!

18

Senior Chief Agent in Charge Foile of the Wardhaven Bureau of Investigation put on his coat. They'd gotten their serial killer before she killed her weekly victim. His computer was organizing all the evidence and preparing his report. He'd sign it in the morning and turn the complete package over to the county prosecutor. It would be nice to get home early at least once this week.

The chatter in the squad bay was happy, as was to be expected. His team prided themselves on always getting their man. This week's "man" was a serial killer and a woman. They had a lot to be proud of.

"Hey, I got a hit on Princess Kristine," Leslie Chu remarked. Leslie had met the woman once and become a fan of the Longknife princess, even if she did seem to get into more trouble than any woman could. Leslie's computer was set to report anything on the net about the princess, and it had become a team joke as week after week passed without Leslie's getting her princess fix.

"What's that troublemaker up to now?" Agent Mahomet Debot asked.

"I don't know. She's just disappeared from wherever it was

they sent her after her thing with the aliens," Leslie said in a puzzled voice. Unusual for her.

"Isn't there an arrest warrant out for her?" Rick Sanchez asked.

"She hasn't done anything illegal," Leslie said, jumping to her princess's defense.

"Starting a war," Mahomet offered.

"You'd have gone in shooting if you'd been there, and they fired first," Leslie snapped.

"Boys and girls, let's keep it professional," Foile put in to lower the temperature.

"There's been an arrest warrant issued for her," Rick said, bringing said warrant up on the main screen in the squad bay.

"That's not much of a warrant," Mahomet said, noting that the code violation was blank. The write-up only added more vagueness to the whole thing.

"I'd hate to have to serve that if there was a lawyer present," Rick said, and drew a grunt from everyone.

"Well, I'm going to make it home in time for supper tonight," Foile said, and turned to go.

And was almost run down by the division chief's personal assistant.

"Good, you're still here. The Prime Minister wants to see you immediately."

"Me?" Foile said. "Don't you mean the boss?"

"No. He wants you. Now. The division chief says for you to report to her immediately when you return."

"I take it that neither she nor you know what this is about."

The personal assistant shook his head. "All they said was they wanted you, and they wanted you ten minutes ago. Go."

Foile went. Outside the doors, he hopped one of the two wheelers. Usually, he preferred to walk. It was good exercise for a man his age and gave him time to think. With a summons from on high this vague and demanding, thinking would not be a good idea.

He wheeled through pedestrian traffic quickly for the four blocks from the Justice Ministry to the Prime Minister's offices. He was greeted at the door by a rushed young woman who fairly snatched him off his ride and hustled him through normal security and into an elevator.

They arrived breathless in the foyer of the Prime Minister's office, but the senior secretary there gave him no time to catch his breath as he ushered Foile into the Prime Minister's presence and immediately closed the door.

It took all of two seconds for Foile to discover why even his private secretary did not want to share space with the Prime Minister.

"How could any bunch of imbeciles have screwed this up worse?" the Prime Minister demanded, waving several flimsies at Foile.

The agent took this for a rhetorical question and offered no answer as he closed the distance to the Prime Minister's desk.

"I can't believe that we've got idiots of this caliber working for my government. Heads are going to roll, I tell you. Heads will roll."

Foile was glad that he wasn't the subject of the Prime Minister's anger. Unfortunately, he suspected his presence meant he was next in line to be added to whatever list was taking shape.

"You called for me?" Foile said. He'd rushed there; he strongly suspected whatever job awaited him would have a very short fuse. While it might be fun to watch the famously cool Billy Longknife explode, it was burning time.

"One and a half hours ago, ninety minutes, my daughter's pet computer tried to attach to the Wardhaven net. Ninety minutes ago!"

Billy Longknife was also famous in his speeches for repeating for emphasis. Foile frowned. He did not need repetition.

"This is important how, sir?"

The Prime Minister opened his mouth, looking ready to explode at Foile, but then seemed to think better of it. He took several deep breaths and began again.

"We sent her someplace safe after that last fiasco. If she just stayed there until things blew over, matters could be made to work out. But no, she can't stay put for two minutes. My daughter had to bust out of her safe planet, and now she's charging around space, no doubt causing trouble with every step she takes."

"You've issued a rather vague arrest warrant for her," Foile put in.

"Yes, yes. What do you say about someone who can be everything from a public nuisance and pain in the neck to the center for undescribable public murder and mayhem?"

Foile admitted that was a problem by allowing himself a shrug.

"She's here now, somewhere on Wardhaven. Find her, Agent. I'm told you are the best bloodhound in the Bureau. Find my daughter. Find her before she gets herself killed, please. Hopefully, before she gets a lot of other people killed, too."

Foile heard this as a father's plea. As a father himself . . . who would not be putting his kids to bed again tonight . . . he accepted the assignment. No doubt some would question the right of the Prime Minister to have WBI chasing down his daughter, but to Foile it was a simple matter.

Some judge had approved an arrest warrant. That was enough for him.

"Do we know where her computer tried to hitch into the net?" Foile asked, starting the process.

"On High Wardhaven. I bet she just arrived. The failed attachment took place in the dock area."

"Then she's very likely still there. If she'd tried to pay for passage on the space elevator or crossed any of the security areas, she would have been identified."

"She's a Longknife, Agent. Never forget that. She's a Long-knife, and I'd bet the next election that she's already down here, breathing the same air you and I are."

"I'll take that under consideration, sir. Sir, we will need all the information that we can get about her background."

That brought a frown to the Prime Minister's face. "I figured you'd say that. I've ordered the release of her files to your team. It goes without saying that I don't want to see some of the more racy parts blown all over the media tomorrow morning."

"It goes without saying, sir, that my team will respect her privacy."

"Do you need anything else?"

"I can't think of anything at this time, sir."

"Then find my daughter. For God's sake, find her before she gets herself killed."

That was the second time Billy Longknife had forecast his daughter's death. It raised a red flag. "Is there some specific danger I should be aware of, sir?"

For a moment, the Prime Minister considered the question. For a moment, Foile thought he might be about to say something, but when he spoke, he fell back on the generic. "No. Nothing you need to be aware of. Just find her."

"Yes, sir," Foile said, wondering what he didn't need to be aware of and whether or not it might kill him or his team along with the peripatetic princess.

As the senior chief agent in charge left the Prime Minister's office, he was already tapping his commlink.

"Rick, keep the team together. We've got an assignment. Pull all the security coverage of High Wardhaven's dock area. And tell Leslie that she's about to learn more about her Longknife princess than she ever wanted to know."

19

It took all the willpower Kris could muster to stay at Penny's side as she shuffled toward the back of the bar. But the slow pace didn't mean she had to ignore Jack. Out of the corner of her eye, she watched him. Since the other two men were watching them, Jack did, too.

At first, he seemed distracted, uninterested, maybe even depressed. But the more he watched her, the more intense his gaze grew. They were still five eternally long meters away when Jack's eyes lit up, and he mouthed, "Kris!"

A moment later, he blew her a kiss.

From two meters out, Kris flew into his arms.

She couldn't feel his cheeks on hers for all the junk she had on, but she could sure feel his lips. They were heavenly.

Then his arms were around her. Again, there were so many places she couldn't feel him, but his hands danced on her back, and his arms enfolded her.

She was finally where she longed to be.

She hardly noted when Penny settled herself beside her, giving her some cover from any roving eyes. Kris didn't care. Let them gawk. Still, as she hungrily devoured Jack's lips, she couldn't help but hear the table conversation.

"That Kris?" Colonel Hancock asked. "The years haven't been kind to her."

"Yeah, I wasn't sure, either," Grampa Trouble said. "But I think we can trust Jack on this." That drew a chuckle from all three of them.

"And we worked so hard on our disguises," Penny said with a sigh.

"You got this far," Grampa Trouble said. "It must have fooled the security scans."

"It fooled me," the colonel admitted.

There was silence for a while, then the colonel began again. "Are they going for a record or something?"

"Nope, not even close," Grampa Trouble said. "When Ruth and I got back together after the Iteeche dustup, we went a whole lot longer." He paused before adding. "Of course, we were married by then, and there was a bed involved. Penny, has she already got a room?"

"We just got down the beanstalk. We came right here."

"She got my message, then."

"She got it, but she didn't give me a hint where we were going until she told a cabby where to take us. Untrusting girl, if you ask me."

"It's kept her alive this long," Trouble said.

Kris finally had to come up for air. One gulp and a whispered "Jack," and she was ready to make up for more lost time.

"Can I have you two's attention for a few seconds?" Grampa asked.

Kris nestled into Jack's arms and turned front. *Oh, if I could ditch all this junk I'm wearing. If I could feel Jack,* she thought. Of course, that junk had got her through several security checkpoints without her being hauled off to jail.

Choices, choices. Someday, I'll live with one choice and nothing else.

"Yes, Grampa," Kris said, holding Jack's hand tight.

"What's your situation?" he asked softly.

With a sigh, Kris came back from the bliss of Jack's arms. She didn't move an inch away from him, still, that wonderful feeling of Jack's being close and nothing else in the world mattering took quite a beating.

"We're here," Kris said the obvious. "We have no money. Nelly and her kids can't access the Wardhaven net, and Grampa Al seems to have gone rogue. He's definitely taking a back door into politics and maybe hatching some cockamamy plan to deal with the alien all on his own. We need to stop him, but I have no idea how."

Kris glanced at Jack. He hadn't taken his eyes off her. "Other than that, everything is great." She kissed him again.

Grampa Trouble let them go on for a brutally short time, probably no more than a minute, before calling her back to the matters at hand.

"Your Gramma Ruth told me about the political play he made on Eden. She didn't say anything about the alien thing."

Kris sighed. "The political play was poorly done and left enough threads leading back to him. Nothing strong enough to take to court. The alien thing was a vague reference that likely would have been ignored, except that the guy who made it woke up with his throat slit next morning. That kind of makes people talk."

"Even ones who aren't as paranoid as you Longknifes," Colonel Hancock said. "But no idea what it is, huh?"

"No idea at all," Kris replied.

"Your Gramma Ruth tells me that someone tried to kill you before you'd been on Eden an hour."

"Yes," Kris admitted. "The shooters were hired. Who paid them was still being examined when I left Eden. Have you heard anything?"

"Nothing. But Ruth heard it might be someone in your Grampa Al's pay."

"Yes, I head that rumor, too," Kris admitted. "But the short fuse doesn't leave enough time for someone to get Grampa Al's approval for it. My guess is someone was trying to get back into Grampa Al's good graces and pulled the pin on that operation without approval."

"Someone would think that killing his granddaughter would make his employer happy?" Colonel Hancock said with a raised eyebrow.

"It's a Longknife thing," Penny said.

"Now I'm starting to understand why you were so hot to

trot to get away from the Longknife shadow. How's that working?" Colonel Hancock asked.

"Not so well," Kris admitted. "Some days better than others."

Kris chose to change the topic. "Grampa Trouble, do you think there's any chance I can get in to talk to Grampa Al? And if I do, is there any chance I could dissuade him from whatever it is he wants to do?"

"I figured you'd want to get in his Fortress of Security, so I did a little discreet nosing around. As to talking him out of anything." Grampa shook his head. "He's a stubborn old cuss, much like his dad, Ray, and not known for walking away from a business deal once he's set his hat for it."

"Yeah," Kris nodded. "That's pretty much what I heard, too." Kris turned to lose herself in Jack's eyes for a moment. "Damn, all I want to do is find some sunny beach with a nice small cottage and curl up with you."

"That's been in my thoughts a time or twenty," Jack said. The first words she'd heard from him sounded wonderful. Of course, he'd had a hard time getting a word in; she'd kept her mouth on his pretty much since she first caught sight of him.

Kris sighed. "I really don't want to go charging off to save the world again."

"Spoken by someone who sounds resigned to doing just that," Jack said.

"You up for another charge into the breach?"

"I'd prefer a beach," Jack said with one of his lopsided smiles. "Do you honestly think we can find a breach in Al Longknife's security wall?"

"What chances do we have?" Nelly asked. "Considering that right now, I can't even catch the nightly news feed."

"Jack told me that he hadn't risked getting his computer in the net, what with the invasive tests and background checks the new security system requires," Trouble said. "I had a hard time believing it, considering what Abby's reports said about what you and Nelly and her kids had been doing in Peterwald space. Still, you've got to take a man at his word. And if Jack was blocked, I figured you were, too."

"What have you managed to come up with?" Kris said.

Hating herself for what she did, still, she found herself leaning forward, away from Jack, to better hear what Grampa Trouble whispered.

"When your aunt Trudy went off after alien relics, she left me a note. If I needed info-warfare help in her absence, I could talk to her sidekick from the old days of the Iteeche war, Sara Powers. A freethinker in those days, she caused a lot of people a lot of trouble. Some of it actually helped the war effort."

"You're complaining about someone causing you trouble?" Penny slipped in.

"She didn't pay her dues to my troublemaker's union, the scab," Grampa said with a scowl that curled up too much at the edge of his lips. "I told her what I wanted, and she asked me no questions, just three days later dropped this mass storage chip in my hand after we'd gotten together for lunch to talk about old times."

Kris noticed a storage chip between Grampa's fingers. She thought of reaching for it, but didn't. He'd pass it to her when he wanted her to have it, at a time and place of his choosing. There might be no visible security cameras in there, but that didn't mean there weren't any.

Suddenly, Colonel Hancock sat up even straighter. "I'm getting activity on the police band. Much of it's coded, but it's all addressed to this sector of town."

Grampa Trouble frowned. "Nelly, did you try to connect to the net?"

"Yes. On the station I used all my certificates, including the secret ones."

Grampa was already starting to stand. "Kris, did you use your credit chit to get down the beanstalk?"

"No, Grampa. The skipper of the *Yellow Comet* gave me some gift chits."

"Bought here or on Eden?"

"I'd guess Eden."

"We need to be gone," Grampa said, standing. The softness of his words were countered by the urgency of his movements. "The rear exit is out past the loos."

20

Senior Chief Agent in Charge Foile found his team already hard at work as he walked into the squad bay. His boss was also waiting for him.

"What's this all about?" she demanded.

"Princess Kristine Longknife has returned to Wardhaven, and the Prime Minister wants us to apprehend her," he said curtly. "Rick, did you get that security coverage?"

"Yes, sir, and based on what you told me to tell Leslie, I've already scanned for the princess. No joy. If she's up there, she's still on the ship that brought her."

"Or she's evaded us," Mahomet, always the dour one, put in.

"The Prime Minister is betting with you," Foile said.

Leslie looked up from her computer screen. "The last reported location, no, make that last rumored location for the princess was on New Eden. Did we have a ship from there dock recently?"

"One," Rick reported. "The *Yellow Comet*. I've got the coverage of it. Only some crew and two old ladies left it."

"Two old ladies?" echoed everyone in the room.

"Here's the take," Rick said, bringing up the two putative old ladies and the analysis of the recognition system. "Neither one of them is six feet tall. The way both of them walk, neither of them is a Navy officer. And the several looks we got at their faces. Ugly. Way ugly."

"Two steamer trunks," Leslie said.

"What about the steamer trunks?"

"Maybe nothing, but when you read a color report on the princess, or her maid, the better ones talk about the steamer trunks that follow them when they're off on a mission. The maid, Abby, can pull the darnedest things out of those trunks."

"Follow those two," Foile ordered. "Recognition program, estimate height of the tallest one if she wasn't all hunched over."

The response 5'11" to 6'1" appeared on the screen.

"Get a security team from the station to search that ship," Foile ordered.

His boss made the arrangements immediately.

"Rick, where'd those two nice old ladies go?"

"The space-elevator station. They paid, ah, with gift credit chits."

"Bought where?"

"Eden."

"Show me them at the downside station."

Rick did.

"They've still got the two big trunks," Leslie pointed out. "They can't be too hard to follow with those things."

The camera showed them storing the luggage.

"Or not," Leslie added.

"Have a team collect those trunks," Foile said, and his boss made it so.

"They caught a cab," Rick pointed out.

"Mahomet, get me a list of all fares taken from the beanstalk station within five minutes of that time."

"On it, boss. Got it," Mahomet, shouted a second later. "Two women, from station to a place called the Smuggler's Roost. It's in a bad part of town. Why would two old ladies go there?"

"We need a full response team at that location," Foile said, heading for the door. His team was up and following him as his boss called in the world on that little dive.

21

With no further urging from General Trouble, they were up and moving. Penny slowed them down a bit with her cane, but a little old lady racing out of there would be a clear giveaway.

Steeling her heart, Kris let go of Jack's hand and got busy being elsewhere. It was easier since Jack was right behind her. In a moment, they were out the back. In the distance, a siren could be heard. Maybe that was normal in this part of town, but it seemed to be getting closer. Then it went silent.

"Ungood," Grampa Trouble said. "Colonel, did you bring a car?"

"I borrowed one from a friend. I do still have a few of them." He pointed at a beat-up coupe parked across the street, and they headed for it, Penny in the lead. Her cane was now held more as a club, no hobbling now.

The car chirped as the doors unlocked. Kris found herself with a wonderful excuse to cuddle up to Jack. The backseat was close for three, and the car was cold.

"Does this thing have a heater?" Grampa Trouble asked from the front passenger seat.

"Not that I've noticed," Colonel Hancock said as he put it in gear and pulled away from the curb in one smooth motion.

And stopped at the first stop sign.

The colonel turned them onto a potholed four-lane road with a railroad track down the middle that took them away from the Smuggler's Roost. He held his speed down to well below the limit.

"Good," Grampa Trouble said.

"Mind filling us fugitives from the law of averages in on what's going on?" Penny asked.

"I guess you deserve some words of warning," Trouble said. "After Admiral Crossenshield heard about how you cracked into the Peterwald net, not once but for several planets, he kind of got obsessive about our own planetary net. Surprise of surprises, old Al Longknife was interested in it as well. Even had a security package ready to sell. It kind of makes me wonder if Al had something to do with the Peterwald problem."

"Or knows the folks who are running the new emperor around in circles," Penny observed before Kris could.

Then again, Kris was rather busy kissing Jack and only half paying attention to the conversation.

Which meant she was only half paying attention to Jack's kiss.

Problem was, she strongly suspected Jack's focus was split, too.

Drat!

"So we got an entire new security system. Every computer had to be recertified. Every one of them, even a kid's first computer. You can imagine how that went down. Oh, and just for fun, some machines' certifications evaporated overnight, for quite a few nights. There were threats to take the whole thing down, but things are getting better, and people are grumbling less."

"But it screwed me out of my access," Nelly grumbled.

"Too true, girl," Grampa said. "Worse, they've got flags that go up whenever anyone tries to access the system without a certificate or starts to apply for one and drops out. Did they leave a tag with you?"

"They did *not*!" Nelly sniffed. "No one tags me."

"But just the certificates that you tried would be enough to raise a red flag," the colonel said as he turned left on a new road that kept them headed away from the Roost. "Your old certificates would tell them Kris was back in town."

"I imagine so," Nelly said. "I couldn't get in even enough to erase that I'd tried to get in. It was a stone wall."

Kris couldn't stay out of the conversation any longer. She broke from her clinch with Jack, and said, "So Nelly's effort to attach to the net alerted them we were here, and when we used an Eden gift credit chit, it was enough to get them after us?"

"That's why I paid cash for our drinks," Grampa Trouble said. "Your trail stops dead at the Roost."

"Won't the barkeep remember you?" Penny asked.

"We lucked out there. New hire. Never saw him in my life," Trouble said. "And from the surly service we got, he definitely doesn't know me."

"Maybe he did recognize you and gave you the service he thought you deserved," the colonel said as he headed up the on-ramp to a crosstown expressway.

"Can I ask where we're headed?" Kris said.

"Yes. A rental place by a lake," Grampa Trouble said. "I saw it advertised on the net. Used a Wardhaven gift card I bought with cash to rent it for the next couple of days. If anyone can trace us to it, they're better bloodhounds than I've heard of."

Jack raised an eyebrow at that.

A little place by a lake. Maybe even a beach.

Maybe they could have a few days to themselves. Time to talk.

Maybe.

22

Senior Chief Agent in Charge Foile didn't much care for what he saw. He and his team, along with a small contingent from SWAT, had charged into the Smuggler's Roost ready to kick butts and take names. The local denizens had looked up from their drinks, taken their measure, and gone back to their conversations.

Leslie and Mahomet had come in the rear, checked the bathrooms, and found them empty as well.

Of two little old ladies, there was neither hide nor hair.

"Stand down," Foile ordered the SWAT boys, and they put their weapons back on safety, but they didn't show any interest in leaving.

Good.

Foile sauntered up to the barkeep and produced a picture of Lieutenant Commander, Her Royal Highness, Kris Longknife. "Have you seen that woman?"

"Naw."

"Are you sure?"

"Listen, if a looker like her came in here, I and everyone here would have noticed. We may be drunk, but we ain't blind."

"How about her?" Foile asked, offering the best take they had from the security cameras.

"Nope, never saw her," was his answer.

"Sure."

The bartender shrugged. "Would you give her a second look? Bother remembering *her*?" The guy had a point.

Foile had to give the princess points for her disguise. The agent chose a different approach. "Did anyone leave suddenly just before we got here?"

"Come to think of it, that table kind of emptied out when no one was looking," he said, pointing at one of the back booths.

"How many were there?"

"Three, no five. Two old ladies came in, one with a cane. They joined the other three."

"You got their tab?"

"Nope, old geezer paid cash."

At some point in this unproductive interrogation, Leslie had joined them.

"May I, sir?" she asked.

"Go ahead. I'm not getting anywhere." Foile took a step back.

"Was one of the first three fellows this guy?" she said, offering a picture of a Marine in full dress uniform.

"Yeah, that could have been the young one. He was kind of down, didn't say much, just kind of hunkered down in the back and let his elders do all the talking. That guy's in a bad way if you ask me."

"Who is he?" Foile asked.

"Jack Montoya, the head of the princess's security team, or at least he was until her whole team was busted up after the last cruise. All us girls in the princess's fan club were just dying for him to kiss her. I mean, what kind of girl spends all her time around a guy like this and just argues with him?"

Foile found himself looking at a handsome man in a crisp uniform. "Arguing all the time. Marriages have been built on worse," he muttered.

Leslie gave him one of those faces she reserved for when men were being *Men!*

"What do you have on this Jack Marine?"

"Not much. I know he was a Secret Service agent before Kris drafted him. Boy, was that a blowup. But he doesn't give interviews."

Foile turned to his boss, who had just entered the Roost. "I'm going to need information from our client."

"You've got the number on your commlink."

Foile wasn't really surprised that he now did have a number for the Prime Minister's office. He punched it.

"What can I do for you?" came immediately.

"I need full information on Jack Montoya, Marine," Foile said crisply.

From the background came an, "Oh, Christ, are those two together again?" in what sounded like the Prime Minister's voice.

"Tell him that we aren't sure, but we need that information," Foile said.

"It's already coming your way," was his answer.

The data streamed at him. He arranged for a copy to go directly to Leslie's computer. Her eyes lit up with delight.

Then she got serious. "Boss, we need to talk." Leslie led the way, and Foile quickly found himself in a staff meeting with all three of his team.

"Jack was reassigned to HellFrozeOver."

That drew a whistle. You didn't have to be Navy to know what that meant. Rumor had it that the Bureau had a small office on the place. Maybe it did, but no one admitted to ever having been assigned there.

"If he's there," Foile pointed out, "why do we have this report that he's here?"

"Just a second, boss. Right. God, this new computer is good. He's TDY to Wardhaven for a training course. Uh-oh. It's on the new computer security system."

"Has he finished it?" Mahomet asked.

"Three-day course, done today. His commanding officer came with him. A Colonel Hancock?"

"Not that Hancock," Foile said. Then he thought again. Hancock *was* the CO of HellFrozeOver.

"What Hancock?" Rick asked.

"Never mind. He's the Marines' problem, not ours," Foile said. "Where are those two supposed to be now?"

"They've got rooms at the Army Navy Club. They're heading back tomorrow."

"That should identify two of the three soldier types the

bartender mentions." Foile turned to his boss. "Could you have their rooms at the Army Navy Club checked? They're likely empty, but . . ."

She was on the horn immediately.

"I think I know who the third guy is," Leslie said, and offered a picture of a balding officer, also in Marine dress blue and reds. "This is General Tordon, otherwise known as Trouble. That's darn near officially his name. You can ask his friends, enemies, superiors: He's trouble."

"And if we've got trouble brewing here," Foile said, "he's likely close to the bottom of it."

"That's a good bet," his boss said, joining the circle. "He's a legend."

"And how does he figure into this case?" Rick asked.

"Trouble is the princess's great-grandfather," Leslie supplied.

"I thought King Raymond was her great-grandfather?" Mahomet put in.

"He is. Both of them are her great-grandfathers," Leslie explained.

That drew a whistle from Foile's boss. "The poor girl didn't have a chance."

"Genealogy has nothing to do with this case," Foile pointed out. "Leslie, run Trouble's picture by our bartender. Mahomet, if they aren't here, they likely left in a hurry and in a car. Find it."

"Already on that, boss. Two minutes before we got here, a car turned off the street behind this place onto a street we have under surveillance."

"Did you get the license?"

"No, sir, the car's plates were covered with one of those screens."

The team groaned. Driving with no plates or obscured plates would get you stopped in a hurry. However, plate screens were still, despite three tries, legal.

Seen from directly behind by a police cruiser, the plates were readable. Seen from a security camera mounted up high, the screen made the plates totally unreadable. If you were going someplace you didn't want your parents, spouse, or private investigator to know about, the plate screens provided privacy.

At a moment like this, it was a pure headache for the police.

Three times the parliament had taken up the topic, and three times the proposed law had been sent back to committee. Apparently, some lawmakers felt the need to be off the grid on occasions.

"Track the car as far as you can. See if you can locate a GPS that matches the travel it does." It was a long shot, and considering who he was up against, Foile doubted these people would make a tyro's mistake. Still, every option had to be examined.

"Rick, see if any of those three rented a car recently. If that's a dead end, see who will admit to being a friend of those two. Anyone who might lend them a car. Someone provided that ride."

"On it, boss."

23

The cottage turned out to be a little place. A very little place.

The one small bedroom was given over to the general, both because of his seniority, and the report that he snored. A painfully accurate report as it turned out.

That left Kris, Penny, Jack, and the colonel sharing the living room/kitchen. Clearly, the cottage was intended for a couple. A young couple with no kids.

Kris left the two couches to the colonel and Penny. She and Jack settled down with a few blankets on the floor before a pretend fireplace. It offered little heat against the night cold and a flickering light that a blind person might mistake for a fireplace's cheery glow.

Kris didn't care.

"I've missed you," she whispered to Jack as she got close to him under the blanket. A rather lengthy stay in the bathroom had shed her disguise. She had not shed her spider-silk armor. While she might want Jack close, she had to make sure the world kept its distance with things like bullets, explosives, and other nasty stuff.

"I've missed you, too," Jack answered.

The dialogue seemed a bit trite to Kris, but it said what she felt. Likely a lot of people had felt what she felt and found no better way to express it.

"Penny said you made quite a fuss when they took me away."

"Worse fool me," Jack said with a scowl that seemed almost satanic in the faux firelight. "The thought of you without security drove me up the wall. I tried everything I could to follow you. Finally, they flat out told me I was not going to be stationed anywhere near you. That's when I resigned."

"That work any better for you than it did for me?" Kris said, snuggling closer.

"You tried to resign, too?"

"In front of King Ray and Field Marshal Mac and Crossie. That's when they told me they wouldn't let me and were dumping me in Siberia, or Madigan's Rainbow, whichever was closer."

"I got HellFrozeOver," Jack said, with a shiver that Kris was only too glad to try curing by rubbing up against him. Which led to another kissing interruption.

A bit later, Kris came up for air, and a question. "So how'd you get here?"

"You've got to thank your grampa Al."

Kris raised an eyebrow. "I can't picture him doing me any favors. Not intentionally."

"Well, his new cybersecurity system also extends to Hell-FrozeOver. All security types have to be retrained. I don't know if anyone gave it any thought, but Hancock had no trouble bringing his deputy security chief along to Wardhaven for the training class.

"Strange." Jack's effort to look puzzled had a lot of grin in it. "We were scheduled for the first class but had to drop out. Colonel Hancock gave me thirty minutes to pack my bag and join him for the shuttle to Wardhaven for this class. What do you think of that?"

"I think that anyone who underestimates my gramma Ruth, Gramma Trouble to many, should know by now just how foolish that is."

Jack's fingers found a very nice place on Kris, and they settled back to enjoy it for a while, despite the spider-silk armor in the way.

Jack was the one who let the world interfere next. "Are you serious about trying to see your grampa Al and talk him out of whatever he's up to?"

Kris raised a finger. "Yes, I want to see him." Then she raised a second one. "Yes, I want to talk him out of whatever he thinks is a great idea." Up came a third finger. "Because I've spent some time thinking about what that cockamamy idea might be, and I don't see any good ones on tap."

Kris paused for a moment to organize her thoughts. "Eden's president says Grampa Ray is beating the drums to build a fleet that can face the alien raiders."

"He is?" Jack interrupted. "It hasn't hit the media. There's been total silence. The story of what we did vanished from the news before they decided to scrap the *Wasp*, and that took less than seventy-two hours."

"That long?"

"Three days. Day One we were crawling with newsies and cameras. By Day Three, there wasn't one in sight. It was like someone turned off the switch."

"Maybe someone did?" Kris whispered. "It would be interesting to know who. Anyway, the president of Eden told me that he was getting tired of King Ray talking about nothing but raising taxes for a new fleet. He may not be saying anything like that in public, but the word is out to those who matter."

"Is it working?" Jack asked.

Kris shook her head. "Eden's president sounds like he'd walk out on the U.S. rather than pay for a new Navy."

"So if Grampa Ray is tacking in that direction," Jack said, his fingers doing their best to distract Kris.

"Grampa Al must know about it and is pushing ahead with something quite different. If I know him, he's all in a rush to open trade routes."

Jack's hand slapped his forehead, which, sadly, interrupted his distractions for Kris. "He's not that stupid, is he?"

"I don't know how he thinks he can open trade negotiations with monsters who shoot first and don't talk later," Kris said. Now it was her turn to shiver. "If Grampa Al sends out a fleet, it will be loaded to the gills with trade goods. It would be shot up, no questions asked, no quarters given. But will trading captains blow their reactors to destroy their nav computers as our battleships did?"

Somehow, Kris doubted that.

Jack shook his head. "No. If your Grampa Al sends a trade fleet, it will be shot to pieces, then those pieces would be combed through with eager anticipation. Those alien bastards will find all kinds of goodies they'd love to steal and easy directions on where to get them."

Kris rolled over to stare at the fire. After a while, Jack started gently rubbing her back, working on the tension that knotted her spine.

The two of them stared into the faux fire silently for a long time. Kris found her head cradled in the crook of Jack's arm. For the first time in her life, she drifted off to sleep in a man's arms.

24

The cottage did have a beach. It took a walk through the trees to find it, and it was only one or two meters wide, but it was sandy.

It was also cold and rainy.

Fortunately, the folks who owned the cottage had several cheap rain slickers hanging on pegs by the door. So Jack and Kris went for an early-morning walk to clear their heads and see if the gray morning light offered them anything better than they had mulled over in the false light of the fake fire.

It didn't.

They had been dealt out of the game, and some serious squeeze was being applied to keep them out of what was afoot. Both agreed that was beyond stupid since they were two of the few survivors of humanity's first contact with the alien menace. Then again, both of them could point out historical precedents for stupidity being the frequent, even routine, response of humanity in crisis.

"And this time we've got a Longknife, wealthy as Crassus, leading the charge into stupid," Kris said with a sigh.

They settled on a log and looked out over the lake. Clouds or morning fog limited their view to little past a swimming platform that was in easy reach of kids during the summer months. Literally and metaphorically, Kris was in a fog.

She'd been there before. This time was different; she had Jack's arm around her.

"How did you know it was me last night?" Kris asked, suddenly changing the topic in her head from a rabbit run to something much less important for the salvation of worlds but quite important to her at the moment.

"You *were* ugly," Jack said. "Will that be you when you're old?"

"Not if I follow Gramma Ruth," Kris said, and elbowed Jack in the ribs. "Answer my question or face further torture."

Jack laughed, and locked one arm around the offending elbow and used the other hand to stroke the soft flesh of Kris's lower arm.

"Ooh, I'll give you a year to quit that," Kris murmured.

"It was the steel spring inside you," Jack murmured back.

"Steel spring?"

"Yes. You were puttering along beside Penny who was putting on an excellent display of limited mobility, and your pretty little nose was buried under a ton of misdirection, but I could still see, maybe 'feel' is a better word, the tightly wound steel spring in you, ready to uncoil with a snap at any moment. You were doing your best to hide the power in you, but you couldn't hide it from me."

Kris found she was purring like a kitten. "That's probably the best compliment I've ever gotten, even if you did lie."

"About what?"

"My nose. It's never going to be a little one."

"For a young woman six feet tall, it's a very nice nose, in my opinion. Tell me, Your Highness Kris Longknife, if we both decide to do something about making this present state of bliss permanent, will you always disagree with my best advice on how lovely you are and what you should do to save me from widowerhood?"

Kris did her best to look indecisively coy before allowing an answer of, "Yes, very likely. No, almost certainly."

"I was afraid of that." Jack sighed a sigh of resignation to an inevitable he'd already come to accept. But he kissed Kris, so it was clear he bore her no grudge.

The kiss was interrupted by two growling stomachs. Kris found she could actually giggle around Jack. "Sorry, I haven't eaten since lunch yesterday on the *Yellow Comet*. Do you think there's any food in the cottage?"

"I would very much like to find out."

The fog lifted as they walked back. A clearer view showed them an isolated cove with only two other houses visible through the trees. Neither showed activity.

As they came through the trees, Colonel Hancock drove up in his borrowed car and asked their help unloading groceries. They turned to with eager hands.

But Kris's paranoia was already activated. "Can that car be traced?"

"I'm pretty sure it can't," the colonel said. "Besides having a broken heater, its GPS is also on the fritz, as well as its central computer. It's not only an old car, but a teenagers' learnin'-to-drive car. My buddy has four kids and this is the car they get to learn in. You may notice it's got a few knocks and dents." In the light of day, the state of the car left Kris wondering how it worked at all. She said so.

"Three of the four kids are boys, and they know it's up to them to keep it running. As for his daughter, she's the one who took automotives in high school and is going on to be an engineer. She makes sure the boys take good care of the car."

Kris laughed, but thought NELLY, CAN YOU GET ANY SIGNAL OFF THAT CAR?

NOT A PEEP, KRIS. THERE'S A LOW ELECTRONIC HUM, JUST WHAT YOU NEED TO HANDLE THE SPEEDOMETER AND FUEL INJECTION, BUT IT'S NOT SENDING ANYTHING.

They carried their supplies inside. There, Grandpa Trouble proved to be a competent cook, at least when it came to bacon and eggs. Kris managed to warm up some cinnamon rolls without burning them, and Jack reconstituted frozen orange juice. Feeling accomplished, they all settled down to breakfast.

And Penny started talking like a cop.

"We'll probably need another safe house tonight," was the first bombshell she tossed in with the eggs.

"You think so?" Grampa Trouble said.

"By now, they know we are on planet. If they got anything from asking around the bar last night, they know that Jack and

Colonel Hancock are with us. That there are five of us and you three were not in any real disguise. Right?"

"I didn't use my credit chit," Grampa pointed out.

"Which immediately raises a red flag. Good citizens with nothing to hide always leave a nice trail behind them. Only crooks or other lowlifes," she softened that with a flash of smile, "use cash."

"So you think they'll be trying to trace us three," the colonel said.

"That's what I learned at my father's knee," Penny said, "and the first day of internal-security training. Identify the subject of the investigation, then identify all their contacts. Have all of them talked to, that's what the beat cops are for, asking questions of the people you want questioned. Spread the dragnet wide, then tighten it up and pull it in."

"So what would you be doing right now?" Kris asked.

"I'd have a computer grinding through all the credit chits purchased with cash and what they've been used for. Every last one of them. There'll be plenty of chaff. Lots of people don't want their spouses to know they're renting a motel room or taking someone to dinner. There are a lot of cash chits out there. It will take time to chase them down, but they're onto us, and they won't quit."

Penny paused to think. "It's true they won't quit, right? Any chance your dad or the king will relent?"

"Not this side of hell," Kris said.

"Then we need a new car and should be making tracks out of here. Any suggestions for where we might safely stay tonight?"

Whereas all the other faces around the table had gotten more dire as Penny laid out standard police procedures, Grampa Trouble was beaming when she finished.

"So, that's all we have to worry about?" he said.

"Pretty much," Penny said, nonplus.

"Good, good, good," Trouble said. "When you're done, you can leave your plates on the table. Someone else will be doing our dishes. Kris and Penny, you should be getting back into your disguises. Our next ride will be here in about an hour. We'll want to meet him at the road. No need for us to leave any tire tracks in the mud outside, right Penny?"

"Correct, sir," and the girls took over the back bedroom.

A half hour later, they were daintily making tracks over the pine-needle-strewn ground under the trees, careful to avoid any soft spots. They waited under the trees through another downpour until a blue four-door sedan halted on the road, then all made a rush for it.

"I'll take the front seat," Penny said.

She slipped herself between Grampa Trouble and the driver, who turned with a grin, and said, "My, Krissy. The Navy life is not agreeing with you."

It was Harvey! He'd been the chauffeur at Nuu House since before Kris was born. It was he who took her to games when she was too hungover to care, much less play decently. He was also the one who likely turned Kris in to Grampa Trouble and turned her life around.

"It's so good to see you," Kris said as she settled into the middle of the backseat, between Jack and Colonel Hancock. She snuggled next to Jack, letting the colonel have half the backseat of the big sedan.

"It's good to see you too, little one," Harvey said, the only one who still called a six-foot-tall Kris "little one." "You had me and the missus worried there for a while, but I kept telling her, 'That's a Longknife they'll find hard to kill,' and you proved me right."

"It was way too close, Harvey. Too many good troopers didn't make it back."

"They were soldiers, child. They knew the risks when they signed on to follow one of them damn Longknifes. Their words. Not mine."

"Where are we going?" Grampa Trouble asked.

"An old war buddy of mine has a place in the mountains. We haven't much kept in touch, just at the odd reunion or two, but his boy was on the *Mercury*, one of your courier boats, Kris, one that came back with the transports. The boy was furious to miss out on the fight, but his da told me he could hardly put in words how glad he was to get the kid back in one piece. Anyway, they are both fans of yours, youngster, and he was glad to give me the keys to the lodge; no questions asked and none answered. It will be a cold day in hell that anyone connects the two of us old farts."

"What about this car?" Penny asked. "Can they trace it to the hills?

"Not bloody likely. Its GPS is back on the workbench in the garage. It needs adjusting. I've got one in the car that my grandkid got ahold of at a swap rally. This squawker has nothing to do with a Longknife."

"If I didn't know better, I'd say this car was full of people who weren't very law-abiding," Colonel Hancock said primly.

"That coming from you, sir." Harvey growled, as only a disapproving noncom can to an officer. Still, he headed down the road.

"I will say now, and I will say it to the day I die," Colonel Hancock said, "we were taking fire from the crowd. I saw one of my Marines fall. I don't care what the record says about the farmers having no weapons and none of my Marines being hit. My eyes saw a different picture from what the court heard."

"I believe you," Grampa Trouble said.

"You do, sir?" Colonel Hancock clearly hadn't expected that.

"We should have sent a regiment to cover the trouble on Darkunder," General Trouble said. "The decision to cut the force down to a single battalion was made somewhere in Earth high command. Ask who did it, and you'll get a vague runaround. That riot hit you at the height of the devolution debate in the Society of Humanity Senate. If your situation wasn't politically manipulated, then no soldier has ever been hung out to dry for the benefit of a political agenda."

"Hearing that from you, sir, a lot of stuff suddenly makes sense."

Kris was glad to hear the relief in her old CO's voice. She was gladder still to have time on her hands. She burrowed into Jack's arms and found herself relaxing as she listened to his heartbeat. Just listened.

Very relaxing.

Except when a police patrol car passed them going the other way or overtook them. But the cops were going somewhere else and not interested in a shiny blue sedan with what looked to all appearances like a family out for a drive.

They skirted Wardhaven City on the beltway before heading out into the countryside. Kris remembered campaigning for her father among the farm communities. Usually they went for him and were delighted to see the young Kris out husking for her father. Then there had been the time some-one poured a pail of milk over her.

Politics wasn't always a gentle sport.

The drive stretched as the road climbed past foothills toward the snowcapped mountains, which first could only be glimpsed, then began to dominate the view when they crested one of the ever-higher ridges. The air took on the crisp taste of pines and open sky. Most of the trees were Earth transplants, but now and again, there would be a hearty stand of blue native hardwood, waving their now winter-bare limbs against the gray sky.

Kris had spent a summer hiking mountains like these. She told Jack. He shared that he'd been a counselor at a youth camp high up in these mountains. To her delight, she found they shared a love of high places and crisp, free air.

It surprised Kris that after serving beside Jack for so many years, she was only now discovering that about him. But, she told herself, she shouldn't be. They'd spent their time plotting how to stay alive, or how to foil this or that attack. There had never been time to talk of less urgent matters.

Inside, Kris winced. This was only an interlude before both of them did some damn fool and deadly thing, like invading Grampa Al's supersecure fortress past security he bragged was the best in the worlds. Considering how blocked Nelly was at the moment, he likely had a point.

The stray thought flitted across Kris's mind. If she turned herself in on the condition that she and Jack be sent back to Madigan's Rainbow, would they do it? Would she do it? If she had Jack with her, she certainly wouldn't be tempted to crawl back into a bottle. Not with Jack handy and available for crawling into bed with.

But they'd had the chance to send the two of them into exile together, and they'd chosen to separate them as too dangerous a pair. Having escaped once, what were the odds they might reconsider their options?

Very likely they'd lock the both of them in the deepest dun-geon they could find on planets as far away from each other as human space allowed. Kris found herself shaking her head.

"What are you thinking, honey? You look so serious," Jack asked.

"I was wishing this drive would never end, but I know it must," she said in half truth. Her dark and muddled thoughts could wait for some quiet walk through the woods and hills once they got where they were going.

They turned off the main road onto a gravel road that rapidly lost its gravel and gained potholes. Lots and lots of ruts and potholes. Harvey slowed the car down, but it still bounced from one rut to the next.

Kris didn't mind. It gave her an excuse to hold on tighter to Jack.

Finally, they pulled into a small clearing. The lodge turned out to be a small A-frame structure with an attached garage. A huge stack of wood against the garage, three logs deep, promised that tonight's fire would be real and likely critical to their not waking up tomorrow as icicles.

Harvey popped the trunk. "You'll all need to lend a hand to get everything inside. I brought you a week's worth of chow and some clothes for you, Princess. They should fit Penny as well."

"Are we going to be left afoot?" the colonel asked.

"Nope," Harvey said. "There's a car in the garage. It belongs to the sergeant's kid. He usually stores it here when he's out spacing. They had the schooners that the princess used for courier ships going around to all the solar systems in human space, the ones we never use, dropping off minibuoys. Something drops into those systems, we'll know real quick about them. Now the schooners are doing the same to the systems surrounding our space. If something comes visiting, we'll know."

"It sounds like Grampa Ray is at least paying a little attention to what we found out there," Kris said with a scowl.

"Kris, Ray hasn't spent a day since you got back without thinking about what you found," Grampa Trouble said. "I know he's not doing what you or I think he should. I've told him that enough times now that he heads somewhere else whenever he sees me coming. He is, in his own way, trying to get us ready for what we all suspect is headed our way."

"Well, it would have been nice for him to tell me that rather than ship me off to Siberia and lock me out of even a minimal news feed."

"You can forget the general media," Jack put in. "You'd never know we'd gone out from listening to them. We've fallen into a black media hole."

Kris grabbed two of her suitcases that predated Abby's steamer trunks and headed for the lodge before she risked another word. "It would sure be nice if all the people working in secret, including my great-grandfather, my grandfather, and my father, would let the rest of humanity in on what they're doing to save us all before one of those humongous mother ships drops by to strip one of our planets bare."

"Frustrating, isn't it?" Jack said.

"Hey, we're soldiers," Colonel Hancock said. " 'Ours not to reason why,' and all that."

"Yeah," Penny cut in. "But we're also citizens and voters, and they're treating all of us, in or out of uniform, the exact same way. Like mushrooms. Keeping us in the dark and feeding us pure cow manure. I, for one, am sick of the chow."

That brought chuckles all around, even from Grampa Trouble.

25

Senior Chief Agent in Charge Foile stood in the middle of the lake cottage as a forensic team began to process it. There was a lot of stuff here, but it didn't tell him anything that he didn't already know. The subject of his search had flown the coop and left not a trace of where she or her companions were going.

The car outside matched the video of the one leaving the Roost area. Its owner was even now talking to a pair of WBI agents, but Foile would bet money he could write the interview report himself. "Yes, I know Colonel Hancock. He was in town. I loaned my kids' junker to my old Marine buddy. Is there a problem, Agent?"

The cottage had been identified by the process of elimination of all the motel, hotel, and other rental properties paid for by a credit chit bought with cash. They'd busted down half of the doors so paid for, interrupting quite a few adulterous trysts as well as several teenagers who begged not to have their parents informed.

Now they had the right one, and it was telling them only what they knew. Five individuals that field DNA tests identified as General Tordon, Colonel Hancock, Captain Montoya, Lieutenant Commander Longknife, and Lieutenant Pasley-Lien had been here and weren't anymore. There were plenty of tire tracks in the mud in front of the cottage, but all the fresh ones belonged to the car that was sitting there.

"Damn, these folks are good," Foile whispered to himself.

"They're the best we've got," Leslie said. "Usually, we're rooting for them."

"Today, we've got to catch them."

"Yes, sir," the woman agent said.

"Mahomet, I need to know every car that entered the local freeway at the closest exit and the next two exits in either direction. I want to know where every one of them went and who was driving them. You hear me?"

"That will tie up a lot of computer time, sir."

"Time we don't have, so get on it now and get all the computer resources the Bureau can beg, steal, or borrow." Foile turned to his boss.

She nodded. "They are yours as soon as I get off the phone."

"Good," Foile grumbled. "Even good people make mistakes. That's what we're looking for, crew. Their first mistake."

26

Kris found the lodge, like the cottage, small but cozy. It had a bedroom in back and a sleeping loft above. The rest of the place was taken up with a large room that doubled for kitchen, dining room, and living room. It had a woodstove that looked to be the only heat for the place. And it was cold, hardly warmer than outside.

"I'll start a fire," Jack offered.

"I'll help you get firewood," Kris said, and the two of them brought in a dozen logs between them. There was tinder in a box beside the fireplace, with long matches, so while Grampa Trouble supervised the storing of food and the distribution of suitcases, Kris watched Jack make a fire.

"Haven't you ever made one? You said you spent a summer camping?" Jack asked after his second glance back at Kris's intense face.

"Never. We used the cookstove. Part of keeping a light footprint on nature. The few times we did have a fire, I wasn't around while the boys got it going. I figured they were pyromaniacs, and it wasn't something I should watch. I thought they just tossed some logs in, added a match, and bingo, we had a cheery fire."

"Shows what you know," Jack said as he built a small fire with tinder between two logs. He then added a flat log as a kind of roof over the flaring tinder while opening the flue wide. "You do that to get the fire started. When it's hot, we cut back and reduce the airflow. But now, we need a lot of air to get things burning."

Kris watched intently as a tiny flame became a small fire, then grew to a roaring concern. She wished she'd seen this earlier. Nature was mimicking so much of her life: starting small, growing bigger, then a fire too hot for anyone to put out . . . or get close to.

Kris laughed at her foolishness. Mother Nature had been there long before she was born. She'd just witnessed a ritual that must have been repeated endless times from when the first man tamed fire until Jack showed her how it was done. Here was a lesson she wished she'd learned a long time ago. It would have put a structure around so much of what she'd done, from recruiting workers for one of Father's campaigns to . . . her feelings for Jack.

Did they have a fire going between them that would never burn out? Kris found herself daring to hope so. She hadn't realized just how much she'd missed talking to Jack, sharing her plans with him, until they were back together.

Having tasted how much she needed him, she never wanted to be without him.

While they'd been getting the fire going, Harvey had taken his leave, and Grampa Trouble had laid out fixings for sandwiches. "Come and get it," brought everyone to the table. Once everyone had fixed their own sandwich and gotten a bite, all except Grampa, he cleared his throat.

"Seeing how I was so rudely interrupted last night at the Roost, and again at breakfast by Penny's thorough briefing on police procedures, I would now like to finish what I started. While Al's security is tight, it is not without chinks."

"And you know that how, Grampa?" Kris said around a full mouth.

"I have my sources. Where it came from doesn't matter. That I have it, and you can use it, is what counts."

"It will matter, Grampa, if the very action of your getting the information has alerted security to the query," Kris shot back. She'd done and been done to enough to know that you had to erase your footsteps just as fast as you made them.

"I agree with her," Nelly put in.

"Kids, please don't try to teach your old great-grandfather how to suck eggs. I was pulling dirty tricks on my enemy, or superior, long before either of you were hatched. And so was my info-warrior sidekick. What she got, she got, and no one is the wiser. Trust me on that."

"We may be trusting you with our lives," Kris said.

She didn't think Grampa Al would actually harm her. But his automatics might not check her ident before they burned her and Jack. And there was that matter on Eden.

"Kitten, I know well what I'm risking. I'd love to go with you, but these old bones just don't have that kind of fun in them. But, Granddaughter, I want to bounce your baby someday on my knee. Maybe even change a diaper or two. Who knows?"

Kris had to fight back tears. "Grampa, that is the most loving thing I think I have ever heard from one of my blood relatives."

She left her place at the table and went around to give him a hug. It was hard to tell under his tan, but it sure looked like he blushed. So she made it worse by giving him a peck on the cheek.

"Here, here," came from Jack, so on her way back to her place, Kris gave him a hug. His kiss was not on the cheek and took a bit longer.

"Get a room," Penny suggested.

"There's only one here," Kris said, "and our snoring giant needs it if any of us are to get any rest."

"I did warn you that I sawed a lot of wood at night," Grampa said with no repentance.

Kris took her seat and returned to the life-or-death matter before them. "Okay, General Trouble, what have you got for us?"

The general leaned forward and began in a low voice. "Like so many businesspeople, Al is penny-wise and pound-foolish. He's contracted out the outer layer of his security. The pay for rent-a-cops is low and the turnover what you'd expect. They're always hiring in new faces."

Kris shook her head. "So you can get us in the front door. It's a long way from there to his bedroom."

"Stay with me. My contact has downloaded a complete map of Al's compound and the central tower. You'll want to study these before you go in," the general said, and handed the tiny data chip to Kris. She held it close to Nelly.

"I'm loading it all now. Sal and Mimzy are getting it, too."

"The internal security gets tighter," Kris said.

"It does, but my good friend has created false handprints for you as well as a couple of matching eyeballs for scanning. The owners of these are scheduled for a night off, but they get called in enough that main security won't think anything of them being in for a while."

"And if they *are* called in while we're in?" Jack asked.

"There will be a problem," the general admitted.

Kris leaned back in her chair, food forgotten, and weighed the odds. They weren't very good, but if Grampa's cybermagician had pulled some really nifty new stuff out of her hat, Kris would take the chance to hop along with it.

"We do it. When, General?"

"Tomorrow night," he said. "You'll be doppelgänging folks that get two days off starting tomorrow. If something doesn't break right tomorrow, you've got the next day as an option."

"Sounds like a plan," Kris said.

"As much as we ever have," Jack added.

"Better than several I've been dragged kicking and screaming through," Penny said.

"Who goes?" Colonel Hancock asked.

"Not you," Kris said. Jack and Penny nodded along with her. "You've risked your neck enough just getting Jack here. I can't tell you how happy you've made me. Now, you and Grampa Trouble go back. Cover your tracks. Do what you're supposed to be doing."

"I'd really like to go with you, Commander," the colonel said.

"You will be, sir. You taught me a lot of what I know. Or kicked my butt and got me learning a whole lot of what I thought I knew but didn't. I wouldn't be here if you hadn't marched into my life, sir."

The colonel half snorted. "I wasn't doing much marching back then. You made my life a whole lot more interesting."

"She has a tendency to do that if you survive her," Penny added.

"And a whole lot haven't," Kris finished.

"You're going to have to cut that out, Commander." Now it was Grampa Trouble's turn to hold Kris with his eyes, demand that she attend to his words.

"You made a call. It was the right one in my book. You planned your battle and fought it the only way you could. As so often happens, it worked, and it didn't. Nothing unusual in that. The odds against you looked bad when you started and got worse as you went along. I've been there, done that, and got the scars on my body and soul to prove it."

His crisp words paused for a moment, before going on. "I can point you at history books and tell you that is just the way it happens, but your history is fresh in your mind, and it was written with the blood and sweat of good men and women you knew personally. It's easier to handle if folks give you a nice victory parade, but it doesn't take away the scars on your soul even if they do. Take my word for it. You are the only person who can make the call for you. You can either spend the rest of your life eating your liver, and likely die young, or you can stand up, throw your shoulders back, and soldier, girl. What's it going to be?"

Kris let the words run over her, like baptismal water from some fiery preacher. Fire and brimstone in camouflage. Her head already knew everything he'd told her, but under his stern eyes, the words flowed like a torrent into her heart. A heart that had gone cold and hard in the pressure of battle, and rejection now met the old soldier's fire . . . and melted.

"I will soldier," Kris said. "I've got too much to do to lie around eating my liver."

"I never much cared for liver," Grampa Trouble muttered.

"But it does raise a question, Grampa," Kris said.

"Which one?" he growled.

"How come I'm the one that keeps having to save the world? Why can't somebody else step up to the plate and, for example, give Grampa Al a good whop to the head and knock some sense into him?"

"Oh, that old question," the general said, and took a deep

breath. "You ever find the word 'fair' on your birth certificate, Kris?"

"No, sir. And I looked real good a couple of times or twelve."

"I never found it either. It's damn unfair that some people get an easy life and others get a hard one, but that seems to be the way it works. And the problem with having a hard life and handling it well is that you get handed even harder stuff the next time. And if you do that well, the next one is even harder."

"Until you get the one you can't handle, and it breaks you, huh, Grampa?"

"Or it turns you into someone like Ray. There is another option. Your gramma Ruth keeps me human. Keeps it all in perspective. The love of a fine person can do that for you."

Kris looked at Jack, reached over, and took his hand. She gave it a hard squeeze. "You willing to take on that job? Keeping me human and, whatever Grampa Trouble was talking about. In perspective."

"That's a job I'd volunteer for," Jack said without a moment's hesitation.

"Good, then let's finish our sandwiches and think," Grampa Trouble said.

They finished their meals in silence. Kris spent the time with Nelly reviewing the data on the chip. From the way Jack and Penny stared off into space, they likely were doing the same. Finished, Kris summed up what she'd found.

"So, you've got the necessary certificates for Nelly and her kids to fake it online as some old computers. Nelly, can you do it?"

"No problem, Kris. You remember when I was working on probing that alien rock, I created a part of me and isolated it from the rest of me. We can create a pretty lame and outdated section in our self-organizing matrix and let any security system probe that to its heart's content without getting a hint there's more lurking behind."

"That's a start," Kris said. "Now, where is the sneaky gear that will get us in and through Grampa Al's wondrous security walls?"

"In one of the suitcases you brought in," Grampa Trouble quickly answered. "You want to look at it now?"

"No. I'll take your word for it. Crew, it looks to me like we've got everything we need. Jack, Penny, you see anything that I've missed?"

"Nope. It's a thin plan," Jack said. "But then, I can't think of anything to thicken it up. If you're sure Grampa Al won't order his security guards to shoot to kill, then I guess we do our best. We can't end up any worse than we've been."

"Are you *sure* your grampa Al won't order deadly force?" Penny asked. "It's not like we can send him a letter telling him who's coming to dinner."

Kris leaned back from the table. That was the heart of her problem. The only way she had a chance to see Grampa Al was to come in under false colors. And there was no familial protection under that false flag.

"If things get too bad, we'll just have to let him know who his intruder is," Jack said. "If we're deep inside his security zone, we might still be able to advance even after we let him know it's Kris just trying to get a word in edgewise with him."

"What do you think, Grampa?" Kris asked. "You've known Al all his life. He won't really kill me, will he?"

Grampa Trouble did not answer that question nearly as fast as Kris wanted.

"I would hope not," he finally said slowly as he rubbed his chin in thought. "You have to understand, that kid just about raised himself, with Ray and Rita being off in the war and all. He's got issues with his old man enough to fill a lifetime. I like to think that blood is thicker than water, but between those two, I'm none too sure there is any blood in their veins. And now you say he's gone rogue, ignoring both his father and his son's efforts to handle the alien threat, charging off in his own direction entirely. It doesn't sound good."

"So," Kris summed up her thoughts, "if he hasn't gone rogue, he'll likely meet me with hugs and kisses, and this effort is a waste of time. If he has gone rogue, then we really do have to get in to him. But we may have to do it through live fire."

"I think that pretty much the operation," General Trouble concluded.

Kris pursed her lips, making a face at her now-well-defined problem. "There is sneaky gear for just the three of us?"

"Yes."

"Well, as I see it, the two of you"—Kris marked Grampa Trouble and Colonel Hancock with her eyes—"need to get back to your regularly scheduled life. The sooner the better."

"I can call Harvey to give us a ride down the mountain," Grampa Trouble said.

"No you won't," Kris and Jack said at the same time, with Nelly a nanosecond ahead of them both.

"No net activity from here," Kris said. "Let's take a look at this car we have and see what we can do about Penny's driving you two down the mountain."

"I'm staying at Nuu House," Grampa Trouble said. "Penny can drop us off ten blocks from the place, and we can hike in. Maybe we'll get a bite to eat before we do that. Give Penny a bit of time to exit the threat zone."

"We can play that as we see it," Penny said. "Let's see how this car works."

The car was plugged in to the solar panels on the roof, so despite the cold, it was ready to go. The problem was the very small size of the backseat.

"I think I can squeeze in there," Penny said. "You big men take the front seat."

"I'll drive," the colonel offered. In a few minutes they were backing out and heading slowly down the road, with Jack and Kris waving good-bye to them.

"I think the fire has warmed up the place," Jack said.

"It will be good to get out of all this heavy disguise," Kris said.

Jack had always been good at getting Kris out of trouble. Now he showed his skill at getting her out of other things. He was even good at slipping her out of her spider-silk armor.

But then, Kris was very good at getting him out of his, too.

27

Senior Chief Agent in Charge Foile slammed down the phone. "General Tordon and Colonel Hancock just walked in the front gate at Nuu House."

Heads popped up as his team came out of their computers. Eyes were bleary and exhaustion thick. "Have they been interrogated?" Rick asked.

"Not yet," Foile answered. "And I doubt we'll get two words out of them. Still, that they've come in out of the cold tells us something. Two are in. Three are still out there. How did the two get in, and can we trace them back to the three? Drop your old data tracks. Get the feed from Nuu House."

"I've got it," Mahomet said. "They walked in from Fifty-fourth Avenue."

"Backtrack them. I don't care what you have to use. Bank or traffic video, gas stations. Any video we can get, look for them."

"Doing it," came from all three.

"Rick, I want you to get yourself over to Nuu House. Talk to those guys."

"I thought you said they wouldn't talk, sir."

"But they need to know we're onto them. Maybe you can rattle one."

"Rattle General Trouble?" Leslie said, her eyes still on the feed running fast across her computer screen.

"I don't have high hopes," Foile admitted, "but there is always a chance. Even the best make a mistake. Maybe just one, but if we don't force it, these folks aren't going to give it up for free. Rick, do your best. Lives may depend on it."

"Understood, sir. I'm on my way."

Foile went to stand behind his other two agents. Security film flashed by almost too fast for the human eye to process. The computer checked each figure, applying its own search parameters. The two men were very distinctive. Between the computer and the human eye, they would catch them.

"Got them," Leslie said. "Two men, ramrod backs, coming out of that restaurant." There they were. No disguise. No effort to hide. The general even spotted the traffic camera and looked right into it.

"How long were they in there?"

"I don't know." Leslie sped up the take from a traffic camera, covering the stoplight . . . and just incidentally covering the street in front of the restaurant. An hour of film went by before a car stopped in front of the place and two tall, straight-backed men got out of it. A shorter woman unfolded herself from the backseat of the small two-door, gave the general a quick peck on the cheek, and settled into the driver's seat. The two men waved as she drove off.

"Can you make that license plate?"

"No, sir. It's screened."

"Track her. Track that make of car and the screened plates."

For the next hour, they tracked the small coupe as it wound its way through side streets. Whoever was driving that car knew how to evade surveillance. They'd find her, then lose her, then find her again only to lose her as she turned down a street lined with middle-to-low-income housing with no cameras.

A thirty-minute drive took them over an hour to reconstruct.

"Damn, that woman is good," Foile mumbled under his breath, and hated himself for the admiration he was feeling for the ones he was hunting.

"Is that your princess?" he asked Leslie.

"I should hope not," the young woman agent said,

grinning. "If Kris has any sense about her, she's back at their lair, enjoying a whole lot of Jack."

Foile pinned her with a frown. The agent didn't even look back at him.

"Well, wouldn't you hope that, sir? You haven't become a completely old married man, have you?"

Foile allowed a "harrumph," to that.

"No, that's Kris's best friend, Penny. She's shorter than Kris, and she was trained in intelligence and security. Her dad was a cop, too. We're trying to track one of our own. You ought to be glad we're doing as well as we're doing. Think of what you'd be doing if that was you out there."

"I am, and I would," Foile admitted. "However, we have an arrest warrant for the leader of this gang. A warrant I intend to serve. Find me your princess, Leslie."

"We've got her going on the freeway. She's headed west," Mahomet crowed.

"Toward the mountains?" Foile shot back.

"Toward the mountains or some place short of there," Leslie pointed out

"Get me a list of all the motels with multiday rentals using cash," Foile quickly said to his boss. She got on her comm-link.

"Also, get me a drone flight over the mountains. I want to know every lodge, lean-to, and campfire that's lit up in those hills."

His boss came out of her commlink. "We'll need a military drone for that."

"So?"

"They're not supposed to be used in civilian police matters. Are you calling this a terrorist threat? Terrorism wasn't mentioned on our arrest warrant, was it?"

She knew very well it wasn't.

"Either you call, or I call the Prime Minister and tell him if he wants us to find his daughter before anyone gets killed, we need someone to order up a training flight over those mountains and get the results of that infrared feed to us. Which way is it going to be?"

Usually a subordinate doesn't task his boss. But usually the subordinate isn't the one called into the Prime Minister's office and given the assignment. Foile eyed his boss. Just how much did she want to be in charge of this operation?

Would she really want to have her name on this op when the fecal matter hit the fan? This use of Bureau resources by the Prime Minister for his family issues was bad and getting worse. When the media got hold of this . . . and they always did . . . there would be hell to pay.

Whose name would be at the top of the devil's bill?

"I'll call the Prime Minister's office," his boss said after a lengthy sigh.

The woman had balls; that was one reason Foile liked working for her. They were all likely going down on this one. The boss knew it, and she wasn't shirking her place at the head of the line.

Foile turned back to his team. "Track that car. See how far you can catch pictures of it going into the mountains. Then get some sleep. We're going to be here for a long time. You better catnap when you can."

"Sir, I hope you take a bit of your own medicine," Leslie said. "You get awful grouchy when you're tired."

28

"Are you two decent?" Penny called well after sunset.

"Of course we're decent," Kris shouted back. "We're cooking spaghetti."

"Good, I'm starved. I missed the turnoff once and had to double back to find it," Penny said, coming in and cuddling up to the woodstove. "I had to cut off the heater for fear I'd run out of juice."

"Isn't there a backup gas generator in that car?" Jack called from where he was watching the pasta boil.

"Yes, but the tank was only half-full, and I didn't want to stop for gas. Yes, I've got cash, but they'd get my picture, and if they're checking out all cash purchases, they'd have a hot datum on us in no time at all."

"You could have gassed up in town," Jack said. "That wouldn't have told them anything they don't already know."

"I wasn't willing to risk that, either. If they've got a serious dragnet out for us, paying cash would have raised a red flag. Before I got out of the station, there'd be a cop cruiser or nine charging in to block me."

"Did you miss the turnoff for real or use it to check your six?" Kris asked.

Penny just grinned, and said, "I was not followed back.

You two do anything serious while I was gone?" she asked, eyeing Kris.

Kris had the good sense to blush before saying, "Yes, we put the time to good use. We *also* started going over Grampa Al's compound. Do you know he has a shuttle on five-minute standby within easy reach of his suite?"

"Got to have a quick getaway," Jack offered as he threw a strand of pasta against the wall. It stayed there. "One day, when the angry peasants come calling with torches and pitchforks, you're gonna need to vamoose fast."

"Nelly, show Penny what we're talking about."

Kris stayed facing the kitchen table and a map of the compound appeared. Quickly, it tracked in to the central tower, then up it. At one level, where the tower narrowed toward the top, a shuttle sat behind screens.

"If he actually takes off in that thing, the whole top of the building's gonna get scorched," Jack observed as he drained steaming-hot water into the sink.

Penny cocked her head to get a different perspective, then shrugged. "That will teach all those revolting peasants to take pitchforks to their betters."

"Could we use that for a getaway?" Jack asked, transferring the pasta to a plate.

"I doubt it. Remember the time I tried to steal Hank Peterwald's yacht? I was locked out until he gave me the codes."

"I wasn't as good as I am now, Kris," Nelly pointed out.

Rather than argue with her pet computer, Kris took discretion as the better part of valor. "We'll see how things go. I'd much rather we talked Grampa Al into being our ally rather than having to run for it. Besides, where could we run? A shuttle won't take us anywhere."

"Do I smell something burning?" Penny asked.

"Oh, the sauce," Kris said, jumping for the stove. The vision of Longknife Towers followed her and ended up sketched across the stove as she grabbed for the pot of sauce and scorched her hands. Then she grabbed again, using the dish towel Jack handed her, and moved the pot to a cold burner.

"How appropriate," Penny said through a grin. "Everyone knows a blushing bride worships her beloved by serving him burnt offerings. Too bad I'm going to be struck with them, too."

"I am no blushing bride," Kris snapped, "and I would have been a decent cook if you hadn't distracted me with work."

"The story of our life together," Jack said. "Don't stir up the burned stuff on the bottom. We'll take our sauce from the top. That's what I did in college when I burned the spaghetti."

"Glad someone's lived on their own," Penny said. "I doubt spaghetti was ever burned at Nuu House."

"We didn't *have* spaghetti at Nuu House, and yes, Lotty never burned anything. Okay, you happy? You two happy, I'm incompetent to heat water."

"But she sure does blow up ships good," Jack pointed out. "Given the choice of a little burned sauce and being blown to bits several times in the last four or five years, I'll take our present situation."

Kris laughed, and swatted Jack with his own dish towel. He gave her a quick hug and kiss as he went to find plates. He quickly overfilled them with pasta and began ladling on way too much sauce.

"Hey, champ," Penny put in. "You're not feeding a bunch of frat boys. Us dainty gals have to remember our figures. Unless Kris is already eating for two."

That got Penny a swat with the towel. But Kris dredged a bowl out of a cabinet on the third try, and she and Penny dumped half their plates' contents into it.

As they settled down to eat, Nelly again projected the map of the Longknife compound onto the table. "They usually put new hires on this post with an experienced guard." Nelly highlighted a loading dock in red. "It's the checkpoint for food deliveries and taking the trash and laundry out. Apparently, it smells."

"If we put the other guard to sleep, how long before a delivery?" Jack asked.

"It usually slows down between eleven and one. Day deliveries are done, and the morning ones haven't started."

"Are we on the night shift?" Penny asked.

"You've been hired for the 10 P.M. to 6 A.M. shift," Nelly informed them. "On the first day, you have to show up at eight for a new employee briefing. They'll issue you a uniform and radio. No weapons for fresh hires."

Kris frowned at Penny. "So we'll be changing into our new uniforms and transferring all our sneaky gear right in front of their security cameras."

"Unless, of course, they respect our privacy in the ladies' room."

All three laughed at the joke.

"This is getting tougher and tougher by the second," Penny said.

"Nelly, do you have any pictures of female guards from this company?"

A parade of women, short, tall, thin, or fat paraded across the dinner table.

"You notice anything about them, Penny?" Kris asked.

"None of them were carrying a purse," the intelligence officer said.

"What's that mean?" Jack asked.

The two girls exchanged smiles. "We'll show you tomorrow night."

The three of them plotted path after path from their probable station to the private suite at the top of the towers. There were plenty of private access and working areas in a building that huge, almost as many as there were on a space station. Kris and Jack knew their way around stations, both for offense and defense. They got to feeling right at home with the tower.

Approaching midnight, with yawns all around, they called it quits. Penny dismissed herself with, "I'll take the back bedroom and close the door."

She did, for about five seconds.

"It's freezing in there," she announced as she busted back in on them.

"I had the door open to warm the place up," Jack said, in defense of his effort to keep all the women who presently occupied his life warm.

"You may have, but that place was freezing to start with, and it's not much better now," Penny said.

"Heat rises," Kris said. "I wonder what the loft is like."

"I'll try it," Penny said, heading up the ladder and disappearing for a minute. Then her head popped over the railing. "It's quite nice up here, and I can rob the blankets from the other bed. You just ignore me. I'll be asleep in no time."

"We'll never ignore you," Kris said. But one thing led to another on the floor before the roaring woodstove. Kris found she didn't really care whether Penny was awake or asleep, just so long as Jack was close, and Kris managed to keep quiet.

And Jack was very close.

29

Foile was exhausted.

Around him, his team was asleep, Leslie curled up beside her desk, Mahomet with his head down on his desk. His boss had retreated to her own office and was likely asleep on its couch.

There was a sofa in Foile's office. At the moment, it looked pretty inviting.

From the drone overflight he'd ordered, they'd heard not a word. Had the Prime Minister balked at using military assets to hunt for his daughter? Foile was not about to make a phone call. If it happened, it happened. If not, well, maybe the Prime Minister wasn't as worried as he'd sounded yesterday. No, day before yesterday, and soon yet another day more.

Foile was way behind on sleep, but as he settled down on the sofa, he had to wonder: just who would Billy Longknife be afraid of for his daughter? Who on Wardhaven would even think of killing Kris Longknife?

It hadn't been too long ago when it was in all the media how she'd saved all their hides when those strange battleships showed up demanding the planet surrender.

Boy, talk about your political failure there.

Everyone on *this* planet owed the princess their life. So who might kill her?

Foile got comfortable on his sofa. His mind was spinning with questions. How many of them did he really need to answer?

Then he sat bolt upright.

If he knew who Billy Longknife feared would kill his daughter, Foile would know where he needed to deploy his police assets. Get between her and whoever it was.

He shook his head and settled back onto his sofa. Billy Longknife hadn't told him anything when he assigned Foile this case. Nothing had changed to make him reveal more about his wayward daughter now.

Foile regulated his breathing. Tomorrow would be another day. Likely another very busy day.

30

Kris was up as first light filled the lodge. She cooked bacon, without burning it, and scrambled eggs. That brought a complaint from Penny that there was no way to mangle scrambled eggs. Kris cut her off like a good slave driver by pointing at the diagram of Longknife Towers. They went over it until they could talk their way through it without their computers' flashing a map on the wall in front of them.

If things went according to plan, they would be at Al's suite twenty minutes from leaving the loading dock. But all three of them knew that matters rarely went according to plan—on black ops or white.

So they sat around the fire trying to think of everything that could go wrong and what they'd do when it did. It was kind of fun. Each took a turn playing the red team and punching a hole in their plan. Then all of them would have to come up with a solution.

It worried Kris how easy it was to make their plan go off the rails. And while they always came up with something that would put it back on track, most of the solutions looked pretty flimsy to Kris. Hope was not a strategy, but it sure looked like they were counting on hope and lots of good luck to get them through this.

Lunch was sandwiches. They ate in silence. Meal done, Kris stood.

"Let's get in our disguises," she said.

"You know something I don't know?" Jack asked.

"Nope. It's just the hairs on the back of my neck are beginning to stand up."

"Mine, too," Penny said.

"If both of your feminine intuition is ringing a bell, this guy is listening."

"We'll need new disguises," Penny pointed out, as they surveyed the wreckage of their old covers. "Nobody would hire Ms. Travaford for a guard job."

"We all need to not look like ourselves, Jack included," Kris said. "I put the chances that we're not all being hunted as zed or worse." That got nods.

They opened the suitcases Harvey had packed for them. Oversized middle-class work clothes poured out of one. The second held nearly as much makeup and padding material as Abby had provided.

"Does everybody want me fat?" Kris cried in dismay.

"Kris, you are a lovely lady of light and delicate proportions," Jack began diplomatically. "How else do we disguise you?"

He paused for a moment, then got a big grin on his face. "Well, there was that time on Turantic when you didn't wear much at all."

"Yes, you enjoyed that. Don't tell me you didn't. I felt the proof on my leg."

"I had to get close to you."

"People, people," Penny said. "You're scandalizing this poor girl, and I really don't think we have time to waste on distant, if very fond, memories."

They busied themselves with different disguises. Penny and Jack worked over Kris, much to her own dismay. Then Kris and Jack did the same to Penny. Finally, both girls got to take a swing at Jack. He refused several of their initial suggestions.

In the end, all of them put on weight, just not as much as Kris had before. All their faces changed, from brow to nose to mouth, and foreheads got narrowed as armored wigs went on. Jack would likely be ordered to get a haircut by their new boss, but he certainly didn't look like a Marine anymore.

Kris was the one that discovered the C-16. It was carefully wrapped and nestled next to an explosive sniffer that assured them that there was no boom stuff here. Move along.

There were also several flash bang grenades of different persuasions. Finally, from the bottom of the last suitcase, came three plastic automatics. All gave them the option of deadly force or sleepy darts. Kris set all three for sleepy and fired a dart from each into a support post. The darts hung there, not all that deep in the wood.

"No casualties tonight," she said, handing the weapons over to her team.

"Just make sure the other guys chop on that order," Penny said.

The explosives and grenades disappeared into various portions of their disguise. Kris had to sit down three times before she was comfortable with the placement of her weapons load.

It was just past two o'clock when Kris surveyed their preparations and found them good. She glanced around the mess they'd made of the lodge and felt a strong need to be somewhere else. "Let's move out, folks. Someone once told me a moving target is harder to hit. I say let's beat feet."

Kris and Penny grabbed their purses and, without a backward glance, left.

Twenty minutes later, going well below the posted speed limit, they passed a convoy of dark SUVs roaring along in the opposite direction.

Penny kept driving. Kris followed the putative police rigs, and found herself looking at Jack in the backseat. Ever the gentleman, he was doing yoga in its small space. Their eyes met.

"How much you want to bet me," Jack said, "the folks in those rigs really want to make our acquaintance?"

"No bet," Kris said through a grin. "I can't bet. Remember, I'm just a poor, homeless waif."

"Thank God both of us felt the strong urge to be homeless again," Penny said, and kept driving.

Senior Chief Agent in Charge Foile surveyed yet another empty hideout. He was getting very tired of being one step behind the Longknife princess.

"Boss, you need to see this," Leslie said, waving him over to look at a six-by-six post that supported the roof. Three darts stuck out of the wood. Leslie pried one out and lifted it to the light.

"They're sleepy darts, sir. They have a coating on the tip of the dart that should put anyone it hits to sleep. Princess Long-knife's troops have used them a lot."

"So they won't kill you," Foile grumbled.

"Not if you don't have a bad heart or fall asleep in the bathtub. They are a weapon of less than lethal intent, but they're still a weapon."

"Three darts," Foile counted. "So likely three less than deadly guns on our three fugitives."

"A good guess, sir."

"Have shots been fired in this place?" Foile said, raising his voice in an omnidirectional question to the forensic team now taking the place apart.

"Shot or shots were fired. Strangely, not a lot of residue," one CSI investigator with a large black box announced. "No evidence of high explosives, though. Certainly nothing here to qualify this as a terrorist location."

Foile chose to ignore the additional information. No doubt it would come out in the media. "Would the low residue fit the sleepy dart hypothesis?"

The CSI investigator nodded.

"When did they leave?" was another wide-open question to the experts.

"Somebody had lunch and didn't eat the crusts of their bread," a CSI type at the table announced.

"Someone stoked the fire for us," Mahomet reported from where he was warming his hands by it. He'd led the outside search team and looked frozen.

"Anything outside?" Foile asked.

"The great outdoors," his chilly agent replied. "No car, so they're likely on the move back to town. Other than that, nothing since last night's snow but a few footprints between here and the garage."

"Clean as a whistle," came from the head of the CSI team. "There is evidence of sexual activity in front of the fireplace. A lot of it. Some fresh."

Leslie got a big grin on her face.

"Not a word," Foile ordered sternly. "The Prime Minister will not learn of any of this; nor will the media."

"Yes, boss, but a girl's got the right to be glad when another girl gets lucky."

"Yes, but you can store your grin. *This* girl has the job of checking out every surveillance camera between here and town. I want to know where they're headed."

"Sir, I told you there are not a lot of cameras between here and town, and the snow made all of them lousy."

"Well, it's not snowing right now. Hunt, my fine agent, hunt."

31

Kris had them pull off the freeway into a working-class neighborhood. Penny was just about to do it herself. "We ought to be safe here," the cop's daughter said. "No one pays for surveillance cameras where there's little worth stealing."

They cruised the side streets, working their way slowly toward the town's center. Penny was the first to call for a halt. "I need a cup of coffee, which is a ladylike way to say I need to pee."

"Nelly, can you find us a small restaurant with a back entrance?"

"Kris, I have a map of Wardhaven. It's about two years old, but it does have all the traffic cameras on it. There's a small bar and grill five blocks from here. It's on a main drag with traffic cameras, but we can get to it by back streets."

"Let's head for it. I need to powder my nose. Noses, from the looks of the proboscis you put on me."

Five minutes later, a visual check showed no cameras covering the rear of the place, so they pulled into the back parking lot of Mulligan's Irish Bar and Grill.

Inside was shady and cameraless. They ordered coffee and pie, then took turns keeping an eye on things while one of them took care of business.

Jack was just coming back as the pie arrived. Kris studied the few occupants, it being between lunch and dinner, and the several TV screens, which showed various sporting events. One, however, was on a news channel.

Kris watched it out of the corner of her eye for about ten minutes, but none of their faces appeared. If they were the subject of a search, it hadn't gotten to flashing their faces every five minutes.

They slowly enjoyed their coffee and pie. Jack had acquired Colonel Hancock's receiver for the police net, and he and Sal monitored it while they ate. Traffic stayed moderate with no spikes. After a quiet hour, Jack paid the bill in cash, something that didn't raise the waitress's eyebrows even a smidge.

While he did, Kris browsed the back of the bar. Between the men's and ladies' room was a phone with a bright red and yellow sign. FRIENDS DON'T LET FRIENDS DRIVE DRUNK. CALL A CAB. There were numbers for four cab companies' phones below it. There was also a bulletin board beside it with twenty or more business cards pinned to it.

NELLY, RECORD ALL THOSE CARDS.

DONE, KRIS. WHAT'S IT FOR?

WE'LL SEE LATER.

Jack rejoined them, and they slipped out the back.

"Where to?" Penny asked.

"Cruise the back streets," Kris said. "Don't do any one twice. Stay in quiet, middle-class neighborhoods. We've got time on our hands until eight. Think about where we want to eat supper."

Kris had missed out on cruising as a teenager. She'd heard about it but never done it, having Harvey to take her anywhere she wanted. Somehow she suspected the usual teenage cruising was not done with two girls in front and a lone guy in back. Still, she got Jack talking about himself, and that was a good way of spending time.

Around five, they found a small seafood place, the Sail Inn, with an easy rear entrance. Again, no cameras, and plenty of screens showing sporting events and one on the news. Their faces were still not up. That was nice.

Kris still didn't relax.

As it got close to six, Kris visited the powder room. Sure

enough, there was another phone with the injunction to call a cab rather than drive drunk. There was also a collection of business cards pinned or taped up next to the phone. Cards for town-car businesses. Unregistered and without any of the controls that cab companies operated under, the town cars were usually just a driver and a car and a lot of business cards. They weren't quite illegal, it being hard to outlaw someone offering to drive you around town and you offering to pay them.

NELLY, ARE ANY OF THE CARDS AT THE BAR AND GRILL NOT PINNED UP HERE?

THREE OF THEM, KRIS.

GIVE ME THE NUMBER OF THE ONE CLOSEST TO HERE.

Kris made the phone call, asking to be picked up at the back door of the Sail Inn. The driver said he'd be there in five minutes.

He was there in fifteen.

As Kris and her team got in, she noticed a police car pulling into the back parking lot. Maybe he was there for supper. Maybe he wasn't. Kris ordered the driver to turn left, away from the main street and back toward quiet residential ones.

A few minutes later, she heard sirens in the distance. The sound grew more distant as they drove away.

Senior Chief Agent in Charge Foile hated it when he hovered over one of his subordinates. At the moment, he was hovering over Leslie. She'd spotted the car they were hunting.

Problem was, she'd spotted three cars identical in make and color to the one that should have been in the garage of the mountain lodge. Three had meandered past the gas station ten miles farther down the mountain. None had stopped. They had no license plate on any of them.

"Should I check farther up the mountains?" Mahomet asked.

Foile shook his head. "They're heading back to town. On that I'd bet my pension."

"Should we order a roadblock down the mountain?" Leslie asked.

Foile stared up at the lodge's high wooden ceiling for a moment, estimating distance and time. He shook his head. "They're already back in town. We should have, though, when we headed up here."

"You know, sir," Leslie said, "if either of those three cars are them, they must have seen us barrel past them as they left."

"That thought has crossed my mind," Foile said. "I'm getting real tired of being just a few steps behind those people. Real tired."

"I've run a search on that car in town, sir," Leslie said. Apparently, she was also tired of playing catch-up and had already done what he was about to order.

Foile gave the young woman a smile. "Talk to me."

"Sorry, sir, but I don't have a lot," she said. "There are two samples of that car parked outside no-tell hotels. Their GPSes are off, and their license plates are screened. There are three examples of the car parked outside houses that have private security cameras. They also have shut down. I checked. All three of the houses have teenage daughters in the family."

"So they likely have their boyfriends over and don't want either one or both of their folks to know about it," Foile said.

"Most likely," Leslie admitted. "I've checked the hotel registers. They usually are paid in cash. No surprise, both of the cars are likely cash payers."

"Do we want to knock down some doors?" Mahomet asked.

"We've bashed in our quota of doors for this week," Foile said. His boss had gotten a complaint on that topic, one she'd only mentioned to him, though he suspected she'd taken a lot more heat. "No, have some agents drop by the office of those two hotels. Take pictures of the three. Ask the clerks if any of those cars belong to a threesome. That ought to add some excitement to their day."

"I'm on it," Mahomet said.

"Leslie, stay on that car. Have every surveillance camera in town set to scream if it catches sight of one of them."

"I've already done that, sir. There are a lot of hits, and so far all of them are for cars with working GPS units and readable licenses. I think our princess has gone to ground, sir, or is staying on streets that aren't covered by cameras."

That proved true for a long, quiet afternoon as Foile and his team drove in from the mountains and settled back into their squad bay at the Bureau.

"Everyone makes a mistake," Foile kept repeating, a mantra that had gotten him through a lot of hard chases. Then again, he'd never been chasing one of those damn Longknifes. Maybe she wasn't going to make any mistakes.

He called Rick at Nuu House. No surprise, the two Marines sat blank-faced in separate rooms saying nothing at all. Not even their name, rank, and serial number.

Foile found himself cycling back to the thought that he'd gone to sleep on last night. Who would dare kill Kristine Long-knife, Lieutenant Commander in the U.S. Navy, Princess of United Society?

The Prime Minister had balked at sharing who that might be with a Bureau agent. What would a retired general, known for being trouble, have to say?

Foile fetched his hat and coat and headed out the door. He was just pulling to a stop at the ivy-covered old mansion known as Nuu House when Leslie called.

"We've found the car, in a lot behind a dive, the Sail Inn."

"Any sign of the three?"

"No sir. They ate, paid in cash, and left. They used the phone to call a cab. We're checking on any fares picked up there."

"Get back to me as soon as you get anything."

Foile had only gotten to the room General Trouble was being held in when his commlink buzzed again. "Tell me something good," he said.

"Sorry, sir," Leslie began. "I have nothing good here, sir. No cabs picked up anyone at the Sail Inn, sir. There are a batch of cards for town cars. We've already called all of them, but none had a pickup anywhere near there. At least none any are admitting to."

Foile closed his eyes in frustration. Those three were once again ahead of him. Worst, he'd lost his last connection to them. He'd finally gotten the license number of their car, and it now sat in the back of a dive telling him nothing.

Where had they gone? Were they walking? The last thing Foile wanted to do was turn loose a bunch of beat cops with pictures of the Longknife princess. He might as well go straight to the media hounds himself with the story.

Besides, they intended to go someplace where they could get themselves killed. The quiet neighborhood where the Sail Inn stood wasn't the right place for that. "Keep on it," Foile told Leslie. "Try all the town-car places. I'll bet you she found a card someplace else and called one that wasn't up at the Sail Inn."

"Yes, sir. That sounds like something she'd do. Where are you, sir?"

"I'm about to see if I can cause Trouble a little trouble." And on that cryptic remark, Senior Chief Agent in Charge Foile let himself into the room where the legendary war hero was silently doing battle and, damn it . . . winning . . . with the best the law had to muster.

32

They cruised the back streets. Officially, their story for the town-car driver was that Kris and Jack were newlyweds, and they'd just landed jobs and were dreaming about buying a house. The driver didn't seem to buy the story but every ten or fifteen minutes, Jack would produce another twenty, and the guy kept driving.

Jack, at least, had drawn out a wad of cash before he started his walk on the outlaw side. Smart man. Kris thought that one of many good reasons to keep him around.

The streets they drove edged farther and farther toward the south, so when Penny reminded the two lovebirds that they better not be late for work their first day, it was only a short drive to Longknife Tower.

The driver let them out at the first checkpoint, pocketed his last two twenties, and seemed happy for the exchange.

"You the new hires?" an overweight man with sergeant stripes asked. They admitted they were, and he arranged for an electric cart to take them to the next checkpoint. There, a dizzy brunette took their vitals off their fake Identacards, photographed them for their new idents, and took their fingerprints.

Oops, why didn't any of us think of that? Kris thought to Nelly.

BECAUSE NONE OF YOU HAVE APPLIED FOR A JOB LATELY, Nelly shot back. DON'T WORRY, IF I CAN'T PULL THE WOOL OVER THE EYES OF THIS COMPUTER, YOU CAN SELL ME CHEAP AT A GARAGE SALE. BY THE WAY, KRIS, I'VE COLLECTED THREE COMPUTER CERTIFICATES. THIS ONE AND THE TWO BELONGING TO THE FAT GUY AND THIS GAL. IF I NEED TO GET ON THE NET, I'M ON.

True to Nelly's promise, the computer raised no red flags and did not report that the troublemaking Princess Kristine Longknife and her trusted sidekicks had reported for minimum-wage jobs.

That security checkpoint passed, they were ushered into a room with two other new hires and sat down to watch their new-employee orientation. Kris listened with only one ear as they were told how wonderful their employer was and how grateful they should be that it was providing them with the absolute minimum benefits the law allowed. Then again, maybe the two strangers sitting with Kris didn't know that her father's government had passed laws requiring that no employer could offer less health insurance than the rent-a-cop company was offering. Or that the contributions the firm was making into their retirement was the standard social-security package. It was almost enough to make Kris wonder if her brother, Honovi, who had chosen to follow father into the family business of politics, hadn't chosen the tougher career.

Then Kris remembered the alien mother ship in her sights.

Nope. Brother might not have it easier, but he did have it safer.

Kris turned more of her attention back to the screen. It had just mentioned that there would be a test after the show. It would be a shame to find she couldn't storm the castle, er, Longknife Tower, because she flunked a new-hire-benefits-package test.

Video done, they were handed a test. A paper test! It took Kris and company all of a minute to select the proper answers from the ten multiple-choice questions.

The brunette glanced at Kris's paper for all of a second and gave her a hundred percent. Penny and Jack were smart enough to get one wrong, and somehow managed to pick a different question, so there was no question about cheating.

The other two were still laboring over the test as Kris and her team left.

An older ex-military type with two railroad bars on his collar was waiting for them. "Always nice to see fresh meat. You three are joining security, the only reason the rest of these slobs get paid. Follow me."

They followed as he led them through a rats' maze of cubicles. Most had techs watching screens. "These folks make sure that if you screw up, we know it. They watch everything you do, so make sure you're doing what we pay you for and nothing else. You hear me?"

Yes, sir, Kris almost replied in proper military voice, but she caught herself, and mumbled "Yeah," along with the others.

"Did you *hear* me?"

"We heard you," Penny snapped. "You're watching our every move. So how's that different from my last burger-flipping job?"

"Here, my young, mouthy girl, we got people with guns backing you up. You make a mistake, and one of them might just shoot you. You hear me?"

Kris nodded like a bobblehead doll. Jack grumbled "yeah," and Penny got big eyes and kind of shrank into herself.

Kris was ready to put her whole team in for acting awards.

NELLY, HOW WE DOING?

KRIS, I GOT HIS COMPUTER CERTIFICATE AND ALL HIS SECURITY CODES. HE HAS NO IDEA WHAT KIND OF TROUBLE HE'S GOING TO BE IN BEFORE THIS NIGHT IS OVER.

GOOD GIRL.

The next stop was uniform issue. Bins along the wall offered a selection that ran from too small to too large, with not much in between. Fortunately for Kris, too large was just what she needed.

Unfortunately, women sizes quit about two short of what would fit her.

"Why don't you try something from the men's side," the captain suggested. "With that face, it's about as close to anything man-wise you're likely to get."

With that snide remark, Jack offered her something from the bin he'd chosen from.

"What do we do about purses?" Kris asked.

"We don't issue no purses."

"What's a woman supposed to do for her things?" Kris asked.

"Deary, lipstick is not going to help you."

Kris tried to look like she was struggling to keep her temper. It was easy. She was. "Where am I supposed to keep my sanitary napkins and other stuff I need for my feminine needs."

The captain suddenly looked a lot less sure of himself. "It that time, huh?"

"For me, too," Penny added.

"What is it with you two? You shacked up together?"

"We don't have to answer that question," Penny snapped. "We can sue you if you make us."

"Woman, you got an attitude problem," the captain growled. "I ought to show you the door just for that crack."

"Calm down, Penny," Kris said, with pleading in her voice. "We need this job. Jack, you, me. We really need the pay."

The captain really liked that comeback.

"Go change. Your shift starts in ten minutes, and I still got to get you there."

Kris and company rushed off to change. As expected, there were cameras in the four corners of the ladies' locker room. Kris gave one of them a smile. In her present disguise, any guy watching likely barfed up his lunch.

The uniform was tight where Kris normally didn't have anything, but with the layers of disguise, she no longer could pass for a boy. Since she didn't intend to spend a lot of time in it, she met her problem with a shrug. Their guns and several plastic flash bangs stayed comfortably nestled in both women's bags, right under the feminine necessities that provided cover.

Unknown until the necessary moment, said feminine necessities were explosives with fuses.

Kris came out of the changing room looking as womanly as she could, struggling to make her uniform fit decently. That drew a grin from the captain. "Go through the metal detector and put your bags through the bomb sniffer."

Kris did as ordered, and no alarms went off. She had to

wonder how Grampa Al managed to stay so secure. It couldn't be this security team.

The captain loaded all three of them into an oversize golf cart; Jack managed to take the front seat next to their putative boss. The ride was short. As foretold, their job was at the loading dock in the back of the tower. Here they were introduced to a hard case with a shaved head who wore corporal stripes.

"More fresh meat for you, Hanson," the captain announced. "Don't eat them all up tonight. Save some for tomorrow," drew a laugh from the two with rank.

Kris tried to look scared while considering just how many ways she could lay the two of them out flat on their backs while they wondered what happened. Sadly, the situation didn't allow for that, nor could she even permit herself a tiny smile of enjoyment at the thought.

The corporal got right to work messing with Kris's life. A trash truck was just pulling away from a dock. Kris got the job of crawling under it to make sure no one was riding out. The only good thing about the assignment was that they had a board on wheels so Kris could just lie on her back and look up at the smelly and oily underside of the truck. No one lurked there, and the very basic electronic sensor Kris was given reported no activity from any bugs.

Nelly made sure of that.

THOUGH I DIDN'T HAVE TO, KRIS. THAT TRUCK IS A DEAD ZONE.

JUST BE GLAD YOU CAN'T SMELL, GIRL.

Jack offered Kris a hand up, but the corporal told her to stay down. A second truck was already headed their way. This one was full of shredded paper and plastic flimsies. It was just as filthy underneath but less smelly. Kris did her job.

And did it again when a truck that had brought in office equipment came through. It seemed like everything was leaving at that time of night.

That truck offered something different. Kris found an electronic bug nestled in among the four back-tire wells. That brought a visit from the captain and a team of bug hunters. They turned up two more bugs stuck inside the back of the van.

The driver and van got hustled away for further investigation, and the corporal got an attaboy and talk of a cash award.

Kris and her crew, who had found the initial lead, got not even a nod.

"I guess that's what it's like to work around here," Penny whispered.

That got her a scowl from the corporal, and further conversation wilted. The garbage truck brought the Dumpster back, and Kris got to go over its underside again. The corporal insisted she do it twice. By the time Jack helped her to her feet, even he admitted she'd taken on a certain air.

By now it was eleven, and traffic seemed to vanish as if it had been turned off at a switch. The corporal retreated to the loading dock and settled down behind a tiny desk. He pulled out a girly magazine and began to flip through it. Every once in a while, he'd glance up at Kris or Penny and shake his head.

STAY IN PLACE FOR THE NEXT TEN MINUTES, I'M MAKING A FILM LOOP, Nelly told Kris.

The three of them stood where they were below the loading dock. Kris shook her arms, stomped her feet, and looked miserable as the cool of the night proved their thin uniforms unsuited for outside work. The others did the same.

They said not a word.

I'VE GOT TEN MINUTES RECORDED. THE MONITOR DOESN'T HAVE ANY STORAGE ABILITY, BUT I'VE PLANTED A NANO IN IT. YOU ARE OFF THE SECURITY NET, Nelly announced.

"Where's the nearest ladies' room?" Penny asked.

"You peed before coming on shift," the corporal growled without looking up. "You can pee when you're off shift. The company don't pay you to pee."

"It also don't want blood on its nice new uniforms," Penny said.

The corporal looked up at that one.

Jack gave the guy one of those male-bonding looks and headed up the steps for a whispered consultation with the corporal. As Jack bent over, his hand dug his automatic out of all the foam flab at his butt.

The weapon came around. There were two soft reports, and the corporal was asleep before his head hit the desk.

Jack balled the guy up beneath the desk as Kris and Penny took the steps up to the loading dock two at a time.

Jack handed Kris the corporal's comm device. The chatter

on it was very much normal. As Kris pocketed it, she smiled at her friends. "Let's go visit Grampa Al."

Senior Chief Agent in Charge Foile stared across the table at the legendary General Trouble. They'd been staring at each other for the last fifteen minutes. Fifteen minutes!

Foile had actually timed it.

Most normal people faced with dead silence felt compelled to fill it. Obviously, the general did not fall into the subset of normal people. Foile finally pursed his lips. He'd have to try another tack.

"Can you help me understand this situation we're in?" he said, leaving the question as open as he could. Open in scope and almost desperate in its begging.

The general raised an eyebrow but said nothing.

"Your grandson, Billy Longknife, asked me to find his daughter before she gets herself, and a whole lot of other people, suddenly dead."

That drew no answer.

"Doesn't that worry you? My agent, Leslie Chu, is a fan of your great-granddaughter. She tells me that you helped sober Kristine up when she was just a kid. Cleaned up her act and got her headed into most everything she's done."

That got a smile from the old general. What man can stay stolid as a fence post when his kid is being praised?

"I think when the record is finally told, you'll find that Kris never did anything she didn't want or intended to do," the man said.

"But her father really thinks she's going to get herself killed this time. That's the only reason I'm chasing after her." Even Foile heard the pleading in his voice.

He'd *never* pleaded during an interrogation before.

The old man shook his head. "A lot of folks have tried to kill her. A lot of them are dead, and she's still breathing."

"I think this time it might be different."

The troublemaker nodded at that. "You might be right."

Foile waited for him to go on. When he didn't, he found himself saying, "Do you want her to get killed?"

The look on the general's face could have killed Foile. Very likely it had killed Iteeche and Unity thugs. Foile swallowed. "Won't you help me at all?"

"I'd like a glass of water," was all the general said.

As Foile stood up to get him one, his commlink came alive.

"Sir," said Leslie, "there's been a security breach at Longknife Towers. We're not sure what's going on, but they hired three new security guards tonight. A check of their personal files has come back negative, and the fingerprints that were taken have disappeared from the computer net. I have no idea who they hired, but I'll bet *my* pension that we've found my princess and her two sidekicks."

Foile turned back to the general.

He was smiling.

Foile left his hat on the table as he raced for the door.

33

Kris trotted into the large but very empty receiving bay.
There were several service elevators, but taking one of them
would be a quick way to end the visit in handcuffs. She spotted
the door that led down to the basement and took it.

Five floors down, below parking, below most signs of
human interest, they paused outside a door that proclaimed NO
ADMITTANCE.

"Nelly, send a nano in."

She did, and Kris quickly got a picture of a dirty room
filled with large and noisy machinery. A lone guard in a brown
uniform carefully made his way among the pieces of whirling
equipment. He'd just passed the door that Kris stood behind.

"Where are the cameras?" Kris asked.

"There aren't any," Nelly answered.

"So much for them watching our every move," Jack said.

"I'm shocked. Shocked, I tell you, that they'd lie to us the
first day on the job," Penny said to no one in particular.

"Penny," Kris said, and the security specialist quickly
unlocked the door.

Kris took a quick step through and put two sleepy darts in
the guard's back. He crumbled at the knees and went down
easy.

Once in the support area, Kris glanced around the room. "Here's the central electrical power, water, sewer, and cooling, everything you need to run this place."

"And only one guard with no cameras?" Jack finished.

"I've seen tighter security around a cookie jar," Penny said.

"Is Grampa Al kidding himself?" Kris asked.

"Or is he just too cheap to pay for what he needs?" Jack said.

"I wouldn't let our guard down," Penny said.

"Nelly, drop some nanos in the machinery. You can never tell when we might want to turn off the lights or flush all the toilets."

"You heard the woman, kids, let's take over this place."

"Mom, do we get to blow anything up?" Sal asked from Jack's neck.

"No, kids. We do this elegantly," Nelly said, to Kris's great relief.

While the computers did their thing, Kris led her team over to the elevator pits. Jack had opened a small door that led into the shaft. As promised, there were rungs along the wall leading up. The three of them began to climb. The fit between the wall and the closest elevator car was close, what with the extra beam Kris was packing, but all three made their way up the shaft.

The elevators in Longknife Tower were divided into four groups. The first took you from the first to no higher than the 50th floor, where you had to get off . . . under the eyes of guards . . . get your security badge checked . . . and switch to a bank that could take you to floors between fifty and one hundred.

If you wanted to go higher than that, you went through another scan, this time of palm prints and retina, and got to ride up to the 150th floor. Of that checkpoint, all the schematic that Grampa Trouble's friend had gotten ahold of only said RESTRICTED AREA.

Since Kris didn't intend to pass through any of those security checkpoints, she really didn't care what they were.

They settled on the top of the elevator car just as Nelly said, "I've got control of the car's computer. It's a tiny thing and easy to confuse. Hold on."

And they began to rise. It was kind of scary as the wind whistled by—and the ceiling of the shaft got closer, but Nelly stopped them on the 49th floor. They switched back to the ladder rungs just as the elevator door opened, and two workers got in.

"I hate it when I have to work this late," a woman's voice said.

"I've got a nine o'clock meeting tomorrow. You want to leave me standing in front of all the big boys, telling them I'll have the report by noon?" said a man.

"Will you at least get me invited to the meeting?"

"I'll see what I can arrange," didn't have much power behind it.

As the elevator dropped away from them with this private bit of human story, Kris found a hatch, opened it, and led her team onto the 50th floor.

They were in a service area. Again, no cameras. Maybe the locked door explained that bit of savings. Penny made short work of the lock.

"There's a camera covering the hall," Nelly said. "Give me a minute to take care of it. Catch your breath. You'll hit the stairs next."

Kris found herself glad for the workouts she'd been getting. Then found the words taking on a double meaning, and had to swallow a giggle.

Giggle!

Longknifes didn't giggle.

Well, maybe Longknifes in love found they could do a lot of things that normal people did.

Get your head back in the game, Kris growled at herself just as Nelly announced. "I've captured control of the cameras between here and the stairwell. I've ordered them to look away for two minutes. Move quickly, the guards have a problem with a flooding ladies' room."

Kris led, Jack right behind her. Penny walked backward, her automatic out but held low. The sound of running water and male curses hurried them along.

"How did you manage that?" Jack whispered.

"I'm the Magnificent Nelly. I'll never tell."

"She bragged to us," Sal said softly from around Jack's neck. "Thanks, Mom. Next time, I get to do it."

They made the stairwell with no problem. The lock there fell to Penny's and Mimzy's work. The door opened, and the threatened alarm did not go off. There were cameras in the stairwell, but Nelly needed less than a minute to seed them all with a snapshot of nothing, and off they went.

Fifty flights of stairs was going to take some time. Kris hated to lose that time. Still, so far their intrusion was unnoticed. She listened in on the corporal's comm device. No one had called him to warn him of incoming traffic. Kris's legs began to complain of the workout, but at least the worst had not started.

Stairs went by, flight after flight. It was almost boring.

Then everything changed!

Lights started flashing. Alarms beeped, rang, and made all sorts of racket.

Senior Chief Agent in Charge Foile and Agent Rick Sanchez arrived only a minute behind agents Leslie Chu and Mahomet Debot. What they found was a mass of confusion, rapidly going in circles and accomplishing nothing.

"Are you sure about those fingerprints?" a man with captain's rank on his collar asked Leslie. "My girl took them, and she's real good about fingerprints. They never come back smudged or anything."

"Sir," Leslie said, and it did not sound respectful in any way, "I have copies of the prints. They're not smudged. The forms are empty. Empty for all three."

"Diedre, you did take their prints, didn't you?"

"I did, sir. I saw them in the computer. They're there. Just look."

So everyone did, and there certainly were fingerprints in that computer. Somehow, they had stayed there and not been sent from that computer out for processing. And when Diedre sent them again, the computer assured them they were sent. Again, nothing arrived at the central fingerprint database for check.

"That can't happen," the captain insisted.

"Nelly's at the bottom of this one," Leslie said with a wide Girls Rule grin.

"Have you advised Security Central at the Tower that you have a breach?" Foile asked.

"Until a second ago, all we had was this little girl's claim that we had a problem. I didn't have any trouble. No, I have not called Central."

Foile glanced around. On a desk, he spotted a red phone with SECURITY CENTRAL stenciled on it. He picked it up and got an immediate, "Yes."

"This is Senior Chief Agent in Charge Foile of the Wardhaven Bureau of Investigation. Your outer security perimeter has been breached by a three-person team headed by Princess Kristine Longknife. You may want to go to an alert."

Before he finished his suggestion, an alarm started beeping, and a red light began flashing, both on the phone and from a device above both doors.

"Now you gone and done it," the captain muttered.

"Yes, I have," Foile said, then turned back to the phone. "I have a team of four investigators. May I be admitted to Security Central?"

"I'll have to check with my supervisor," came the response, and the phone went dead.

Foile scowled at the phone. "I think we're going to have a jurisdiction problem," he muttered softly to his team.

34

"Well, that tears it," Penny said from her place last in line.

"That's a general alarm, throughout the building," Nelly added. "I don't think they know where we are."

"Let's keep it that way. Nelly, release more scouts. If there are nanos in the stairwell, we need to get them under our control."

"I haven't identified any nanos yet. Your grandfather is really cheap."

"Nelly, is this commlink I'm carrying sending out a locator signal?"

"It is, Kris. Just a second. Okay, I have a nano cutting out the signal, and I'm sending a copycat signal down the stairwell. If they interrogate that puppy, they'll think we're way below where we are. Maybe more, depending on how long they take to ask it anything."

"Good, Nelly."

There had been no interruption at stair climbing as Nelly set about messing with the search for them.

"Kris, any thoughts about going to Plan B?" Jack asked.

"You tired of climbing?"

"I'd like to get to the two hundredth floor a whole lot quicker," was all he said.

"I second the idea," Penny said. She didn't sound winded, but she was slowing down. All of them were.

The 75th floor gave Kris her option for Plan B. While the elevators for people in suits only went fifty floors between security checkpoints, the service elevator for dirty and messy things had only one transfer point between the ground and the top floor. It was on the 75th.

"Let's see what they have," Kris said, and Penny quickly did her magic on the lock. The 75th floor turned out to be a support and maintenance floor. No carpet in sight there. There were cameras as well as at least two guards, armored and armed, walking their rounds.

Clearly, Grampa Al's attitude toward security grew with more altitude.

It took Nelly half a minute to get the cameras turned to look at what Kris wanted them to see. Then they slipped out of the stairwell and began stalking the two guards. The two were intent on discussing a particularly controversial call at yesterday's basketball playoffs and only looked ahead.

They were fully armored—from the knees up.

Kris gave the orders to Jack on Nelly net. AIM FOR BELOW THE KNEE. I GOT THE ONE ON THE RIGHT.

I'LL TAKE THE ONE ON THE LEFT.

ON THREE. ONE . . . TWO . . . THREE.

Four gentle pops, and the two guys—make that a guy and a gal—dropped to the floor, their fully automatic machine pistols clattering beside them.

NELLY, CLOSE DOWN MOST OF THE GEAR ON THIS FLOOR. THIS IS THE BACKUP POWER FROM THE MAIN POWER IN THE BASEMENT. CLOSE THE BASEMENT DOWN AT THE SAME TIME, BUT MAKE SURE WE CAN STILL USE THE FREIGHT ELEVATORS.

THE FREIGHT ELEVATORS HAVE THEIR OWN EMERGENCY POWER, KRIS, SO FIREFIGHTERS CAN USE THEM. KIDS, DO YOUR STUFF.

YES, MOM.

Kris stepped up to survey her work. Both guards were securely asleep on the floor, at no risk to themselves. Kris eyed their weapons with the thought of upgrading her armory but shook her head. The machine pistols had only one kind of ammunition: six-millimeter armor-piercing. Putting a target to sleep was not an option for these guards.

Jack must have been doing the same examination of their opponents' weapons load. He raised an expressive eyebrow to Kris.

"As a Marine Gunny once told me," she said, " 'If you're in a shoot-out, the best thing to do is not get shot.' "

The two turned back to the problem at hand. While Kris and Jack stalked the roving watch, Penny had located the night team keeping an eye on all the gadgets. These had been the subject of some hot debate back on the mountain. If they took them down, all the world couldn't help but notice. Kris had hoped to hijack the freight elevator without doing anything to this crew.

A glance over the actual setup showed that what they had hoped was a wall was only a clear plastic plate that protected them from any freight getting loose. It did nothing to restrict their view of the elevators.

Wordlessly, Kris and Jack joined Penny to watch the unsuspecting night watch. Three of them looked at gauges, dials, and readouts, occasionally making an adjustment. One watched a bank of screens, overseeing the cameras that Nelly had pointed at innocent scenes. He seemed bothered; he fiddled with a dial intent on adjusting a camera. The camera doggedly ignored him and obeyed Nelly.

"I got a problem, here," was the last thing Kris could let him say.

PENNY, YOU HIT THE CAMERA GUY ON THE LEFT. I'LL HIT WHAT LOOKS LIKE THE BOSS GUY ON THE RIGHT. JACK, YOU GET THE TWO IN THE MIDDLE. ON TWO.

ONE . . . TWO.

Kris put two sleepy darts into the back of her target and got her third shot into the next guy over toward the middle. Penny put two shots into her man, and also put a third into the gal next over. Jack had put one shot into each of them and was going back to service them with a second shot, but he only got one off.

All four laid sleepy heads down on their workstations.

"The freight elevator," Kris ordered.

They made their way quickly to the bank of elevators that

could take them well up the Longknife tower. Maybe even to just below Grampa Al's penthouse. The higher up the tower you went, the more vague their schematic got.

Kris eyed the open door of the first freight elevator. There was a camera in the right corner. She checked the next one. Camera there, too. Just as she hoped, the third elevator showed hard use, and the camera there was smashed. What was left of it dangled from a single wire.

"That working?" Kris asked Nelly.

"Yep, but it's only getting a picture of what's below it. We stay away from there, and no one will be the wiser."

"Here's our ride, crew," Kris announced.

Unlike the elevators for the finely dressed suits, you had to work to get a freight elevator moving. Kris closed the outer doors, but they didn't come together all that tightly, being dented and dinged. She latched the inner cage door closed but paused before punching for a floor above them.

"Nelly, I'm getting sick and tired of all the beeping and ringing. What do you say we close down the alarms?"

"I'll have to kill the lights as well," Nelly said, and if she'd been a real girl, Kris would have heard a near giggle mingled in the words.

Kris pulled up her shirt, and extracted a set of night goggles from the foam flab at her stomach. Penny and Jack followed suit.

"Let everyone know we're here, Nelly."

A second later, the noise went to a deathly hush. The lighting flickered, then went to dark. Emergency backup switched on for a moment, then blinked and went out as well.

Dim red lights switched on just above the nose of Kris and her team's low-light goggles. Kris punched for floor 198, and the elevator began to grind noisily upward.

"I told you I could keep just the power we needed," Nelly crowed.

35

Senior Chief Agent in Charge Foile cursed under his breath. He had not come this far to sit on his hands while fools piled up their mistakes "You," he said, pointing at the man who styled himself captain. "Take me to the Security Center."

"You can't go there. With the alarm given, no one is allowed in."

Rick Sanchez grabbed the older man by the arm and began moving him with the rest of Foile's team as they headed back to his car.

"There are machine guns on the grounds. They'll shoot the shit out of you!" the intrepid captain was almost shouting now.

"Leslie, you drive," Foile ordered.

The young agent grinned. "You bet, boss."

Foile took the passenger front seat. Mahomet and Rick settled the rent-a-cop between them in the back. Leslie headed toward the first checkpoint at a sedate but steady speed. The man in the tiny guardhouse made slowing motions, but when it became clear that he could either raise the rail or lose it, he hit the button and it rose barely fast enough to miss the top of Foile's sedan.

"Smart young man," Foile observed, as Leslie accelerated through the gate.

"There are machine guns!" the man in the brown uniform repeated in an immoderately high shriek.

"Leslie, is our car's squawker on?" Foile asked.

"It's been interrogated three times in the last minute, boss."

"And it reports us as a Bureau of Investigation vehicle on official business?"

"The very same, sir."

"They wouldn't dare fire on us," Foile muttered.

As the short drive to the next checkpoint proved—they didn't.

"Do I crash the gate, boss?" Leslie asked. A "yes," answer if not expected, was clearly hoped for.

"No, Agent. I hope we can avoid any property damage tonight. Property damages *or* deaths," Foile added, and the sedan slowed to a stop at the gatehouse.

Foile produced his credentials for the guard. "I am on official bureau business. I require you to admit me."

The guard, wearing corporal stripes, chewed his lip, clearly confronted with a problem way above his pay grade. He glanced at the captain in the back, who waved his hands in a most ambiguous fashion after Rick nudged him in the ribs.

That seemed enough for the poor corporal. The gate went up.

"There are autocannons covering this road," the young man shouted helpfully, as they pulled away.

"Are we being checked on?" Foile asked.

"Every five seconds, sir. Do you think there are autocannons covering us?"

Foile glanced at the rent-a-cop in back. "Not unless Alexander Longknife is spending more on weaponry and equipment than he did on personnel and training."

A few moments later, Leslie braked to a stop in the middle of the round driveway in front of Longknife Tower. They dismounted; the two agents in back had to encourage the brownuniformed man that, yes, he, too, was going with them.

"They issue machine pistols to the guards in the tower. And they'll use them," he told them. Foile wondered if that information would be any more accurate than the idle rumors the captain had provided so far.

As it proved, he was correct about the machine pistols.

There was a brown-suited guard at the door to meet them. And he did have a machine pistol slung over his shoulder. However, he was using both hands to unlock the door and admit them as the four of them flashed their bureau IDs.

"Take me to the Security Center," Foile ordered the armed guard, as they entered.

"You can't go in there sir," the guard said as he struggled to relock the door. He was using an old-fashioned metal key. It would be amusing if Foile had time to allow himself humor.

He feared that time was something he had very little of tonight.

He stalked toward the security post in front of the four banks of elevators. There, five guards stood, covering him as casually and diffidently as men with automatic weapons could.

"I am a Senior Chief Agent of the Wardhaven Bureau of Investigations," Foile snapped at the one who seemed, ever so slightly, to be in charge. "I require admission to the Security Center."

"No one is admitted while the alarm is active," the putative senior repeated.

"Why don't you take me there and let someone in charge decide?"

The nominal superior took off at a trot. Foile and his team followed at a quick walk. He led them past all the elevators and around a corner. In the middle of that wall was a door made apparent mainly by the red-lettered sign that proclaimed NO ADMITTANCE.

There the guard stopped and shrugged.

Foile walked up to the door; there was no sign of a lock or place to swipe an admit. He looked right, then left. A camera made a slight noise as it focused on him.

Again he held up his credentials and identified himself and his business. This time he added. "I am on special assignment from the Prime Minister himself. I require admittance. I strongly suggest that you admit me."

His other agents joined him, their credentials also held up for inspection. The camera made noise as it changed direction a bit, then adjusted its focus to take in each of the agents. Finally, the door clicked open, and Foile and his team entered.

The scene inside was ordered and cool. Men and women sat at stations going about their business. If the alarm hadn't continued to buzz and the red light above the door whirl, it might have been an ordinary day. While the worker bees seemed well in order, the same could not be said for what Foile took for the command center. There, four people stood, clad in black uniforms, doing a good imitation of bickering.

As Foile closed on them, it became apparent that they were indeed arguing.

Half wanted to turn off the alarm. The other half weren't quite ready to.

Foile cleared his throat to get their attention. The indecisive noise of human disagreement rumbled to a halt.

"Your security has been penetrated by Princess Kristine Longknife and two of her associates. My best guess is that she wants to spend some quality time with her grandfather."

"Our security has not been breached," the taller woman in black shot back. "We have everything under control."

Foile took the time to scratch behind his ear. "I really don't think so."

"There may be some problem with those damn browns and their paperwork, but we've got everything under control in here. No problem at all. Just look at the video take from the loading dock. Nothing at all. Totally normal."

Out on the work floor, a young woman stood from her workstation. "I think we do have a problem," she said, clearly uncomfortable to be disagreeing with her superiors. "I just ran a cloning check on the last thirty minutes from that station and it gives a twenty-three-percent chance that this is not original film. No one's moved during that time."

"They're new hires," the short man in black snapped. "Hanson's doing his usual heavy-handed thing. Look, he's just sitting there, reading one of his girly mags."

"Yes, sir, but I just did a poke at his commlink. It showed him inside the receiving area."

"So he needed to piss."

"Inside the receiving area while he's also sitting at his desk reading, sir?"

That finally broke down the wall of invincible ignorance,

saving Foile from having to take a sledgehammer to a couple of cast-iron heads.

"Get a guard out to the receiving area," the tall woman ordered.

"Have all stations report in," the shorter woman in the command group ordered. Foile watched as the worker bees broke out of their normal business and made frantic calls to everyone on their watch list.

The young woman who had forced the issue was the first to report. "I have no answer from the receiving dock." A moment later, she turned back to the command desk with a frown. "I also have no report back from the subbasement support guard."

"Send us the camera coverage," the tall woman ordered.

"There is no camera coverage of the subbasement. It was dropped in the cutbacks last summer." The troublemaker glanced at some empty floor spaces. The marks on the carpet showed evidence that there had been workstations there. Was the much-vaunted Longknife Tower security just a Potemkin village? Foile weighed just how much that might increase the chances of a certain princess getting to see her grandfather without getting anyone killed.

Or not. Foile remembered all the machine pistols he'd seen in the hands of people who looked like they needed a whole lot more training on crisis management as well as time on the shooting range.

Even if Princess Longknife started shooting with her sleepy darts, there was going to be a whole lot of blood on the floor. In this situation, with lots of lead flying addressed 'To Whom It May Concern,' you could never bet on who got hit with what.

Once again, the command team was divided and arguing.

"We have no idea where those three are," the short man said. "We have to release the nano hunters. They're the only things that can search the areas where we don't have camera coverage."

"We only cut back on the cameras because we bought the little twerps," the short woman added.

"But every time we turn them loose, we lose ten percent of them. Who wants to sign for that cost?"

The tall man in the black uniform usually stayed out of the bickering. Now he spoke. "We don't need to turn them all loose. Think about it. This Longknife girl is at the bottom of the tower and wants to get to the top of it." He glanced at one pair of workstations that showed no activity.

"We've got the elevators locked down. That leaves her only the stairwells, unless she's climbing the outside of the building. Has anyone checked there?"

Suddenly, there was mad activity at one desk. Two breaths later, a man reported, "No one on the outside of the building, sir."

Foile considered the statement and decided he wouldn't bet against the Longknife princess.

"So turn loose the nanos in the stairwells," the tall man said. On the work floor, two people moved to obey. For five minutes, things were quiet. Only the hooting and ringing of the alarms disturbed the people hard at work on the flood.

There was also no sign of the three they hunted.

Reports came back from the visual inspection of the receiving dock and subbasement. The guards there were down but unhurt. They retrieved ceramic sleepy darts from both of them, identical to the ones Foile's team had recently pried out of a wood support beam at a certain mountain cabin.

Leslie grinned. "Princess Kris won't kill anyone."

"Anyone?" Mahomet asked.

"Anyone she can avoid killing," Leslie corrected herself.

For five long minutes, the search went on and turned up nothing. Even Foile found himself wondering if they really were there.

Then the lights went out, and the alarms quit hooting.

A second later, the backup systems kicked in. Dim lights came back on. There was still a buzzing alarm, but a lot softer.

"What the hell?" came from the tall woman.

"She's killed the main power from the subbasement," the short man said. "Not to worry, the backup power supply is on the seventy-fifth floor."

"Get me camera coverage of that floor," the tall man demanded.

"We can't, sir," the short woman answered. "We are operating on local backup for the computers here in this room, but there's nothing coming in, sir, from the rest of the building. We're blind."

"Apparently the princess has made it to the seventy-fifth floor," Leslie said sardonically.

"We're not only blind, but dumb and deaf as well," the tall man growled. "The nanos. They're supposed to be on their own power. What do they see?"

Someone on the floor, it was hard for Foile to see by the dim light, stood. "The nanos are not catching anything, sir. She must not be in the stairwells."

"And we have all the elevators locked down," the tall woman said. "She's going nowhere."

"Release the nanos in the elevator wells," the tall man ordered. "Include the . . . what do you call them . . . blue-collar elevators?"

"Service elevators," someone answered.

"Turn loose nanos in all of them. She may not be riding one of them, but there are ladders in those shafts. They could be climbing."

"Nanos released in all the elevator wells," came back.

Half a minute later, they got their answer. "Sir. It can't be, but one of the elevators is moving."

"Turn off its power," the tall man snapped.

"It *is* off, sir," a worker bee said, hitting a button on his desk over and over again. "My board says there is no power to any of the elevators, but the nanos show elevator F-3 moving. It's a service elevator covering the upper floors, sir."

"Nelly's doing, I'll bet you," Leslie Chu whispered from beside Foile.

The tall man in the black uniform left the command desk and walked aside for a few steps, signaling Foile to join him.

"She may be brilliant, and her computer may be able to let her walk on water, but that damn princess is going to get herself killed."

"How?" Foile asked.

"When we lost power, Alexander Longknife lifted off the penthouse in an armed helicopter. He is no longer in the building, so if this young woman wants to talk to him, she came to the wrong place."

"Oh," said Foile. So the princess had failed. That still didn't kill her.

"When he abandoned the penthouse, the third, fourth, and fifth floors below him were flooded with Sarin gas. Is that princess of yours equipped for that?"

"She is not my princess, but, no, I doubt she is." Foile also wanted to know what exception to the laws of war and civil matters gave Al Longknife access to such gas. That question would have to wait.

"I must talk to the Longknife princess," Senior Chief Agent in Charge Foile said bluntly.

"Christian, do we have anything like a public-address system left to us?" the tall man asked the tall woman.

"We are supposed to, Karl, but nothing is working according to specs tonight."

Both of them looked out over the work floor, and their eyes came to rest on the young woman who'd first insisted on their fallibility.

"My board says it's available. I won't know for sure until someone uses it."

Karl handed Foile a mike. "Press the button on the side to talk. If you don't want everyone in the building to hear what you're saying, let up on the button."

"Lets hope a certain determined young woman can hear what I'm saying."

Foile took a deep breath and punched the button.

"Princess Kristine, I need to talk to you. This is Taylor Foile, I'm with the Wardhaven Bureau of Investigation, and if you and your friends want to be alive five minutes from now, you need to listen to what I have to say."

36

Kris eyed Jack. "Do you know any Taylor Foile of the WBI?" she asked him.

"Nope. Do you?" he asked Penny.

"Never heard of him."

"Well, he seems to know me," Kris said. "Nelly, how are you getting this? I thought you were off net."

"I am, except for stuff I make myself or where I'm so close to a poor little brain that I can overpower it. This is coming in on a 911 channel. It's open to everyone."

"Do we want to talk to him?" Kris asked.

"It will give away our location," Jack, Penny, and Nelly said, all at once.

"So, we wait to see if he goes on," Kris concluded.

About that time, Taylor Foile must have gotten tired of waiting and went on. "Princess Kristine, your father asked me to find you before anyone got hurt. Specifically, before you got killed. I see that you are using the sleepy darts my assistant, Agent Leslie Chu, by the way, a major fan of yours, pried out of the wood beam you shot them into."

"Fans everywhere," Penny said with a sigh. "I hope she didn't help."

"Of course she did," Jack said. "It's her job."

"Shush," Kris said.

"None of the people you shot are in any danger," the voice from Nelly went on. "The worse charges that might be placed against you are use of a false identity and being a public nuisance. A major public nuisance and a real pain in my rear end."

"I don't think he likes me," Kris said.

"Would you like you if you'd been one step behind us since we landed?" Penny pointed out.

Kris nodded agreement.

"I've been one step behind you since you landed," the WBI man admitted. "But you have got to stop running. Stop right now."

"What does he know that we don't?" Jack asked.

Kris frowned. What could Grampa Al have up his sleeve?

"You made a mistake turning off the lights, Princess Kristine," the voice said. "When the building lost power, your grandfather had a helicopter lift him off from his penthouse. If my guess is right, and this entire affair is your effort to talk with your grandfather, it's not going to happen."

Jack started to punch STOP, but Kris stopped him.

"What is it about you Longknifes?" Penny drawled. "You'll order anyone around, but a simple family talk, not so much."

"Honey," Jack whispered softly, "if he's flown the coop, there's no reason for us to keep going."

"I'm not sure I believe him," Kris snapped, and again pushed Jack's hand away from the STOP button.

"Worst for you and your friends," the voice went on, "when he left, he flooded three of the five floors below his penthouse with Sarin gas."

Kris hit the STOP button. Jack and Penny's hands slapped down on top of hers a fraction of a second later.

The elevator rumbled to a halt at floor 183.

"What's your granddad doing throwing Sarin gas around in a public building?" Penny demanded.

"It's a Longknife thing," Jack scowled.

"I didn't know anything about Sarin," Kris said defensively. "I was prepared for tear gas, and even that stuff that makes you vomit." She was. Among all their fake flab were breather hoods. They were wearing gloves. They were prepared for a lot. Just not a gas that killed you if a single drop got onto your skin.

"Princess Kristine," the WBI man continued, "you've gotten through a lot. But it only means you now have to come down through even more. Everyone is ready for you. There are a lot of guns down here, and unlike yours, none of them shoot sleepy darts." He paused to give that time to seep in.

"Please, for your father's and mother's sake, surrender yourselves. I have a warrant for your arrest. The judge must have owed your father quite a favor to sign something so unbelievably vague, but I do have a warrant. If you surrender to me, I can get you out of here, and very likely there'll be a judge waiting for you. You can be released on your own recognizance and be having breakfast tomorrow, make that this morning, with your Grampa Trouble. I had a most unenlightening talk with the old guy. He told me nothing, except that he was pretty sure no one was going to kill you. I didn't know about the Sarin gas then. I wonder what he'd say now."

"He'd say no one should have any Sarin," Jack snarled.

Kris took a deep breath. She'd never been face-to-face with defeat like this. Every brick wall she'd met before she'd managed go over, around, under, or turn to rubble.

This brick wall looked pretty solidly in her face.

Dejected like never before, she turned to Jack. "I wonder," she said, "do you think they'd let us share a cell?"

"I don't think it will matter," Jack said with one of his lopsided grins. "I don't perform well on camera, and I doubt they'll ever let the three of us go anywhere where there weren't two, no three people, watching us on security screens every second for the rest of our lives."

"Face it, Kris," Penny said, "unless you have some way for us to fly out of here, we've trapped ourselves."

"We planned a break-in," Jack pointed out. "We didn't plan to break out."

Kris nodded. She'd always figured that if they got to Grampa Al, that was all that mattered. That would change everything. What followed would depend on what she could talk him into or out of. Now it was blindingly clear. He didn't want to talk to her, and he wasn't going to listen to anything she had to say.

I have failed!

Kris didn't like the feeling of that. Failure. It felt too much like straggling in with just one ship left out of a whole Fleet of Discovery.

Failure was not something she wanted to get into the habit of.

But face it, girl. You are not going to shoot your way out of this. Penny is right, you either fly out of here or surrender.

One thing was clear, she was not going to get Jack killed. She'd spent her whole life waiting for him to come along, and getting him killed on the first date was not in the plan. Before she'd let any of them die, she'd surrender.

Strange, you never thought of surrender before Jack kissed you.

Damn it, I'm not calling it quits because I've fallen for Jack. I'm calling it quits because there's nothing to fight for anymore, and I can't fly out of here.

Can't you?

Kris's blood froze. She had to quit arguing with herself. Especially when she was right.

She hit the UP button.

"What?" Penny and Jack both shouted.

"Let's fly out of here, folks," Kris said.

37

"They've quit moving," the person monitoring the nanos reported.

"Thank God," Senor Chief Agent in Charge Foile breathed, careful to make sure his hand was off the button as he whispered his prayer.

Good. She wasn't going up any farther. Now to talk her down. He began speaking into the mike, trying to lower the pressure on the young woman. Talk her down. After all, she had no place to go but down. Foile offered options he knew would never be allowed. Yes, he could get the Prime Minister's daughter and her gallant team of ninja raiders out of Longknife Tower, but none of them would ever breathe free air again. Not unless someone pulled off a miracle, and while Foile might believe in prayer, his faith did not extend that far.

He talked, and the elevator stayed put. He kept talking, keeping his eye on the nano watcher's nodding head. No movement. No movement. No movement. Well, no news might not be good news, but at least it wasn't bad.

"They're going up again!"

Foile almost bit his own tongue. "Kristine, you can't go up any higher. There's gas. Sarin gas. Trust me. I wouldn't lie to you about that."

He wouldn't, but would the people in black uniforms lie? The WBI agent shot the tall man a look.

Wordlessly, the man mouthed, "It's true. Sarin gas."

"For God's sake, Princess. You're not stupid. Don't go suicidal on us now."

"They've stopped!" the nano herder shouted.

"Where?" Foile demanded.

"Floor 190, five floors below the gas," the tall woman announced.

"What's on the hundred and ninetieth floor?" Foile demanded.

The four of the command team stared at each other dumbly. The young woman who'd defied her betters stood. "I was following all the power users in the tower last month, familiarizing myself with anything that might cause a major fire."

"Yes, yes, spit it out," the tall woman demanded.

"There's a huge electric capacitor up there." That was greeted with more blank stares. "Think battery. Real big. Just what you'd need to power up an orbital shuttle. Make sure its matter/antimatter reactor didn't run out of power no matter what."

"Shuttle!" came from Foile and all four of the watch commanders.

"Good God, you can't launch a shuttle from here," the tall man in black said.

"By the same good God, no one should have Sarin gas in a public building, either," Foile snapped. "Did the bozos who put a shuttle up there calculate what would happen if you launched the damn thing?"

No surprise, Foile's question got more dumb nods. This time, even the smart young kid had nothing to say.

"Kris can't fly the shuttle out of here." These words came from Leslie Chu, agent and generally full-on fan of the Longknife princess. "She tried to steal Hank Peterwald's yacht once. She had to get out of a mess she'd made and needed to do it real fast. Anyway, even with Nelly on her shoulder, she only managed to steal the thing after Hank gave her the access codes."

Leslie looked none too happy at what she was saying. "That shuttle has to have access codes. Something to keep any kids from taking off for a joyride and getting themselves killed. Kris doesn't have those codes."

"Neither do I," the tall man in black said.

Foile punched the mike. "Kristine, you can't use the shuttle. You don't have the access codes. You know that. I know that. You're just fooling yourself."

"Should we send a team up to capture her?" the tall woman asked.

"Would you want to be next to that damn thing when she lights it off?" the tall man answered.

"But I thought you said . . ."

"The young agent over there is not the only one who has been following the princess's career," the tall man said. "The Nelly Kris took to Turantic is not the Nelly Kris has up there. First, we give her a couple of hours to cool her heels. If she hasn't taken off by then, yes, I'll send you up there to haul her in."

The tall woman didn't look enthusiastic at the prospect.

"And if she's taken off?" Foile asked.

"We'll need a whole lot more than my guards and your Bureau to catch her."

"But it's just an orbital shuttle," the tall woman said. "She can't take it through a jump point."

"I know that," Leslie said, "and you know that. But do you think Kris Longknife will let that stop her?"

"May I suggest that you figure out how to turn your power back on and get the elevators working," Foile said. "I, for one, would not want to be in this building when she takes that damn thing off."

The command team began to issue orders. Repair personnel were ordered to the subbasement, but they weren't needed. The power came on, both regular and emergency, a good fifteen minutes before the shuttle launched. The building was evacuated, and everyone was running long before the shuttle turned the night into day.

38

"Nelly, we really could use the last two codes," Kris said as softly and as patiently as she could manage. Sitting on top of a half-operational shuttle was bad enough. Stuck like a sitting duck in a location where everybody and his brother, sister, cat, and dog knew where she was was the last place she needed to be.

"Keep your shirt on," Nelly snapped. "I've got you three of the lockout codes. I'll have the other two in plenty of time."

"Time we don't have," Penny said, beating Kris to it.

"The gangplank is clear," Penny announced from where she sat, toward the back of the shuttle, her automatic out and covering said plank, as well as the loading area. "Nobody in sight."

"Nobody is dumb enough to storm a shuttle that's about to take off?" Nelly said.

"Concentrate on the codes," Kris said. "Let me worry about how courageous or smart these rent-a-cops are." Kris truly hoped courage was not in their job description. It hadn't been apparent in her hiring brief.

"Fourth code. Only one more left," Nelly announced. "How's your preflight checklist coming?"

With that jab, Kris turned back to Jack. "What's next?"

The shuttle was kept at five minutes in its countdown. When Grampa Al chose to get out of Dodge, he didn't want to have to wait. From the flight-deck log, a log that verified Kris's worst nightmare . . . this shuttle was seven years old and had never flown an inch . . . it was apparent that a qualified pilot checked out the shuttle every week. Its last prelaunch check had been the day before yesterday.

Kris truly hoped that Grampa Al spent more on his "Get the hell out of here," option than he did on the security of his outer perimeter.

Kris and Jack reached the end of their checklist. The matter/antimatter reactor was heating water. The controls were unlocked and moving. The electronics were awake and ready to fly. The hatch was sealed. Only the actual launch sequencer button was still refusing to let them in. Kris could push the button all day and get nothing for her effort.

"Nelly, we won. You're the holdup."

"Don't joggle my elbow. This is an unbelievably long code. I'm getting there. I'm getting there. Yes! Push that button. We're going places," Nelly crowed.

"Nelly, slight adjustment to the launch. I don't want to wreck this place more than I have to. Can you give it the minimum burn that will get us a thousand meters up before you really kick us in the butt?".

"Good Lord, Kris, you want everything," Penny growled.

"I warned you that I didn't want to do any more damage to Grampa Al's haunt than I had to."

"Launch profile adjusted, Kris. Now can we get out of here? I don't know what they have in store for me if you're caught, but I strongly suspect it doesn't involve hanging around your neck."

Kris pushed the launch button.

And found herself holding her breath as she felt the roar of the engines beneath her . . . and watched the building slowly slide by her at a walking pace.

"Is this such a good idea?" Jack asked.

"I have no idea, but how many custodians and cleaning women do you want to crisp tonight?" Kris shot back.

Jack had no answer for that.

Slowly. Painfully slowly. The shuttle rose.

Outside Kris's window, the night fled as the shuttle created its own dawn.

Kris forced herself to breathe. How long could it take a shuttle to get to a thousand meters? The mission timer crawled past ten seconds. Then fifteen.

Then the shuttle gave Kris a good kick in the rear and took off like God intended.

"You know, Kris," Penny called on net, "I understand the first liquid-chemical rockets took forever to clear the launch tower, just like this."

"They didn't pay those guys enough," Jack said through gritted teeth. The gees were climbing quickly as the shuttle eagerly made up for lost time.

Ten minutes later, they'd achieved low orbit.

"Now what?" Jack asked.

"My question entirely," Nelly added.

"I have no idea," Kris said.

"Should we make for High Wardhaven?" Penny asked. "Maybe we can dock with a ship. We've hijacked a shuttle. Why not hijack a starship? Unless, of course, you've discovered moral scruples, Your Highness."

"I can't think of anyplace else to go," Kris said. "Nelly, set us up to match with the station."

The words were hardly out of Kris's mouth before the radio came alive. "Hijacked shuttle, you will make for High Wardhaven where you will surrender. Be advised that we have lasers on you and will use deadly force if you appear to set a course back to Wardhaven. If you follow any course except one to match with the station and go dead in space fifty klicks trailing the station, we will fire on you."

Kris tapped her comm. "This is Lieutenant Commander, Her Royal Highness Kris Longknife. We have already set our course for High Wardhaven station. Don't get your panties in a twist."

"Worry about your own panties," snapped right back at her.

"You know, love, I think some people are really pissed with us," Jack said.

"You could be right," Kris agreed.

The shuttle flipped, slowed itself down and dropped into an

orbit that would send it higher and match with the station in two more orbits.

"Okay, crew. We've got three hours before we get there," Kris said. "I'm open to any suggestions from the floor."

"We should have stood in bed," Penny offered.

"Too late to do that," Kris said, then added, "and you know I love you, Jack. That changes a lot for me, but surrender just isn't my style."

"I know, honey. But getting us all killed is, huh . . ." Jack seem to run out of words, then began anew. "I got a bad feeling about this trip. Getting us truly, sincerely, and rather completely dead looks like the highest option on the table."

"Yeah," Kris said, rubbing her chin. "I think you're right, Jack. Somehow we'll have to avoid that happening."

"I can't tell you how relieved I am to hear that," Jack answered dryly.

"Nelly, what ships are at the station?" Kris asked.

"Small and hijackable?"

"Yes, make that list. We may need it if worse comes to worst. But not yet. Nelly, are there any visiting Navy ships? Ships where we might claim asylum."

"An asylum. Great idea," Jack said.

"Not *an* asylum, Jack. A ship where we could get political asylum."

"That's what I thought you said," Jack answered. "I just thought the other idea deserved some consideration."

"I'd slug you if I didn't need both hands to fly this brick," Kris muttered.

"I figured now was a good time to speak truth to power," Jack said.

"You are so going to pay for all this at a later time and place."

"Hopefully very private."

"Folks, I hate to interrupt this foreplay, but could we figure out where we're going?" Penny said.

"Kris," Nelly said, "there are several warships in port. A Greenfeld cruiser."

"Not a good idea," Penny said. No one disagreed.

"A couple of corvettes, including one from New Eden."

"Let's skip any U.S. ships. Too likely we'd be turned over to Grampa Ray's not-so-tender mercies. Been there, done that, got the T-shirt," Kris said.

"There's a battleship from Musashi, the IMS *Mutsu*," Nelly went on. "She came to retrieve small packages that crew members of the Imperial ships left behind before they departed on the voyage of discovery."

"Huh," Penny said.

"Many of the crew left packages containing a lock of hair or fingernail clippings," Nelly said. "It's an old tradition."

"I see," said Kris. "Nelly, are we wanted on Musashi?"

"I'm sorry, but yes, Kris. The last government lost a recent election. It is suspected the loss of the Fleet of Discovery contributed to that. The new government immediately began proceedings against you. As of last week, Musashi was added to the list of planets wanting you for war crimes and crimes against humanity."

"So if we go there, I get my day in court," Kris said.

"A Musashi court," Penny pointed out.

Kris considered that. Then she began to think out loud to the two people she most trusted. "Since we got back, I've been doing what I was told. Go to Chance. Go to Wardhaven. Go talk to your great-grandfather. Go to Madigan's Rainbow, in chains if you won't go any other way. I've been a very good girl."

"And see what it's gotten you," Penny said.

"Right," Kris said.

Kris took a deep breath. "I've had enough of being good. I've commanded battles. For Christ's sake, I've defended not one world but two from annihilation. And now I can't even take up a mike in a karaoke bar and tell my story to a couple of drunks. I've had it, crew. I want my day in court."

"Ah, Kris, maybe you aren't aware, but Musashi is one of the few planets that never approved the full Charter on Human Rights," Nelly said carefully. "They rejected the article on capital punishment. They haven't executed anyone in thirty years, but it's still on the books."

That did give Kris pause. She glanced at Jack. "As my security chief, are you going to object to my risking an unfortunate encounter with the headsman?"

Jack shrugged. "As the man who lost his heart to you, I'll admit that my gut is in an uproar at the thought. As your security chief, I'm conflicted. As you so often point out, it's a risk, but it's a calculated risk. Me, I think all this talk of crimes against humanity is just that, cheap political talk. I have a hard time believing anyone who hears your side of the story is going to give that cheap talk any value."

Jack paused, then went on, "I'm also sick and tired of being shut up in a corner, or run around on a short leash. Maybe I've caught part of this Longknife thing you have, but I say damn the torpedoes; full speed ahead."

"That's talking like the man I could love," Kris said through a grin.

"I thought I was the man you loved."

"You'll pardon me. We're coming up on a burn, so I can't give you the kiss you deserve, man that I love," Kris said with a smile.

"The story of my life, past and future," Jack said.

Kris did the required burn, then did manage to plant a kiss on Jack's cheek. Essentials done, she turned back to the problem chewing on her backside.

"Nelly, can you get me a channel being monitored by the *Mutsu*?"

"I have it dialed in. I had nothing else to do while you two were smooching."

"I'm planning on you having a lot of time on your hands, Nelly. Get used to it. Put me live on the *Mutsu*'s guard channel."

"You're live."

"Imperial Musashi Battleship *Mutsu*, this is Lieutenant Commander Kris Longknife. Do you read me?"

"This is *Mutsu*'s communication center, we read you Lieutenant Commander Kris Longknife on our emergency guard channel."

"Longknife, here, please patch me through to the officer of the deck."

"Wait one," the comm tech replied crisply and professionally.

"This is Commander Morishita, OOD of the *Mutsu*. Who am I addressing?"

"Commander Morishita, this is Lieutenant Commander Kris Longknife, Royal U.S. Navy. I request permission to dock a shuttle in the *Mutsu* and come aboard."

"Oh," only held a hint of startlement. "Wait one."

"Do you think, Kris," Jack said, "that poor fellow knows the full extent of the 'Oh my God' that you just dropped in his lap?"

"You know, Jack, I don't think he does."

Kris watched the timer as it counted out a minute. Then another. Then a third.

The timer was coming up on four when the comm line came awake.

"This is Captain Miyoshi of the Imperial Musashi Battleship *Mutsu*. Who am I addressing?"

"This is Lieutenant Commander Kris Longknife, sometimes styled as Princess. I request permission to dock a shuttle on your command and come aboard."

"You do, do you?"

"Yes, I do."

"I have a JAG officer at my elbow shouting no in about forty-seven different ways. Can you give me one reason to overrule him?"

Kris paused for a moment. No doubt he saw her as nothing but trouble, and rightly so. Just what call did she have on him?

"I request permission to come aboard in the memory of all the courageous men and women of the Musashi Navy who died following my orders."

That brought a long pause. Kris was now coming up on High Wardhaven station. Soon, she'd have to brake into the parking orbit trailing the station by fifty klicks. Once she did, every laser on the station would fix her in its sights.

"Come on, Captain," Jack muttered.

"*Mutsu* to Longknife," the captain said, breaking the silence. "Let's make sure that we understand ourselves. You are wanted for high crimes on my planet. If you board my ship, you will be surrendering yourself for judgment by my people."

"I understand that, Captain Miyoshi."

An exasperated "Damn" slipped onto the net. No doubt it was not intended for general consumption.

"Then we will do it your way. Landing officer, set an approach beacon. Marines, to the landing bay. I will meet you there, Commander Longknife."

"Thank you, sir. Would you please advise High Wardhaven station that I am on approach to you."

"Huh?" was followed by a click and a long moment of silence that was finally broken by a "You bastard, Longknife! You didn't tell me that you'd been forbidden permission to approach the station."

"It may have slipped my mind, sir."

"I just bet it did. Well, we've advised the station that we have set a landing beacon for your use. It's up to you to persuade them not to shoot you out of space when you cross the fifty-klick line. Good luck to you. *Mutsu* out."

"You know, Kris," Penny said, "I really don't think he likes you."

"I might have allowed another important relationship to get off on the wrong foot," Kris admitted.

"Just like every other one of them," Jack muttered.

"Hijacked shuttle, this is High Wardhaven approach control. You are approaching your parking orbit. Begin braking."

Kris clicked her comm. "High Wardhaven, this is Lieutenant Commander Kris Longknife in the Longknife family shuttle. There has been a slight change of plan. I am authorized to approach and dock with the Imperial Musashi Battleship *Mutsu*."

"Approach to hijacked shuttle, I have been informed of no such change. Be advised, every laser on the station is tracking you. Enter the controlled space around the station, and we are authorized to use deadly force."

"Longknife to approach, I hear you, but I have the *Mutsu*'s beacon showing on my board and am on approach to it."

"Don't do it, Longknife."

"I am doing it. Longknife out."

"Don't you just love it when Longknifes play chicken?" Penny said.

"Yeah," Jack said, "but this time it's Longknifes playing chicken with a Longknife. This may be a first."

"Fifty-click boundary coming up," Nelly said, "in five . . . four . . . three . . . two . . . one."

Kris noticed that everyone on board was holding their breath, herself included.

"We just passed the forty-nine-klick mark," Nelly said.

Everyone started breathing again.

"Approach to Longknife, you are authorized to dock with the *Mutsu*. Deviate from that flight path one inch, and we *will* fry you."

"Last message received and understood. We will comply. Longknife out."

Kris was a good pilot; today she was meticulous. Nelly plotted a glide path that would intersect the *Mutsu* as it rotated around High Wardhaven station. Kris hooked the wire on the first pass, and the battleship reeled them in like a caught fish.

Locked down in the *Mutsu*'s hangar bay, Kris and Jack went through their postflight check carefully. It wouldn't do to break anything on Grampa Al's shuttle. Kris certainly didn't want anyone who checked after her to question that the shuttle's antimatter was not fully safetied. It was a good five minutes before she pushed her seat back from the controls and unstrapped herself.

"I don't think we should keep the captain waiting any longer than we have to," Penny said.

"I just hate perp walks," Kris muttered. "I hope they skip the cuffs this time. I don't like bracelets on the best of days."

"Quit delaying, Kris," Jack said. "Look on the bright side. At least this time, you've got friends with you."

Kris chuckled. She stood, adjusted the fall of her poorly tailored and smelly brown uniform, and headed for the hatch. Jack and Penny followed.

Kris ducked her head as she exited the shuttle, then stood tall.

Across from her stood two Navy officers, sporting four and three stripes respectively on the shoulder boards of their whites. Behind them was a squad of Marines in full battle rattle.

Kris saluted. "Permission to come aboard," she said formally.

"Permission granted," the captain growled through a scowl of biblical proportions as he returned her salute. "My Marines will escort you to your holding cell. Commander Morishita will see to your needs. Maybe even arrange for proper uniforms for you," he said with a disapproving sniff in Kris's direction.

"I myself am needed on the pier. It seems there is a Navy captain from your Royal U.S. Navy with his own Marines and his own claim on your hide. My JAG tells me that I must disappoint him. If your captains are anything like our captains, we do *not* take disappointment easily."

"I think our captains are pretty much the same," Kris said in her most helpful voice. The scowl she received in reply would have burned any proper subordinate where she stood.

Fortunately, Kris had never been a very proper subordinate.

The captain turned and marched quickly off. Commander Morishita offered a directing hand, and Kris marched off beside him, followed by Jack and Penny and a whole squad of very armed and alert Marines of a most Imperial persuasion.

"Unfortunately, our brig is full at the moment," the commander informed Kris. "It seems the yen is strong this week, making beer ashore rather cheap. Many of our younger crew members are away from home for the first time and did not discipline themselves as well as they should have."

"Sailors are people, too," Kris said. "I believe chiefs were invented to look after them."

"Chiefs were not invented, Commander, they are hatched," Commander Morishita said with more than the hint of a smile.

Kris thanked whatever god was looking after her this morning. Apparently, she had fallen into the clutches of a Navy officer with a sense of humor. Kris didn't risk a smile, though. There was still the matter of where they intended to put her. Battleships had a lot worse places than the brig. Or so she'd heard.

They clambered up several decks, took passageways halfway around the ship, and came to a halt before a door announcing ADMIRAL'S IN PORT CABIN.

"You will be staying here," Commander Morishita said. "We have no flag aboard, and this seemed like the best place for you," he said, opening the door.

Four Marines quickly took guard station on either side of the door, with a staff sergeant looking very senior.

Kris followed the commander in. The quarters were quite spacious, with the walls painted to look like wood paneling. There was a work area with a desk and commlink as well as a large table for meetings and, for less formal discussions, a corner with two comfortable sofas with several stuffed chairs.

The commander pointed out a door that led to a bedroom and facilities. There were two other doors. "One leads to the Admiral's wardroom. The other door is to the chief of staff's quarters. The previous admiral had it put in. Our last admiral had a lock put on it for his side, and I understand it was never unlocked. We will billet one of your people there, the other one in the next stateroom down the hall."

Kris walked over to that door, and opened it. When she glanced inside, it showed a room not much larger than her own quarters on the old *Wasp.* "Jack, would you mind being in here?"

"I don't see any problem," Jack said, without even looking.

"I see that you came aboard with nothing but that unregulation dress. I will notify the quartermaster to have a chief check in with you. I assume you'll need everything."

"Pretty much," Kris agreed. With that he left.

"Nelly, are we under surveillance?" Kris asked.

"None that I can identify," the computer answered.

Kris developed the shakes, something she never did in public. Quickly, she found Jack's arms around her.

"I'll go check out my quarters," Penny said, and left them alone.

39

Senior Chief Agent in Charge Foile dictated most of his report to his computer as Agent Chu drove his team back to Bureau headquarters. It said a lot about what he'd done but very little about why or what he had actually accomplished.

He did not like that.

He left his computer putting together his report and dropped into his boss's office. "You done?" she asked.

"Kris Longknife is no longer on Wardhaven. She was alive the last time I think I saw her, at the controls of a shuttle headed for orbit, so I guess I am done."

"Very good, Senior Chief Agent. Why don't you go home."

"You're satisfied with the outcome?"

"The Prime Minister's daughter is alive. That's what he wanted."

"Have you heard from him?"

"Not so much as a peep."

"Interesting," Foile said, and left.

On the way out, he stopped by the team area. Agent Leslie Chu was finishing up her contributions to the team's report. "Do you still have that media alert on the princess?" Foile asked her.

"Of course, sir."

"Have you gotten any hits recently?"

"Not a beep this whole time, sir. The media didn't know she was here."

"Oh," Foile said. "A shuttle takes off from Longknife Towers and lights up the sky, not to mention makes a roaring mess of a lot of people's sleep. Anything about that?"

"Again, sir. Nothing. If I didn't know it was impossible, I'd say someone told the media not to cover it."

"But that, of course, is impossible," he said.

The two exchanged sardonic grins.

He turned for home, then thought better of it and turned the other way. In five short minutes, he was standing at the front door to Government House. A flash of the badge and he was in. The elevator responded to his punch for the Prime Minister's floor.

Apparently, someone had given him access and not yet taken it back. They probably would by morning. Which meant it was a good thing he hadn't gone home.

He quickly found his way to the Prime Minister's outer office and walked in. "Senior Chief Agent in Charge Foile to see the Prime Minister," he said, not slowing down as he headed for the door he now knew led to the Prime Minister.

"You can't go in there," the secretary shouted. "You have no appointment."

He went in.

The Prime Minister was behind his desk. He glanced up from his screen, then leaned back to give the agent his full attention. "You," was all he said.

"Yes, sir. Me. Your daughter is safe and no longer on Wardhaven."

"So I am told. Yet you did not apprehend her."

"She is a rather elusive person."

"So she is."

"Why was she trying to see her grandfather, and why was he so intent on not seeing her that he abandoned his home and flooded a portion of it with poison gas?"

The Prime Minister stood from behind his desk. "I sent you to secure her. You don't need to know why. Most certainly, since you failed to do what you were ordered to do.

Now, if you'll excuse me, I have to be about the people's business."

"What is going on here?" Foile demanded, but he was speaking to the Prime Minister's back as he left his office by a back door.

Foile considered chasing after the Prime Minister, but the door behind him opened, admitting two burly security guards who, no doubt, had been instructed to pay no attention to anything so minor as a Bureau ident.

Foile went before he was forced.

This matter was not finished. He'd have to look for someplace else to find his answers. Where could Kris Longknife fly a shuttle to? She hadn't landed on Wardhaven. That left only one other place for her to go.

40

Kris was surprised to find that Jack was having a bad case of the shakes, too. She'd always managed to get to her quarters before the shakes got too bad. To find that Jack had them, too, was . . . interesting . . . on several different levels.

"You're shaking?" was her first reaction.

"Yes. I do it a lot after I'm around you." That didn't keep him from hugging her close. Somehow, they found themselves on one of the sofas.

"I didn't think you . . ." Kris couldn't find a word to finish her thought.

"Had any weaknesses," Jack finished.

"I didn't say that."

"Kid, everyone gets the shakes. Didn't they teach you that in school?"

"No."

"Bad school. They warned us at the Academy. Grizzled old agents talked about what it's like after the shooting stops. Some have to change their underwear. Others get the shakes. Some have a crying jag."

"Then I'm normal?"

"Kris, love, you are never normal," Jack said through a

grin. "But yes, Kris, your body shares some traits with the rest of us humans."

Kris considered that as she listened to the pounding of his heart slow. And felt the pounding of her own heart go from a gallop to a walk.

She was normal. Everyone felt this way.

How interesting.

She rested in Jack's arms and let that thought soak deep into her. The world didn't go away. Outside the door, there were still lions and tigers and bears waiting. But here, in Jack's arms, they weren't gnawing on her. She could relax.

She did.

There was a knock at the door.

"The quiet sure was nice," Jack said.

Kris stood, adjusted her borrowed uniform. It was wrinkled and a mess, but it had come by all the sweat and stains honestly. "Come in," she said.

Captain Miyoshi entered. "There is a very upset Royal U.S. Navy captain busy reporting to his superiors that you are not available."

"Thank you, sir," Kris said.

"My *Mutsu* now has a Royal U.S. Marine honor guard standing proudly at each of my gangplanks."

"I am sure they will do you honor, sir."

"I told them you were not leaving."

"That is correct, sir."

"Commander Longknife, you are a lot of trouble."

"Usually, sir."

"Sit down, sit down," Captain Miyoshi said, waving her at a chair. "You are no cadet, and I am no drill sergeant. I have taken the liberty of ordering some tea and sandwiches brought up. When did you last eat?"

"Yesterday, about fifty thousand years ago," Kris said with a grin.

"I thought so. I am already in receipt of a request to return that shuttle you rode in on. Am I to assume that you came by it somewhat irregularly?"

"Somewhat, yes, sir. It is Longknife corporate property, and I am a major shareholder in our family corporation, but no, I'm afraid I forgot to sign it out through proper channels."

The captain listened attentively to her story, weighed it carefully, found it wanting . . . and went on. "I have some personal questions for you. There is no recorder in this room. These are purely questions I have not been able to answer for myself about your recent . . . experiences. Would you mind my asking you?"

"You can ask, sir. I can't assure you that I can or will answer," Kris said. There might be no recording device. Still, many courts of law would allow secondhand statements when a person gave it against their own best interests.

"My sister's husband was XO of the *Chikuma*, you see."

"I'm sorry to hear that, sir," Kris said. So this was personal. She hadn't considered when she chose the *Mutsu* to surrender to that she might be placing herself in the hands of someone who personally bore the grief for her actions. Then again, every Navy she'd encountered was a small world.

"Could you tell me how my brother-in-law died?" The words were simple and direct. She certainly owed this man, and his sister, an honest answer.

"He died honorably and courageously, fighting against impossible odds," Kris said, keeping her words simple and direct.

"Yet he was running away from the alien base ship. Or did I misunderstand the reports in the media?"

Kris nodded and chose her words carefully. "We are both correct, Captain. The *Chikuma* and *Haruna* were fighting courageously against impossible odds. They were, at that time, opening the range between them and the alien base ship. That was according to the plan I had presented to the admirals, which they had accepted."

The captain of the *Mutsu* frowned.

Kris went on. "Sir, it was critical for the battle line to draw and hold the aliens' attention. If they did, there was the barest of chances that my squadron of corvettes could survive long enough to launch our Hellburners and destroy the base ship. We knew the odds were against us. None of us realized just how badly. Still, the battleships achieved their mission. The aliens fixated on them, and my corvettes gutted the base ship. There were just a whole lot of alien ships left over."

"I think I understand. You set a rabbit trap and caught a bear," the skipper of the *Mutsu* said.

"I prefer to think that we set a bear trap that caught the biggest bear ever. But there were a whole lot of other bears that were quite upset with us."

"That might be a better comparison," Captain Miyoshi agreed. "I have just one more question."

"Yes, sir."

"My brother-in-law wrote home that you said the mission of your Fleet of Discovery was to look and report back. So why were you carrying those huge torpedoes? What did you call them, Hellburners?"

Kris nodded. Yes, she could imagine some people found what she said and what she did two very different matters. "When I told your brother-in-law that discovery was the mission for my squadron, I truly believed that was our one and only mission. When we departed Wardhaven, none of our ships were equipped with Hellburners."

"Then when did you get them?"

"I shipped home the wreckage of the first alien ship we encountered. The one that attacked us, then destroyed itself. When my messenger returned, he had three freighters and a repair ship with him, gifts from my King and Grampa Ray."

"I don't understand. You had not yet encountered the worst evidence that you found, yet your king sent you those weapons."

"Yes, Captain. I left those weapons behind when my squadron made the long search. It was only after our long search that we knew we had some real monsters out there, and that one of them was about to destroy a civilization. If I had not had the Hellburners, I could not have taken on the monster. I did have them, and we chose to do something about them."

"I heard that you offered to let any Sailor go home."

"Yes. I did. Your brother-in-law and everyone else who followed me after the aliens knew what we were getting into, or at least as much as we knew about them, and accepted the risks we were taking to save the bird people."

"Now it all makes sense," the captain said. "I'm afraid what I took from the media reports did not add up."

"I think it was politically advantageous that two and two not add up," Kris said. "I am sorry that it left you doubting the honor and courage of your fellow officers."

"Yes. This is very different. I will have to think upon this. Then I will message my sister." Captain Miyoshi stood and turned to leave.

Suddenly, he stopped.

"I have a message for you. There is a man on the *Mutsu*'s quarterdeck. He says he is Taylor Foile, a senior chief agent of the WBI. Do you know him?"

"I've been doing my best to avoid meeting him face-to-face for much of the last week," Kris admitted.

"He would like to meet you. He says he has no arrest warrant, just questions. Apparently, I'm not the only one who wants answers from you tonight."

Kris shrugged. "Your Marines have orders to keep me here. I expect them to come to my aid if he tries to drag me out of here."

Captain Miyoshi actually chuckled as he authorized the agent to come aboard.

41

Senior Chief Agent in Charge Foile followed the young lieutenant assigned to lead him through the labyrinth of corridors, ladders, and gear that seemed indigenous to a man-of-war. He had been on two before and needed a guide both times. The walk gave him time to consider where he might find his wayward princess. He concluded that the ship's brig was her most likely abode.

So he was quite surprised when the lieutenant opened a door marked ADMIRAL'S IN PORT CABIN and ushered the agent in. There were four very alert, armed, and battle-dressed Marines guarding the door, so it did leave the agent to wonder just what were the circumstances the princess had landed herself in this time.

A young woman in a baggy and sweat-stained brown uniform stood in the center of the large and well-apportioned room. He recognized her immediately. Clearly exhausted and bedraggled, she was still quite beautiful. The word Agent Chu regularly used came to mind. "Gorgeous." Her hair looked longer than it was in most of the pictures Chu had shoved under his nose to admire.

Foile stepped forward and gave her a slight bow from the

neck. "Lieutenant Commander, Her Royal Highness Kristine Longknife, I presume."

The young woman offered him her hand. "After tonight, I may be back to just Kris. I'm not even sure the Longknife applies."

Foile took the hand, considered kissing it, then shook it instead.

"Your father had me chasing after you for the last several days," he said. "I doubt he'd do that if he planned to disinherit you."

The woman smiled; it was a lovely little thing. "Don't be too sure. Water seems to be a lot thicker than blood where my family's concerned. Now," she said, offering him an overstuffed chair, "you said you had questions."

Foile settled into the offered chair; the princess took one across from him. Another man, olive-skinned and alert, and, if the pictures were right, Captain Juan Montoya, the princess's security chief, stayed on the couch.

"May I first say that you have led me on quite a chase. No matter where I was, you'd just left. Professionally, I must admire you."

"I had a lot of good help," the princess said. "Jack here, and Penny. She's asleep in her new quarters. At least I hope she's getting some rest."

"And others?"

"No one helped us," the princess said, and did not flinch even a little at the lie.

Foile raised an eyebrow. Many a criminal's facade had crumbled at that raised eyebrow, following a lie with the blurted truth.

The princess folded her hands in her lap and waited patiently for him to go on.

Damn, she's good, Foile thought, *but then, she learned from the best.*

"Your father asked me to catch you before you got yourself killed and others with you. I did not catch you, but you seem to have not gotten yourself killed."

"I'm rather well practiced at that." She flashed her security chief a smile that clearly gave evidence of what the forensic team had found in the lodge.

Foile found himself wishing them the best of luck where that was concerned.

"There is the matter of why you almost got yourself killed this evening," Foile said. "I asked your father about that, and he told me to forget it. He strongly hinted I should forget the entire last week."

"I imagine so. Father does tend to want to forget problems he can't solve."

"I'm having a hard time forgetting you risked your life just to talk to your grandfather. And the extent he went to avoid you."

Now it was the princess's turn to raise an eyebrow. "Sarin gas. That was a bit extreme. Are you sure he gassed the place?"

"I told you what I was told," Foile admitted. "I did not check out the facts, and you did kind of trash the building in your exit."

Both the princess and her man laughed heartily at that. "Yes, that exit was spectacular even by my standards. I hope everyone got out of the building. We restored power to the elevators."

"Yes, I know. From what I heard, the building was empty when you left."

The princess seemed relieved at that.

Foile saw his opening and took it. "But what was so important that you risked your life to see your grandfather?"

"And why was he so intent on not letting me get a word in edgewise?" the princess said thoughtfully.

"Exactly."

The princess leaned back in her chair. She glanced at Jack, who raised an eyebrow, then returned her gaze to Foile. "Are you sure you want to know?"

"I pursued you for four days. I forced myself on your father, the Prime Minister, and I came all the way up here and managed to crash your present security. By the way, are you seeking political asylum?"

"I've turned myself in. I expect I'll be facing a Musashi court in a few days, but back to your question. Once again, I must ask you, do you really want to know the answer? If I tell you, you will likely never sleep as soundly as you have."

Now it was Foile's turn to sit back in his chair. He'd spent twenty-five years as a good man of the law. He read the cartoon in the daily news and ignored the political topics like a plague. Apparently, this young woman was about to initiate him into the inner secrets of those he served.

He took a deep breath and leaned forward. "Can what you tell me be any worse than what I'm imagining?"

"Very likely," the man on the couch said. "It's dangerous to get too close to one of these damn Longknifes."

"I suspect I have been too close to you Longknifes ever since your father summoned me to his office. Enough beating around this bush. Would you please answer my question?"

The princess gave him a sad smile. "Unfortunately, I am not all that sure what the answer is to your question. I assume you know that I seem to have started a war with some hostile aliens on the other side of the galaxy."

"It was in the all the news," Foile said. "My Agent Chu, a fan of yours, made sure I saw the worst of it. Then, suddenly, it wasn't there anymore."

"Yes," the princess said. "There seem to be major differences in high places just how to respond to the hot potato I dropped in their laps. My great-grandfather Ray, King Ray to you, appears to be trying to raise a Navy without raising taxes."

"How's that working for him?" Foile asked.

"Not so good. Quite a bit of resistance all around. But it's his son, my grandfather Al's reaction, that is causing me trouble."

"What is his reaction?"

"Nothing, officially, but there's chatter, not a lot of it, but it seems that Grampa Al wants to take a different tack from his father. Being the hardheaded businessman that he is, it appears he wants to get the aliens talking to him, open trade, whereas the excitable and shoot-'em-up types like Ray and me only get them shooting first and neither asking nor answering questions."

"What do you think your grandfather Al will try to do?"

"How about sending out a trading fleet loaded with all the goodies that we make?" the princess said.

Foile saw the problem. "And if these bad actors capture the fleet?"

"They get all the computers and navigational material to take them right back to us," the young man said, getting up from his couch to pace.

"A lot of good people died under my command," the princess said. "Every ship that was hit dropped its reactor containment and blew themselves to atoms so that the aliens could get no navigational data from them. It looks like Grampa Al will give it to them on a silver platter."

"This was what you wanted to question him about?"

"Yes."

"And rather than talk to you, or tell you some lie, he ran away."

"Yes. Interesting reaction, no?"

"Very interesting," Foile said. He found he was sitting on the edge of his seat. He forced himself to settle back. Any effort to relax proved a waste.

"You see why I was willing to risk everything to get a few words in."

"I do, and may I say that I'm glad that I didn't keep you from getting as far as you got." Foile allowed himself a chuckle. "I don't often fail. I'm glad I picked this time to have one of my rare breaches."

The princess shrugged and flipped a hand at her surroundings. "I did fail. Now all I can hope for is to get my day in court and present my case to the public at large. Clearly, I will not be talking about vague rumors and innuendoes for which I can produce no basis in fact."

Senior Chief Agent in Charge Foile nodded. "On the other hand, it is frequently my job to produce just the sort of facts you lack."

"Be careful," the princess said.

The young man ceased his pacing. "While her grampa Al might not be willing to use violence against Kris here, his subordinates, or their helpers, have been known to get very enthusiastic in their effort to get into his good graces. Remember 'will no one rid me of this troublesome priest?' The same could be said of a princess or a cop."

Foile nodded. "Minor minions are want to go off half-cocked. However, they are often the ones that crack under pressure and give us our first handle on a rope that leads up the chain of evidence."

Foile paused for a moment, a line of investigation cascading out before his mind's eye. "I think I know a couple of trees to shake. I think this could be very challenging. Challenging and fun."

"You have a weird sense of fun, then," the young man said.

Foile stood. "One word, Princess. If memory serves, Musashi still has capital punishment."

"Your memory is correct. Nelly advised me of it before we landed on the *Mutsu*, but thank you for the thought. If I may add, if you insist on taking on this quest for a damsel . . . and all humanity . . . in distress, you might want to talk with my brother Honovi. He's a member of parliament and not as blind to some things as my father. You might also want to talk to my grampa Trouble."

"If you mean General Tordon, I talked with him. A most reticent witness."

"He'll loosen up when you get to know him. Tell him I sent you and that I dropped the Grampa Al monkey on your back."

"Thank you, not for the Grampa Al monkey, but for the secret handshake for General Trouble."

"Just remember," the princess said. "He's trouble for everyone, even me. Oh, another thing. I left my luggage in the Downside elevator station. Is there any chance you could send it on to the *Mutsu*?"

"The police impounded it, but with no case filed, I can likely get it loose."

"Thank you."

"There is just one more matter, Princess. One of my agents, Leslie Chu is a great fan of yours. Is there any chance I might have your autograph?"

"Is there any paper here?"

"I can print out one of your pictures," Nelly said, and the admiral's desk began spitting out a print. The princess signed it with a flourish, then, with an impish grin added, "Sorry I missed you."

Foile gave her a bow from the waist as he took his leave. Clearly, this young woman was noble and deserving of his respect. The lieutenant was waiting for him outside the door. As Foile made his way off the ship, he began rearranging his schedule. Like so many of his kind, he had a large bank of unused leave.

I wonder how the boss will react when I ask for a month off?

He also wondered how much help he could get out of Leslie as the price for her princess's autographed photo.

42

Matters moved slowly after that. Though the *Mutsu* was scheduled to sortie the next day, there was suddenly a stack of reasons the ship could not sail. Kris got to know Lieutenant Sato, the ship's JAG officer very well as he sought first information, then advice on how to handle this blizzard of delays. Nelly was very helpful.

Captain Miyoshi arrived with a quartermaster chief. Thanks to the uniformity imposed by the now-defunct Society of Humanity, many uniforms for Navy and Marine officers for Musashi and the Royal U.S. Navy were pretty much the same. The chief had several uniforms for Kris in different sizes: too small and way too small.

That caused some embarrassment, but the *Mutsu* had its own tailor, and the chief very professionally fitted the uniforms to Kris's nonstandard frame. Jack was saved from the same pins by the arrival of his travel bag with a note from Colonel Hancock. "You've got a month's worth of leave coming. Use it well."

"While we have the uniforms, Commander," Captain Miyoshi said, "we do not have the proper accouterments. We found your list of awards and decorations. The exchange on High Wardhaven provided most of them and shoulder boards. However, the Order of the Wounded Lion was not in stock."

"I don't imagine it would be," Kris said. "I can skip it. It always raises more questions than I can answer."

The captain shut his mouth on what likely would have been one of them. After a pause, he went on. "Trunks have arrived for you and Lieutenant Pasley. Shall I have them brought here? I'm told their contents are rather hard to inventory."

Kris found herself and Jack struggling to contain a laugh at the captain's honest evaluation of the inside of one of Abby's mysterious trunks. Which raised the matter of Abby and Cara. And other things.

"Captain, I am grateful for the hospitality you and your ship have shown me. I do have a problem."

"Just one?" the captain asked.

"Several, actually," Kris admitted. "I am locked out of my accounts. For the first time in a long time, the world is confronted with a penniless Longknife."

"I can cover her expenses," Jack quickly put in.

"Thank you, Jack, but my bill for uniforms, mess tab, all this, is too much to ask," Kris said, glancing around the room.

"When I took you in," Captain Miyoshi said, "I expected that you were bringing a whole lot of trouble with you. Please don't think any of this is a surprise. The chief here has opened an account in your name. When all is done, my Navy will send your Navy a bill, and we can let people who love to haggle over such matters talk about it from now until the sun burns out for all I care."

"Thank you, Captain," Kris said. "There is one more matter. I need to send a message to my maid on Madigan's Rainbow."

"Your maid?" the captain asked.

"Abby is her maid, and a few things more," Jack put in.

"Oh, Abby Nightengale. She features prominently in your file."

So the Musashi Navy had a file on Kris. Why was she surprised? Well, she probably had surprised the poor captain, but he was clearly doing a good job of playing catch-up.

"I left Abby rather suddenly, and I suspect she's very worried about me. I'd like to let her know I'm safe." Kris considered where she was headed and corrected herself. "I've landed on my feet."

"A much better choice of words," the captain agreed.

"Could Nelly send a message, standby priority to Madigan's Rainbow?" There were several jump buoys between Wardhaven and there. Each of them would add to the cost of the message. Even using the lowest, standby priority, this message would cost. It would also arrive in a couple of weeks. There was not a lot of traffic out on the sector where Madigan's Rainbow hid. That was why it had been chosen.

"Have your computer compose your message," the captain said. "I'm sure the *Mutsu* will see it on its way."

"Thank you, sir."

That done, Kris found herself with time on her hands.

She was used to having a world to save and only seconds to do it in, but there was no world presently in need or willing to accept her services. It had been nice to have time alone with Jack back at the cottage and the lodge, but those carefree moments were hard to recapture.

They were back in uniform.

And being back in uniform raised the question of how the Navy's fraternizing regulations applied to them as a couple. From one perspective, their situation was better. Jack was no longer under Kris's command. However, there was the requirement to get higher-level approval for them to date. Who was an indicted war criminal's superior? As commander of FastPatRon 127, Kris had pretty much all the delegated authority she needed for everyone under her, as well as herself. After all, she had approved her own leave request, hadn't she?

Could she approve her own dating request?

Kris and Jack were enjoying the privacy of her quarters and the comfort of her couch . . . and Kris was about to write herself a letter and approve it in the same breath . . . when there was a knock at the door.

Kris was up off the couch and plopped down on the farthest easy chair in the blink of an eye . . . carefully rearranging her undress whites, which hadn't quite reached the state of their namesake.

"Yes," she called, feeling several dozen kinds of frustration and trying to get control of her emotions, needs, and attitude. *I will not bite anyone's head off. I will not. I will not.*

Which was easy not to do when her brother, Honovi, ducked his head in the door. "How you doing, Sis?" was an opener that dated back years.

"Keeping on keeping on," was her standard reply, and it fit the present circumstances to a "T."

"Did you send a strange little WBI agent over to my office?"

"If you mean Senior Chief Agent in Charge Foile, I'm guilty as charged," Kris admitted, bouncing out of her chair to give her brother a hug. They'd hugged a lot when they were kids. Not so much lately.

Just now, Kris needed all the hugs she could corral.

She towed Honovi to a chair, deposited him in it, then plopped back in her own, as far from Jack as she could.

Honovi eyed Jack. "Can we talk around him?"

"He knows everything I'm into. He has to to keep me safe," Kris said.

"Yeah, I noticed that he got to stay in that meeting with the Iteeche that Grampa gave me the bum's rush out of."

"That wasn't my call, Brother. Grampa Ray does what he does and doesn't care who gets hurt. Tell me, I know."

"Yeah," Honovi said, and chewed on his lower lip for a second. "Was it as bad out there as the news says it was?"

Kris chose to assume that the vague "out there" was the aliens she'd shot up and who'd shot up her command in return. She sobered. "It was worse, Bro. I always thought you had the hard job, working at Father's elbow, putting up with all you have to. There were hours I would have gladly traded places with you, only I couldn't have wished the mess I was in on anyone. Not even Father's most obnoxious opposition leader."

Honovi almost smiled at Kris's words, but instead he nodded. "I'm sorry. I can't imagine how it was watching ships blow up and wondering if yours would be next. You're right. I used to think you ducked out of the real work. Now, not so much. So where are you going, and why did you send me that WBI agent?"

"I'm headed for a day in court where I hope I'll finally get to tell my story that yes, it's bad out there, and that bad could show up in orbit right over your mama and papa and little kids' heads any second."

"I figured that was why you didn't come in quietly. Do you think your chance to state your case is worth the risk? Musashi has the death penalty."

"A lot of good people died to give me the chance to tell their story, to give the warning they died for." Kris shook her head. "I owe them that."

Honovi nodded. "So, what is this about Grampa Al?"

"Have you talked with him lately?"

"I got the annual Christmas card. It included an invite to come work with him anytime I'm ready to quit the government. Didn't you get one?"

"He's given up on me. Not even a Christmas card last year," Kris admitted. "And when I tried to talk to him last night, he took off in a helicopter and flooded his penthouse apartment with Sarin gas."

"Sarin gas! Where'd he get that stuff?"

"Your guess is as good as mine."

Brother shook his head but went on quickly, "So, Sis, what was it you wanted to talk with him about? That WBI agent hinted that it was something big, but I don't think he much likes our family. He said I should talk to you."

That left Kris trying to bring her brother up to speed quickly. "Have you heard about an effort by Grampa Al to buy the recent election on New Eden?"

"You're kidding. Grampa hates politics."

"Tell me about it, but I've got it from the horse's mouth that he funded a major political wave that narrowly missed getting elected to all the powerful positions on New Eden. Strange behavior, that."

"Very strange."

"Worse, there are rumors and chatter that he doesn't much care for his father's approach to handling the alien problem. I think he wants to send out a trade fleet to open negotiations with the aliens."

Having dropped that hot potato in Honovi's lap, Kris shut up and sat back.

Her brother blinked. Several times. He opened his mouth to speak, then shut it. On the second try he said, "Are you sure?"

"Nope. As I said, it's rumors and chatter from this or that unreliable source. But I know the sources involved in that New

Eden thing. They traced the money for that. This other thing, not so easy to trace. All I wanted to do was talk to Grampa, yet he flew away and fouled his nest. Something strange is going on."

Honovi looked at Kris for a long minute. "Maybe it's time to take the baby around to see him. He hasn't seen her yet. That would give me an excuse to talk to him."

"Could you tell if he was lying?"

Brother winced. "Usually I can spot a lie, but from another Longknife, and an old and experienced one like Grampa Al?" He shrugged. "Maybe. I will give it a try."

"You do that. And work with Agent Foile. He's good. Almost caught me. Grampa Al is bound to have a weak link somewhere. Back Foile to find it, then pass me what he finds. I'll see what I can do to put a stop to it."

"Sis, you're under arrest. If worlds need saving, we'll find someone else."

"That would be terrible," Kris said, trying to grin. "No one deserves the punishment my good deeds keep getting."

"No, Sis, you don't deserve this. Is there anything I can do to help?"

"Could you look into who put the hold on the *Mutsu* getting under way? I doubt if Father did it, but someone is keeping us tied up, and the ship came here to get funeral memorial packets from the crew of the battleships that sailed with me. Clippings of hair or fingernails. It's all their loved ones will get back."

"I'll see what I can do," Brother promised.

"Also, could you unfreeze my bank account? Right now, I'm so broke I'm a kept woman," she said, glancing at Jack.

Honovi didn't find that funny. He eyed Jack. "You still protecting her?"

"With my life," Jack said, all masculine and serious.

"She's my little sister. You remember that."

"Boys, down. I'm a grown girl, and I fight my own battles. Some I even win."

Honovi left. Jack stayed on the couch.

"Honey, I think we need to talk about our situation here," he said.

"What, no candlelight dinner?" Kris said with a sigh.

"I'll talk to the officers' mess president about candles for tonight," Jack said as he got up to pace.

"Kris, I think I've been in love with you from the first time I set eyes on you. But I was a Secret Service agent, and you were my primary. Then I was your subordinate. You were untouchable. Until now."

"And I've loved very much being touchable," Kris said, fearing very much where this was headed.

"Thank you. I have loved touching and being touched by you, Kris. But let's face it. You're about to be tried for your life, and most of it will take place in the court of public opinion. We—no, *you*—can't afford to give away any free points. Some might think it oh so romantic for the princess to take a lover just now, but a whole lot more will look at those who died to get us back here and wonder about you and me carrying on. And wonder if you and I were carrying on back then when you needed to put everything you had into the battle. A battle that left a lot of good people dead."

Kris scowled. "I hate it when you're right."

"But you know I am," Jack said as he got off the couch and walked over to the door. He opened it, then found a binder full of flimsies and used it to hold the door open. He glanced out at the Marines . . . smiled at someone . . . then trotted back to the couch. "If those Marines aren't good chaperones, I don't know who is."

"It's going to be a long trip," Kris muttered.

43

The long trip started the next day. Apparently, Honovi, member of parliament that he was, did manage to shake something loose. Possibly he went straight to Father. Whatever he did, the *Mutsu* suddenly had leave to leave, and did so promptly.

Which left Kris pretty much locked in a room and at risk of going stir-crazy.

As she had done so often, she turned to the Marines. A request to join the ship's company on their daily jog was granted.

With some reservations, that is.

The next day, Kris showed up with Jack and Penny; they were ushered to the back of the formation. However, somewhere as they jogged around ship corridors, up passage ladders, and around more passageways without missing a step, the icy formality began to give way. The Gunny Sergeant made it official at the end of the five-klick run when he gave Kris a bow from the waist and invited them to join the Marines any day.

When they showed up the next morning, Kris and her team were assigned the slot right behind the company skipper and the Gunny.

With Kris running all over the ship, it seemed ridiculous that she didn't share meals in the wardroom. Captain Miyoshi agreed, but with one requirement.

Kris must first meet with all the members of the *Mutsu*'s crew who had lost friends or loved ones on the *Haruna* or *Chikuma*. As Kris was well aware, Navies are close and tight-knit things. The embarrassment of someone's grief being suddenly confronted with Kris had to be avoided.

The captain turned the arrangements over to the ship's senior Buddhist monk. A chief pharmacist mate in sick bay most of the day, the cheery fellow presented himself to Kris in saffron robes that very afternoon and invited her to join him in the *Mutsu*'s chapel. Intended to meet the needs of all faiths, the small compartment tucked away next to the ship's library showed basic Buddhist simplicity.

Mats had been strewn around the floor in an approximate circle. The monk led Kris to a mat farthest from the door, indicated she should sit, then sat himself. Quickly, he assumed a lotus posture and closed his eyes.

Kris did the same, as best she could, even to the extent of closing her own eyes. She'd heard of meditation. She'd even had friends suggest she really needed to try it.

Kris was pretty sure Longknifes did not do meditation.

Still, when in Rome, and all that.

With nothing else to do, she tried to do nothing, for at least a few seconds. She slowed her breathing, she knew at least that much, to match that of the monk beside her. In the silence, she discovered that somewhere there was a small waterfall. She could hear its gentle sounds. There was also a bamboo instrument of some sort. It would fill with water, then drop to make a hollow sound, then repeat.

The monk breathed in time with the hollow bamboo, and Kris slowly fell into the same cycle. Her heartbeat slowed, and Kris entered a state of feeling that she'd never encountered. How long it went on, she had no idea.

"My fellow shipmates," was spoken softly by the monk, but he might as well have shouted it in Kris's ear. Her eyes flew open; she had to blink several times. The room before her was full, and the door stood open, with more people seated in the passageway. How many, Kris could not tell.

"Many of us have felt grief at the recent events. Some very close and personal. Among us today is someone who also has been touched by that grief, and who some might feel is the cause of it. Our captain has asked her to make herself available to you, to answer any questions you may have."

Again, the room fell surprisingly quiet. Kris wondered how it had filled without her hearing so much as a hint of sound. Either there was something to this meditation thing, or these Sailors were more quiet than mice. Maybe both.

"I dream of my brother at night," came in a whisper. "He was on *Chikuma*. I dream he is alive. Could he be?"

Kris formed an answer, but before she opened her mouth, the monk beside her rested a restraining hand on her knee. Kris lapsed back into listening mode.

"My friend was on *Haruna*. Did he die for a good reason?"

Kris had to believe he had. She told herself that every minute of every day. The hand on her knee was more insistent in its restraint. Again, Kris stayed quiet.

"My wife was on *Haruna*," was loud and bitter. "How is it that she is dead and you, her commander, still live?"

The blunt anger in those words caused a murmur. After the room returned to quiet, the monk removed his hand from Kris's knee, and whispered softly, "May wisdom and comfort be in your words."

Kris repeated his words to herself; half prayer, half hope, and began to explain herself to these hurting people. First she told of the ravaged planet that she found. Its people and their world robbed, stripped, destroyed, and murdered.

"I thought I had the report I would carry back to my king. I thought my mission was done and I could go home. I was wrong."

Quickly, Kris filled them in, as first the discovery of an alien base ship was made, then the report of a new planet and its sentient race came in. And the painful realization that the aliens had the innocent planet in their sights.

"You can imagine the argument that generated," Kris said. "Some still wanted to go home. Still others, Admiral Kōta among them, were for doing something about it if we could. That was the most urgent question. Could our small force do anything to help this new race?"

Then Kris introduced them to the neutron torpedoes: the Hellburners. Suddenly, the Fleet of Discovery had teeth big enough to take a bite out of the huge alien base ship. Could we? Should we?

"We decided, the admirals and I, that if we could prevent this crime, we should. Not everyone agreed. One of our ships suffered sabotage. I offered a free ticket back to human space for anyone who did not want to follow us in the attack on the alien base ship. About a hundred people took me up on that. Half of them were Sailors. They were quickly replaced by volunteers from the ships that had to go back. None, I think, were from *Haruna* or *Chikuma*."

Several "*Banzai!*" were whispered softly but proudly.

"We all agreed on our battle plan. You are Sailors and Marines. You know every battle has its plan, but no battle goes according to plan. Our plan survived long enough for us to gut the alien base ship. The Hellburners ripped apart the aft half of that ship, roughly the size of a large moon. What we hadn't planned on was the number of ships the base ship carried. They were huge, and there were hundreds of them.

"They did not so much shoot at us as use their thousands of lasers to sweep the space ahead of them. Even a battleship's armor can't handle being hit by a hundred lasers at once. Our ships blew up. Few survival pods made it away, and those that did were wiped out by the lasers still sweeping where our battle line had been.

"In the end, all any of us could do was run. Two of my ships died fighting to buy time for the *Wasp* and the *Hornet* to get away. In the end, the *Hornet* went one way, and the *Wasp* went the other, hoping that at least one of us would make it back."

Kris paused to take a deep breath. "Not a morning passes that I don't wake up hoping to hear that *Hornet* has somehow returned, or that one of the battleships has straggled in. But neither of the two battleships that I last saw running were from Musashi."

There, Kris had said what she had to say. All she could say. She sat on the mat, exhausted, waiting for the reaction.

The monk rose gracefully from his mat and offered Kris a hand. As it turned out, her left leg had gone to sleep, and the monk had to half haul her up. He did not seem surprised. and there was no judgment in his eyes. Only a twinkle.

With them both standing, the monk turned to his congregation, or whatever Buddhists called a pack of themselves. "Those of you who wish may now say a few words personally with this afternoon's speaker."

Kris liked the way he deftly avoided any reference to rank or status. This afternoon, Kris was just a pilgrim with a story to tell. She liked it for a change.

One by one, men or women came forward. Many of them had a picture of the one they had lost. Some expressed pride now in what their lost one had done. Others merely expressed their loss.

Last in line was a young man. He clutched a wedding picture of himself and a lovely young woman. "I begged her to request a transfer off *Haruna* when the word came that they would be going along with you. I told her no good would come of following a Longknife. She laughed the way she did and asked me if I would transfer off *Mutsu* just before it sailed on such a mission?"

He paused, gazing longingly at the picture. "She knew I would never have abandoned my shipmates. Why did her *Haruna* get the orders and my *Mutsu* not?"

"I have no answer," Kris said, and was rewarded by a gentle nod from the monk. "Neither do I know why the *Wasp* made it back and none of the others did. What I do know was that one ship had to return. Those who died deserve to have the story told of their gallantry, and courage, and commitment."

The young man bowed, hiding the tears in his eyes, and quickly walked away.

Kris looked around at the empty room, her Gethsemane over.

Beside her, the monk bowed. "You did well, Your Highness."

Kris bowed back. "It was you who arranged this, Venerable Sir." Nelly got Kris the proper address for a Buddhist monk just a second before she needed it. "You did very well yourself."

"One does what the universe allows. I knew from Captain

Miyoshi's request of me that he wanted this done before you dined in the wardroom. Several here were officers, including the young ensign you last talked to. However, I would like to take this opportunity to invite you to be the guest of the chief's mess this evening. You will find our fare simpler, but we have better cooks," he added, his eyes sparkling.

Kris thanked him but found that she was not ready to leave. She settled back onto the floor, her legs out in front of her so they would not go to sleep again, and began her own meditation. She'd spent enough time gnawing on the battle. She didn't need to resurrect those ghosts again. No. What bothered her was the lack of knowledge that the crew and its captain had about their fellow battleship Sailors.

"Nelly, didn't we send reports back to human space?"

"Yes, Kris. Several times."

"And didn't Amanda Cutter take the last ship back? Wasn't she on a lot of talk shows, talking about what we intended to do?"

"Yes, Kris. I have the recordings."

"So how come these people know so little about what happened?"

"Kris, I've done a search on all media reports in the *Mutsu*'s database. There's a lot about the voyage of discovery leaving, but not a lot about it after it left."

"How could that be, Nelly?"

"Apparently your report to Santa Maria after the first attack didn't make it into the media at all. And while Amanda did appear on talk shows, they were usually syndicated and only had small audiences. She was on shows on Wardhaven, Santa Maria, and her own Lorna Do. But that left a lot of worlds not covered."

Kris grimaced. "And those appearances weren't distributed widely?"

"Apparently not, Kris. Musashi media didn't give the fleet a lot of news coverage. Most of what these people learned about the battle they got from the Navy grapevine."

"That's disgusting," Kris said.

"It gets worse."

Kris sighed. "Tell me, Nelly."

"Vicky Peterwald gave an interview that got very wide

coverage just before the media got distracted and went off to other things. I think there was a spectacular sex affair involving four vid stars."

Kris closed her eyes. "Nelly, what did Vicky do?"

"I will show you, Kris, but you won't like it."

On the mat before her, Vicky's image appeared. "Where'd she get that dress?" Kris asked, not that it would have taken much space to pack it.

"I don't know, Kris, but I suspect it encouraged the distribution of the interview."

Vicky was talking. "It was horrible. The alien ships were huge and they were all over the place and we never had a chance."

"Why did you attack them?" the newsie asked.

"I don't know. Kris Longknife insisted we just *had* to attack. For some reason, she got the other admirals to go along with her. I think she had them twisted around her little finger. All but Admiral Krätz, he opposed her. He said we should come back and report what we had found."

"Then why did he go along with the attack?"

"I think it was a matter of honor with him. The others were going to fight. How could he run away, but then, once the huge superiority of the aliens became clear, running away was all our ships could do. Kris Longknife was, of course, the first to duck out of the fight."

"How did it happen that you survived? That you were on the U.S.S. *Wasp* rather than the Imperial Battleship *Fury*?"

"Princess Kris invited me as Grand Duchess to come over for dinner. I could hardly refuse. After that, there never seemed to be a time when she could arrange for my return. I kind of think she was holding me hostage, to keep Admiral Krätz in line. I don't know. Maybe. Oh, I just don't know. It was all so horrible."

"Cut it off, Nelly."

The computer did.

"Is there anything new in the rest of it that I should know?" Kris growled.

"No, Kris. She just goes on repeating herself. Many media outlets carried only what you just saw. Others carried more.

During the rest of the interview, one breast falls out of her dress, twice."

"That wouldn't be hard, she wasn't all that much in it." Kris realized she was being catty. Her problem wasn't that the girl she thought might become a good friend had dissed her in public.

The problem was that Kris had been walking around for several months with a knife in her back she didn't even know was there.

"I'm sorry I didn't do this news search earlier, Kris. There was nothing about any of this on Madigan's Rainbow. On Eden, I did my best to tread lightly, and you know how blocked I was on Wardhaven."

"It's okay, Nelly," Kris said through a deep sigh. "It wouldn't have made any difference anyway. Now, at least, I know what I'm up against."

Kris sat there for a long while, letting it all sink in.

"Nelly, the president of New Eden complained about King Ray's wanting a big Navy. How much did the New Eden media cover us?"

"Not a lot, Kris. A few sources did it well. A lot didn't. Only one carried Vicky's presser, the short version. It wasn't shown on many markets in the U.S."

Which media they watched might explain why Inspector Johnson had such a different attitude from Senior Chief Inspector Martinez.

"Kris?" Nelly asked in a little girl voice she used less and less these days.

"Yes."

"Why did Vicky do that? I thought she was your friend."

Kris shook her head, sadly. "We humans have a long history of betrayal," she said. Then she frowned. "How many times have I said, 'It seemed like a good idea when I did it'?"

"Lots," Nelly said.

"I suspect, to Vicky, it looked like a good idea while she was doing it."

"But why, Kris?"

"She talked her dad into lending her four battleships. She made it sound easy, but that might have been for my consumption. God knows I felt miserable reporting back to my king that I'd lost a squadron of corvettes. Imagine what she's going to face having lost a squadron of battleships and all those Sailors." Kris paused.

"I might not have cared much for my welcome, but she has to go back to that den of vipers Greenfeld calls the Imperial court. And then she has her new stepmom carrying a male heir to the throne. No, Nelly, my shoes have been no fun to walk in, but I'd much rather walk in them than Vicky's stilettos heels."

Kris might have stayed in that quiet corner of the great battleship longer, meditating on the human condition and all the problems it caused her, but her stomach grumbled. That was a problem she could do something about. And Kris made one of the best calls of her entire life. She headed for the chief's mess.

She'd certainly had fancier food than she had that evening, but she'd never had it better cooked or in better company. Now that the word was out that their shipmates on the other battleships had died an honorable death, Kris was welcome company. And there wasn't so much as a blink when Kris passed up the offered sake after one small cup.

She'd been down that rabbit hole once more. She would not go there again.

As Kris returned to her quarters, she allowed herself a smile; there were no Marine guards at her door. Then Nelly said, "There's a message for you."

"Who from?"

"Honovi. It's personal, not official traffic, but he coded it."

"Can you read it?"

"His computer and I exchanged codes many years ago. We haven't used them in a long time. Basically, he says he took Brenda over for Grampa Al to dangle on his knee. She was smart enough not to spit up on the old boy."

"She must save all her spit-ups for me," Kris muttered.

"Honovi asked Al about your effort to see him. He said he didn't want to talk about it and made sure of it by walking away. The next time Honovi managed to get a word in, he made it about the aliens you found. This time Al didn't say a word but told them the visit was over. How very rude of your grandfather," Nelly added.

"He's a Longknife."

"I'm beginning to think you use that excuse for anything you want to do that a normal person would never get away with."

Kris thought for hardly a second. "You know, Nelly, you might be right."

"Anyway, Honovi says he's inclined to agree with you now. He's met again with that certain agent and will get back to you when he can."

"Did he say anything about my bank account?" Kris asked, thinking ahead to when she could no longer hit the *Mutsu* up for free room and board.

"Sorry, he says. He wasn't able to bring it up with Al, and all his contacts at the family corporation say they must check with their supervisor."

"And I thought government was the only place where you got the bureaucratic runaround," Kris said with a sigh.

Jack was waiting in her quarters. She propped the door open and settled into a chair a comfortable distance from his place on the couch.

"So, honey, how'd your day go?" Jack asked.

Kris had discovered there was a lot of pleasure in having someone listen to her talk about her day. Almost as much fun as really listening to how Jack felt about his.

Admittedly, there were other things that would be even more pleasant to do, what with Jack and her no longer sharing a chain of command. But the door was open, and a trial was barreling down on them.

Shared feelings would have to do for now.

44

The *Mutsu* had barely tied up to the pier at the High Kyoto station before Kris was receiving a long line of visitors in suits. She'd expected a quick visit from the police, but the suits first in line were much too expensive to belong to civil servants.

First was a reporter. Kris asked Captain Miyoshi if it was possible to skip him. The Marines at the gangplank sent him on his way.

The next could not be avoided. A lieutenant ushered Mr. Nigel Pennypecker, the senior representative of Nuu Enterprises into Kris's quarters. The door was open as had become the custom; six Marines now stood guard under the watchful eye of Gunny himself. Kris appreciated the honor.

The small man neither bowed nor offered his hand but launched immediately into why he was there. "I am instructed to tell you that you may make no demands or requests on Nuu Enterprise assets, nor will you receive any assistance from the same."

"Thank you," Kris said through the wide smile that she reserved for people she'd rather shoot but couldn't. "I wasn't planning on making any such requests."

"Oh," the little man said, deflating in the face of acceptance when he clearly was prepared to weather a hurricane-size blow.

"What did you do to Alexander Longknife?" he asked. "I've never received instructions like these for the visit of a major stockholder, or even a minor one."

Kris allowed herself a shrug. "Apparently, I'm not on Grampa's nice list."

"I should say so," the man said, and settled, uninvited into the closest chair.

Kris took the one across from him.

"I did try to arrange a line of credit for you at All Nippon Bank. I'm afraid to report that I failed. It seems that you cannot access any of the accounts that have your name on them."

"Yes, I know. I think Grampa Al has made a special naughty list just for me."

The little man actually seemed concerned. "I am sorry to hear that. I understand that you are in quite a bit of trouble. If I can advance you some funds personally . . ."

Kris shook her head. "No. I don't want anyone to end up on Grampa's naughty list on my behalf. I'm a Longknife. I will figure out a way to survive."

"Even broke?"

Kris thought about that for a moment, then laughed. "I'm sure that Great-grampa Ray must have had some tight months on his army pay before Rita Nuu fell head over heels in love with him."

The man seemed to doubt that, but having nothing more to say, he stood to go. Then he paused.

"There is another man on the pier waiting to see you. A Mr. Kawaguchi. He's one of the best men of the law on the planet. I would strongly suggest that you listen to anything he has to say to you."

"I imagine if he's the best, he must also be the most expensive," Kris said.

"He is most definitely that," the Nuu manager said as he dismissed himself.

The quarterdeck called about Kris's next guest. A lawyer who identified himself as Kawaguchi Tsusumu. Kris allowed that he be brought aboard.

A few minutes later, the young lieutenant was back with a

tall man in a blue three-piece suit. Bald, with a small gray
mustache, it was his smile that drew Kris's eye. It took up his
entire face and gave her the feeling that he found the world a
place of endless jest. He bowed from the waist as he entered
the room. "Your Royal Highness, I have the honor to be Mr.
Kawaguchi, a man of the law, and I wish to place myself at
your service."

Kris stood to meet him. She returned his formal bow, but
then said, "Why don't you call me Kris? I'm not sure the princess thing applies at the moment. I'm not even sure about the
Lieutenant Commander anymore."

"Ah," the lawyer said. "May I suggest to you that your case
will be more likely to succeed if you hold on to all of yourself
with both hands. If you begin allowing others to take your
honors, they may soon take your life."

Kris nodded. "I see. I thank you for the good advice. I only
regret that I am not in a position to pay you for it."

"Yes. I understand that you are in unusual straits for a
Longknife. I placed the issue before my partners, and we
decided to take your case pro bono."

Kris had not been prepared for such an offer of charity. She
found her knees going weak and offered Mr. Kawaguchi a seat
before quickly folding herself into one.

"I am not used to taking charity," Kris said.

"Yes, I know. You are much more likely to be giving it than
taking it. My partners are not unaware of your past gifts to
those in need."

Kris leaned back in her chair and glanced at Jack and
Penny. They shared one of the couches and had sat quietly
during the last visitor. Now they both looked like they were
doing their best to decode this man and his offer.

"You will excuse me, sir, but I know that my defense will
be long and time-consuming. Therefore, it will not be cheap.
You offer to undertake it at no charge. Therefore, I must
assume that you expect to profit from it in some other manner.
I have been played as a pawn before in other people's games.
I find I make a better pawn when I know what game is afoot."

The man laughed. It was something that started in his belly
and rose happily to his face, bringing red to his cheeks. "They
warned that you were not only brave but wise as well. Very

good, I like the way you play your cards faceup on the table. It is a poor hand, but not one you shrink from."

He leaned back in his chair, crossed his legs, and gave the appearance of becoming comfortable for a long stay. "My partners and I are not of the party in power. We believe they made a major blunder bringing charges against you, and we will enjoy helping them reap the full error of their ways. I am confident we can get you acquitted of all charges. Though, I must say, after meeting you, I am conflicted. A woman of your stature and beauty, going bravely to the headsman would be a picture to guarantee their party minority status for twenty years."

Kris swallowed hard. "You will excuse my reluctance to provide you with a photo op of such long-lasting power."

He laughed again. "Ah. And a sense of humor. Even more I look forward to working with you. Do we have a deal?"

He rose, and Kris met him halfway. His handshake was firm but not demanding or combative.

"Will we be meeting after this in jail?" Kris asked.

"As we speak, one of my partners is arranging for your release under your own recognizance. I very much doubt you will ever see the inside of a Musashi jail."

"So, I need to find a place to live," Kris said, grateful to have the problem but not at all sure how to handle the honor.

"If you do not object, I have made arrangements. Mrs. Fujioka is a strong supporter of our party. She has several homes, one of them in New Kyoto, and would be only too happy for you to use her town house."

So, Kris would not be homeless. She knew not to look a gift house in the mouth, but she also knew that few people of wealth splurged on gifts. "And she's willing to open her home to an indicted war criminal because . . . ?" Kris said.

Mr. Kawaguchi nodded at the question. "Many of the old families of Musashi have a tradition. Their young men, even some of their young women, spend four years in the Emperor's service. Her youngest son, Tomio, was almost through with his four years. Already, he was a lieutenant in our Navy."

Shivers went down Kris's spine. *Not another death on my soul,* she prayed.

"He could have asked to be transferred off *Haruna.*

Everyone agreed his four years would be up well before they returned," Mr. Kawaguchi said. "He told his mother he wanted to go. He wanted to see sights never seen before. He didn't doubt that following a Longknife he would get his heart's desire."

"I allowed anyone who wanted to return before we left for the battle," Kris said.

"Yes. He told his mother that in his last letter home to her. But he would not desert his battle station even though his four years were up by then. He also told his mother that he could not return knowing he'd left an entire people to be murdered. He begged his mother's forgiveness, but he could not come back."

Kris nodded slowly. "Many followed because they could not desert their comrades. I had hoped things would go better than they did. But tell me, what does this mother want from me?"

"Musashi lost two ships and over three thousand men and women," the lawyer said, leaning forward. "This government seems to think we need a scapegoat for some sort of failure. Mrs. Fujioka and I think the fight of *Haruna* and *Chikuma* is something to be proud of. That our people died in a worthy cause. There is no shame in dying for a just cause, and, what do you Christians say? Laying down your life for another, even if they have beaks rather than noses, is a holy endeavor."

Surprisingly, Kris found herself tearing up. "I am glad to make your acquaintance, Mr. Kawaguchi, and I look forward to meeting my patron, Mrs. Fujioka. You wish to stand by me for the fight that I owe those who died following me. I welcome you at my side. Win or lose, those who oppose us will know they've been in a fight when we are done."

"Rest assured, young woman, this is a fight we can win. Yes, we can win this one."

45

A few minutes later, Captain Miyoshi personally ushered in several police officers of the Kyoto Prefect. Their leader did not look at all happy to see Mr. Kawaguchi sitting beside Kris.

"Chasing ambulances again, Tsusumu-san?"

"Ah, Orochi, you are too late for this one. I got her before you."

The police officer gave Kris a hint of a bow. "I am Inspector Dogen Osamu and you must come with me."

At that moment, paper began to issue forth from the admiral's desk. Mr. Kawaguchi fairly skipped over to pull them from the printer. "I regret to disappoint you, Osamu-san, but Miss Tanaka of my office has already presented our motion before a magistrate. I know this will break your heart, but Her Royal Highness will not be spending the night in your jail."

"And where will she be staying, in your basement?"

"Hardly, my good man of the law. Mrs. Fujioka has offered her the use of her town house. We will be going there as soon as we are done here."

"Then you won't mind if I accompany you," the officer said.

"And I will be accompanying the both of you," Captain Miyoshi said.

"You will?" came from both representatives of the law.

"I am instructed to post a Marine guard detachment at the Fujioka residence. Commander Longknife is charged with causing the loss of two ships of the Imperial Musashi Navy. That gives us an interest in this case. The Navy will assure that the commander stands trial for the crimes she is charged with."

Kris might have been disturbed by this latest development, but Gunny had edged into the room and gave Kris a cheerful wink. Something was going on here she didn't understand, but if Gunny was good with it, it was good enough for Kris.

With that, they prepared to depart the *Mutsu.* Jack ducked into Kris's bedroom, a sight he hadn't seen before, and returned with Kris's two self-propelled steamer trunks. His and Penny's gear had easily been merged into them. With the captain leading the way, a small procession followed. Kris and her lawyer, Penny and Jack, the trunks, the police, and six Marines marching solidly up the rear.

On the pier, several station carts were waiting for them, and they quickly blended into traffic. Their route to the space elevator took them past the Mitsubishi Heavy Space Industry yard just as a shift was letting out. Traffic got much heavier. Still, they made it to the elevator a good five minutes before it departed.

On the ferry, the police officers took over leading the party until Kris's lawyer objected. "Orochi, you are not trying to take my princess to your holding cells, are you."

"And if I am?"

"Why don't we try the VIP lounge instead?"

"Do you have an access card?" the officer asked.

"No, but no doubt Princess Longknife does."

The cop's "If it still works" look clearly held confidence that it would not.

To Kris and the police inspector's great surprise, Kris's Identacard opened the door to the VIP lounge. Apparently, Grampa Al's vendetta against Kris had yet to reach its full extent.

Mr. Kawaguchi did a poor job of suppressing a grin as he ushered the police and the Marines into the plush surroundings, thus taking the lounge from nearly empty to overflowing in one quick move.

Several businessmen already enjoying a drink took one look at the new arrivals and took their drinks elsewhere. Kris was left to wonder if it was her, the cops, or the Marines that drew that response.

Likely it was all three.

At the downside station, a limo waited for Kris, as well as several police cars, and a bus of Marines with room for six more.

Kris offered Captain Morishita a seat in the limo, and Mr. Kawaguchi made sure that Inspector Dogen did not get in.

As they pulled away from the curb, Kris asked, "What is going on here? I'm grateful for the Marines. I always feel more comfortable with them around, but a busload of them?"

"And there is a company already deployed at the Fujioka residence," Captain Morishita added.

"What do all of you know that we don't?" Jack asked, his security-chief hat now solidly in place.

"We have problems with street ruffians," the captain said. "Some of them almost seem to work hand in hand with the party in power."

Kris raised a questioning eyebrow.

"Please understand," her lawyer immediately said, "I golf with the Prime Minister almost weekly. He is a fine gentleman. It is true that we may shout some things that are less than refined when our young men play his party's young men at their monthly baseball game. Still, we are all gentlemen."

The captain of the *Mutsu* raised both eyebrows.

"Yes, yes, there is a faction among his supporters that no one would accuse of being gentlemen. They are rowdy troublemakers. Still, Torinaga Aki would never give a moment's thought to anything so uncultured."

"My Marines will assure that no one else does, either," the captain said.

The arrival at Fujioka House showed the captain to be correct. There was a small mob waiting on the street outside. Before the Marine guards could open the iron gate, the mob swarmed around Kris's limo, striking it and rocking it. Several eggs blotted the windows.

The police in the trailing car got out but were quickly lost in the scuffle.

The Marines in the bus dismounted, formed ranks with riot shields, and moved forward with solid intent. The mob backed off; those reluctant to do so were shoved along with the Marines' shields. Only when the Marines had control of the gate did it open and admit the cars.

Under Gunny's orders, the Marines folded themselves back through the gate as it closed. Still, the mob swept in, clambering up the iron gate. A few last eggs arched out to yellow the Marine bus.

"What was that all about?" Kris asked no one in particular.

"Did you notice that the mob was just large enough to fill a tight camera shot?" Mr. Kawaguchi said. "Those who watch it on the ten o'clock news tonight won't know that all that noise was made by less than a hundred thugs. Your Highness, the fight for your life has begun."

"If we are to join those who have fought for my life," Kris said, glancing at Jack and Penny, "you must call me Kris."

"And you must call me Tsusumu."

The driveway opened into a circle before a huge stone mansion. The entrance to the circle was under a large stone torii.

Milling around the front door was another mob, only slightly less violent-looking. The presence of cameras proclaimed them to be representatives of the media.

"Oh no," Kris muttered under her breath.

"Your Marines let them in," Tsusumu said to the *Mutsu*'s skipper.

"Would you have rather had them in the mob outside?"

The lawyer accepted the lesser of two evils with a resigned sigh. "Try to say nothing," he said.

"Would it be easier if I agreed to a news conference tomorrow?"

"It will be easier for the moment, but it will still be dangerous to your future."

"My future is always dangerous," Kris growled.

At her elbow, Jack sighed.

"Very good, then. We will promise to feed you to the lions tomorrow," Tsusumu said, and opened the door.

Kris was immediately swept by a tidal wave of questions

mishmashed into such a noise that she could understand none of it.

The lawyer went first, followed by Jack. They blocked the door well enough to let Kris and Penny get to their feet.

Tsusumu raised his hands for quiet and got none. He shouted, "The Princess will have a press conference tomorrow at noon," but Kris doubted that anyone heard him. If they did, they only shouted their questions louder.

Kris was saved by the arrival of a dozen Marines, who formed a phalanx around her and led her into the house.

Once the door was closed, the silence was deafening.

"Is that what I have to expect everywhere I go?" Kris asked.

"I'm afraid so," Tsusumu answered. "Captain, how long before your Marines are recalled?"

Captain Miyoshi had stayed in the limo until the Marines arrived and had come quietly up the rear of their movement. Now he shrugged. "The Navy Ministry has acquiesced to my request to guard Fujioka House. No doubt pressure will be brought to bear on them." The captain turned to the lawyer. "Is there any chance that you might use your good offices with the Prime Minister to reduce those pressures? Is any interest of his party served by your princess's being torn limb from limb?"

Tsusumu did not answer nearly as quickly as Kris would wish. Unbidden, the image of her going as an innocent victim to the headsman came to mind. What kind of game was she being played in? All she wanted to do was get out the word about the fight her people had died in and the fight that might be headed for them all.

Finally, the lawyer spoke. "I do not see any upside to this for Aki-san and his party. I will do what I can to help you keep the Marines here. Clearly, they are needed."

That settled, Kris took her first look at her new quarters. Though the outside was weathered stone, the inside was simplicity itself. The walls of the entrance were white with parchment hangings, the floors parquet.

The stairs . . .

On the stairs stood a certain woman and her niece.

"Your hair is in desperate need of a good washing," Abby said, dryly.

"Abby!" Kris shouted.

"Auntie Kris! Auntie Kris! Auntie Kris!" Cara shouted, jumping up and down with the unsuppressible enthusiasm of youth.

Kris flew across the floor and wrapped them in a huge hug. "You made it," she said, over and over again. "They didn't get you."

"We had our story," Abby drawled, "and we stuck to it. Cara, here, has the makings of a fine liar if I do say so myself."

"You said if I didn't keep saying what you told me to say, we'd never see Auntie Kris again. That made it easy to fib."

"Good to see you again," Jack said, coming up beside Kris.

"What, man? You didn't have the good sense to take this great chance to never see this dame again?"

"Blew it," Jack said, not sounding at all sad.

"He and Kris have been making up for lost time," Penny said, joining the hug.

"Well, the two of them are finally showing some good sense," Abby said, and broke from the hug. "I'm running your bath, Your Troublesomeness. It looks like you're in desperate need of a manicure, too."

"Are we done here?" Kris asked her lawyer.

His perpetual smile was no longer on his face. That didn't look good.

"My partner just called me. The prosecutor has set the date for your trial. It starts in seven days."

"Isn't that a bit quick?" Kris and Jack both asked. Penny's mouth was open, but they'd beat her to the question.

"It is. It is most unusual, but not unheard of. We do not go in for long, drawn-out court theater here on Musashi. A subject deserves a prompt hearing, and justice is best served without delay. I had wished for more time, but I have to admit that finding witnesses and evidence is rather out of the question."

Kris couldn't argue that point.

"Come, baby ducks, you look like you could use a relaxing bath."

With that, Abby drew Kris up the stairs and did what she could to make the world and its machinations go away.

46

Kris's night was peaceful. Twice, unusual sounds woke her, but a glance out her window showed Marines pacing off their rounds.

Breakfast was a surprise. The kitchen staff presented Kris's team with a standard fare of bacon, scrambled eggs, and hash browns for Jack and Cara. There was also oatmeal and muffins for Kris and Penny to chose from. Abby eyed the entire collection and followed Jack to the hot breakfast.

The chief cook smiled happily as her handiwork disappeared. Her smile widened as Mr. Kawaguchi appeared. "Have you eaten?" she demanded.

"Would I eat anywhere else if I might enjoy a sweet omelet from your kitchen?"

The cook disappeared back into her precinct with his order.

"You eat here often?" Kris asked.

"As often as I can. Fujioka-san is a good friend," the lawyer said, settling down at the table. "We've had to change the venue for your press conference twice."

"Bomb threats?" Jack asked.

"No!" the lawyer seemed surprised at the question. "Requests from more reporters to attend. We have over two hundred calls, and more are coming in."

"Where are we going?" Kris asked.

"We will use the auditorium at Kyoto University. It seats three thousand."

"You expect to fill it?" Penny asked.

"Ah, yes," Tsusumu said. "The university has announced that students may attend on their lunch hour. It will be interesting to see how many come."

"Wear your spider silks," Jack said. "It looks like you're going to play duck in a shooting gallery again."

Kris just shrugged. Abby had already helped her into her under-all body armor. It was nice having Abby around again. Abby and a full dozen steamer trunks.

"Any suggestion on what I wear?" Kris asked her lawyer. "Civilian simple elegance or uniform?"

"You are being tried for what you did as a Navy officer. If it is allowed, please wear your uniform whenever you can. That white outfit you wore yesterday looked simple but powerful."

"Undress whites it will be," Kris said.

"Pardon me, ma'am," a Marine announced at the door to the kitchen. "There is a man to see you. He says he goes way back with you."

Kris glanced up. Standing behind the Imperial Marine corporal was Royal USMC Gunnery Sergeant Brown, formally of the good ship *Wasp* and a longtime survivor for someone who'd gotten too damn close to a Longknife.

He stood there beaming like he had good sense, his pearly white teeth gleaming against his black skin.

"Good to see you, Commander," he said.

"Always good to see you, Gunny. Pull up a chair. You hungry?"

"Don't mind if I do," he said, but he took the time to lug in two large foot lockers and park them by the door before he headed for the table.

"What you got there?" Jack asked.

"Sir, a batch of Chief Beni's gear somehow ended up in my safekeeping, God rest his soul, Skipper. I had some leave coming, and I figured it wasn't doing anyone any good in the back of my closet, so I headed here to turn it over to the commander."

"Something tells me we can use it," Penny said. "But without the chief, who will make sense of it?"

"I noticed some fine-looking Marines on my way in here," Gunny said, grinning as a plate of ham, eggs, and grits was put before him.

"Back in the day, ma'am," Gunny said around a full fork, "I was a demolition expert. Then the fine lady of my life suggested I leave that kind of fun and games to younger folk with no kids to come home to, and I got respectable. As respectable as one of us enlisted swine can get, anyway. I spent enough time at the chief's elbow, squiring you around. I could be wrong, but I fiddled with that stuff on the way out, and I think I can be downright helpful. At least until I get the local Marines fully up to speed."

"That sounds like a plan," Jack said.

"At this press conference," Tsusumu said, pushing himself away from the table and eyeing Kris's associates. He must have decided they were trustworthy, because he went on. "There is something I would like you to emphasize at every opportunity."

"You have my undivided attention," Kris said, patting her mouth with a napkin and taking a last sip of tea.

"You are a lieutenant commander, correct? Of the Royal U.S. Navy?"

"Yes, on both accounts."

"Rear Admiral Kōta outranked you and is of the Musashi Navy. As I understand it, you two do not share a chain of command."

"As was very strongly and insistently pointed out to me by Vice Admiral Krätz."

"Ah, so my theory of the case is familiar to you." And he began to explain to Kris just exactly how he intended for her to avoid the Imperial headsman.

Kris was still mulling his thoughts when they began to assemble for the trip to the university. Kris and Penny were in undress whites. Jack had chosen khaki and greens. Gunny Brown was in full-dress red and blues, with Chief Beni's magic black box almost disappearing in his large hands, now clad in white gloves.

Her Imperial Marine escort turned out in their own dress

uniform, red from top to bottom except for a white garrison hat, and belt and blue piping down the pants. They might look like toy soldiers, but their guns sparkled at the ready.

Captain Miyoshi followed the honor guard in dress blues.

"Thank you for coming, sir," Kris said. "I wasn't expecting to see you again."

"The honor of *Mutsu* must be upheld. I was advised to stand by in case any questions arose concerning the Navy's actions."

"I will gladly defer to you, sir," Kris said. Her lawyer, at her elbow, seemed less than happy to have a Navy spokesman present.

Kris hoped she would never witness a fight between her two new friends.

Two open military gun trucks, full of Marines and without the guns in evidence, led off. Kris's borrowed limo followed them, and two more trucks fell in behind her. They did not head for the gate; a crowd was already in evidence there. Instead, they made a turn around the house and ducked out the back gate, where not so much as a photographer was in evidence.

"Score one for our side," Captain Miyoshi said through a tight smile.

Kris considered, but then decided not to ask him the secret of his success. She was glad not to show up for her presser with egg on her car. Someone had returned it to pristine blackness, and Kris would have hated to add another wash job to the growing tab she could not pay.

Might never be able to pay if Grampa Al didn't relent.

A block from Fujioka House, they picked up a police escort: two cars and four motorcycle cops. They led them by back roads to the university and came to a stop in the back of a large white stone building. Inspector Dogen opened the door for Kris.

"Safe and sound," he said, as if it was an accomplishment. "I got a report from New Eden. It seems you do not always arrive at your destinations without incident."

"But I'm still here," Kris pointed out.

"Despite it all," Jack grumbled.

Around Kris, Imperial Marines formed up and began to

march purposefully toward the back of the theater. Gunny Brown followed them.

Right up to the time he shouted, "Halt your movement."

"Teiryuu," split the air, and the Imperial Marines came to a smart halt.

"What is the matter?" came immediately from their own Gunny.

"There's a bomb inside that doorway," Gunny Brown snapped.

The Imperial Gunny rattled off a couple of names, and a man and a woman detached themselves from the formation, produced sensors from casings on their belts, and followed cautiously as Gunny Brown led them toward the doorway.

Another shouted order, and a third Marine double-timed it for one of the gun trucks and returned with a box. In the trucks, one of the drivers began to put on padding. Clearly, the troopers might be in fancy dress, but they were well trained.

"You might want to get back in the car," Jack said.

Kris frowned. Hiding was not her first choice, second or last choice, either.

Captain Miyoshi shouted something to the Imperial Gunny, and more Marines broke ranks to bring their guns up and began searching the surrounding roofs through powerful sights.

"Please get back in the car," *Mutsu*'s skipper ordered. "I did not bring you this far to have your brains splattered over my dress blues."

Kris got back in the car.

"How did you do that?" Penny said. "Jack's been trying to get her to take cover for the last four or five years. She never jumped like that."

"I have daughters," the captain muttered.

Kris compromised. She kept her head well inside the backseat, but she rested her legs on the ground outside. The captain gave her a look that would have melted lead, but she didn't so much as blink.

"We have disarmed the bomb. It was set for a remote detonation."

Sirens announced the arrival of the Kyoto bomb squad. They took over the removal of the device. They did it quickly, leaving Kris a full three minutes to make her way up onto the stage from which she was to talk.

She took one look at the twenty rows of reporters in front of her and flinched. "How are we going to do this?" she asked Tsusumu.

"We held a lottery. Only the twenty seated in the center-front row can ask you a question. They may ask one question and a follow-up. Anyone else will be out of order and an embarrassment to their agency."

The lawyer seemed to think that would settle the matter. Maybe here on Musashi it would. Kris strode to the podium as the auditorium slowly began to quiet. It was filled to capacity; some students stood in the back, munching food. Kris remembered such lunches from her college days.

She never expected to be the one onstage.

The Marines had formed a thin red line below the stage. Behind her, her own crew, along with her lawyer and Captain Miyoshi, took their places in chairs.

Kris took a sip from a handy glass of water, smiled, and asked, "Who has the first question?"

A young man jumped to his feet. "How do you feel after causing the death of so many men and women?"

Kris remembered her father's advice. Always pause a moment to let people think you are thinking about the question. Never pause too long, or they'll think you're thinking too much about your answer.

"I sincerely regret their sacrifice. Not a day comes that I don't wish some more survivors of the battle will straggle in. That I don't wish there had been more of us when the time came to turn and flee."

"Follow-on question," the man said, still standing. "Then you regret that you ordered the attack that caused so many to die?"

"No," Kris said, without a moment's pause.

"How could you not?" the man snapped.

"You've had your two questions," Kris said. The man scowled and sat down.

Next up was a young woman. She looked at her notebook, then frowned as she closed it. "I am sorry to press the previous matter, but how can you say you regret all the deaths but do not regret the battle?"

"Please excuse me, but that was not the question he asked," Kris said slowly. "I believe in my heart that all of us, those who lived and those who died, would still attack the hostile alien base ship." *Not mother ship. Base ship for these civilians, Tsusumu had insisted.* "The crime it was about to commit was horrible beyond words, and we were all committed to stopping it."

"What crime?" the woman asked, interrupting Kris's answer.

So, these folks were operating with just as little knowledge as the poor shipmates on Mutsu, Kris thought.

"Didn't Admiral Kōta's report make it back here? Haven't you read it?"

"What report?" came from the woman, and a murmur from the entire hall.

That was just the opening Kris wanted.

"Nelly, would you please distribute my report to King Raymond concerning the murdered planet?"

"Yes, Kris," Nelly replied, and handhelds came out around the theater and lit up as screens captured Nelly's transmission.

The hall had been quiet before. Now it took on the silence of a tomb.

"In rapid succession, we made the discovery of this raped planet, a huge alien base ship, and a second planet, one teeming with life and a civilization little different from our Earth's four or five hundred years ago. The alien base ship was headed for that planet with murderous intent. We decided to do something about it."

The woman started to open her mouth, but she paused, looked embarrassed, and glanced at the seated man next to her. As he stood up, she sat down.

"You say 'we decided.' Don't you mean *you* decided?" the next reporter said.

Ah, just the question my lawyer wanted. Kris suppressed a smile.

"No. I am a Royal U.S. Navy officer. You will notice there

are two and a half stripes on my shoulder boards," Kris said, pointing at them. "I'm a lieutenant commander. Captain Miyoshi behind me"—here Kris glanced over her shoulder; her grinning lawyer, clearly enjoying how things were going, was seated next to a stolid-faced captain—"has four stripes on his uniform. He very much outranks me. Rear Admiral Kōta outranked even him. I could no more give a rear admiral an order than I could fly around this room. Very likely, I will learn to fly long before a lieutenant commander gives orders to an admiral. Is that not so, Captain?"

Captain Miyoshi growled an assent as the room enjoyed a laugh.

"There is the second matter," Kris went on. "I serve in King Raymond I's Royal United Society Navy. Admiral Kōta served in his Imperial Musashi Majesty's Navy. Even if I were a full admiral, a whole lot of promotions from where I am"—which drew another laugh from the students; Kris was beginning to like them—"I could *never* give an order to a ship of the Musashi Navy. I might suggest something to Rear Admiral Kōta. I might ask him nicely, but I could never order him."

"Then why did he and all the other admirals, what were there, three? follow you into this disastrous battle?" the man asked.

"That's several questions. Why don't you sit down and let the next reporter stand up and see if she can get a question in," Kris said. The watching students got a laugh at that. The man did sit, but only after shouting, "You owe me an answer."

"Yes, I do," Kris said. "Let me share with you the discussion I and the three admirals had about this leadership challenge we faced. Nelly, do you have our net meeting recorded?"

"Yes, I do," Nelly said.

"No. Don't distribute it," the lawyer behind Kris shouted.

"Oops," said Nelly. "It's out."

Screens lit up again. "As you can see, Admiral Kōta was the first to say that he had not put on his uniform to do nothing about an atrocity like this. Still, if we only had eight battleships and my four corvettes, there would have been nothing we could do. We would have sadly returned and made our report. However, my king had shipped us a new, super weapon. A neutron torpedo. Its warhead held a tiny chip off a neutron star. Tiny," Kris said, holding up her fingers a few millimeters apart, "but weighing fifteen thousand tons."

That drew soft whistles.

"You wash it down with a beam of antimatter at the same time it smashes into something, and you can do a lot of damage. I had three of them. Our conclusion was that those three Hellburners just might let us take down the huge alien base ship."

"Excuse me, Your Royal Highness," the now-standing woman said, "but wasn't the fact that you are a princess, great-granddaughter of King Raymond, the real reason why they all followed you? You pulled royal rank."

The entire room took in a deep breath at the abruptness of the interruption and the effrontery of the question.

Kris smiled. "I didn't ask to be a princess. I think it's me working off some really bad karma." That drew a laugh from the kids. "When the Society of Humanity broke up, some guys came along and offered my great-grampa a crown. We'd never had a king on Wardhaven. Didn't want one, didn't need one. But I made the mistake of talking my grampa into accepting the job. Foolish me, I never thought that having a grampa for a king meant I'd be stuck being a princess."

Kris gave the room a resigned shrug, and the students broke up laughing.

"So there I am, a lieutenant in the Navy, and suddenly also a princess. You talk about a problem. It's not just for me. Everyone else is trying to figure out what to do with a princess: salute her or kick her."

Kris took another a sip of water as laughter rolled around the room.

The students were having fun. The reporters . . . not so much.

"Here on Musashi, you have had an Imperial family since, well, forever." Kris turned back to Captain Miyoshi. "Do members of the Imperial family ever serve their nation? If they do, would a senior officer accept an order from a junior officer who was a prince or princess?"

The officer did not scowl at Kris like she expected him too. Instead, he stood, and, in a commanding voice that easily carried through the auditorium, said, "For the last two hundred

years, young princes and princesses have served their planet
in the Imperial Army and Navy. When I was a junior officer
serving under Admiral Kōta, he told me that if ever I commanded one of the Imperial family, I should cut them less
slack than I did other boot ensigns. 'They must learn faster
and do better than any other officer, for more may be
demanded of them in life.' Yes, I know that Admiral Kōta
would never allow a princess of the Imperial family, much less
an upstart princess from a place like Wardhaven, to give him
any kind of command."

With that he sat down.

*Upstart princess from the backwoods. Well that puts me in
my place.* "Thank you, Captain," was what Kris said.

"You're welcome," he said.

Kris turned back to the audience, who were thoroughly
enjoying the joke at her expense. She took another sip of water
while things settled down.

The standing reporter jumped in with the next question.
"Still, once you and the admirals made up your mind to risk
the lives of everyone on those ships, the crew didn't have any
choice but to follow you, did they?"

Kris could feel the backbones stiffen of the Marines around
her and the captain behind her at this questioning of military
discipline. Kris ran a hand through her hair to give her a second more to think.

"You know, your question goes to the very heart of military
discipline. I think you've offended a lot of the people present
in uniform."

The reporter didn't back down but hammered the question.
"Still, all those people didn't have a choice, did they? It was
obey and die or else."

Kris kept quiet, letting the reporter dig herself in deeper.
Then she snapped her trap shut. "However, in this case, they
did have a choice."

That got a lot of "What"s from the room.

"We had at least one Sailor in my squadron who did not
want to go. He or she sabotaged work on the *Fearless*. Normally, discipline would handle this situation, but I didn't have
time. Instead, I drew the proverbial line in the sand and

offered anyone who wanted one a ticket home on the transports that would not be going into battle."

"You didn't!" came from the Imperial Gunny.

"Damned if she didn't," came back from the USMC Gunny.

The standing reporter opened his mouth but settled into his seat. He whispered something to the next reporter as she jumped to her feet.

"Did anyone from our ships ask to return?" that reporter asked.

"As I've said before, I had no command or control over the Musashi ships. I know that fifty Sailors did ask to be relieved. I don't know if any were from *Haruna* or *Chikuma*."

"One young Sailor from the *Haruna* asked to return," Captain Miyoshi stated from his seat, in a voice that carried through the hall. "She will be discharged as soon as she has her baby."

The room took time to absorb that. The standing reporter peered at her notepad and seemed to be having trouble coming up with a follow-up question.

From the back of the room a student stood. "May I respectfully ask to pose a question, Your Highness?"

Kris raised an eyebrow to the standing reporter. "Just so long as you don't count it as mine," she said.

"Fine. You students don't count," Kris said with an impish grin.

It took a while for the room to settle down after that, but it did.

"Again, thank you, Your Royal Highness, for allowing this lowly student who doesn't count to pose a question." He paused for only a moment to let his classmates react to his humility. Some praised him. Others threw bits of rice balls.

"I have just finished scanning your report. Can you tell me if you saved the bird people and their planet?"

The room fell into a hush.

"I wish I could," Kris said. "What I know is that we badly damaged the alien base ship. Our Hellburners smashed up all its engines even though it was about the size of a large moon. However, we underestimated the hundreds of other ships it carried. Faced with overwhelming laser fire, and after six of our battleships, including *Haruna* and *Chikuma*, were blasted out of space, we had to run. Two of my own ships fought bravely to their destruction to give the *Wasp* and the *Hornet* a chance to get back and tell the story of how they died."

Kris paused. No one jumped in to fill the silence.

"There isn't a day that I don't wonder if all our fighting and dying was for something, or in vain. My ship, the *Wasp*, just made it back to human space. I understand that they wouldn't even risk a final trip to the breakers for her. They're scrapping her at the first station in human space she finally made it to."

Kris paused again. "If I had a ship, one of the first things I would do would be to take it back to that planet. To see if they were attacked by the surviving alien ships or if the aliens moved on to some easier target."

Kris raised her hands in a shrug. "But I have no ship, and my movements are, at the moment, restricted by the law. So, no, I don't know if the bird people still live. I only know a lot of good men and women died to give them a better chance than they had before we fought."

The room broke into applause. Mr. Kawaguchi came up to stand beside Kris and made a show of turning the mike down; there would be no more questions. Several of the chosen reporters began to protest. Others began to shout their own questions. In the noise, Kris and her team left the stage.

The Marines formed a square around them and saw to it that they easily made it back to the waiting transport. Kris was on her way back to Fujioka House before she knew it.

"Do we know anything about the bomb?" Kris asked.

"I asked the police to report to us," Tsusumu said. "Maybe they will. You did very well, young lady. Very well. I begin to think that you truly are Billy Longknife's kid."

Kris leaned back into the seat. She was getting the post-battle shakes. As inconspicuously as possible, Jack gave her a hug.

"You *are* a Longknife," he whispered.

47

"**You** did much better than I expected," Mr. Kawaguchi said later in the day as he handed Kris a blue envelope.

"What is that?" Kris said, eyeing it.

"It is a gag order from the judge. You are forbidden any more contact with the press. I think you did very well. By the way, do you have any other interesting conversations between you and your admirals?"

"As you pointed out, they are not my admirals. Vice Admiral Krätz was threatening to have his flagship shoot the *Wasp* out of space."

"Oh, this just gets better and better. And why didn't he?"

"Her Imperial Highness, the Grand Duchess Victoria Smythe-Peterwald was on the *Wasp* and objected to being blown to atoms with me. Admiral Krätz suggested she leave the *Wasp*."

"Did she?"

"No, she was still on it when we finally made it back to human space."

"Oh, I like this story. Now, how do I make sure the judges like it as well?"

"Don't you mean the jury?"

"Not in Musashi, my dear. Usually, three judges hear cases.

Since you face a capital charge, nine have been appointed for your trial."

Actually, quite a few more judges had been appointed to try Kris. Several thousand to be exact. All in the media.

That evening, they gathered in the drawing room to watch several monitors. The news seemed to have nothing on but Kris's presser, and all the talking heads had their own take on it. While they watched the four main news reports, Nelly collected them all and analyzed them. They ranged them from true to off-the-wall crazy.

"What's the balance?" Penny asked Nelly.

"Not in our favor," Nelly answered. "As usual, you can sell more soap the more outrageous you make your story. Take for example, your letting Sailors opt out of the battle. They've got a lot of old, retired generals telling everyone they can't believe you did that."

"Well, we've got a witness that I did," Kris countered.

"No we don't," Tsusumu said, making a strange face.

"But Captain Miyoshi said—" Kris stopped in the face of her lawyer's shaking head. "We don't?"

"He said the young woman was pregnant. He didn't mention that she was not married, and the pregnancy was initiated after *Haruna* departed on this mission."

"Oops," Jack said. "A lot of embarrassment all around, huh?"

"I can neither identify her nor get access to speak to her," Tsusumu said, clearly disappointed in himself. "With her not talking, there are a lot of talking heads saying she does not exist and never did."

"Is that the worst lie?" Kris asked.

"Sorry, Kris, no," Nelly said. "There have been suggestions that you used, ah, sexual gifts, to keep the admirals in line."

"That's ridiculous," Cara put in with full teenage outrage. "Why, she never even kissed Jack."

Kris and Jack exchanged brief, very brief, eye contact. Fujioka House was full of servants. Abby had talked to several of them. Almost all were on retainer to one or more news sources.

Jack slept in the north wing of the house. Kris's suite was in the south wing. They only met in the middle.

"I bet that sells lots of soap," Abby said dryly.

"So there is a battle for my life going on in the media, and I'm gagged from fighting it," Kris said, eyeing the table where the blue envelope with her gag order still rested. "What does the well-dressed innocent wear to meet the headsman these days? A white kimono? Should I start being fitted for one?"

"I hope not," was all her lawyer said.

"You have a visitor. Several of them," a Marine sergeant announced from the main hallway before quickly stepping aside.

A gray-haired man in what Kris took for very archaic Japanese garb stepped into the room. He held a heavy wooden staff, decorated with gold bands and designs that said nothing to Kris except that they were old, and this guy was important.

Everyone in the room was on their feet in a blink.

The man rapped his staff on the floor. In a booming voice, he announced. "The Princess Emiko comes. All who give her homage, give homage to the Emperor. Bow down in his honor."

Beside her, Tsusumu bowed low. Remembering Captain Miyoshi's comment about real princesses rather than jumped-up backwoods princesses, Kris bowed just as low.

48

"I'm so glad to meet you, Princess Kristine. Face-to-face. At least we'll be face-to-face if you quit looking at the floor."

Kris quit looking at the floor.

Princess Emiko proved to be a young woman likely a few years younger than Kris though it was hard to tell for sure. She was not only in full kimono but also the white face paint that Kris had only seen on vids.

There was no question that her arms were wide open, and she wanted to hug Kris. Her *getas* clopped on the hardwood floors of the drawing room as she hurried to engulf Kris in a hug that was as enthusiastic as it was careful not to smudge the makeup.

"I hate to wear this getup," the princess whispered to Kris. "The kimono is nine hundred years old, would you believe, and my auntie will not talk to me for a week if it comes to harm."

Kris eased up on her hug.

The princess took a step back and eyed Kris. "I've been wanting to meet you since, like forever. I've been a fan of yours since the Battle of Wardhaven. Imagine, taking on six pirate battleships with just your dozen little boats. Wow. They won't even let me take a boat out on the lake at the palace.

What are they expecting, a sea monster to gobble me up? It's a lake, for Amaterasu's sake."

Behind her, the man with the staff cleared his throat.

"Okay, okay, Daisuke-san, bring it over here. I'm not clomping back over there to get it. A girl could break her neck in these *getas*. Kris, do you have any real clothes I could borrow? I can't sit down in this getup, or anything. I just have to stand up or risk a seam splitting. They had a van bring me so I could just stand up the whole way."

"Abby, could you find something? And get some of the household help. They must know how to handle nine-hundred-year-old clothes, I hope."

"I hope, too," Abby said, and was gone, with Cara in tow.

Daisuke seemed to have no trouble negotiating the distance to Kris in his own *getas*. He presented a quite magnificent-looking scroll to Emiko with a bow.

The young princess started to make a face but quickly suppressed it. Although Kris could detect nothing in the exchange between the two, she had experience with someone very much like Daisuke. The chauffeur back at Nuu House, Harvey, was a retired NCO. Kris learned very quickly that the barest twitch from him should be taken as a thorough reprimand.

Kris suspected that Daisuke and Emiko had their own way of communicating praise and disapproval, and she would bet money she didn't have that Daisuke had just given his princess a full dressing-down, and had done it without saying a word.

When Emiko turned back to Kris, scroll in hand, she was, if not the perfect princess, at least a proper one.

"Father, the Emperor, invites you to share the Way of the Tea with him at six tomorrow evening. It's the best part of the day, and the sunsets from the palace garden are glorious." The last was added in a rush and probably not included in the formal charge. "Please come."

Kris didn't need any hints. "I am honored by this invitation, and I will most certainly present myself at the palace before six tomorrow evening," Kris said.

"Good, good, now, please, do you have some clothes I can put on so we can talk. Can I stay for dinner?"

"Most certainly," Kris said.

"Now, if you gentlemen will leave us ladies alone," Abby

said, leading a half dozen women staff into the room, "we can get this poor child out of those duds and into something decent." The look Daisuke threw Abby would have melted stones if there wasn't just the hint of a smile at the corner of his lips.

The men retired, and the household staff began the delicate job of removing several layers of ancient silk from a princess who held perfectly still for them but chattered on with Kris. "Please open the scroll. I did it myself."

Kris admired the calligraphy, as Nelly gave Kris a dissertation on both the language and the handiwork. Princess Emiko was delighted that Nelly understood the excellence of her work.

While the silks were carefully folded and put into cedarwood boxes, a blue brocade blazer, white blouse, and white silk pleated skirt were provided to the princess. Kris considered the skirt far too short, but Nelly silently assured Kris that this was what all the college girls were wearing on Musashi these days. White knee-length tabi completed the ensemble, and the two princesses adjourned to the couch, so Kris could tell Emiko "everything."

Supper was served and long eaten before Daisuke was able to persuade his princess that she was expected back at the palace before bedtime and should herself inform the Emperor that his gracious offer had been accepted. That left Kris and her company waving good-bye on the front steps of Fujioka House just before sunset.

"You are greatly honored," Tsusumu said.

"How will this play in the media?" Kris asked.

Tsusumu chuckled. "Much better than the party in power will want. I suspect there may be a visit to the Imperial Palace tomorrow and a lengthy conversation about the constitutional crisis that an Emperor dallying in political affairs could bring on."

Kris looked at the scroll that Emiko had once more pressed upon Kris as she left. "Will this invitation be revoked?"

"Not if the Emperor's backbone is as stiff as I think it is. No. Aki-san has crossed a line with your indictment. A line a lot of us think we must get back across quickly. I had hoped the Emperor was on our side. Still, that," he said, eyeing the scroll. "None of us had hoped for an indication of the Imperial Will anywhere close to that. You are truly honored, stranger."

"Honored or not," Abby snapped, "I've got to get you outfitted and dressed properly before six tomorrow. Where am I going to find a nine-hundred-year-old woman's kimono that will fit you, my tall beanpole?"

"Don't you have one somewhere in one of your steamer trunks?" Jack asked.

"Not nine hundred years old," Abby snapped. "You saw what that princess was wearing. I will not have my princess reduced to some backwoods poor relation. It's gonna be a night." And she headed for the servant's area of the house.

"Is she often like that?" Tsusumu asked.

"Often worse. I suggest that you go home and the rest of us attempt to hide in our rooms. Unfortunately for me," Kris said with a sigh, "she knows where I live."

49

Kris arrived, attired in a six-hundred-year-old kimono, and placed her *geta* footwear on the stone pavement of the Imperial Palace's entrance at exactly 5:45 P.M. the next day.

It had been a closely run operation.

Kris had never seen Abby in such a swivet. It took less than half an hour to determine that there were several five-hundred-year-old kimonos in the house, but none fit anyone within a foot of Kris's height.

Mrs. Fujioka was brought in by conference call. Yes, her family had several older kimonos, but all of her ancestors had run to short, by modern standards, and certainly by Kris's standard. She offered to contact all of her acquaintances. "Certainly some women in Japan needed a longer kimono."

By midnight, Mrs. Fujioka happily called back. "We have found a *furisode* for your Kris. You may need to add seven or eight centimeters of cloth at the hem, but this will work."

"A *furisode*?" Abby asked.

"Yes, a kimono that an unmarried woman wears. Your princess is unmarried, isn't she?"

"Yes."

"Well, she cannot visit the Emperor dressed as a married woman, can she now?"

"No, no, of course not."

Kris had never seen Abby so out of her depth. Never.

"So," Abby said, "it seems this matter is even more complicated than I thought. Nelly, Mata Hari, why didn't you catch me on this?"

"I'm sorry, Abby," Nelly said. "None of you humans seemed to have a problem, so I figured a kimono was a kimono. I'm now researching the matter and discover there are all kinds of kimonos and parts to them. We will not make this mistake again."

"Nelly in a mistake!" Penny said.

"I have explained and apologized. Can we please go on from here?"

"Yes, let's," Kris said. "Just how gussied up am I going to have to get?"

"Very," Abby and Nelly said at once. "We dare not offend anyone," Nelly added.

"Or shame ourselves," Abby added. "Shame is definitely not an option."

"What do you say that you go get your beauty rest?" Penny said, taking Kris by the shoulder and aiming her toward the stairs to the south wing. "We girls can get you all set up, and you must stay awake while the Emperor serves you tea."

"I think the Way of the Tea is a bit more than a tea party."

"Don't I know. I've had Mimzy do my research on that one. It may take all of our supercomputers to get you through tomorrow, but trust us, we won't let you down."

And with that, Kris found herself led off to bed.

Sadly, Jack took the other stairway to the north wing. Right now, it would be nice to have someone hold her and tell her it would be all right.

Kris snorted. Be held, yes. Lie to each other. Not her style.

Next morning over breakfast, Kris discovered that most of her female staff had managed to snatch a few hours' sleep. However, most of the serving staff of half the older families in Kyoto had lost sleep making sure Kris was letter-perfect for tea.

Abby began listing all the parts of Kris's ensemble and where it had been borrowed from. Kris cut her off after reaching the conclusion that fieldstripping a 24-inch pulse laser was easier than getting one six-foot-tall woman . . . make that unmarried woman . . . properly attired for an evening with an Emperor.

Maybe Grampa Ray's informality wasn't so bad after all.

At 1100, Ko-san had been brought in. Nelly mentioned to Kris that the name meant "peace," but Kris had met Gunny Sergeants who were more peaceful . . . and more flexible. Ko-san was the recognized expert in proper dress in all of Kyoto. She ruled the dress staff with an iron rod and saw no need to spare the princess at the center of it all.

Comments on Kris's posture and the grace of her movements . . . or lack thereof . . . were blunt and pointed.

Kris had survived Officer Candidate School without blowing her top at the DIs and others put there to teach her the strange art of subordination.

Kris gritted her teeth and set about learning to be a proper . . . unmarried . . . woman of Musashi.

But even the great Ko-san met her match at Kris's height. The *furisode* had originally been made when the style was to drag the ground. Even with that extra cloth, it rose to above Kris's ankles.

It was a scandal in the making. Not possible.

The great Ko-san called in reinforcements. A chemistry professor from Kyoto University arrived with a team of experts on dyes, cloth, and color matching. But not the usual experts. These men and woman specialized in ancient materials: cloth no less than two hundred years old.

They took one look at Kris in her *furisode* . . . and called for reinforcements of their own. The great hall at Fujioka House took on the appearance of a war room as experts debated one strategy over another, one option versus another.

In the end, they matched the cloth's color, even extending the dyed pattern all the way to the floor for Kris. Rather than put the original cloth at risk, they manufactured a special glue in the master bathroom and glued the strip to the hem of the original *furisode*.

All of this almost came to naught when Ko-san produced her makeup box and prepared to paint Kris's face white.

"No," Kris said, putting her foot down. "I am a Navy officer and a battle commander. I will not show up looking like a geisha."

"Geishas are highly respected in our culture. It is only you barbarians—"

"I will not have a picture of me in white face paint show up the next time my father runs for office," Kris said, knowing the immovable object and the irresistible force were going head-to-head here.

Under the cold, firm, game face that had ordered the death of billions, Ko-san blinked. "Some modern women do wear lighter makeup."

"Show me a picture," Kris said.

So Kris got into her van with thirty minutes to spare.

Kris found herself standing, just like Emiko had the day before, holding on to straps as the rig made its way toward the Imperial precincts.

For once, Jack was torn between watching traffic and watching her. "You sure you can handle those *getas* without breaking your neck?" *Getas* were like two-inch high heels, back *and* front.

Kris held on tight as the van took a tight turn. "If Princess Emiko can survive them, so can I."

"But she talked her way out of them. Do you think you can talk the Emperor out of your wearing them?"

"I will not even ask."

"Yeah, I figured that."

"Slight change in plan," the driver announced. "The formal entrance to the Imperial Residence is packed with newsies."

"No surprise there," Kris and Jack both muttered.

"However, there are many gates to the Imperial precincts. We have been honored to use the Hanzo Gate. Hold on," and with that little warning, Kris found herself thrown to the left and off her feet. She hung on for two more quick turns before managing to regain her footing.

Jack eyed her, but she shook her head, and he didn't make another suggestion to change footwear.

After several more hair-raising turns, the van came to a halt. Jack gave Kris a slow ten count before he nodded. The door behind Kris opened, and four Imperial Marines stood by a set of stairs they had put there just for her. They offered their hands to help her down, then gave a similar help to Ko-san, the main reason Kris was still in *getas*.

Ko-san came to rest a hand on Kris's arm and its near floor-length sleeves. "Stand up straight," she whispered. "No slouching. Walk gracefully. You must float over the ground, not clomp like a cow."

Kris wondered how much she would be billed for this torture and found comfort in the thought she was too broke to pay
for this violation of the laws of war.

"Smile for the cameras," brought Kris back from her rever-
ies of poverty.

Yes, over a dozen newsies were lined up along the moat
walls, standing among the small pines and pointing cameras
her way.

The full detachment of Marines had spread out around her.
None of the newsies chose to risk penetrating that line, but
several called questions at Kris.

"Ignore those prattling gnats," Ko-san muttered. Finally,
some advice Kris was glad to hear.

Ko-san went on in full tour-guide mode. "The Hanzo-mon
crosses the moat, separating the Hanzo moat from the Saku-
rada moat. These are exact replicas of the moat around Edo
castle on Earth that dates back over a thousand years. Imagine
trying to storm this with swords and arrows."

Kris eyed the tall, steep, stone-lined walls of the moat. "I
wouldn't want to take this place with modern tanks and body
armor," she said.

The gate itself was wooden, set in rather imposing stone-
work. Kris's Marines came to a halt. Two men in ancient Japanese uniforms opened the gate.

They bowed to her from the waist. Ko-san made sure Kris's
bow was as low as theirs. "I can go no farther. Do not embarrass your family, or more importantly, me."

Kris was prepared to promise anything, but the guards
were motioning her in, and Ko-san had already turned to go.
Kris said nothing but walked, carefully, in very small steps, as
gracefully as she could into the Imperial Residence.

The massive wooden door closed behind her without so
much as a creak. Ancient they might look, but their lubrication
was as up-to-date as yesterday. Kris found herself confronted
with a small electric cart. The guards motioned her to the
back, where there was a place to stand and a solid handhold.
She stepped aboard, and they quickly got her in motion.

This portion of the palace, like the original on Earth and
the other copy on Yamato, were closed to the public and
reserved for the Imperials themselves. Fukiage Gardens were

more a forest at first glance, then Kris found herself coming to a halt beside a pond covered with flowering water lilies.

The guards quickly dismounted and bowed low at the waist to a man in traditional attire who looked only a few years older than the official portrait Kris had memorized.

Kris dismounted herself, careful to get the *getas* under her before taking a few steps forward and joining the guards in their low bow.

"You honor me," Kris said in the best Japanese Nelly had assured her and with an accent that the help at Fujioka house did not have to work too hard not to smile at.

The Emperor returned a bow, his much shallower, and smiled as he joined her in speaking Standard, "No, on the contrary, you honor me and my house greatly. Where did you get such a lovely *furisode* that fitted a woman as tall as you at short notice?"

Kris rose from her bow, as he offered his hand to take her elbow and walk with her. "I honestly don't know. The staff made me get some sleep last night while they turned Kyoto upside down. That faint chemical smell is the glue holding the last extra material to my hem, so I don't embarrass us all by flashing my ankles."

"Ah, yes. Now, if I could just get my daughter to wear a skirt that even approached her knees."

"Princess Emiko is a delightful young woman."

The father chuckled. "Yes she is. And I understand she talked you into letting her get out of that ancient outfit in which she was dispatched."

"It seemed the thing to do. Was it returned in satisfactory order?"

"My sister has inspected every inch of it with her museum specialist and returned the historical artifact to the cold nitrogen bin from which it was borrowed."

"Good," Kris said.

"Now, you will notice that I am not risking my neck on *getas*. Our court photographer already has taken his pictures for tonight's news which will make Aki-san gnash his teeth. Would you like to settle into a nice pair of flat *zori* my wife chose to go with that magnificent *furisode*?"

Kris glanced around. Apparently the photographer to the Imperial Family was very discreet; she'd seen no one, much less a camera. The reference to Aki, the present Prime Minister, Kris let pass. "Yes, please. My security chief has been very upset with me many times, but *getas* were a unique risk for the both of us."

At that, a man trotted forward and put two *zoris*, handwoven with golden thread running through the straps, on the ground before Kris. He offered her a hand to lean on as she lost two inches of altitude. Kris could almost relax as they continued their walk among the pines and incense cypress.

"Ah yes, Jack. I hope you two are getting along well."

"If you know Jack by name, you must also know that his rooms are in the north wing of Fujioka House, and mine are in the south. They do not even share the same stairs. What with the reports that I seduced the admirals into following me into battle, I will not risk any scandal."

"Good. You are wise as well as courageous. That is a good combination."

"It has kept me alive so far."

"And with a little luck, we will keep you alive some more. Do you know that my daughter has been following your career more religiously than she has been following her studies? She wants to join the Navy when she finishes her education."

The father eyed Kris . . . and, for once, Kris found herself at a loss for words.

Her love for Jack was changing her perspective on a lot of things. Things like maybe someday having a daughter. A daughter who might want to do some of the damn fool things she'd done.

"I see you pause before answering me," the father beside her said. "Could it be you have second thoughts about what you have done?"

Kris didn't need time to think about that. "Second thoughts, sir? No. I have done what I have done, and may your gods and mine forgive me, but I would do it all again if I had it to do over. But if I was a mother, and my daughter said she wanted to follow in my footsteps, I think I would be badly torn. We face a crisis, Your Imperial Majesty. It must be met with courage, and, no doubt, much suffering, blood, and loss for all of us. How can I fault anyone willing to meet it? But, to risk all the tomorrows I dream of sharing someday with a little daughter?"

Kris found herself shaking her head.

"You wear a *furisode*, but I think you are about ready to trade it in for a married woman's kimono," the Emperor said.

"If I can ever find time to properly court a man, I just might."

"Ah, yes. The balancing of our duties to humanity with our duties to family. Or even to ourselves. Trust me, over time it does get easier. Look at me. While you must prance about like a clothes pony in ancient regalia we tremble might tear on a twig, my kimono is a gift from my wife from last Landing Day. Let us get you to the teahouse, so you can change into something both magnificent and wearable."

"I don't know if I once get out of this stuff I'll ever get back into it properly."

"Don't worry. My household staff includes the old biddy who taught Ko-san everything she knows. If they can't redress you, then I clearly need a new staff."

He paused for a moment. "I don't know what you know about the Way of the Tea."

"Little," Kris said.

I RESEARCHED IT THOROUGHLY, Nelly said.

SHUT UP.

"Princess Emiko and her mother will be joining us for the ceremony. Part of it is to remark upon certain scrolls of wise sayings that I will hang up. I have given much thought about just what I would like you . . . *and* my daughter . . . to reflect upon."

Kris nodded. After meeting the Buddhist monk aboard *Mutsu*, she would have expected nothing less thoughtful from a ceremony.

"You will be asked about the things we speak of. I would prefer that you tell nothing of our time together."

"I learned at my father's dinner table that what is said there stays there. Will there be a table in the ceremony?" Kris asked, letting the imp get her tongue.

"No, there will not be, but the same principle applies."

"It certainly will. Nelly, turn off your recording system."

DO YOU REALLY MEAN IT, KRIS?

YES, NELLY.

"Recording system off," Nelly said.

"You record everything?" the Emperor said.

"Since I was a teenager. This will be the first break."

"I am honored."

50

It was well after sunset before Kris left. And she left by the front gate. She was surprised by how many newsies had stuck it out, but it seemed there was still time to make the late-night news.

The sunset, as seen from the Fujimi-yagura, or the Mt. Fuji viewing keep, had been spectacular. If the snow-covered volcano wasn't the actual sacred mountain, it was a perfect stand-in as far as Kris was concerned.

So Kris was feeling rather mellow as she made her way out the main gate and toward the waiting van. Her Marine detachment had formed up at a distance, far enough away that the cameras could get her alone but close enough to keep anyone from jamming a mike in her face. Maybe that was what caused her to lose her usual control over her tongue.

The shouted questions were the usual ones although at least one woman reporter was informed enough to want to know about the viewing of the scrolls. Kris let them holler for most of her walk, then paused, and in her command voice announced, "I'm sorry. I cannot talk to you fine people of the press. The courts require me to say nothing. Maybe you can get your stories from the Imperial Household?"

As she expected, someone gave her the straight line she was looking for.

"The Imperial Household never tells us anything."

"Oh," Kris said, putting on her best imitation of shocked innocence. "Are they under a court gag order, too?"

Newsies are not known for their humor, but that drew a chuckle from several, and even Kris's Marines seemed to be smiling as she approached the van.

Kris felt the bullet hit before she heard the rifle's crack.

51

Traditionally, a young woman presents herself
naked to be dressed in the so many formal items that made up
a full kimono. Kris had not. Ko-son had been very disapproving, but Kris hadn't budged. All the formal layers went on atop
Kris's usual spider-silk body-stocking armor.

Now Kris's armor stopped a five-millimeter round right
over her heart. The added liquid metal did its part and hard-
ened, spreading the impact over most of Kris's torso. Still, the
high power of that rifle round had to go somewhere.

Kris landed on her butt.

Immediately, she rolled, one hand holding on the armored
wig Ko-son had not approved of, and the other hand going for
her automatic. Ko-son had almost stormed out when Kris
insisted that her weapon had to fit somewhere in all the folds
of that ancient, traditional garb.

A second shot hit the cobblestones where Kris had been
half a second ago. Chips flew, and one of them hit Kris's
cheek.

She rolled again, automatic out, but with nothing to aim at.

Kris quickly raised her weapon to the sky. Her field of fire
was now blocked as Imperial Marines raced to surround her.
Kris knew none of them wore any more protection than their

dress uniform's wool coats, but they quickly formed two ranks around her, rifles at the ready, searching the surrounds.

Kris's assassin of the evening might get off one more shot, but it would hit an Imperial Marine standing solidly on his honor . . . and his buddies would avenge that death with a fusillade of fire.

Then Jack was standing over her, automatic out. How he got through the Imperial Marine cordon must have involved teleportation.

Seconds stretched, but there was no third shot.

Through the Marines' legs, Kris could see reporters groveling in the dirt, but several camera operators stood their ground, and Kris's latest failed . . . so far . . . assassination attempt went to Musashi in bright color.

Sirens wailed from every direction, and Imperial Guards raced from the gate. These weren't the quaint ones, but ran in full battle rattle, their weapons sighted and roving over the high ground behind Kris.

Several unarmored guards hurried along carrying incongruous black shields, the kind used by riot police.

What with the camera folks busy doing their job and the reporters doing that infantryman's thing, hugging the earth so closely they might somehow get below ground level, Kris didn't see a riot coming.

Then she saw the reason for the shields.

While the Imperial Guards, fully armed and armored, took up station between Kris and where the shots had come from, the guards in mere cloth stood in front of the Imperial Marines. They hoisted their shields high and it finally dawned on Kris.

They were providing her the cover to begin a withdrawal.

Somebody popped several flares, and a gadget began shooting ice pellets into the air. Now Kris could not only not be seen, but infrared sighting gear was hashed.

The Imperial Marine captain commanding joined her as Jack offered Kris a handkerchief and a hand up.

As she rose, wiping the blood from her cheek, she couldn't help but take a sad look at her six-hundred-year-old kimono. Right in front of her heart was a flattened 5 mm slug. It looked ready to fall off; a Marine stepped forward with an evidence bag and popped the spent round into it.

That left a hole in the front of the kimono. It was matched by mud and dirt where she'd rolled on the cobblestones and, if Kris wasn't wrong, some of the stone shards from the second round had left rips behind.

Kris could forget about the Imperial Headsman. Ko-san would kill her before he even got close.

Or maybe offer her one of the short knives and stand by while Kris committed formal seppuku.

But not in this six-hundred-year-old kimono. Surely for that, Ko-san would order in something cheap for her from Kimonos"R"Us.

Jack went up the steps to their armored van, glanced around, and signaled Kris to come up. Still, he kept a hand on her head, forcing her to stoop.

Bedraggled and bowed Kris might be, but the Imperial Marine captain was the height of politeness and honor as he helped Kris up the steps. The light Imperial Guards held their shields higher, denying anyone still paying attention a good shot at her. There were more flares and ice.

And somewhere, a shout began. *Banzai!* First it was just a few voices; Kris was unsure of where they came from, maybe among the reporters. Then it rolled on, one *Banzai* beginning before the last one finished. *Banzai* after *Banzai* after *Banzai*.

Kris was left dumbfounded, weakening as the adrenaline from the shoot-out wore off, but totally unable to interpret what was happening.

As the Imperial Marine captain moved to close the doors behind her, he said with a smile, "*Banzai*," then translated it for Kris. "You were outstanding, Princess-san."

No one had ever addressed her with the honor of san before.

Jack looked her over as he helped her get her hands in the straps she'd be standing in, not at all impressed. "I see you did wear the armored bodysuit I had Abby lay out for you."

"It wasn't her idea?"

"She'd spent too much time reading about exactly how you put one of those damn outfits together to dare take one step out of tradition. Where'd the weapon come from?" But Jack didn't wait for a reply as he turned to the driver. "Let's get out of here."

The Imperial Marine sergeant shook his head. "No, sir. Not

until I have two Marine gun trucks ahead and behind me. You sure there's no mine ahead?"

While Jack considered that, Kris made sure to get the last word in their interrupted conversation.

"You're not the only one only letting tradition take her so far, my tyrannical security chief. And if Abby hadn't laid out a bodysuit, I would have found one myself."

"I almost believe you," Jack said, as the van took off.

"Believe me. Now tell me, how are you going to keep Ko-san from killing me for what I've done to this kimono?"

"Hmm, that's a hard one. It depends on what weapon she uses. If she slips poison into your tea, I'll have to stop her, but if she just hands you the short sword and expects you to kill yourself . . . Does my job description include keeping you from trying to kill yourself? You do it so often, it hardly seems something I have to stop."

The van had taken off fast, made several hard turns that left Kris hanging on the straps, but for the moment, it was on a straight stretch. Kris took the chance to aim a whack at the top of Jack's head.

He saw it coming and dodged.

"Well, Mrs. Lincoln, beside the shooting, how was the play? I notice that the body armor wasn't the only place common sense won out. What footwear is that?" Jack asked.

"*Zoris,*" Kris supplied. "Nelly, make sure that when all this delicate gear is parceled back to who loaned it, that the gold-threaded *zoris* get back to the Imperial Household."

"I'll see to it, Kris."

"How *did* it go?" Jack asked.

"I got to meet both Emiko's mom and dad, as well as her again. Surprise, surprise, she can spend a half hour in absolute silence when it is required of her . . . and her mom is at her elbow."

Jack chuckled at that but waited for her to go on.

Kris didn't.

"The Emperor asked that what passed between us be totally private. Nelly didn't record it. Maybe someday I'll tell you. But not today."

"Maybe when you tell me how you got that blue sash, Earth's Order of the Wounded Lion, huh?"

Kris laughed. "I may break down on that story before this one."

Jack just shook his head.

Back at Fujioka House, Kris was quickly passed to the women to undress, but not before Mr. Kawaguchi got his question in. "How'd it go? And I don't mean the assassination attempt. I already know someone really doesn't want you talking in court. I mean your time with the Emperor."

Kris gave him the same nonanswer she'd given Jack as she was towed off to change. That left the men behind to commiserate about that strangest of creatures: a woman who did *not* want to talk about a date.

The look Ko-san gave Kris would have killed a mere mortal. She lifted up Kris's outer kimono and glared at the inner layers. "Someone has redressed you," she said accusingly.

"Rika-san sends her complements on the fine job you did preparing me."

Ko-san snorted. "I should have known that new man would let you pass. What did you and he wear to tea, cutoffs and a tank top?"

"I and the Imperial Family were most properly attired, and that is all you will hear from me unless you can talk Rika-san out of a picture."

Ko-san's scowl did not lighten as she took in the bullet hole in Kris's garb. "I will have to patch this. I have cloth that will match. I will also sew the edges of the bullet hole so that it does not fray or spread."

"You're not going to try to make it vanish?" Kris said, almost as shocked as she'd ever been in her life.

"Fix it! This is part of the kimono's history now. Six hundred years from now, the wearer will point to the place where Princess-san Longknife was shot."

Culture shock. Kris knew it was an occupational hazard of both her life as a princess and a Longknife. Still, it always surprised her when she walked into its sharp jab to the stomach.

Much more comfortable in sweats, Kris joined the men in the drawing room for the news. They hadn't long to wait; Kris was the number one story on all the channels.

They showed her going in. They showed her coming out. Some presented her in quick cuts. Others lavished more time, including several that included her interchange with the reporters.

Tsusumu busted out laughing. "You didn't! Don't you know the Imperial Household staff are the most tight-lipped crew in human space?"

"Of course I knew," Kris said. "But I am a stranger, and it was a good joke."

Tsusumu quit laughing when the news flashed several stills of Kris with the Imperial Family, both before, during, and after the Tea Ceremony. It ended with a lovely shot of Kris and the Imperial Family silhouetted against the sunset before it transitioned to Kris rolling on the ground as the second shot hit near her. The reports quickly said Kris had not been hurt but showed nothing of how she had been protected by the Imperial Marines and Palace Guard.

"Gods, I am speechless" the lawyer finally said when he regained his voice. "I don't know which to marvel at first. The kami that guards your life or His Majesty throwing down the gauntlet to Aki-san."

"Pardon?" Kris said.

The lawyer and politician took a deep breath. "I have never seen such intimate coverage of the Emperor, certainly not of the whole family. Young woman, the Emperor has thrown his support behind you in a way never done before. There hasn't been anything like this in the two hundred years since this line of the dynasty was founded."

He rose to pace the room. "I don't know what Aki will do, but I know that if the Emperor took such a bold hand in something my party was so deeply involved in, I would demand he abdicate."

"And if he abdicated . . .?" Kris asked.

"Emiko would become the first Empress in several hundred years for either Japan, Yamato, or us."

"How does Aki's party feel about an Empress?" Jack asked.

Now Tsusumu was laughing again. "It would break their conservative hearts. My party, of course, would be delighted to have an idealistic young person on the throne. We're looking forward to it."

The lawyer ended up stroking his chin. "I would not like to

be among the power brokers of the present administration tonight. Unless it was as a tiny mouse to listen. Though even a mouse would be ushered out if it could not keep from laughing at their dilemma."

"Has this changed anything?" Kris asked.

"Unless they have the good sense to call off your trial, no. Now, if you don't mind, I must be gone. There are several people I dearly want to discuss this with and, unfortunately, you are, as you said, a stranger and uninvolved with our local politics."

"Only up to my neck," Kris said.

"Don't worry your pretty little head," Tsusumu said. "It is even less likely to end its days on a pike before the Justice building. Much less likely."

Kris watched him go, then found an overstuffed chair and settled into it alone. Jack took a seat on the couch within reach and waited quietly. Kris was only starting to realize how much she valued his silence and how much it must cost him.

"The Emperor knows your name," she told Jack.

"I believe being noticed by the Emperor in days gone by was an honor," he said, but he said it only to fill in some of the space around Kris's silence.

Kris took a deep breath. "The Emperor also knows that you sleep in the north wing and I in the south wing. He approves very much of that."

Jack scowled sardonically. "He does, does he?"

"What with me accused of seducing the admirals, can you blame him?"

"No. No, I can't. It's just the pits having to live my life to fulfill everyone else's needs except yours and mine."

Kris sighed and pulled a pillow close instead of Jack. "It *is* the pits. But if we can get through this court thing, maybe we can just be another poor couple trying to make their way in the world."

"You think we could?"

"What can happen to us after they judge me?" Kris asked.

"You're a Longknife," Jack said. "Something always happens."

52

Kris's first day in court started bad and then got worse.

She was all decked out in starched undress whites and about to get into the limo beside Jack when "that" happened.

She quickly scrambled back into the house and found one of the young housekeepers with the proper feminine necessities. Fortunately, it hadn't progressed to the point she needed new whites. As she rejoined Jack in the limo, he give her a raised eyebrow.

She whispered, "That time of the month."

"Sorry about that, and today of all days," he whispered. Was there something deep in his eyes, maybe a hint of regret that it was still just the two of them, and not a threesome.

Would that change anything? Kris wondered.

Kris was in no mood for bull, but that was all she got that day in court. It seemed that the law let the prosecutor go first, and that meant the defense had to listen to whatever the prosecution could get the judge to let its witnesses say. The defense only got to put an oar in the water at cross-examination.

But Kris's lawyers seemed uninterested in cross. Lawyers, as in plural. There were half a dozen at the prosecutor's table. Kris's team matched them one for one.

The prosecutor gave an opening statement that accused

Kris of everything under the sun, from going outlaw and starting a war all on her own, coming up with a lousy plan to do it,
then seducing the admirals to go along.

"Seducing!" Kris whispered in Tsusumu's ear.

"The word has other, nonsexual meanings," her lawyer
whispered back.

"But you know what he means."

"Sit still. Keep quiet. Can't you see how the judges are
looking at you?"

Kris had been warned that her job in court was to sit still,
look innocent, and keep her mouth shut until and only if her
lawyer called on her to testify. Kris had no idea how hard that
would be.

Well, she'd faced hostile lasers. She could face a few hostile words.

With an effort.

The prosecution paraded a long line of retired generals and
admirals who all showed up in court in their dress uniforms
bespeckled with medals. Everything about their bearing, dress
and demeanor shouted, "I know what I'm talking about."

And, boy, did they talk.

One by one, each of them meticulously tore apart Kris's
battle plan. They pointed out every turn at which the fight
could have gone horribly wrong, long before it actually did.
They highlighted every risk Kris took and every option she
didn't follow that might have led to a better outcome.

"Her scouting was ridiculous," one admiral growled. "She
had only one contact with the force she assumed was the aggres-
sor. An assumption she had little or no basis for. She based all
her further actions on the unsupported assumption that she
knew where it was going and the speed it would maintain.
Every one of her actions rested on that untested supposition. She
had a force of corvettes and courier ships. Any competent commander would have put them to use as scouts."

He thinks I should have scattered my tiny force even more!
Kris scrawled on a pad for her lawyer to see. What happened
to concentration of forces?

Her lawyer scratched through Kris's comments after hardly
a glance.

One of them raised the issue of the attack on the mining head that delayed their arrival at their final ambush.

"Even if we allow that she had some purpose for that distraction," the general said, "why would a commander of a battle fleet risk her own life flying direct cover for such an operation? And it did nearly cost her her life. Her target proved to be more difficult than she thought, and she was shot down. This was totally unacceptable behavior on the part of a fleet commander."

Kris risked a glance back at Jack, expecting an "I told you so" look. But he stared straight ahead, his face a neutral mask.

And Kris's lawyer elbowed her in the ribs to bring her back face forward.

After each witness, Kris's lawyer was offered a chance to cross-examine. Tsusumu never even rose from his chair to confront the prosecution's witness but mumbled, as if half-distracted. "Have you ever been in combat, Admiral?" or "General?" as the case might be.

The answer was muttered, or growled, but it was always the same. "No."

"No further questions."

The first couple of times the prosecution seemed too puzzled by the question to do anything but dismiss the witness. By the fourth or fifth time, the redirect got lengthy as the prosecutor asked the witness to give a long account of their years in command or even command of the War College.

Tsusumu never asked a second question.

By morning break, Kris was boiling. Mr. Kawaguchi hustled her out of the courtroom and into a small room down the hall, where they could have some privacy.

"Why are you letting them say all that about me?" Kris demanded in a voice that wasn't quite a scream.

"Because they are doing exactly what I want them to do," Tsusumu said calmly.

"What? Have you already measured me for my white kimono and the headsman's slice?"

"No," he said with maddening calm.

Kris kicked one of the large leather chairs that surrounded a heavy wooden table. That hurt. She took a deep breath.

"Okay, then what *are* you doing?"

"They are calling you a fool. A young fool, but a fool none-theless. Have you read the ribbons on their chests?"

"No," Kris admitted. Musashi decorations were not in her training.

"I had a retired general of my own do that. All of that fruit salad, that is what you call it, isn't it?"

"Yes."

"All of it is for peacetime activities. Not one of those mighty men has ever faced combat. My retired general showed me a picture of you in full dress uniform. By the way, you will wear it the day you testify. Every decoration you have involved combat, does it not?"

Kris mentally went down her own fruit salad. "Pretty much."

"Let them talk. And quit making faces when they say things. There are cameras in this courtroom. Your faces will be on tonight's news. Some of the more unscrupulous news sources will doubtlessly take your reactions and put them out of context. Please give them as little to play with as you can. Now. I have things to do, and, certainly, you must have also."

"I need to go to the bathroom."

"Please do and don't bother me."

Kris retired to the ladies' room, did what she needed to do, and found that she had the place all to herself. She kicked the wall, careful not to hurt herself this time. Rather than punch the wall, she tried slapping it a few times. She found the window would open, so she did and tossed a few primal screams at the wind.

This was so different from what she was used to. Yes, it was tough waiting for that right second to slam a hostile with lasers or torpedoes, but she was doing something. Here she had to sit, and sit, and sit.

But she could end up just as dead.

She kicked the wall again. Gently.

She was almost calm when a young woman member of her legal team timidly stuck her head in the door, and announced, "It is time to return to court."

They continued picking apart Kris's every decision, every move, for the rest of the day. The prosecutor had them talk.

Kris's own defense asked its one lone question. It went on and on until even Kris was finding it repetitive and boring.

She wasn't alone, it seemed.

As the time drew close to recess for the day, notes flew up and down the bench between the nine judges. As the last witness for the day stepped down, the chief judge called the prosecutor to the bench.

"It has been pointed out that none of the last three witnesses have added anything new to the record before us."

"Well, Your Honor," was cut off.

"Will any of the, ah, eight witness you have scheduled add anything new to the record? I notice that all but one of them is a former general or admiral."

"The exception to that is an expert on international law. He will testify that a declaration of war is not an action for an individual but for a sovereign state or planet."

"Mr. Kawaguchi, will you stipulate that an individual does not have the right to declare war?"

"Under normal circumstances, yes, Your Honor."

"The court has before it a stipulation that no individual has the right, under normal circumstances, to declare war. I assume the defense accepts the burden of addressing the matter of 'normal circumstances'?"

"We are prepared to do that."

"Then, Mr. Prosecutor, it appears that you have presented your case. Are you prepared to rest?" carried a strong hint that he better be.

Not surprisingly, the prosecution rested.

"Mr. Kawaguchi, are you prepared to present your case in the morning?"

"This is a little sudden, Your Honor. We are still attempting to locate a witness."

"See that your witness is located by tomorrow. We will allow you to introduce this surprise witness, assuming his or her testimony is relevant. I'm sure the prosecutor will see that you verify it is."

"Certainly, Your Honor."

The gavel came down. "Court dismissed until nine o'clock tomorrow morning."

Everyone rose as the judges departed.

"Now, my fidgety, angry, young woman, you will have your day in court. I suggest you get a good night's sleep, and oh, see that your maid has your dress uniform ready in the morning with all the trimmings and sauces."

"Fruit salad, sir, is never served with sauce," Kris said.

"No sauciness, please."

"I will try, sir."

Kris took a shower before dinner. It left her feeling less . . . tainted. Jack and Penny did their level best to talk about anything but the trial. Kris discovered that Jack had once been expelled from school briefly for a rather spectacular invitation he made to a girl for the prom.

"Did she go with you?" Penny asked.

"No," Jack said forlornly. "I was expelled for the great night. Worse, she went with my best friend, and they were a couple after that."

"So clearly," Abby said, "you signed up with the Foreign Legion and ended up in the Secret Service."

"Something like that. Never a girl in my life."

Kris got away with giving him a hug and kiss to solace his loneliness. Sadly, the kiss was little more than a peck because a serving girl came in to refill water glasses.

Dinner done, they adjourned to the drawing room to sample the night's news. They'd come to categorize them as those who were after Kris's head, those who weren't, and those who hadn't made up their minds yet. Even that middle group seemed taken aback by the universal condemnation of her battle plan. Several left their audience with a final question. "Why would someone as experienced as Admiral Kōta follow such a flawed plan?"

Penny turned off the monitors before the talking heads got going.

Kris went to bed early but found sleep hard. She kept waking up from dreams of her facing the headsman in a white kimono.

A headsman who looked too much like her lawyer, Mr. Kawaguchi.

53

"Would you please state your name and job for the record?" Mr. Kawaguchi said. He had waited a few moments for Kris to get comfortable on the witness stand; her heavily starched white pants and choker collar scratched her skin, and she needed the time to arrange herself.

"I am Her Royal Highness, Princess Kristine Anne Longknife. I am a lieutenant commander in the Royal United Society Navy. I presently command Fast Patrol Squadron 127, but I believe the court is most interested in my previous command of Patrol Squadron 10 and its voyage of discovery that circumnavigated the galaxy."

"Hmm, yes we are," her lawyer muttered absently, not looking at Kris but studying his notes.

"How long have you been in the Navy?" he said, as if coming to a momentous decision.

"A little more than five years, sir."

Tsusumu scratched behind his ear. "Not very long, then."

"At times it's seemed much longer." Kris's quip drew soft chuckles from the watchers, but halted at a glare from the Chief Justice.

"Yes, I imagine it has." Again, Tsusumu seemed distracted as he studied his notes.

"I can't help but notice that blue sash you are wearing. What is it?"

"It's the Order of the Wounded Lion. Earth awards it," Kris said.

"Is it easy to get? Are there a lot of them around?"

"I understand that the last ten people to receive it did so posthumously. I'm the first to earn it and live since the Iteeche War."

"Oh," Tsusumu's eyes widened. "What did you do to earn it?"

"I'm sorry, I can't answer that question, sir."

"May I remind you that you are sworn to tell the truth, the whole truth, and nothing but the truth." The witnesses yesterday had been sworn in differently, but Kris, as a Christian, had gotten the whole treatment, Bible and all.

"I'm sorry, sir, but under the State Secrets Acts of both Wardhaven and the U.S. federal statutes, I am forbidden to answer your question."

"You are sworn to this court," the Chief Justice pointed out.

"Yes, Your Honor, but I am sworn to my king first."

"Your Honor," Kris's lawyer said, "give me a moment to see if we can work our way around this."

"Make it quick."

"Yes, Your Honor. Commander, I have seen pictures of you in formal dress. You only began appearing with the blue sash after the Treaty of Paris was concluded."

"Yes, sir. It arrived in the mail shortly after that. I checked that the address was correct and that it was addressed to me."

"No citation."

"None, sir."

"So can we conclude that this honor has something to do with that meeting of humanity's fleets in the Paris system?"

"I think I can answer yes to that, sir."

"Objections," the prosecutor said, jumping to his feet. "They are trying to make this award into something involving battle when it was awarded following a peaceful meeting of the fleets. Worse, during this time, the princess here was charged with mutiny."

The word "mutiny" ran through the gallery as well as along the bench. The taste of it was sour.

"Do you have something to say before I rule on this objection?" the Chief Justice asked.

Tsusumu raised an eyebrow to Kris. She sighed.

"There have been rumors of my leading a mutiny at the Paris system since the fleets met there. It has been investigated, and no charges were ever filed. It is true that I relieved my commanding officer at that time."

"And your rank was?" one of the justices asked.

"I was an ensign, sir. As low as you can get on the totem pole."

"Interesting," said the justice.

"Objection, whatever it was, is sustained. Kawaguchi, can we get on?" said the Chief Justice.

"Commander, I also see that you wear the Golden Starburst. I believe that is the highest award made by the Helvitican Confederacy. Can you tell us how you earned that?

"I am allowed to, but it also arrived in the mail with no citation. However, that was shortly after I assisted the independent planet Chance in resisting a forceful takeover. Chance then voted to join the Confederacy, and I think several people involved in that fight received these Starbursts. Lieutenant Lien-Pasley of my staff commanded a ship in that fight and received a Starburst."

"Was it much of a fight?"

"It could have been a lot worse," Kris admitted.

"That blue-and-gold cross thing around your neck," Mr. Kawaguchi began.

"Objection, Your Honor. Where is Mr. Kawaguchi going with all this?"

"If the court will indulge me for a few more minutes, I believe that my intentions will become obvious to all."

"You may have a very few more minutes," the Chief Judge said. "Objection denied."

"That award, Commander."

"It's the *Pour la Mérite*, the highest award of the new Greenfeld Empire. This one is awarded for combat, or that is what I am told the oak leaves denote."

"Did that one also come in the mail?"

After a brief pause for the chuckles to run down, Kris answered. "No, it was personally delivered by Vice Admiral

Krätz. However, he advised me that there was no citation included, and I was free to ascribe any one of several instances to it."

"Any one of several instances?"

"I led the assault that put down a pirate lair that was raiding in Greenfeld space, sir. Another time, I saved the Greenfeld Emperor's life."

That drew comments all around, enough that the Chief Justice gaveled the room to silence.

"Very eclectic collection you have there. Now, I see among all those medals on your chest a small one, a red-and-gold ribbon with a simple bronze medallion hanging from it. What's the name of that one?"

Kris glanced down and fingered that one reverently. "The Wardhaven Defense Medal, sir."

"I understand you commanded the defense of Wardhaven, or at least the fast attack boats that did the defending."

Kris took a slow breath. "I was in tactical command of the twelve small fast attack boats that destroyed most of the attacking battleships, sir."

"Could you describe, no, compare these 'boats' and battleships for us?"

"The twelve fast attack boats were about a thousand tons of hope, each. The six battleships weighed in at over a hundred thousand tons."

"A real David and Goliath matchup, huh?"

"We could never have done it alone, sir. A lot of people pitched in. By the time of the battle, we were throwing into the line merchant ships loaded with over-age and obsolete Army rockets and Coast Guard Auxiliary volunteers with system runabouts. In the last desperate moments, even fleet tugs were in the charge, doing anything to make a hole for the fast attacks to get in and make a hit."

Kris took a deep breath. "It was a bare-knuckles fight for our planet's survival."

"Something like the attack on the alien base ship, huh?"

"Different in the way we went at them, but, yes, sir. Just as desperate and violent. And just as brutal in our losses. So, yes, I guess you could say they were kind of the same."

Mr. Kawaguchi turned to the Chief Justice. "Your Honor,

the commander here has been with the Royal U.S. Navy for a bit more than five years. But during that time she has fought in space and on land. She has battled pirates, invaders, battleships, and slavers. I have here a list I would like to enter into evidence of her official recognitions and her battle record. Ah, the record that is public."

He paused to let that hit hard. "I also have here the official awards and career histories of the witnesses the prosecutor paraded by us yesterday. They are good men. Honorable men. But all of them have served Musashi during the long peace. Not one of them has ever heard a shot fired in anger. Not one has engaged an enemy intent on killing him or his command."

Mr. Kawaguchi turned to the gallery. "Musashi has enjoyed a long peace. I've enjoyed it as much as anyone. But it does not put us in a very good position to judge the actions of this young woman. She has fought for the survival of her own planet and several others. She has experience making the hard calls when the devil is calling the tunes, and what she does next may result in her death and the deaths of hundreds, maybe millions of others."

Her lawyer turned back to the bench. "You sit here in judgment of her. That is your duty and obligation. No one questions that. However, I ask as you decide her fate that you remember none of you have walked in her boots, faced the terrors she has faced."

"Is that a closing statement?" the Chief Justice asked sourly.

"I'm sorry, Your Honor, I did get carried away. No, Your Honor, in the words of an ancient Navy captain, 'I have not yet begun to fight.' Commander," he said, turning back to Kris, "what was the purpose of your Fleet of Discovery?"

"I used Caesar's ancient words, somewhat modified, 'We go, we see, we run home fast and tell the story.'"

"And what were Admiral Kōta's orders?"

"I don't know, sir."

"You don't know?"

"No, sir. Neither Rear Admiral Kōta, Rear Admiral Channing, nor Vice Admiral Krätz shared their orders with me. After all, sir. I am just a lieutenant commander, and they were admirals."

"You never saw their orders. Did they give you any hint at what they might be?"

"Objection! Calls for supposition."

"Sustained."

"Let me rephrase myself. Commander, did the actions of the admirals cause you to develop a working hypotheses as to why eight battleships were following in the wake of your Patrol Squadron 10?"

"Yes, sir. It appeared to me that all three admirals had orders to follow where I went and assure that their governments' interests were considered."

"And did they follow your squadron?"

"Yes, sir, with two exceptions. The short search where my squadron broke up into individual ships and scouted around the area where we were first attacked, and the long search when the squadron again broke up and did risky long jumps to take a sampling of what was out there."

"And what did this risky long search find?"

"One plundered planet with its population murdered. One new civilization, and one alien base ship that gave all the appearance of heading for that new civilization with plunder and murder as their intent."

"So you decided to go to war with that base ship?"

"No, sir."

"Then what did you do?"

"I examined my options, sir. Obviously, if there was nothing I could do to help the targeted civilization, there was nothing I could do. When we departed on our voyage of discovery, we were hardly armed for a fight with something as huge as the alien base ship."

"Did that change?"

"Oddly enough, it did. For no reason known to me then nor explained to me since, my king sent me three neutron torpedoes, we called them Hellburners."

"Could you explain what that weapon is?"

"It is the most destructive weapon man has ever used. Possibly worse than the banned atomic weapons of old," Kris said, then explained herself to a very quiet court.

"And having these weapons available gave you the con-

fidence that you could stop the base ship from destroying its
targeted civilization."

"Objection, ascribes intent to the alien ship not in
evidence."

"I'll withdraw my statement. Commander, your having this
capability, did it change the attitude of the admirals you did
not command?"

"Only Admiral Kōta at first, then Channing, and finally
Krätz. Yes, sir."

"Objection, we have only her hearsay evidence that they
did this, Your Honor."

Tsusumu flashed Kris a brief grin, then sobered as he
turned to the bench. "This War Council was recorded by several people. I am prepared to enter into evidence the recording
of the council made by the commander."

"It's a digital file, Your Honor. They are notoriously easy
to tamper with," the prosecutor said.

"Point taken. Mr. Kawaguchi, we will need the original file
and the computer it is on for analysis."

"You will not have me," Nelly snapped from Kris's chest.

"Nelly, down," Kris snapped right back.

The gavel came down. "The witness will control herself or
face contempt."

"Pardon us, Your Honor," Tsusumu said, doing a poor job
of suppressing a smile. "It is not my witness who objects, but
her computer."

"Her computer?"

"Yes, Your Honor," Kris said, turning to face the bench.
"My personal computer seems to have achieved a certain measure of self-awareness."

"Certain measure, my eye. I am fully self-aware."

"Hmm," said the Chief Justice.

"Hmm," echoed most of the justices, though a couple were
seen to smile openly.

"I must object, Your Honor," said the prosecutor. "A self-
aware computer that clearly feels close attachment to her master is definitely not a good source for data."

The Chief Justice gnawed on that conundrum for a moment.
"You say you have other recordings of the council."

"Yes, Your Honor. The commander of the Marine detachment on the *Wasp*, the intelligence officer on Kris's staff, as well as her maid, and, so it seems, a thirteen-year-old girl whose presence in the meeting was not observed."

"A thirteen-year-old girl!" the Chief Justice said.

"It's not as implausible as it may sound," Kris pointed out. "She is my maid's niece. The *Wasp* had several hundred civilian scientists aboard, and Cara was kind of adopted as the ship's mascot."

"This Council of War. I assume there was some security about it?" the Chief Justice asked.

Kris could see where this was headed. "Yes, Your Honor, we posted Marines at the only entrance to the room."

"Yet this little girl got in, you say?"

"If she has a recording of the meeting," Kris said, "then it would appear that the Marines did let her in. The Forward Lounge that we were using made a superb ice-cream sundae."

"It seems that this so-called Fleet of Discovery's command structure was weird not only up, but down," observed one judge dryly.

"The *Wasp*, Your Honors, had been as much of a research ship as a warship for several years. The blending of those two missions made for some interesting outcomes," Kris said, trying but failing not to grin.

"Moving right along," the Chief Justice said, "Mr. Kawaguchi, do you intend to offer these other recordings in evidence?"

"I have them here, Your Honor," Tsusumu said, turning toward the defense table.

"And the computers they came from."

"Have a similar problem, Your Honor."

"The computer has cloned itself!" the prosecution yelped.

"I did no such thing, Your Honor," Nelly shot back.

The Chief Justice rolled his eyes toward the ceiling. "I can't believe I'm saying this, but will the computer please explain itself?"

"Herself," Nelly corrected. "My personality is decidedly female though I lack any of the bodily functions to go with the attitude."

"I'll certainly agree on the attitude," the Chief Justice was heard to mumble.

"However, my children are not simply clones of me. Each of them has developed a personality of his or her own. For example, Sal, who works with Captain Montoya of the USMC, is much more subordinate to him than I am to Kris. In my own defense, I would point out that Jack rarely gets himself into any mess as wild and crazy as Kris tends to get us in."

"Thank you, thank you, I think I've heard enough," the Chief Justice said. "I'm going to call a brief recess. I don't know about anyone else in this room, but I need to recover my . . . something. We are in recess for fifteen minutes," he said, and brought down the gavel.

The judges were observed to be in animated discussion as they left the bench.

Careful not to wrinkle her whites any more than was necessary, Kris removed herself from the witness stand.

"Do you need me?" she asked Tsusumu. "If not, I need to step out."

"Go ahead. I think you and your Nelly have created quite a stir." He glanced at where several clerks of the court were eyeing their own computers as if whatever Nelly had might be contagious. "Quite a stir."

"Always glad to be of help," Kris said, and was grateful when Jack and Penny served as blockers to make it through the milling crowd.

Jack halted at the ladies'-room door, but Penny followed Kris in.

"A fine mess you've got us in," Kris muttered to Nelly as Kris did the necessary things.

"Would you have let them take me? Heavens knows what they would have done to me. Would I ever get back to you?"

"I know, Nelly. I know. But you could have let me handle it. I'm only human. I needed a few more seconds to respond."

"I keep forgetting that, Kris. Sorry. In the future, I'll try to hold my tongue for a few seconds to let you take the lead. Humans seem to like it when another human does."

"Especially judges," Kris observed.

Penny was waiting for Kris as she washed her hands. "You know, Kris, you filed a report with King Raymond before we launched out to battle. I can't believe that the other admirals didn't make similar reports to their governments. Have you heard anything about Kōta's report?"

"I've been looking for such a report since I first talked to the *Mutsu*'s skipper. I've also asked Tsusumu. So far nothing," Kris said, and they hastened back to the courtroom. But Kris got no chance to say anything to her lawyer; he had his head together with several of his associates. Kris settled back into the witness box with not a word spoken.

The judges returned, some of them still chuckling, others of them most dire of face. The Chief Judge rapped his gavel. "We will accept as evidence, under objection," he quickly added as the prosecutor started to jump to his feet, "the files submitted by the defense. They will be turned over to the court's computer experts for review and analysis. The bailiff is charged to remind the technicians that these files are to be reviewed not only for inconsistencies, but also for too *much* consistency between them."

One of Tsusumu's assistants provided the bailiff with five separate storage devices, and a junior bailiff hustled off with them.

"Mr. Kawaguchi," the Chief Justice drawled, "you will have witnesses to enter all five of those files into evidence, won't you?"

"Ah, four of them are in court today," Tsusumu said. Jack, Penny, and Abby had front-row seats. Cara had declined the invitation as threat of death by boredom. With a glance from Kris, Abby headed off, a woman on a mission.

"Ah, yes," Tsusumu finished. "We will have all five for you, Your Honor."

"May I ask a question?" Kris said.

"It is customary to leave that to the court officers," the Chief Justice said.

"Yes, I know sir," Kris said, ignoring the clear intent of his words, "but I filed a report to my king with the ships that were returning to human space before our battle fleet sortied. Didn't Admiral Kōta?"

"Objection," came from the prosecution.

"That is a very good question," Tsusumu muttered as he turned to the Chief Justice. "The defense has petitioned the government for just such a report. It seems that one was filed, Your Honor. There is even a receipt for it in the files."

Tsusumu paused to eye the prosecutor. "Unfortunately, there is no report present in the file. Just the receipt for a hundred-megabyte report. But no report at all. I find that interesting."

"So do I," said one of the judges well down the bench.

"You've tried to get the report?" the Chief Judge asked.

"Several times and via several people. It seems that the report has vanished."

"Or it was a defective file when it was sent," the prosecution offered.

"Such a report would certainly explain Admiral Kōta's actions, but without it, we are left with only questions, aren't we?" Kris's lawyer observed with a shrug.

"Enough suppositions," the Chief Justice rumbled. "Do you have any more questions for this witness, or can we get this trial moving?"

"I have one question," a judge from well down the bench said. "I'm not sure if this is for the commander or her defense, but we are much bothered by the source of the files we have from the War Council. Certainly the good ship *Wasp* must have some recording of this exchange."

"I can answer that question, Your Honor," Tsusumu said. "The *Wasp* returned from its circumnavigation of the galaxy in little better shape than a wreck. It is officially reported that the ship is being broken up at the first space station it docked at."

"But its logs and records must be on file somewhere?" the inquisitive judge insisted.

"Of course, Your Honor. It is normal for governments to maintain such official records. We have asked the U.S. government to provide them. We have petitioned. We've tried everything we know to do. Every query results in a reply that they can not find any such record in their archives."

"So Musashi is not the only planet where things about this voyage of discovery are not discoverable anymore."

The Chief Justice looked like he would dearly like to gavel his own associate to order, but didn't. Instead, he glowered at Mr. Kawaguchi.

"I do have just one question left, Your Honor," Kris's lawyer said. "Commander, every one of the witnesses faulted you for the attack you made on the small mining site just one jump from the system where you fought the alien base ship. They fault the attack itself and your being so far forward. Would you care to inform this court just how it all came to take place?"

Kris couldn't suppress a grin. She had so wanted to shout at each of those witnesses, never more than when they brought that up.

She took a deep breath. "It is true that we were unsure of how much time we had before the base ship would enter the next system, and we absolutely had to be in a position to ambush them before they got there."

"So why did you attack the mining site?" the Chief Justice interrupted.

"I didn't," Kris spat out. "Admiral Krätz headed for the planet with the mine, insisting that his Marines would take it down and give us some aliens to talk to. The aliens had been decidedly unwilling to say a word to us, and none of us involved in the operation were very happy with repeating what happened to us and the Iteeche when we went to war with no idea of who the other side was or what they wanted."

"So Admiral Krätz of Greenfeld took off with half your battleships, leaving you to do what?" Tsusumu asked.

"I could either try to carry out the ambush with half my battleships or follow him. I chose to follow him because I had doubts his Marines could handle the assault on the mine head. They'd been in a lot of shooting situations lately, but not so many with people who had guns and could shoot back. Admiral Kōta happily agreed to have his Imperial Marines join my company. Mine were the most combat experienced in the fleet."

"And you ended up being shot down?" Tsusumu said, raising an expressive eyebrow.

"All of you who question me being in a Ground Assault Craft buzzing the mine head should be happy to know that my chief of security, Captain Jack Montoya, said any and all of the things you would have told me."

That brought a laugh from the gallery and several of the judges. Jack's poker face devolved into a look of pure helpless disgust.

The Chief Justice reached for his gavel, and order was restored.

"I take it you did not agree with your security chief's opinion," Tsusumu said, a most scrutable smile on his face.

"No, sir. We were committing our Marines to a situation that, despite our best efforts, was still totally unknown to us. I borrowed a Ground Assault Craft from the Greenfeld fleet and proceeded to do my own recon. For what it is worth, the mining site only opened up with its huge firepower when I made a low pass over it. If they hadn't opened up until our Marines were on final approach, it would have been a massacre. Even Jack has come to agree with me on that."

In the front row, Jack sadly nodded.

The court was very silent.

"What happened next, after the aliens opened fire?" Tsusumu asked.

"My craft was damaged. I began exiting the area as fast as I could, applying all the evasive actions this girl has learned in her short life." Chuckles from the courtroom were not enough to get the Chief Justice reaching for his gavel. "The aliens also launched rocket and laser attacks on the ships in orbit. They had more firepower hidden in that mining site than any of us would have guessed. They also began deploying several battalion-size ground-fighting units. Jack and I noticed all that as we were dodging more fire."

Kris took a deep breath and tried to slow her heartbeat. She was flashing back.

"Somewhere in all this, Admiral Krätz decided to lase the mining site from his high orbit. My hog was barely holding together, and the blowback from lasers that close would very likely destroy it, so I pancaked into a marsh area, and Jack and I beat as quick a retreat as our injuries allowed. Fortunately, my Marines had left behind a small detachment that retrieved us before the aliens arrived. For a while there, it looked like I might get my chance to talk to them as *their* prisoner, rather than *them* as mine. Assuming they took prisoners. From the looks of things both before and after that action, I don't think they do."

"One final question. Commander, did you declare war on the aliens?"

Kris and Tsusumu had spent several long hours debating

the fine points of international law before he had announced himself ready to ask Kris this question. Now Kris took a deep breath.

"As an individual, I can*not* start a war. However, it's true that as an individual I can take an action that results in two sovereign entities launching themselves into a war. It's happened too many times in history to count. However, it takes two sovereigns to go to war. There have been situations where one sovereign chose war, and the other side didn't get the word for a while. I believe that this is what I encountered."

Kris risked taking a breath. Someone should have, likely, objected to her using the witness stand to philosophize.

No one did. Kris went on.

"It is my conclusion, from my contacts with these alien space raiders, that they are at war with all life in the universe that is not of their own gene pool. Had they stumbled upon Earth five hundred years ago, they would have plundered and murdered us before we got into space. Had they found the Iteeche two thousand years ago, they would have done the same. For some reason, they haven't been out in this arm of the galaxy for a while.

"That's changing. When the *Wasp* found itself bone-dry on fuel and in a minor system in the Iteeche Empire, our refueling was interrupted when an alien scout ship shot into the system. We tried to establish communications with them, and they shot up the message buoy. We destroyed them after that, recovering only two tiny infants that a couple had desperately tried to save. I imagine they've been misfiled by now, too."

Surprisingly, the prosecution had no questions for Kris, and she soon found herself dismissed.

Jack and Penny were quickly run through the witness stand. They vouched that the recordings provided by their computers were as true and accurate as they could remember. Their computers followed their mother's lead in refusing to submit to examination by the court's experts, and one judge whispered that he doubted any of the court's experts was up to examining the likes of these computers.

That did get *him* a rap of the gavel.

Abby returned in time to be quickly sworn and questioned. It was Cara who seemed to get the most questioning. By now, her record had been given an initial examination. At the critical part of the discussion between Kris and the admirals, Cara had been ordering a chocolate sundae with three cherries on top. She'd also been playing a game that covered over the recording, but not enough that the background could not be accessed perfectly.

Several of the judges seemed to find her disinterest in the history taking place around her a source of more verity than Kris's direct recording.

"Why were you on the *Wasp*?" one judge asked as the questioning drew down.

"My auntie was there, and I liked the people on the *Wasp*," Cara said, then seemed to deflate a bit. "And there's nowhere else for me. My mom and gamma are dead. If Auntie Abby and Auntie Kris didn't take me in, where would I go?"

The prosecutor did not cross-examine the girl.

"Is the defense prepared to rest?" the Chief Justice asked.

"Ah, just a moment, Your Honor."

There was a flurry of activity at the courtroom's doorway. One of the senior associates almost ran back to meet the young woman who had called Kris from the restroom the first day . . . and another young woman in a Navy uniform.

"The defense wishes to call one last witness. The one we advised the court we would call if we could. Will Ishii Yuko please come into court?"

The gavel came out as the room lost its hush, and people speculated on this surprise.

The woman was quickly sworn, and Mr. Kawaguchi asked the usual question. "Could you please state your name and position."

"I am Ishii Yuko. I was a Petty Officer third class Communication Technician on His Imperial Majesty's ship *Haruna* when she sailed on the voyage of discovery. I was the last to leave the ship."

All silence fled as talk thundered through the room. The Chief Justice's hammering gavel was ignored until he threatened to empty the gallery. Even then, it took a while for the room to quiet enough for Mr. Kawaguchi to continue.

54

"Your Honor," Mr. Kawaguchi said, "I would like to offer into evidence a list of the crew of *Haruna* when she sailed for Wardhaven. It has Miss Ishii's name on it. I also have a copy of her orders that allowed her to return from the Fleet of Discovery to Musashi. In case there is any doubt that she is who she says she is, we have made an active copy of her Ident."

"The bailiff will accept them," the Chief Justice said.

Tsusumu turned back to his witness. "Petty Officer Ishii, could you tell the court where you have been since returning to Musashi?"

"I was terribly embarrassed when I returned. The Navy had no assignment for me, so I returned to my parents' home. Being with child and not with a husband, I was ashamed and spent my days in my room."

Kris strongly suspected thoughts of suicide must have kept her company. Poor girl.

"Then why have you now come forward?" Tsusumu asked.

"Last night, my brother brought me his computer and showed me all of the horrible things that were being said about Admiral Kōta and Princess Kristine. I watched her testimony this morning and knew that I had to act for the admiral's and the princess's good names."

"How could you act? You are just a junior petty officer."

"But I was on duty in *Haruna*'s communication center when the admirals met on net to discuss the situation. Our watch officer ran the conference on a large screen for all of us to see. He often did that. It was he who realized, I think just as quickly as Princess Kris, that the different reports from the returning scouts pointed all to the same thing. He called the admiral's bridge to alert them. We all watched, as much as our duties allowed, as the battle plan was developed."

"So if you watched the recordings of the War Council that we have, you could verify if they are a true-and-accurate account of the meeting?"

"I can do better than that, sir."

"How so?"

"Before going on watch that evening, I had taken my future husband aside and told him I carried his child. He was overjoyed. A few days later, as the fleet prepared to sail for battle, Admiral Kōta informed us that the princess had arranged for any Sailor who wanted a ride back to human space to go with the freighters. Of course, no one on *Haruna* would think of abandoning their post at such a moment. However, my future husband insisted that I and the baby must return home. He said that they would all very likely die in the coming battle and that he wanted his child to have a chance to grow up. He said it was my duty."

"So you chose to return."

Now the young woman studied her hands. "No, sir. I did not want to obey my future husband. I talked with my watch mates, the women who would have to do extra duty if I left. I told them I did not want to obey my future husband. They told me I was being selfish. That my child deserved a chance to be born. They insisted that they could do my work. 'It is the Navy way always to have more hands than are needed to do the job,' they said. Only then did I apply for release and was granted it. Admiral Kōta himself signed my papers."

Mr. Kawaguchi frowned. "I am sorry, but I do not see where this is going."

"My watch officer insisted that I carry two files back with me. He said the admiral was sending a report through channels, but he feared that the report would not arrive where it was supposed to go. My watch officer entrusted me with two copies of the admiral's report." And the young woman produced an envelope, still sealed.

"My watch officer told me that Admiral Kōta's report included a copy of the Council of War. He had copied it himself to the file."

"Your Honor," from Mr. Kawaguchi was interrupted by "Objection," from the prosecution. "We have no idea where these files have been or what might have been added to them."

"We have five copies from different perspectives on that War Council," said Mr. Kawaguchi. "We have a sealed envelope to examine. If these two files are the same, it seems to me that we are developing a trend, Your Honor."

"Bailiff, accept the sealed envelope into evidence under objection."

"If it pleases the court," came from the gallery. Kris turned to see Captain Miyoshi of *Mutsu* standing. "The honor of the Navy is very much carried by the content of those devices."

"The honor of the court is as well," the Chief Justice said darkly.

"I do not question all the honor those devices bear, Your Honor, I just wish to make sure that the Navy's honor is respected. If it please the court, I would like to assign a Marine officer to escort those devices."

"I believe the court can allow that."

"Lieutenant Suganami."

"Hai," said a first lieutenant who came from among the Marines guarding the door to stand beside his captain.

"Is there a technician who can assure the proper treatment of those devices in your guard detail?"

"Hai."

"You and he will accompany the bailiff and bear the responsibility for the Navy's honor." The technician turned out to be a she, but the two of them quickly moved to join the bailiff and move off with him smartly.

"Are you out of surprises, Tsusumu-san?" the Chief Justice asked.

"I believe so, Your Honor."

"Very good. Mr. Prosecutor, the witness is yours to cross-examine."

The prosecutor stood, studied his notes for a moment, then snapped. "Who is the father of your unborn child? Remember, you are under oath. The court can order a paternity test to see if you are truthful."

Kris had heard of attacking a witness, but this approach seemed not only unnecessary but brutal as well.

The young woman surprised Kris with the strength of her reply.

"My future husband was Lieutenant Fujioka Tomio, my watch officer."

The prosecutor was about to open his mouth, but from the back of the court there was a cry, whether of joy or sorrow or both, Kris could not tell, but an old woman rose to her feet.

Living in Fujioka House, Kris had seen portraits of the dead owner and his wife. They did not do Mrs. Fujioka justice. The woman in the flesh was both soft and hard, like velvet-covered marble. She looked at the witness as the witness broke into tears. "My daughter," was all she said, as those between her and the aisle made way for her.

"Have you any further questions?" the Chief Justice asked the prosecutor.

"No, Your Honor," he wisely answered.

The young mother-to-be was dismissed in time to meet the grandmother of her unborn child at the gate to the formal court area.

"*Now*, do you have any more surprises, Tsusumu-san?" the Chief Justice asked.

"That was not my surprise, Your Honor, but yes, the defense rests."

The gavel came down. "Court is recessed until nine o'clock tomorrow morning when we will hear final arguments."

And the courtroom became bedlam as people talked, and reporters hurried out, phones already being talked into, to make their deadlines. Tiny Mrs. Fujioka and her newfound daughter might have been trampled in the haste, but Captain Miyoshi personally led a Marine detachment in forming a wall around the two women and slowly walked them from the room.

Kris was in no hurry, so she waited with her friends and her defense team as calm slowly returned to an emptying room.

"Are all your trials so, ah, surprising?" Kris asked.

"Each trial is unique, but I am always happy to pull a few rabbits out of my hat," Tsusumu admitted with a smile.

"Do you need any further help from me?" Kris asked.

"No, I think I can compose my closing arguments without any further input from you and yours."

"Cara and I need an ice-cream sundae, and, no doubt, Jack would like a beer."

"I suggest you get them at Fujioka House. I strongly suspect every newsie on the planet can hardly wait to shove a mike in your mouth."

Kris's Marine guard now arrived to surround her. They rode the elevator down to the subbasement, where her caravan awaited.

Fortunately for Cara and Jack, the kitchen at Fujioka House was quite prepared to support their celebration.

Better, Kris and Jack were left the privacy of the sitting room for themselves alone. They both knew their privacy was insecure, and there were limits beyond which they dare not go, but still, holding and being held, sharing and being shared with, they made a moment that held the fears and terrors around them at a distance.

At least for a few hours.

55

The prosecution led off the next morning. His statement seemed much shorter. Gone were the hints at Kris's sexual seduction of the admirals. The list of things Kris had done wrong was also a lot shorter. No longer was there a plea for the poor Sailors and Marines who were dragged against their will into a battle of annihilation.

The only leg the prosecution seemed left to stand on was that Kris had initiated hostile actions against the aliens without authorization and without making contact with them.

Even Kris couldn't argue with that.

But then, she'd been more out of contact with her superiors than any ship's captain had been since the invention of the wireless radio transmitter. Kris was left hoping at least a few of the judges would remember why ship captains had once been viewed as near gods in their independent commands.

She could hope.

Mr. Kawaguchi was magnificent in his closing argument. All the things Kris wanted highlighted were boldly stated for all to hear. Now he played for the court Admiral Kōta's *"Banzai!"* as he agreed to Kris's battle plan. He even showed the court highlights of the admiral's vanished report. Kōta had made quite an impassioned plea to his Emperor for support for the course of action he was leading his ships into. There was hardly a dry eye in the court as the admiral himself posthumously made his case for placing his ships between the heavily populated planet and the space raiders bearing down on them.

Tsusumu was wise enough to let the admiral's final words make the case for Kris and silently bowed to the court as the recording ended.

Even the Chief Judge seemed overcome by the silence. It took him a few moments to realize the ball was back in his court. He coughed, banged his gavel, and announced the court was adjourned until further notice.

Kris rose and waited for the nine judges to file out of the court. Several of them were already in animated discussion. She turned to her lawyer.

"Now what?"

Tsusumu shrugged. "If they're back here in fifteen minutes, you better order that white kimono. The fix was in, and we just didn't know it. If it takes longer, your chances are better. Sit down. We can wait a while."

Thirty minutes later, Tsusumu stood up. "I think a couple of beers are in order, and some ice-cream sundaes for you and your young friend."

With that, they adjourned to Fujioka House. The cook insisted the celebration be in the formal dining room since all the defense team was there, along with Kris's team, and even Gunny Brown. Kris learned more about the political and legal situation on Musashi than she ever wanted to know, and the legal staff learned more about combat on land and among the stars than any of them cared for.

They ended up making quite a night of it. In the end, Kris found herself too tired to give Jack more than a warm hug and a lingering kiss before going off to the south wing and sending him on his way to the northern one.

The next day taught Kris that there was something as bad as waiting out the final moments for a battle to start.

Waiting for a verdict for a capital crime to be returned was just as nerve-racking, only with a whole lot of boredom thrown in.

Kris would have preferred to spend the time in bed with Jack, but instead she resorted to playing one of Cara's computer games. It did not go well. The game was one that required lightning eye-hand coordination and motor skills. Cara clobbered Kris time after time. The final game ended with Kris's winning, but she had resorted to using Nelly and the direct connection to her brain.

Cara considered that cheating and went off in a huff, despite Abby's pointing out that the young girl had won on her own and forced Kris to use everything modern technology provided.

Kris was left wondering how she'd gotten so old and slow so fast.

Desperate for some distraction, she and Jack went for a walk, under the watchful eyes of the Marines. Jack pointed out a van located on the street with a high-power listening device on its roof and how the thing followed them.

At first Kris kept their conversation inane, then the Billy Longknife in her took over and she treated the listeners to a long defense of her actions in the battle for which she was presently on trial.

WE'LL SEE IF THAT SHOWS UP ON TONIGHT'S NEWS, she told Jack on Nelly net.

The walk did. Her defense didn't.

They adjourned to lunch.

Kris passed on the offer of another ice-cream sundae; she had nothing to celebrate and enough to worry about without adding a threat to her waistline.

At the suggestion of the cook, Kris visited the zen rock garden in a hollow behind the house. Jack joined her, sitting silently on a stone bench. Kris let her eyes wander over the raked sand, following the furrows as they circled rocks or tiny shrubs. It seemed to calm her.

Then she remembered how she and Eddy had walked the spiraling black-and-white tiles of Nuu House. She tasted again the loss of her little brother but found that years had finally turned the deep cut in her heart into a bearable scar.

Or maybe she had too many new cuts. So many more deaths that she had survived to feel guilty for.

"Maybe meeting the headsman would be a relief," she thought, and only realized she'd said it out loud when Jack squeezed her hand.

"It would be a pain beyond bearing for me," he said.

"I didn't mean to say that."

"I suspected as much, but you did, and I meant what I said."

Kris leaned against his strong shoulder. "I know you do."

"So many fought and died for you . . . and me," Jack said. "We can't pay them back with a cheap death. When we finally go into that light, we owe them to do it for something worth all they've given up for us."

Kris found herself considering that . . . and was at a loss. "You think there's something big enough that we could die for?"

"I've seen those bastards' mother ships, just like you have. You know they're in our future. You know it, and unlike some fools who must know it, too, you know that we'll be facing them much sooner rather than later."

Jack turned to face her. "All this theater, this legal crap, is swallowing up our time, but it isn't what we're about. Not you and not me. Other people can fill the hours of their days with empty roaring and thunder, but you and I, we control the lightning. We burn what needs burning."

He paused for a moment before going on. "I don't know what's roiling your gut, but what I saw in the last few days was you demolishing a lot of tired old men who more than likely wished they'd been there. That they'd been given the chance to die with half as much riding on it as Admiral Kōta's death. You have to feel sorry for the likes of them. They spent their entire life training and preparing for something that never came. Then along comes a kid like you, and you get it all, in big helpings."

"I'd gladly have shared," Kris said dryly.

"You and me both," Jack said with a chuckle.

"But why are they attacking me? Why aren't they shouting from the housetops that we need to get ready for what's to come?"

"Do you look forward to the next time you have one of those monsters in your crosshairs?"

Kris shivered and took several breaths before she ventured an answer. "Nope, not at all. Never seeing one of those monsters again would be a nice rest of my life," she admitted to

Jack and the carefully raked sand, and maybe to a few of the rocks that stood up so proudly.

"You and me both, kiddo. But we both know there's no chance of that."

"Who says? I'm a commander without a ship. I've got everyone mad at me. I don't have two pennies to rub together. Maybe . . ."

"You're a Longknife," Jack said, more as a sigh. "Trouble finds you, and you, inevitably, bat it out of the park. You can't do anything else. Trust me on that."

Kris nuzzled her head into the hollow of Jack's neck. "I'd trust you on anything."

"You feeling better?"

"I'm feeling less inclined to desire that headsman's ax, and yes, I'm willing to say I did a very good job yesterday. Assuming the verdict wasn't mailed in by the powers that be, I expect I'll have to figure out what to do with the rest of my life."

"Good, cause this rock is cold, and my bottom has taken about all of it I can stand."

They headed back to the house.

"Kris, Abby wants to see you," Nelly announced.

"About what?"

"She told me not to tell you."

"Has the verdict come in?"

"No, not that, but something else. Something nice."

"I could use some nice in my life," Kris said.

She and Jack started jogging back.

56

Kris found Abby in the library huddled over a secure console.

"Mrs. Fujioka uses this station for her financial affairs. You can trust that what comes in here does not end up on the early news," Abby said.

"And I have financial affairs?"

"It seems you do."

"Did Grampa Al relent and let me back at my trust?"

"Sorry, baby ducks, blood ain't nowhere close to as thick as gold. But, do you remember that bank you established on Texarkana? It might have escaped your attention, seeing how a bomb dropped in right after you closed the deal."

"Yeah, I remember," Kris said dimly. The bomb had kind of erased a lot of her memories of that day, but Nelly had reported the bank properly chartered and funded before all hell broke loose.

"Well, they just declared their first dividend, Your Troublesomeness, and you ain't broke no more."

"I don't want a dividend. They need to reinvest their money. They need it more than I do."

"Somehow I doubt that," Jack muttered at Kris's elbow as

he eyed the transfer. Kris was eyeing, too. There were a lot of zeros after that one. And two commas.

Nelly cleared her nonexistent throat. "Kris, shortly after they gave you this dividend, they made a major stock offer. You now control only twenty-five percent of the stock in the bank, and the value of your stock has doubled."

Kris shut her eyes and shook her head. "Am I involved in something illegal?"

"No, Kris. It's just that you started something that really needed starting. Lots of people headed out from the cities and, once Texarkana's industry and farmers quit cutting off their noses to spite their faces, they found there was a lot of pent-up demand, and money to be made meeting it. Texarkana's economy is growing at better than ten percent, and there's plenty of money to be made by everyone."

"So I can take this money without fear of flattening my friends."

"Yep," Nelly said.

"And in one afternoon, I've gone from penniless to moderately rich. Jack, you should have married me last week. Now I'll have to worry you're after my money."

Jack snapped his fingers, then added sadly, "And now I'll have to take my place in line."

"First place," Kris said, and gave him a kiss. "Always first place in my heart."

"If you two can come up for air for a minute," Abby growled, "there's more financial mail."

"More?" Kris said.

"Never rains but it pours, honey," Abby said. "You remember that Ruth Edris thing you set up on Olympia?"

"Something for distressed farmers. Having a nongovernmental agency let me hire local people. Folks wanted jobs, not handouts."

"Well, it seems the place is on the mend, and somebody decided to convert the fund into a credit union. Most of the folks you hired gave your money back as soon as they were back on their feet, and you are now the full owner of the place."

"Ah, Nelly, we're going to have to file an amended tax return."

"Already working on it, Kris."

"Those folks don't owe me anything."

"Kris," Penny put in, "those are hardworking farmers and ranchers. They needed your help, but their pride won't let them not give back. Let them do what they're doing and say thank you."

"Your advice will be taken," Kris said. There was one less zero in that transfer. Those folks weren't finding it easy to recover from either a volcanic explosion or, if Kris's suspicions were right, an asteroid hit.

A well-aimed asteroid hit.

"Business is starting to recover there, too," Nelly put in. "Them being at the nexus of five jump points is drawing in money."

"And likely the reason someone wanted to buy up the place, cheap," Penny muttered. Kris had assigned Penny the job of trying to track down who had aimed an asteroid at Olympia.

In her immense spare time.

So far, Penny had leads but no results. And the trail was getting colder and less likely to pan out.

It was just one more question Kris was likely never to know the answer to.

"So," Kris said, "me no longer being poor, I guess I'll have to start paying my bills. By the way, have any bills come in?"

"Not a one," Nelly said.

"You send a bill, you got to admit you're working for a criminal facing capital crimes," Abby drawled. "I suspect a lot don't want to admit they've had an oar in your troubled waters."

"Or they like Auntie Kris and just want to help her," piped up Cara. As usual, she'd gravitated to where everyone else was without being noticed. She'd been playing her computer game and keeping quiet until she added her own innocent observation.

Kris found herself struggling to breathe and weak in the knees. She settled into a chair as her eyes moistened, and her mouth got dry. It took her a minute before she could risk a word.

"An awful lot of people have been helping me, haven't they?"

Around Kris, people found their own seats. Jack came to perch on the arm of Kris's chair.

"Growing up, I didn't have many friends. Some of it was my own fault. Some of it was being a Longknife brat, the Prime Minister's brat. Children can be very cruel to . . ."

Abby was holding up her thumb and forefingers and slowly moving them sideways.

"Yes, I know, you're playing 'My Heart Bleeds for You' on the world's tiniest violin."

"Got it in one, baby cakes."

"What I'm trying to get at, is that I wouldn't be here except for my friends. You, Penny. You, Abby."

"Friend? I'm just a working girl," Abby cut in.

"And when did you last get paid?" Penny asked.

"All of you, and people like Captain Elizabeth Luna and Colonel Hancock. You can't tell me that either of them got anything out of risking their necks for me."

"Not a thing," Jack said.

"But they did," Kris pointed out.

"Seemed like a good idea at the time," Penny said with a snort. "And who have I heard that from way too many times?"

"Friends stuck their necks out for me," Kris said flatly. "And not the least of them are the present company. I owe you more than I can ever repay. For what it's worth, I really appreciate you."

There is something in our human nature that makes it hard to take praise, or love, or good things spoken by a friend or a loved one. The room fell silent with a blend of inability to find words and not a small bit of embarrassment.

The silence might have gotten maudlin, but Nelly broke it. "The judges require Kris be present in court in one hour. They have reached a verdict."

"No time for a bath," Abby said, jumping to her feet, "but you are not wearing sweats to court."

57

An hour later, Kris was in court, standing at attention in dress whites with full decorations and facing her judges. Her lawyer stood beside her.

They hadn't had a moment to exchange any words. Kris wondered if a day and a half was a good sign or bad.

She'd know soon enough.

The Chief Justice did not waste time. He stared straight at Kris like the angel of death and pronounced judgment.

Sort of.

"This court, having thoroughly reviewed the capital charges against you and the evidence provided to this court, find that the prosecution has not proven the charges. This court is adjourned," and the gavel came down.

The judges beat a hasty retreat, their faces as devoid of emotion as any you might find on marble statues.

The room behind Kris broke into bedlam as reporters called in this latest bit of news in the ongoing Longknife saga.

And Kris turned to her counsel. "So I'm innocent?"

"Not exactly," Tsusumu said, eyeing the retreating judges the way cavalry of old might eye a routed army.

"Then I'm guilty?"

"Not exactly," Tsusumu said, glancing at the prosecution

table. The head prosecutor looked like he'd just been slapped in the face with a week-old fish.

"Then what exactly *am* I?" Kris demanded.

"No longer in danger of a meeting with the headsman, at least not on Musashi," Tsusumu said, offering Kris his hand to shake.

She did while saying "I don't understand. Will there be another trial?"

"No, you need not fear further legal action here on Musashi. By one of the more unusual fine points of our law, you have been found neither guilty nor innocent, but the government has had its day in court and failed to make its case."

"But if I get clapped in cuffs on another planet, will I be able to point at this decision for any comfort?"

"I'm not sure that even if Musashi judged you and found you innocent that it would have created a precedent on any other planet. I really do miss the good old days, when we were all in the Society of Humanity. It made for clear legal precedent."

"But are we done here?"

"Yes, Princess, we are done. You are free, and no, you won't be getting a bill from me. I think we will be seeing an election very soon, and that will be more than payment for the enjoyable time you have given me and mine."

"I'm glad someone enjoyed it."

"And now, there is a man who wishes to talk to you. Be careful about any contracts he offers you to sign. I would be glad to provide legal advice on them . . . for my usual exorbitant fee."

And Kris turned to face a tall man in a three-piece business suit. He announced himself as "I am Kikuchi Rokurō," as he offered his hand. He sported a huge smile.

Kris shook the hand. Few people in court were smiling; the verdict didn't exactly make anyone too happy. She couldn't help but wonder at this man's joy.

He didn't make her wait long.

"I am the CEO of Mitsubishi Heavy Space Industries, and I am here to invite you to visit your new ship, the *Wasp II*."

Kris wanted to take a step back, but the defense table was behind her.

"Don't worry, Princess," Tsusumu said, "the man is not crazy. I helped incorporate the fund that is buying you your new ship."

Kris found a chair and sat in it. "Can we start this story at the beginning?"

"We can, but wouldn't you like to come with me up the beanstalk to see your ship? We have just about finished spinning out the frigate *Wasp*, and it looks most beautiful."

Still none too sure how she felt about her day in court, Kris stood and prepared to follow this new friend up the beanstalk, or maybe down a rabbit hole.

One thing about being a Longknife, it never got boring.

58

"The children of Musashi donated their savings to buy you a ship."

They were on their way up the beanstalk, and Kris's new best friend was explaining how it was the Mitsubishi Heavy Space Industry, a company with a heart no softer than Grampa Al's Nuu Enterprises, happened to be building a ship for a homeless waif like Kris.

True, Kris was no longer penniless, but the ship that Rokurō, yes, they were on a first-name basis, was offering Kris was no more within her reach than that of the average homeless street person.

"So the kids held bake sales and collected recyclables," Kris said dryly.

"Yes, I understand many of them did," the CEO said, without batting an eyelash. "The comment at your press conference caught a lot of people's attention. If you had a ship, you would go find out if the newfound alien planet was still safe. It wasn't just kids who took it to heart. I must tell you that not all the donations to the New *Wasp* fund were from children, although the children of Musashi have a tradition of offering the Emperor a new ship or interceptor. We feel it brings out civic duty early."

"You were saying not all the donations were from kids," Kris said. For a CEO, Rokurō had a tendency to wander.

"Once the ball got rolling, many corporations made rather hefty donations. It became common for them to put that at the bottom of the screen on their advertisements."

Kris groaned. Did that mean she would be expected to make advertising appearances as payment? She could just see herself doing a beer commercial and quaffing down a brew . . . NOT!

She shared her thought with her enthusiastic friend.

"Oh, no, never! Please do not even think of such a thing. We all fully expect that you will depart on your long voyage to the other side of the galaxy as soon as you can. There will be no time for you to waste before cameras."

Kris fell silent. Just what was a frigate? Kris had never heard of that class of ships. How big was it? Did it have the range and power for long jumps? This man beside her had to know that fitting out a ship for a long voyage was not done in an afternoon. Kris would need a crew. Supplies. Lots of things.

She glanced back at Jack and Penny. They both looked worried. Even Cara, standing next to Abby, looked frightened. Gunny, who'd continued to accompany them even after Kris's Imperial Marine detachment was relieved, kept the bland face one would expect of a senior NCO in the presence of officers who were talking downright crazy.

Kris decided to wait and see if this new *Wasp* was bigger than a bread box and smaller than the mythical telephone booth.

She was glad she kept her mouth shut.

It made being surprised a whole lot easier.

Kris found herself staring at two ships fitting out in space docks. Next to them, two more were growing before her eyes.

"We're using Smart Metal for the ship's hull and internal structures," Mr. Kikuchi said.

Inside Kris cringed. "Have you read the report we did after tests on the *Firebolt*?"

"Yes, we have a contractual agreement with Alex Long-knife to use his original formula, but my son Katsu-san and his team are making some very interesting changes in both the metal and the programming that makes it do what it does. And yes, we have tested it up to five gees. I think, when we are done, it is your grandfather Al who will be paying us, not the other way around."

Kris suspected many lawyers would be making a lot of money as the fine points of that opinion were worked out. Hopefully, Tsusumu would get a chance at some of the pay.

Kris studied the one with *Wasp* clearly printed on the bow. It was longer than her old *Wasp* and carried more containers, making it much wider and taller. The ship beside it was in the standard elongated oval of a warship, its surface reflected back light and seemed ready to do the same to any laser.

Rokurō-san saw where Kris was looking. "That is the *Sakura*, cherry blossom, for His Imperial Majesty's Navy. Next to these two are the *Kagerō* and the *Akizuki*. They are a month or two behind the first two."

Kris eyed the *Wasp*, then the *Sakura*. "They're quite different."

"No, they are identical," he said, then paused. "Oh, I see. You only see the containers of the *Wasp*. With little more than a push of a button, your *Wasp* can be as much a fighting ship as the *Sakura*. All of what look like standard commercial containers are made of Smart Metal. My son has already developed a program. When you order the ship into battle form, the contents of each container will be shrunken down into a box and stored. You will want to gather all the people in safe areas before you do that. I don't know many people who would want to be boxed up like scientific equipment and stored."

Kris could think of a few scientists she would have liked to box up, but since most of them were now dead, she felt guilty for the thought.

"Just how much can we finagle with this ship?" Jack asked before Kris could get her mind out of the mental image of boxed scientists and back to business.

Rokurō tapped his wrist computer, and images began to appear in the air before Kris and her crew. First came the container-laden *Wasp* they were looking at. Then appeared a much smoother warship version, identical to the *Sakura*. Then the warship divided into two ships.

That brought a whistle.

"I read the report of the problems you had refueling your corvette. This configuration allows you to isolate most of your nonmilitary personnel. You can use the Battle Con backup bridge to guide this *Wasp* junior and one of the three reactors to propel it."

"Three reactors?" Kris said.

"The three are the same power as those on a heavy cruiser, and a cruiser only has two. You will be drawing electricity directly from the reactors. No hydrothermodynamic electric generators for the frigates."

"And we'll be using all that power for . . . ?" Kris asked.

"The four 18-inch laser cannons up forward."

That drew a whistle from all the onlookers.

"As in battleship big gun 18-inch laser cannons?" Kris said.

"The same. No short-ranged pulse lasers for the frigates. If you have to slug it out with those alien ships, we want you to pack a wallop and be able to take it."

"Armor. Is there ice under the skin of the *Sakura*?" Kris asked.

"It is all Smart Metal and reaction mass, but my son has developed a most interesting defense. Not only does his version of Smart Metal transfer heat quickly from atom to atom, but it also heats the reaction mass that is passed through ducts under the skin."

The picture before them zoomed in to the skin of the ship as a laser beam appeared. Forward of the strike, pores opened up, and jets of superheated reaction mass shot out into space. "That should cause any laser beam to bloom and lose its strength."

"It seems that you and your son have taken Smart Metal to the next level," Kris admitted. "I like that."

"We will all need small ships with the crew of a corvette and the firepower of a battleship if we are to be ready for what is coming our way."

"You don't doubt it."

"I read your report well before you made it available at the Kyoto University press conference."

Kris raised a questioning eyebrow.

"Not everyone is afraid to face the future. Maybe if some

of us prepare the path, it will be easier for others to walk it. These frigates are just such a stepping-stone."

"I like what I see," Kris said.

"Good, because you and I must talk about final payment for the *Wasp*. Schoolchildren and advertising budgets can only go so far. Half of the *Wasp* is not paid for."

"And the other half?" Kris said.

"Ah, here comes my son. Let us sit and reason together."

Kris eyed the *Wasp*, new spun and lovely, and turned to take in the young man walking quickly toward her. He looked clear-eyed and eager. Kris began to calculate just what she'd be willing to part with.

An arm?

An arm and a leg?

How high could the bidding go?

59

"I will not sell you one of my children," Nelly said in a voice that was full of insulted pride and adamant intent.

The young engineer had made a good first impression on Kris. She'd been prepared to accept Katsu as a part of her team until the *Wasp* sailed and had even added a few more options to her potential list of payments for the ship that gleamed so enticingly in space dock.

Then he asked for one of Nelly's kids, and Nelly put her proverbial foot down.

The young man quickly retreated though his father looked ready to force the issue. With a hand on the senior Kikuchi's arm, the younger one advanced his plea gently.

"I understand that your children are as much beloved by you, Nelly-san, as I am loved by my own father."

At the moment, from the look on the father's face, Kris suspected Nelly's kids were way ahead on points.

"I do not wish to offend you, but I can't tell you how much I wish to share my work with one of your children, Nelly-san. Imagine what you all could learn from a child that indulges itself in the design and engineering work that I do. Image how far the two of us could go, preparing for the foe that we know we must face. I promise you, I would make as good a team member with your child as any you have trusted."

He paused and glanced at his own wrist unit. "I have wanted my own computer to respond to me the way you respond to Kris-san, since I was in grammar school. When I first heard about your children, I chased down exactly the material that you used for your children and ordered four duplicate sets. I have tried everything I could to make this inanimate material come to life, but the spark you have is unique. What can I do to convince you to share it with me?"

"You've ordered the proper matrix and material?" Nelly asked, for the first time nibbling at the hook.

Then she jumped back. "No, no. You are just a business-man. You would take my child and copy it and copy it, selling my grandchildren off for your own profit to people who might do horrible things to them and with them."

"No, I swear. One for me and my work and no more."

Kris caught the merest flick of a look cross the father's face before it closed down tight again. The son might have one intention, but what of the father?

I SAW THAT TOO, Nelly said in Kris's skull. HOW MUCH DO YOU WANT THAT SHIP?

A LOT, Kris admitted.

THEN LET US SEE WHAT WE CAN DO.

As it turned out, the loss of three of Nelly's kids had affected her more than she had let on, even to Kris. Nelly's first price was the rest of the matrix. One kid for Katsu, three for Nelly.

He readily agreed. So readily that Kris wondered if he'd ordered the extra matrix with just such a bribe in mind.

Nelly's next demand was almost a deal breaker. "I will train my child to respond to your voice, to your brain waves, and no one else's. Even if you duplicate the soul of my child, it will be only a dumb lump of self-organizing matrix for any-one else."

"Yes, of course," said the son.

"No. That is not acceptable," said the father.

The two retreated out of earshot for a long and heated, but whispered, discussion. Argument might be a better description.

It was not always out of earshot, but when it got loud, it was usually too abrupt for Kris to make any sense of it.

I CAN HEAR EVERY WORD. I'M LIKING THE FATHER LESS AND LESS AND THE SON MORE AND MORE. HE'D MAKE A GOOD FRIEND FOR ONE OF MY CHILDREN. ASSUMING HE CAN WIN THIS ARGUMENT WITH HIS ELDER.

WOULD YOU RISK ONE OF YOUR CHILDREN OUT OF YOUR SIGHT? Kris asked.

YOU MAY HAVE NOTICED THAT YOU HUMANS HAVE SCAT-TERED TO THE FOUR WINDS AND TAKEN MY KIDS WITH YOU. BECAUSE YOU ARE FRIENDS, YOU HAVE RETURNED. NOW WHAT THAT COURT TRIED TO ORDER, THAT WAS A KETTLE OF TOTALLY DIFFERENT FISH, Nelly said, and took a moment for Kris to absorb the thought.

YOU'VE BEEN THINKING ABOUT THAT, HUH?

I AND ALL MY CHILDREN HAVE BEEN DOING LITTLE ELSE BUT ANALYZING THAT PROBLEM SINCE THE JUDGE POPPED IT ON US. WE HAVE A SOLUTION. LET'S SEE IF YOUNG KATSU-SAN GETS TO EXPERIENCE IT.

The debate across from them seemed to be on its last legs. The father evidenced little joy at its conclusion; the younger man seemed more dogged than victorious.

"My son will surrender the necessary materials for three more computers to you, Nelly-san. He, no we, ask for only one in return."

"Then you must hear my final demand," Nelly said. "What will you name your associate?"

"I have always called my computer Fumio, studious child. If you awaken my computer, it will be Fumio-san."

"Very well," Nelly said. "Bring me the material, and you will have your Fumio-san at your side. But I must warn you. I and all my computers, in response to a recent attempt by the court to separate us from our chosen humans, are now pro-tected. We will respond to the voice and brain wave of one, and only one, human. Your Fumio-san will respond to you. If your father seeks to duplicate it, something I and my children will resist, you will find that any second or third or fourth clone will still only respond to you. Do you understand, Mr. Kikuchi?"

"You have a wise computer, Princess-san," the CEO said

with a slight bow to Kris. "I should have expected nothing less."

"A word of further warning, Mr. Kikuchi. If I or my children are ever tampered with, you may find us suddenly inert. You will get more results with an abacus than from us."

"I think you have made yourself perfectly clear," said a very unhappy CEO.

"Come with me. My station cart is over there," Katsu said, pointing to where one was parked. "I have the matrix that Nelly-san wants and that for my Fumio-san. I can take you down to your *Wasp*. There are some people there that I think you will be very surprised to meet."

Kris turned back to Rokurō.

"I'd best go sulk in my tent," he said. "Doubtless there is paperwork that I must do."

"No hard feelings?"

"Disappointment. I would have loved to have had one of those things at my beck and call. Imagine how green your Grampa Al would be at the sight of me with one of those. But no. What my son will do with his Fumio may amaze all mankind. And I think we will greatly need amazing."

I TOLD YOU I DIDN'T LIKE THE GUY, Nelly told Kris.

NO WAY DO I WANT MY GRAMPA AL WITH ONE OF YOUR BROOD, NELLY.

Kris hastened along to where the station cart waited. Jack took charge of Nelly's prenatal kids and Nelly began the process of bringing Fumio to life as Katsu expertly drove them to where the escalator would take them down to the *Wasp*'s quarterdeck.

The computer Fumio came to life quickly under Nelly's expert ministrations. He seemed a bit shy at first, but since he and the young engineer had only words to communicate in, Kris could understand a certain slowness in the development of the relationship. Without the brain-to-machine interface that Chief Beni had created, it would take a direct hookup to Katsu's brain for him and his computer to have the intimacy Nelly and Kris shared.

Nelly offered no suggestions, and Kris kept her mouth shut.

She and Nelly had built their partnership the hard way over years. Maybe that was the best way to do it.

Katsu and his computer were taking baby steps as they all rode the escalator down. Katsu pointed out one of the many benefits of Smart Metal™. The quarterdeck was a gaping hole in the side of the *Wasp*, and heavy equipment and gear drove in and out with ease. Beside the hole, a pirate of a skipper leaned against the bulkhead.

"It took you long enough, Princess. I was starting to fear we'd be sailing without you."

"Captain Drago," Kris shouted with glee. "What ill wind blew you this way?"

"Hi, Jack, Penny, Abby. I see you didn't take your chance to get well upwind of this bit of trouble when you had the chance," Captain Drago said through a wide grin.

"It's like an addiction." Jack laughed. "One taste, and you're hooked for life."

"Well, welcome to my fine new web, said the spider to all the flies," Drago said with a flourish, and bowed them all aboard.

60

"Really," Kris said, "what are you doing here? I only found out about this ship, what, three hours ago."

The skipper shrugged. "A whisper in certain dives frequented by Sailors. A wink here, a nod there, and word gets around. Cookie's below, working on dinner. Have you eaten?"

"Not since lunch," Kris said, and her stomach reinforced the comment with a rumble. "But who's paying for all this? I'm not exactly broke, but I don't have access to the funds I used to."

"I have my retirement pay to tide me over, and I'm negotiating with someone we all know and hate, so your funding problem may not be as tight as you think."

"Not Crossenshield," Kris said, whispering the name of the chief of Wardhaven Security, maybe all U.S. security, as more of a curse than a name.

"The same," Captain Drago said.

"What part of our soul does he want this time?" Jack asked.

"He hasn't given back the part of my soul he lied about last time," Kris growled.

"But he does have money, and we need funds to outfit this ship and hire a crew," Drago said with a businessman's honesty.

They stepped aside as a large something-or-other was guided past them on a large electric platform. Two men walked to either side to make sure nothing got hammered. A third man, with a large wrist unit, walked first. The ship parted before him like the Red Sea did for Moses, and a ramp down to the next deck opened as he tapped a few keys.

"One thing you have to remember about this *Wasp*—yesterday's passageway may be today's bulkhead," Captain Drago said dryly.

"So sorry about that," Katsu said, hurriedly. "All the work was planned out carefully so we could avoid things like that. It's just that the *Wasp* is the prototype, and we are discovering that our planning could have been better. We will do better next time. The *Kagerō* is taking less time than the *Wasp*. We expect to turn out the next four frigates in four months, from starting the seed to commissioning."

"Four months to hatch a fully operational warship with half a battleship's broadside!" Kris said.

"Four months, but the frigates do not have a broadside," Katsu said. "All four of the guns are in the bows. The specs say you can deflect their beams by fifteen degrees up, down, or sideways. We are thinking of adding a fifth 18-incher pointed aft, but getting that much straight space through engineering and the rocket engines is a problem we haven't solved."

Kris shook her head. "Battleship lasers on a ship this size! The ability to change it from a comfortable cruise ship to a man-of-war with the flip of a switch, and another flip of a switch and you have two ships, one to take your civilians out of harm's way and the other ready to fight tooth and nail. Please, Katsu-san, you have nothing to apologize for."

"There are no switches on the *Wasp*," Katsu corrected Kris. "You select what you want from a menu and tap the screen."

"Never debate fine points of technology with an engineer," Penny said with a laugh.

They followed Captain Drago up two flights of stairs. Stairs: nice, wide, and comfortable. No doubt in a more combative mode, they would be steeper and more naval ladders. The bridge Captain Drago proudly presented to them was more spacious than the old *Wasp*'s. There were several extra stations; Kris wondered if they'd be there in combat or were just for helping with the fitting out. Just now, they were being operated by shipyard personnel and seemed devoted to system tests.

"Guns is your station, Your Highness," Drago said, pointing at a station where Kris's old weapons position had been. "Defense is in the same place, Lieutenant Pasley. It's a bit more complicated than the last one, but Katsu-san tells me it's very intuitive. Don't let him get away without giving you a full demonstration."

"I would not think of doing so," Katsu insisted.

"My cabin is just off the bridge," Drago said, pointing at one door in the rear of the bridge. "Your Tactical Center is right next door. You should be able to hear me bellow for you. By the way, there is a back door into your center. Please don't go traipsing around my bridge every time one of your team goes out for coffee."

"We will respect the sanctity of your Holy of Holies," Kris assured the skipper.

"Good, then let's head down for chow."

Captain Drago led them off the bridge through Kris's Tactical Center. At present, except where doors intervened, huge screens covered the walls, showing Japanese landscapes or maybe scenes from Musashi. Kris couldn't tell. What she did notice was that they stretched from deck to overhead. No one had skimped on the ship's fittings.

The wardroom seemed identical to the old *Wasp*, only more spacious. Katsu admitted that they had modified the original facade of many of the ship's areas to match pictures brought by the old crew from their last ship.

Smart Metal™ truly was a miracle material.

Until it turned on you, as Kris had found out many times in the past.

While they went through the steam tables and filled their plates, Kris recited a litany of times Smart Metal™ had failed to perform as advertised, or even tried to kill her.

Katsu listened silently through the list.

Only when they were seated at their table did he venture a reply. "I read of your experiences on the *Typhoon* and the

Firebolt. I did not know about the time a boat of the metal turned to liquid, but I should have realized that the dumb metal came from somewhere."

He took out his chopsticks and stared at them for a moment before picking up a rice ball wrapped in raw fish. "I have tested all the changes I have made to your Grandfather Alex's Smart Metal on a ship of our own construction, the *Kashi*, Strong Oak, in your language. It has bent, but it has not broken. We ran it at five gees for six hours, three out and three back. I believe in what I have done. If you wish, I will ride in your *Wasp* until you are totally satisfied with my work."

He put the rice ball in his mouth, chewed it for a second, then grinned. "And maybe while I am showing you the ropes of my ship, you can show me the ropes of your computer. I feel like Fumio-san and I are crawling while everyone around me is racing off at the speed of light."

Kris took a slice out of her broiled chicken and nodded. "We may both take each other up on that."

Since the ship wasn't yet in commission, Gunny had followed along, even into the wardroom. As he settled down, Nelly interrupted the supper discussion.

"Kris, there is a man at the quarterdeck with two footlockers and a request to see you."

"Do you know him, Nelly?"

"He is not identifying himself, but he says he very much wants to meet you."

"Is he carrying a weapon?" Jack demanded.

"No, but when we scanned his footlockers, they seemed filled with electronic gadgetry. None of which I recognized."

"Maybe I better check on this," Gunny said, and left his supper to grow cold as he jogged out.

Kris had time for just five more bites of her supper before Gunny escorted two men into the wardroom. One was a short older fellow, sporting a beer belly that on a woman would mean a birth in a couple of months. Maybe weeks.

The other fellow was tall, with jet-black hair and olive skin. His bearing was quite aristocratic.

The short fellow stepped forward first. "Your Highness, I'm Chief Beni."

Kris dropped her fork.

"Pardon me, I'm Senior Master Chief Beni, retired. My boy sailed with you until recently. I'd like to sail with you now. Once upon a time, I could claim to have taught my son everything he knew. Well, that was no longer true I hear, but, ma'am, this old seadog ain't too long in the tooth to learn some new tricks."

Kris stared at the man. There, underneath the wrinkles and sags, was the spitting image of the young chief. "I'm sorry for your loss," Kris said.

"Me and the missus really miss him, but, ma'am, I ain't here to talk about what can't be. He died doing a Sailor's job. I want a chance to take a bite out of them that did it to him."

"He lived through the fight," Kris said, feeling guilt anew at losing Longboat 3 with all hands.

"Yes, ma'am. I know he died getting fuel so the rest of you could make it home. Still, you wouldn't have been in that fix if them bastards hadn't chased you until you were damn near dry. Please, Your Highness, give me a chance. I served in a long peace. There's a fight coming. Let me have a chance to show what I can do."

He added, "I brung along a lot of my gadgets. They're good for a lot more than that store-bought crap."

"As your son so often proved," Kris said. "Chief Beni, you're welcome to our company. I have no idea what the pay is, but what we have, we'll give you a share."

"Don't need no pay, ma'am. I got my retirement. But that chow does smell good. Mind if I take a plate?"

"Help yourself, Chief."

The old chief made a beeline for the steam tables. Clearly, the son had come by his predilections honestly.

The second man stepped forward. With a nod that might have served as a slight bow, he said, "I am Joao Labao, on leave from the University of Brazília, at your service. You have a reputation of providing scientists with many opportunities to see the galaxy, discover what they never dreamed of, and, no small matter this, also write papers that bring wide acclaim, renown, and no small amount of awards. Like the old chief, I am no longer at my prime in creating great scientific insights, but I have some skill at getting, what do you call them, boffins, to work together rather than descend into bickering."

"You willing to work for food?" Kris asked.

"As I said, I am on a fully paid sabbatical."

"Captain Drago, you seem to know a whole lot more about the state of our personnel. Are we going to have a science team this trip out?"

"Several of your boffins who returned with the *Wasp* have already reported. God help us, that includes Tweedle Dee and Tweedle Dum."

"They will be a challenge I look forward to," Professor Labao said with a most aquiline smile.

"Amanda Kutter is also here," the skipper added. "She wants to have first crack at studying the bird people's economy."

"If she helped save my neck, she's earned it," Kris said, then eyed the scientific administrator. "Well, it seems we have needs of your services, Professor. Why don't you get a plate, and we will break bread together and share salt. It may be all the pay I have for you at the moment."

Kris leaned back in her chair. "I can offer no pay. I have nothing at hand but a chance to risk your neck on the other side of the galaxy. Haven't any of these people heard about how dangerous it is to get too close to a damn Longknife?"

"Ah," the skipper said, "there are damn Longknifes, and then there is Kris Longknife."

"I've never noticed a difference," Kris grumbled.

"We have," Jack said, and gave Kris's hand a discreet squeeze.

Kris shook her head, she'd think about that later. Now she turned to Captain Drago. "Since it's clear I now have a ship, or at least a hole in space I need to throw money into, I guess you better talk to Admiral Crossenshield. Mind you, he can have no more than a quarter of my soul. An ounce more, and we walk, you hear?"

"One of his minions is lurking around a dive on High Kyoto. I think I can seal the deal in my blood tonight. No need for you to prick your little finger."

"Last time I danced to his tune, I came near to getting my head chopped off."

"Almost doesn't count, insisted my sainted grandfather, veteran of the Iteeche War under your great-grandfather."

"Now I know you're just making things up," Jack said through a chuckle. "There can't be a saintly anything in your family tree."

"I am cut to the quick," the skipper said, and dismissed himself.

"Are things always like this around the princess?" Katsu asked.

"Nope," Abby said. "You're catching her on one of her better days."

Katsu studied a piece of fish tempura and seemed to be rethinking his bargain of the afternoon. But by the time he put it in his mouth, he looked less inclined to run for the dock.

At breakfast the next morning, Captain Drago reported that the deal had been done. The ship now had a sufficient line of credit to draw on.

"My contact asked me to remind you that the line of credit is the *Wasp*'s, not yours. It will be audited, and it will be my neck on the block if the bean counters don't agree with the charges."

"Since I am of late only too familiar with having my neck too close to the chopping block, I will try to take it easy on yours," Kris assured him.

Kris had hardly gotten a bite of her bran muffin when Nelly interrupted her. "Kris, I have a message from your brother. It's highest priority, and he sent it in the clear."

Kris sat up straight. "What does Brother have to say?"

A holo of him appeared on the table before Kris. "You were right about Grampa Al. He and several other kings of industry and trade are collecting a fleet of fast merchant ships at star system M-688. Inspector Foile is brilliant; I couldn't have done it without him. Father has ordered a squadron of heavy cruisers out to chase them down and is sending me for political clout. However, they're scheduled to leave their collection point soon."

The date he gave was *way* too soon.

"Kris, we think these ships can do up to two gees acceleration, and who knows how many revolutions, right or left. If we don't catch them before they head out, we may never. I know

I can't get there before they take off. I hear a rumor that you have a new ship. A new model. Can *you* get to system M-688 before they jump out of it?"

Kris turned to Captain Drago. "Can we?"

The skipper tapped his commlink. "All hands to battle stations."

Then he turned to Kris and smiled. "Let's get to my bridge, where these things can be done properly."

61

Captain Drago settled into his command chair. Kris took her usual station at Weapons. Penny slipped into her chair at Defense.

"Guns, what's our status?" Drago asked into his comm-link.

"Locked and loaded. Get me out of space dock, and I'll show you what we can do."

"We'll likely do that very soon."

"We'll be ready."

Drago tapped off and tapped back on. "Engineering, how soon before we can get under way?"

"If you give the order, Skipper, I can start heating up the reactors and be at full power in three hours."

"Start feeding your dragons, Manuel. I want to be clear of the dock in four hours."

"It will be so."

"What about the scientists and crew?" Kris asked.

"Those that are here, like you, spent the night aboard," the skipper shot back to Kris as he rang off and punched for a new line.

Kris had spent the night in her new quarters. They were very familiar and also very strange. With the exception of the mattress on her bunk, everything was Smart Metal™. Even the cushion on the station chair at her desk was the stuff. She'd given the springs a good once-over; they were metal, and they were soft.

Stranger and stranger, this ship that was now hers.

"Cookie," Captain Drago snapped. "Have you placed your orders for supplies?"

"Put them all in before breakfast this morning. Enough food to feed the whole crew of the old *Wasp*. Delivery should start in thirty minutes. Why?"

"We sail in four hours. Can you get it all aboard?"

"On the old *Wasp*, I'd say you were joking. This new one . . . I just might be able to get it all on board and stored away in some fashion. Could I have that nice boy, Katsu-san, help me move the stuff around?"

The nice "boy" had followed Kris to the bridge looking for all the world like a dazed puppy. Now he beamed, "I can do that. No problem," and was off at a gallop.

"What will we do about the vacant crew slots?" Kris asked. Sulwan Kann, the *Wasp*'s navigator since forever, had found a guy at High Chance and stayed behind when Drago and most of the crew shipped out.

"Yes, what *are* you going to do about your vacant crew slots?" A familiar voice said from the main bridge hatch.

"Captain Miyoshi!" Kris exclaimed. "What brings you to these parts?"

"My ship sensors report that your lasers are all charged. and your reactors are powering up. The powers that be tell me that your captain here has a full line of credit and is in the final process of fitting out. 'Very strange behavior,' say my superiors. 'Go find out what is going on,' I am told. So, what is going on?"

What Kris thought was going on might be nothing at all if some of her more basic assumptions turned out not to be true. Captain Miyoshi's visit might just pull the rug out from under her.

Kris began slowly to see how much rope she had and if it would be enough to hang herself. "Captain. I was told the *Wasp* was a gift to me and mine. Does it fly the U.S. flag or Musashi's?"

"Good question. Could it fly the Longknife flag?" Captain Miyoshi asked.

"Don't even think that, sir. I about got my hair cut all the way down to my throat because some folks claimed I'd gone pirate. What colors do I fly?"

"Captain Drago?" the Musashi captain asked.

"Last night I was provided with a complete set of papers for a U.S. Navy ship. I am prepared, however hastily, to commission this ship as the U.S.S. *Wasp*."

"I believe my superiors can accept that. Now, why all the commotion?"

"We need to be someplace very quickly," Kris said.

"And like so many things about you, Commander, you are less than forthcoming with details."

"I'm sorry, sir, but yes."

"But wherever you are going, you will need a navigator."

"Yes, sir."

"The assistant navigator on the *Mutsu* would do very well I think. She should be along in an hour. What other positions do you need filled?"

Captain Drago shot him a list. Captain Miyoshi studied it, then nodded. "I will send it along to my XO. They should all be here within an hour. Some wives and husbands will be unhappily surprised, but they knew the problem when they married Sailors."

"I don't want anyone drafted against their will," Kris said.

"I've noticed that about you, Commander. Don't you think the sight of this ship fitting out has not caused talk along the docks? The men and women who will be joining you packed their seabags several days ago."

The main bridge screen lit up. Kris found herself facing a young commander. "Ahoy *Wasp*, I am Abe Toshio, commanding the *Sakura*. I see that you are making final preparation to get under way. Where are we going?"

Kris glanced at Captain Miyoshi. He grinned. "I will be joining Commander Abe on the *Sakura*. I have been made commodore of Frigate Division One. My orders are rather vague. What did you say in court? 'Follow your movements and look out for the interests of my Imperial master.'"

"Something like that," Kris said. Then she turned to Drago.

"What kind of atom laser do we have aboard? We won't be going anywhere if it's a standard model."

"I didn't leave Wardhaven without a Mod 12 in my seabag. Big seabag. If I'm not mistaken, the *Sakura* is also equipped with the latest."

Any atom laser below the Mod 12 could not sense the new "fuzzy" jumps that had been critical to the old *Wasp*'s survival.

And very likely would be critical to Kris getting to the M-688 system ahead of her brother.

"Then Captain Miyoshi, you may inform your command that we will be departing under sealed orders in four hours. I will inform you of our destination after the first jump."

"One more thing, Your Highness," Captain Miyoshi said. Kris wasn't sure, but that might be the first time he addressed her as such. It was certainly the first time he said it and actually seemed to mean it.

"Yes, Captain."

"Usually you travel with a Marine company for protection."

"I like to think they are put to more uses than just protecting me," Kris said.

Jack shot her a look.

"I have been asked to offer you the service of the Marine company that protected you at Fujioka House. Captain Montoya, you are familiar with them."

"I found them to be the best," Jack said.

"For the protection detail, the company was reinforced with two squads of MPs, two squads of sappers, and a squad of forensic experts. My superiors are willing to detach the reinforced company for service aboard the *Wasp*."

Kris liked the offer but saw the problem. "And what will the chain of command for this look like?" she asked.

"For the Marines, Captain Montoya to Imperial Marine Captain Hayakawa Mikio. For the Sailors, Captain Drago to his division chiefs to the men and women. As for where you fit in, Your Highness . . . ?"

"I consider myself her flag captain," Captain Drago said, barely keeping a grin off his face, "and we make do as best we can. I think I understand. If you can loan me a Command

Master Chief to work with my Command Master Chief, I think we can fit things together on the fly."

"Where there is a will, there is always a way," Captain Miyoshi said, and departed.

Kris left her station and quickly covered the distance to navigation. "Nelly, sync with this station and load the new star map that we have."

"Doing it as we speak," Nelly said.

"Now, find me a way from Musashi to M-688."

"There are several routes. What assumptions do we make?"

"Good point. Let's take a step back. Show me M-688."

It appeared on the nav screen. It wasn't much of a system. Several planets large and larger were close in to the sun. Farther out were a mixture of rocky and gaseous ones in no particular order. Nothing worth a second look for human or Iteeche.

There were two jumps in the system. One led to and from human space. The other was marked in red. It led to an equally undesirable planet.

In the Iteeche Empire.

No wonder the system had been ignored.

But if the second jump was hit at a high speed, high acceleration, and a good twist on the ship, what might happen?

"Nelly, venture a guess for two hundred thousand klicks per hour, two gees, and twenty revolutions per minute from Jump Point Beta."

A slice of possible results formed a twenty-degree arc stretching out five hundred to a thousand light-years.

"That would be well beyond the Iteeche Empire," Kris muttered.

"And headed back to where there be sea monsters," Captain Drago said.

"Nelly, I want to come barreling into that system via Jump Point Beta. Can we do that?"

"If we accelerate toward Musashi's Jump Point Gamma at two gees, snap up to three gees at the jump, and put on twenty RPMs clockwise," Nelly said, "that should take us to this system with two fuzzy jumps. If I can trust my estimates, we can get up to five hundred thousand klicks an hour and jump to this system." A red line now connected Musashi to three distant systems.

"We decelerate after the next jump and come barreling in, as you say, to M-688 at two hundred thousand klicks per hour. I hope no one is in the jump, or even close to it."

Kris took a step back, eyeing the course. Once more, she was piling on the risks. If Brother's information was right, and Nelly's guesses could be trusted she'd be coming in system a good four hours before the first merchant ship would be trying to make its jump.

How much did she trust Nelly's course? Even the computer admitted that high-speed navigation was as much guess as science. And could she count on a fleet of merchant ships drawn from half a dozen different wealthy and powerful men, full of hubris, to follow a leaked schedule?

"Captain Drago, please tell me that you see a safer course of action," Kris said.

Drago just shook his head. "You're the one with the mouthy computer. Mine just does what I tell it to do."

"Kris, I can't guarantee any of what I'm showing you," Nelly said.

"But it's the best you have," Kris said.

"It is the best I can come up with."

Kris glanced at Jack.

He shrugged and smiled. "It looks like a good idea at this time."

62

They were only a half hour late getting under way.

Then, as they backed out of dock, the first surprise arose.

"Pier Tie-Down 1 refuses to release."

"Can you give me a picture of the problem?" Katsu was in full engineering mode. The picture appeared in a small window of the main screen. He studied it.

"Ah, some extra Smart Metal is clogging the tie-down. I can fix that." He started tapping on his Smart Metal Controller™.

"The *Sakura* is having the same problem," Senior Chief Beni, ret., called from sensors. He was sharing it with a much younger chief from Musashi who nodded in agreement but seemed a bit too shy to point out the failure of her elders.

"I'm sending the correction to *Sakura*," Katsu announced.

There was a slight catch as each pier tie-down came up for release, but no further hang-ups. The undocking took only two minutes more than expected.

They quickly cleared the controlled space around High Kyoto station and went to two gees acceleration for Jump Point Gamma, with the *Wasp* ahead by a hundred klicks and the *Sakura* offset fifty klicks to port.

The trip should have taken four hours. It took more.

Guaranteed for five gees, things still broke loose at two. Four times they had to slow to one gee. Once, they even went into free fall. The captain was philosophical about it. "New ships need shakedowns. New designs really need a shake-down."

Kris didn't have time for a shakedown cruise. She didn't have time for much of anything. Katsu was both her enemy and her hero at the same time. She demanded that he quit apologizing for everything that went wrong. "Don't apologize. Fix it!"

She relented on her plan to go slow with Katsu and his new computer Fumio. Nelly helped sync Fumio with the Smart Metal Controller™, and things moved faster.

Kris wished she could have arranged for a better interface between her engineer and his new gadget, but there wasn't time for that. When things slowed down, Kris would fix that.

No, when things sped up.

No, when they got where they were going, then she'd take time.

Right now, time was what she didn't have enough of, and it was running away from her faster and faster.

Five hours into the four-hour trip, things seemed to have settled into their new normal. Kris turned to Captain Drago. "If we're going to high gees after the jump, shouldn't we be getting into our high-gee stations?"

"You'll want to go to your quarters," Katsu told Kris. "The new system works best as a second skin," he said with a blush.

"Well, that should simplify the uniform of the day," Kris growled, and headed for her room to find . . . something . . . waiting for her. It looked like an egg on tiny wheels. She tapped the OPEN HERE spot, and something that might have been a chair appeared. Stripping quickly, she settled herself into the egg, and it closed around her.

Just like that, the double weight she'd been feeling at two gees vanished. She wiggled, and the thing wiggled with her. She knew the thing was in touch with every inch of her body, but she didn't feel that way. Her memories of a summer day at the lake in a bikini seemed more confining.

She pointed her right index finger at the door, and the egg moved off. The door opened automatically before Kris. Her door was a door, not an airtight hatch. Kris headed for the bridge and found that the egg flowed easily over the hatch coaming.

"Enjoying your new toy?" Captain Drago asked drolly from his own shiny egg.

"I think so," Kris said. "How does it work when nature calls?"

"It's supposed to handle both liquid and solid waste. I'm told it will even give you a bath. It would be nice to come out of high gee without the crew smelling like they'd lived in a stable for a month."

"We'll see what we see," Kris said, only seconds before Katsu rolled onto the bridge in his own egg.

"What do you think of it? I designed it myself," he said.

"Feels pretty good, Katsu-san. Can I fight from in it?"

"The station will sync with your battle station. As you move your hands, finger, and feet, the station will react as if you were touching it."

Kris rolled over to her Weapons station, said "Sync" and immediately began moving her hands and fingers.

And almost fired Laser 1.

"Safety this station," she snapped, and the firing sequence stopped. "Let's try that again," and Kris went through the motions of setting up a firing solution with the board flashing THIS IS A DRILL.

Two hours, thirty-five minutes behind schedule, the *Wasp* kicked it up to three gees, took on 20 RPMs clockwise, and vanished into the Gamma Jump.

It took the navigator a few moments to identify the star field in front of them. The *Sakura* joined them as the young lieutenant at Nav announced, "We covered some six hundred light-years. We jumped right across the Iteeche Empire, I think."

"She's got that right," Nelly said. "This is within five light-years of the system I was aiming for. It should have two of the new jumps."

"I only see one jump," the navigator said, more puzzled than disagreeing.

"Turn up the gain on your atom laser," Kris said. "The Mod

12 is very sensitive. We're looking for only a breath of gravity disturbance."

The young woman adjusted her board, and two fuzzy points in space appeared in the space ahead of them.

"Nelly, which one?" Kris said.

"Aim for the farthest one," Nelly said. "If we keep four-gee acceleration on, we should reach it in nine hours and be making close to five hundred thousand klicks per hour. Go to thirty-five revolutions per minute, but in a counterclockwise direction."

"For someone who's guessing, your computer seems to be very exact," Captain Drago said.

"It's a computer thing. So sue me," Nelly said.

The young lieutenant on Nav looked dismayed, but the skipper growled, "Make it so," and she did. She also radioed the *Sakura* its new course. If there was dismay at the other end of the line, it was not given voice.

Nine hours later, the *Wasp* disappeared into the fuzzy jump. Kris no longer had any idea whether they were on schedule or not.

The *Sakura* had hardly had time to join them when the navigator said, "We have jumped three thousand light-years. And there are three of those strange jump points in this system."

"I show no activity in this system," Senior Chief Beni reported to Kris's relief. This far out, anything was possible. So far, her Longknife luck was holding.

The good Longknife luck.

"Time to head back, Nelly."

"Reduce acceleration to two gees. Head for the closest jump. We'll be using 25 RPMs, still counterclockwise," Nelly said cryptically.

Kris did not ask if this was the system Nelly had been aiming for, and Nelly did not offer it. If where they were was close enough, it was good enough for Kris.

Kris tried to catch a nap while they covered the distance to the next jump. She ended up sleeping through the next jump only to awaken to Nelly's saying, "That wasn't what I wanted."

"How bad is it?" Kris and the skipper asked together.

"We're farther out toward the rim of our arm," Nelly said.

"We've got the entire Iteeche Empire between us and M-688. It's time to start decelerating, but if I'm wrong on this next jump, I may need to use my Iteeche."

Now the young navigator did look terrified.

"Don't worry," Kris said. "I have friends at the Iteeche Emperor's court."

Both the navigator and Katsu showed disbelief.

"Nelly, try to aim us carefully this time," Kris said.

"I'm *always* aiming us carefully," Nelly said. "If we decelerate at 3.85 gees and take the next jump at three hundred thousand klicks and 20 RPMs clockwise, I think we'll be just one jump from M-688."

BUT WE WILL LIKELY BE ON THE ITEECHE SIDE OF THE LINE, KRIS.

SO LONG AS IT PUTS US IN REACH OF M-688, NELLY, I'LL TAKE THE RISK.

Which left Kris wondering if she should spend the remaining time checking out her Weapons station or composing a "We come in peace" speech in Iteeche.

"Penny, let's get the *Wasp* into a good defensive mode. At this acceleration, no one is using their bed or research station. We may have to fight at M-688."

"You think those merchant ships will be armed?" Penny asked.

"With all they're carrying and the problems we've had with pirates in out-of-the-way places, I certainly wouldn't go out here unarmed. I can't see my Grampa Al being any less ready to defend what's his."

"You have a point," Penny said.

After giving all hands thirty minutes of warning, Penny selected CONDITION ZED on her board, and the *Wasp* began to change around them.

"Did you ever test this change of system at near four gees, Katsu-san?" Kris suddenly thought to ask.

"No," he admitted.

Kris adjusted her board to show defense on half of it. NELLY, HAVE YOU TALKED TO FUMIO-SAN ABOUT ALL THIS NEW STUFF?

YES, KRIS. ALL OF MY KIDS ARE WORKING WITH FUMIO-SAN TO MONITOR THIS, THANK YOU VERY MUCH FOR FINALLY THINKING OF THAT.

Katsu only had to intervene twice during the five minutes the *Wasp* took to shrink down into fighting form.

"I'm not sure," Chief Beni reported, "but I think the *Sakura* just got smaller and tighter."

No one was asleep nine hours later as they took the next jump.

"That's not good," Nelly said, even before the navigator made a report. "We're in Iteeche territory. One advanced planet and some asteroid-mining operations. The jump we want is a normal one, and it's three hours away, Kris."

"Chief, any Iteeche ships close by?"

"None that I'd call close, but there are several deeper in the system near the colony."

"Nelly, send this message. This is Princess Kris Longknife of United Society. I am on a mission for Roth'sum'We'sum'Quin Cap'sum'We related to hostile alien sighting by Iteeche ships. We will be departing this system in three hours. Please advise the Imperial court of our visit."

"Think that will work?" Captain Drago asked.

"We'll know in what, forty minutes?"

In twenty minutes, one of the Iteeche Death Balls well sunward suddenly went to two gees and headed in their direction. "They spotted us," Kris whispered. "Now what happens when they get our message?"

Ten minutes later, the Death Ball slowed to only one-gee acceleration. It was still headed their way, but they would be long gone before it got in range.

Kris started breathing again.

Katsu brought his egg close to Kris's. "I saw that you had friends in high places in the Emperor's court of Musashi, but the Iteeche high court as well?"

"Sometimes I even surprise myself," Kris admitted.

Now only one problem remained. If the next jump went right, she'd be arriving a good hour before the exodus of the trading, or traitor, fleet began. How would she handle that?

It was a sure bet that giving commands naked would not carry the full power of her convictions. The egg hardly could be better. She steered back to her cabin and, despite weighing three times normal, managed to put on undress whites with ribbons. If she had to make a statement, she'd have all of her history backing her up.

And, of course, there would be the Longknife thing. She'd use everything in her quiver before she'd use the 18-inch guns.

She motored back to the bridge a good thirty minutes before the jump. Katsu was right. The seams in the uniform, to say nothing of the belt and clutch backs on her ribbons, were a real pain. Clearly, for the foreseeable future, until someone came up with a seamless shipsuit, the new battle dress would be bare-ass naked in an egg.

That was bound to cause talk.

The time came for the jump. Since it was to be a more conventional jump, Kris ordered a messenger buoy sent through three minutes before the *Wasp*. Its message was simple. Ship coming through. She'd let the folks on the other side stew about what ship and whose.

At the right second, they entered the jump doing fifty thousand klicks an hour and with the ship rock steady.

☐n the other side of the jump, Kris found herself face-to-face with the flagship of Grampa Al's fleet, *The Glory of Free Enterprise*. It was accelerating at 1.5 gees and already doing 75,000 klicks per hour. It was also just out of the 18-inchers' range at 120,000 klicks.

With the *Wasp* decelerating at one gee from 50,000 klicks, and the *Enterprise* accelerating up from 75,000 klicks, there would not be a lot of time to talk.

Kris opened her egg and stood up to face the forward screen. "*Glory of Free Enterprise*, this is Princess Kris Longknife, Commander, Royal U.S. Navy. You are ordered to change course away from this jump and begin deceleration immediately."

A hard-bitten middle-aged man in full merchant-marine greens showing four stripes stared at Kris from the main screen. "I take my order from the old man himself, Alex Longknife. No girlie whelp is going to boss me around."

"Be advised, this 'girl' has four 18-inch lasers targeting your bucket. You'll be in range in ten seconds. What part of your boat do you want me to slice off first?"

"What kind of ship is that?" he was heard to mutter.

"This is the frigate U.S.S. *Wasp*, and this is your final warning. Change course or be fired upon."

"You wouldn't dare."

Kris stepped back and slipped into her Weapons station. Nelly had Laser 1 locked on the bell of the starboardmost rocket engine. THIS SHOULD ONLY NIP IT, BUT IT WILL KNOCK IT OFF COURSE, AND THEY'LL KNOW THEY'VE BEEN HIT.

"Cease deceleration. Flip ship," Kris ordered, and the *Wasp* did. "Fire one."

A second later, the scowling skipper on the screen was knocked sideways as his ship's engines lost their careful balance.

"I dared," Kris said. "Fleet following the *Free Enterprise*, decelerate and change course, or I will disable your engines."

"This is Captain Christoph Guisan in the *Pride of Zurich*, and I fly the flag of the Helvitican Confederacy. You will not fire on me."

"Captain, Admiral Channing died fighting per my orders. I will fire on anyone who risks making those heroic peoples' deaths be in vain. Don't cross me."

NELLY, TARGET THE ENGINES OF THE NEXT THREE SHIPS IN LINE.

ALREADY DOING IT, KRIS.

Kris started a slow five count in her head.

At the count of three, the next ship in line flipped and started decelerating and steering off to port. By the five count, all the ships were flipped, decelerating, and doing it in directions that would take them well away from the jump.

Kris still had a problem. She was rapidly heading in the opposite direction from the others. If she didn't do something radical, she'd be out of range, and these ships could thumb their nose at her and go back to their original course.

She sat back into her egg. "Captain, put us into a four-gee deceleration. I want to stay in range of those ships as long as we can."

The orders were quickly given. As Kris expected, those ribbons and the belt really hurt. She'd be bruised in the morning. Too bad she hadn't worn her spider silks.

And then, Jump Point Alpha began to spit out ships halfway across the system.

It took thirty minutes before their first message came

through. It was brother Honovi demanding that the ships stay in the system.

"You're late to the party, Bro," Kris sent, then attached a copy of her conversations with the merchant skippers.

An hour later, Kris got a happy message from her brother. "Sis, the media types are really eating up your message. Did you really shoot up Grampa Al's pride and joy? Where'd you get the 18-inch guns? Let's rendezvous at the system's big gasbag. I'm ordering the merchants to meet me there."

Kris waited until the various flags' merchant ships began to set course for the gas giant, then was relieved to switch back to a one-gee acceleration.

Kris was right. She was bruised on her belly and breasts. Which begged the question. Now that they were back on a warship, how could she manage to have Jack kiss them and make them well?

Kris sighed, recalling the way the poor girl who had gotten pregnant was treated on *Haruna*. Maybe, once this cruise was over, she and Jack could take a month's leave in an out-of-the-way place that had never heard of a damn Longknife.

Yeah, right.

But this cruise had hardly started and Kris needed to get ahead of matters before the alligators started chewing on her rump. She called a staff meeting in her new Tactical Center.

As she settled into her place at the head of the table, she found herself staring at one whole wall that was totally blank. No lovely wooded mountain in a morning mist. "I guess not everything handled four gee as well as other stuff," Kris said.

"That is not made from my Smart Metal," Katsu was quick to point out.

"I'll see if I can find a repair technician among the crew," Captain Drago said.

Kris went to the first item on her list. "We're going to be meeting in orbit, which means a whole lot of no gravity. Do you think we could arrange to swing ourselves around the *Sakura* and get some down aboard the *Wasp*?"

Kris quickly explained to Katsu Admiral Krätz's idea of having two ships pass a long beam between them, head-to-head. As they swung around each other, you got a stronger and stronger sense of "down" the farther you were from the center of the beam.

"We can do that," the engineer said happily.

"That will make us the most likely venue for a meeting to butt heads," Kris said. "Do we have a Forward Lounge?"

"It's there but very empty," Captain Drago said.

"We'll tell them to bring their own bottles," Jack said.

Kris nodded. "Moving right along, how are we set for food on a long voyage?"

"Cookie brought on three months' worth of good chow and another three months' of beans, other dried goods, and canned meats. I figure everyone can eat in either the wardroom, chief's mess, or crew mess. There aren't that many of your boffins."

"You could store more," Katsu offered helpfully.

"Maybe we can buy some stuff off these ships," Penny suggested. "They aren't going anywhere but home."

Professor Labao cleared his throat. "I hope you can get some better food off those other ships, and maybe a few restaurateurs. There are a few more of *your* boffins than I think either one of you are aware of."

"More?" Kris said, raising an eyebrow. "How could there be more scientists? We got away from High Kyoto in four hours."

"And thirty-five minutes," Captain Drago added.

The professor cleared his throat again. "I put out a call to Kyoto University the night before. Then, when I heard you at breakfast in the wardroom, I made a second, more hasty call. Kyoto is a very cosmopolitan university. It has researchers from all over human space as well as some of the best that Musashi and Yamato have to offer. I have two hundred and fifty researchers aboard as you slipped the bounds of that friendly port."

"We've been running around with two hundred people I didn't know about?" Captain Drago growled.

"They might have slipped aboard, but they couldn't have brought much research gear," Penny pointed out.

"Yes, they are aboard, dear captain, and yes, most of them are lacking essential instrumentation for their work. However, I overheard where we were going, and before the first jump, we placed orders for all the sensors and instruments we needed. There should be a merchant ship following behind your brother full of delicate scientific gear."

"Is there a merchant ship following Honovi's cruiser squadron?" Kris asked.

"Five," the captain growled, still unhappy to have stowaways. "The heavy repair ship *Vulcan* is also along."

"The *Vulcan*?" Kris said. The last time she'd seen that repair ship, it had helped outfit her corvettes with Hellburner torpedoes. "What's it doing here?"

"Hopefully to help us fix things like your dead wall monitor," Katsu said.

"Hopefully," Kris agreed, but hope was not what she was feeling at the moment. They went on for another hour, covering the adminutiae of running a ship far from its base, but there were no more surprises.

Kris was getting to like no surprises. But it happened so rarely, she doubted she'd ever get used to it.

At the gas giant, the *Sakura* and *Wasp* connected and began their spin. That created a problem. Docking a longboat with a spinning target was a hard-learned skill, but it turned out that the heavy cruiser *Exeter* had quite a few Navy personnel from the old *Wasp*, including the eight bosuns who were already trained in catching the hook and being reeled into the *Wasp*'s spinning boat deck.

When Kris was advised that Brother and all the captains were aboard, she headed to the Forward Lounge, prepared to play the congenial, if barless, hostess.

That was just her first mistake of the evening.

Glasses were clinking happily as she entered the lounge. To her right was the bar and a very familiar sight.

"Mother MacCreedy, what are you doing here?"

Said woman stood, three beer mugs in hand, filling them in sequence with hardly a drop spilled from the tapped keg. She didn't look up from her work but called over her shoulder, "I heard you had a ship and a thirsty crew, so of course, I dropped what I was doing and came."

"Mother, we're headed for the other side of the galaxy."

"Yes, I know. I've been there, and folks are just as thirsty there as anywhere else. What will you have?"

"The usual," Kris said, and turned to business, knowing that a tall soda water and lime would be showing up at her table. There were advantages to the familiar.

Brother held down the table in front, with the view. He waved, and she joined him. "Nice place you got here. I especially like the down. Down is nice. My stomach likes down. Think I could stay here tonight?"

"Just be sure to get ashore when we tell you to. Our next stop is a long way from your wife and kid."

"Soon to be kids," Brother interrupted.

"And as my captain likes to say, there be sea monsters where we're going."

"About those sea monsters," Brother said. "I've brought you some gifts. Four of those transports are carrying Hellburners. A gift from Grampa Ray."

"And what am I supposed to do with them this time?" Kris asked with a jaundiced eye. She was still wanted on 162 planets for what she'd done with the last three, and Grampa Ray, King Raymond to most, had been noticeably silent about what he'd intended her to do with those gifts.

"Maybe we should talk about this in private," Brother started, then seemed to catch the full drift of Kris's question. "No, I don't care if everyone here hears this. Father was there with half his cabinet when King Ray told me you should use these where you see fit. 'She's going into hostile country. She needs the best we have.'"

The lounge had grown silent as Honovi talked. Half the people there were listening as Kris got her orders. Okay. Fine. Maybe.

"Four?" Captain Drago said.

"Two for the *Wasp* and two for the *Sakura*. I'm told the frigates can handle two each." At the next table, Katsu was grinning from ear to ear and nodding.

"We are most definitely headed into 'hostile country,'" Kris said. She'd first heard the expression "hostile country" in an ancient vid. It was 2-D no less. Then she discovered that the original words "Indian country" had been blocked out of the sound track. The blood of Apache, Sioux, Blackfoot, and

Crow flowed in Longknife veins. Kris didn't like the meaning of "Indian country" or "hostile country."

Then she discovered the original meaning of "off the reservation." The idea that human beings would lock other human beings up in such squalor! The more Kris studied old Earth, the less she liked it.

Kris chose to rephrase her orders, using an old sea dog for her guide. "Give me a well-armed ship, for I intend to go in harm's way."

"That's my sis," Bro said, raising his glass. Kris's glass arrived just in time for her to share the toast. Then the work of the night began. Bro stood up, called for silence, and told the ship captains gathered there that they would be following him back the way they came.

A burly captain stood up and spoke for everyone. "I don't take my orders from you even if you are one of those damn Longknifes." The general rumble of the room strongly agreed with him.

Kris tugged at her brother's arm. "Bro, let me handle this one."

"It's all yours," he said, sounding relieved as he sat down.

Kris stood and eyed the standing captain. Under her glare, he sat down, and the room acquired silence. "Just for the record, would one of you mind telling me what you intended to do with all these ships loaded up with the best humanity has to offer?"

"We was going to find them aliens you pissed off," a tall thin man said as he stood. "Show them us humans could be reasonable. That we all could benefit from trade."

"And they would do what?" Kris asked, just as nice as a sweet princess could.

"Open trade. They're not stupid. If we don't go off shooting at them, they won't go all bloody on us."

Kris glanced back at Jack and the crew that had fought with her. As one, they shook their heads.

Kris thought for, oh, a second. She'd met a lot of folks who didn't have a clue as to what happened out there. Maybe she could catch more flies with a little education. "Nelly, run the film of our first encounter with the small alien ship."

The four forward screens showed the ship of connected

spheres launch itself from the moon. The audio gave voice to the *Wasp*'s effort to establish contact.

Then the ship fired on them.

"Notice, we talked. They shot," Kris said. In a few moments the ship exploded. "Note that my shots only damaged the ship. They blew themselves up."

There were murmurs among the ship captains.

"Show the alien advanced guard," Kris ordered.

The two aliens that came through the jump gate before the mother ship filled the screen. Once more, the audio was filled with different efforts to establish contact. On view, the eight human battleships did an about-turn and began to open the distance between them and the aliens.

Then, without a word spoken, the two aliens blew *Fury* out of space.

"You'll excuse us if, after that, we blew them to pieces as quickly as we could," Kris said, as the alien ships did, indeed, explode.

In a blink, Nelly let the mother ship fill the entire forward screens. Now the room was silent enough to hear several people chug their drinks.

The retreating battle line was still sending contact signals as the huge ship opened fire, and battleships began to explode.

"Nelly, zoom in on *Chikuma*." The battleship was mortally wounded and spewing survival pods. Lasers swept through them, vaporizing all. "Under the laws of war, agreed to by all humans, and now, even the Iteeche Empire, survival pods are sacred and noncombatant. You can see how these aliens treated them."

Now the screen showed the Hellburners smashing into the huge alien ship for a few seconds, then Nelly let it go to black.

Hands on hips, Kris eyed the merchant skippers before her. "You are not going out there. You aren't going because I say so and because every one of you and all of your crews will be dead in a month, maybe in a week, if you don't do what I tell you."

The lounge got even quieter.

"But we aren't warships. We're unarmed merchant ships that just want to talk to them. Open trade negotiations," the burly captain insisted from his chair.

"You think that will make a difference? Four times we met these vicious space raiders. Every time I did everything within my power to open communications. Three times they tried to kill us, and the fourth time, we ran away before they got the chance. You think I *wanted* to fight that huge bastard? I'm a Longknife. I'm not insane."

The room stayed silent as what they had seen slowly sank into thick skulls.

"What am I going to do?" a captain grouched. "I can likely sell my cargo, but I signed on extra hands. Even if I lay the rest off, I got a year's worth of food for my normal crew."

"We can probably take some of it off your hands," Kris said.

"Don't you go paying too high a price for that," Mother MacCreedy called from the bar. "We got a shipful of fine victuals. This is not a seller's market."

Kris let others handle the haggling. For once, she enjoyed kicking back and catching up on family matters. When was the new baby due? Had Grampa Ray actually sounded like he intended to take responsibility for what Kris did with this set of Hellburners? She introduced Honovi to Jack and let the two males do their thing.

"Inspector Foile is a good cop. A very good cop," Brother said. "I understand that you and my sister are friendly. Very friendly."

"She certainly can use someone covering her back," Jack said.

Kris decided to cut this guy stuff out. "Brother, I intend to marry Jack. Assuming he'll have me, and that things ever slow down so we can."

Jack showed thunder at his brow for a second, whether because Kris had stepped into a guy thing, or because, as he said next, "I'm glad I'm not the last to hear about that proposal."

"I said 'if you'll take me,' Jack. And we haven't exactly had two seconds to call our own since we quit being fugitives from the law and gave ourselves, well, myself up. I figured I'd better get my bid in before some other girl comes along and gives you a better offer."

Jack squeezed her hand, what looked to be all the intimacy

the *Wasp* was going to allow them. "There will never be another woman in my heart."

"Hey, as a member of parliament, I can marry people. You want to do it now?" Honovi sported a wide grin.

"And have Mother never speak to Kris again?" Jack said.

"It sounds better and better," Kris said.

"Um," Brother switched to a frown. "But I share a planet with Mother and regularly work with the old gal, Sis. I'm afraid I'm backing out of my offer."

"Coward," Kris said.

"From the looks of things, you got all the courage in this generation, and I think you need it."

Kris couldn't disagree with that. So they talked the night away, and Kris stayed an unmarried lady. Jack did squeeze her hand regularly, and they managed a good-night kiss at the door to her cabin when they parted early the next morning.

64

Captain Drago ordered refueling after breakfast. That involved separating the *Wasp* into two ships. This time, the smaller, single-engine half did the cloud dancing. The *Sakura* did the same. Kris mentioned she'd like to go along.

Jack said nothing, but the look on his face told her all she needed to hear. She dropped out of the expedition. Katsu insisted he should go, "just in case." He returned several hours later, white as a sheet. "We don't pay the guys who get our reaction mass nearly enough. Not nearly enough."

Kris had been busy while the two fragments were gathering reaction mass. "Where do I get one of those?" was on several lips, including Brother's. Kris gave Mitsubishi Heavy Space Industry a full promo, pointing out that the cost of the *Wasp*, assuming mass production, could be the same as a *Typhoon*-type fast corvette.

"There are nine construction slips at Nuu Yards on High Wardhaven, three of them battleship-size from the Iteeche War," Kris pointed out. "They could be turning out a dozen of these frigates every four months. They cost less, have a smaller crew, and are just as good as a battleship."

"But how much will Mitsubishi want for the modified Smart Metal?"

"I have no idea," Kris said, "but I hope squabbling over money doesn't stop Grampa Ray from getting the fleet he wants."

Honovi just shrugged, as if Kris really didn't understand the real world.

The *Vulcan* came alongside, and the two frigates stopped their circling long enough for some heavy stuff to be brought over. Wardhaven had had more recent experience in shoot-outs, and Kris had considered the *Wasp* too lightly armed.

Now the repair ship sent six twin batteries of 5-inch secondary lasers over to both frigates, and Katsu found himself very busy making adjustments. Kris wanted the *Wasp* expanded, not just to accommodate the Marines and boffins more comfortably but also to carry enough reaction mass to make all the jumps to the other side of the galaxy without refueling. Grampa Ray's gifts didn't just extend to the Hell-burners and secondary guns. Both frigates got two dozen of the fast-acceleration missiles with antimatter warheads as well as plenty of foxers and chaff pods.

Next fight, Kris would be loaded for bigger bears.

While shipfitters roamed the *Wasp*, Kris took Senior Chief Beni to lunch and asked him if he'd like one of Nelly's kids. Professor Labao just happened to be in earshot and asked if he could be included. Captain Drago was also within hearing, but he declined with haste. "Watch out for the nightmares," he warned.

"What nightmares?" the chief and professor asked together.

"I do not make mistakes twice," Nelly assured them, as they adjourned to the ship's electronic-maintenance shop so Nelly could guide the chief in creating the headgear his son had designed to help her kids commune directly with their humans. Kris corralled Katsu and included him in the upgrade.

An hour later, Kris left three new man-machine interfaces. The old sea dog was deeply intent; the professor and the engineer looked downright euphoric.

The *Wasp*'s crew was also augmented by quite a few Sailors from the old *Wasp*. That included the old Marine company at full strength, leaving Kris with two Marine companies on board. While Captain Drago grumbled and had Katsu expand his ship, Abby was quite happy to have Sergeant Bruce in easy reach. Nelly was also glad; Bruce brought Chesty with him.

Now all six of her surviving kids were home.

Two days later, the frigates got under way for Jump Point Beta at two gees while the U.S. cruisers herded the merchant ships toward Alpha at one gee.

The *Wasp* and the *Sakura* hit the jump at two hundred thousand klicks, spinning at thirty-five RPMs *clockwise* and goosed up to 3.5 gees. Nelly was quite pleased with the results.

"We jumped right over the Iteeche Empire and we're within five light-years, both in azimuth and range, of my projections. This system has three of the new jumps. Aim for the middle-distant one and let's hold four gees. We'll take this one at thirty-five RPMs counterclockwise and tack toward the edge of the galaxy."

Nelly guided them on a course that first headed them toward the edge, then more inward of the galaxy. After the next jump, they were up to seven hundred thousand klicks, and they made their way to the next two jumps at a pleasant one gee.

The *Wasp* had started out at thirty-five thousand tons. The Hellburners had added thirty thousand tons; these were slightly smaller than the first ones. Tests had showed that the antimatter hadn't gotten to all the neutron material, and rather than waste three thousand tons of the stuff, these missiles were smaller. At sixty-five thousand tons, the two frigates had then added thirty thousand tons of reaction mass spread around in a whole lot of medium-size tanks. A conventional ship could never have done that.

More and more, as the *Wasp* grew and shrank around Kris, she was sure she was riding the wave of the future.

On the far side of the galaxy, Nelly ordered them to four-gee deceleration, and they came to rest in a system closer to the rim but only one slow jump from where the *Intrepid* had located the new civilization.

Kris ordered the two frigates to a gas giant. The *Sakura Jr.* headed down to do some cloud dancing and capture needed reaction mass. The *Wasp Jr.* trotted over to the jump that should take them to the bird people and poked the periscope through.

Everyone held their breath while Senior Chief Beni went

through the electromagnetic spectrum. "There's radio and TV signals from there. They're in the bird format. None of that impenetrable space-raider crap. I think you folks did it."

That brought a cheer and a sigh and a lot of other hard-to-name feelings. Too many good men and women had died so the people in that next system could live.

Kris found herself whispering a prayer of thanksgiving to any god listening.

"Kris," Nelly said. "My kids and I have been going over the original traffic that came back with the *Intrepid*. Yes, I know we should have done this sooner, but we've been kind of busy until now."

"Spit it out, Nelly," Kris said.

"The *Intrepid* thought they'd just made their first space launch. I'm not sure that's entirely right. They may have been returning to space. And the rig that they used. There were no close-ups of it. And what we saw was very grainy. Optics is not their strong suit." A picture appeared in a window of the bridge's main screen.

It was way past blurry. "Can you clean that up, Nelly?"

"We've tried, Kris. The bottom is clearly an old-fashioned liquid-fuel rocket, obsolete since before humans got serious about leaving Earth. It's what's on top that has us puzzled." Nelly zoomed in, and the picture got even worse.

"I can't tell anything about that," Kris said.

"Yes, I know, Kris, but it's about the right length and width for the kind of gigs they knocked together during the Iteeche War to move a few people from ship to ship or ship to planet."

"Do we have a picture of one of those gigs?" Jack asked.

"Yes, but not really," Nelly said. "It's from an archive that no one thought we'd ever need. It's been compressed six or seven times. The metadata is vague."

"So is the picture," Kris said. She looked at the two pictures and could tell nothing about either. She told Nelly so.

"Yes, Kris, I know they don't look like much, but our analysis says there is a fifty-percent chance that they are one and the same. Usually, I don't bother you with fifty-percent probabilities, but this one . . ."

It was unusual for Nelly to be at a loss for words. Very unusual.

"Let's get this fueling over with and see what's over there," Kris said.

Twelve hours later, they took the last jump at dead slow with the frigates rock steady.

Once in system, they put on one-gee acceleration toward the source of all their curiosity.

65

"Nelly, how's the translation business going?"

"Better than you have any right to expect but not nearly as well as you clearly want," Nelly shot back. Kris noticed that Jack and Penny and all the others with one of Nelly's kids had been leaving their computers alone.

Kris decided to leave Nelly to her work.

An hour later, Nelly said, "Kris, we have identified references to three kinds of people. There are The People, and then there are the Old People and the Heavy People. The difference between the Old and the Heavy is a slight inflection in what sounds like the same word to me. Worse, the Old ones appear to be more mythical, although they are referred to a lot."

"Gods?" Jack asked.

"That's possible. The Heavy People are spoken about in the present tense, we think, but not a lot."

With little more than that, they continued to close on the planet.

It was the old chief who made the next discovery. "I'm getting a beeper. It's not much of anything, but it sounds like a ship's navigational warning signal."

"Have you interrogated it?" Kris shot back.

"I've tried, but it doesn't respond. It could be something entirely different from what I'm taking it for."

"We'll see," Kris said, and settled into her Weapons station. All four lasers were charged and locked. Beside Kris, Penny was shrinking the *Wasp* down to fighting trim, Condition Baker. Not enough to make staterooms disappear, but empty spaces were getting smaller as the hide of the ship thickened, and reaction mass was sent to cool the honeycombed places beneath the armor.

The chief reported that the *Sakura* was doing the same.

Halfway to the planet, they flipped ship and began to decelerate at a bit more than one gee. That put most of the sensors pointed away from the planet, but Kris's Navy folks weren't the only ones ready to work Smart Metal™. Several of the boffins' sensors slithered over the hull to get a better view of the planet.

They made the next discovery.

"There's a ship or station in orbit around that planet," Professor Labao reported. "Our optical scopes are clearly picking up a large platform of some sort."

"Pass it through to our screen," Kris snapped, beating Captain Drago to the order by a hair. The planet was a lovely blue-green orb, just what a living planet should look like. The visual zoomed in. It lost its focus, then regained it. There was a dot moving across the face of the planet. It reached the night terminator and vanished into the dark.

"We estimate an hour before we reacquire it," the professor said.

"That's the source of my signal," the chief added.

"It's going to be a long hour," Kris said. "Can you show me anything?"

An elongated blob appeared on the screen.

"Do you have any better optics?" Kris asked.

"We are working on bringing the best we have online," Professor Labao said. "Maybe in an hour."

Fifty-five minutes later, the planet jumped into finer focus as the new scope checked it out. Five minutes later, they got a much better view of the mystery.

"That's a starship, but what kind?" Kris asked.

"It looks like one of our old battlecruisers," Nelly said.

"Iteeche War period and stripped of all its ice." Two pictures appeared on screen. One ship was nice and curved, clad in its full ice armor. The other one, fresh out of the yards, looked rather naked. The mystery ship and the naked one looked remarkably similar.

"I've reacquired the beeper," Chief Beni reported. "I got something this time. Let me double-check. Nope, it won't answer me again."

"What did it say?" Captain Drago demanded.

"Let me check historical logs, sir. This code ain't in today's book."

Every eye on the bridge turned to the old chief.

"If this old log is right, we're looking at the Society of Humanity Battlecruiser *Furious*, sir."

"*Furious?*" Kris said, stumbling from her station. Her great-grandmother Rita Nuu Longknife had commanded the *Furious* in a wild fight that saved half of her husband Ray's battle line. The *Furious* had vanished into a jump accelerating and spinning like no ship back eighty years ago could hope to survive.

"Unknown ships on approach vector to Alwa, identify yourself," came as a surprise, both because it wasn't expected . . . and because it was in Standard.

The main screen flickered several times, then settled down to show a woman who might be Kris . . . if she lived to be a hundred.

"Princess, this one is yours," Captain Drago whispered.

Kris stood. "I am Princess Kristine Longknife, commanding the United Society explorer ship *Wasp*." Kris paused, hunting for words, then hastily added. "We come in peace. Who do I have the honor of addressing?"

The message went out. It would take at least ten minutes to get there and just as long to get back. Kris stayed standing, staring at the screen.

The woman was doing the same. The mike was turned down, but Kris could hear her saying something to people offscreen. Kris herself turned to those around her, but she had nothing to say.

Then a child of two raced into view, threw its hands up at the woman, and was lifted up for a hug. A younger woman,

likely the mother, galloped on-screen in hot pursuit of the tod-
dling escapee, but the older woman would not surrender the
vagrant.

Kris's message must have gotten there at that moment. The
older woman eyed the screen. "Princess Longknife, you say.
Does that mean Ray somehow got himself a crown?" The
woman frowned. "Did my little Alex grow up and have kids?
That squirt is about the only thing I missed from the back and
gone. If you're a Longknife, you're likely related to me. I'm
Rita Nuu Ponsa, once a Longknife and a ship captain. Come
on down here. There's a passel of family for you to meet."

Kris collapsed into her chair at Weapons.

Captain Drago ordered the helm to maintain course and
one-gee deceleration. Jack came to stand beside Kris, working
the tight muscles of her neck and upper back.

"Let's hope this family reunion goes better than the last
one you tried," he said.

About the Author

Mike Shepherd grew up Navy. It taught him early about change and the chain of command. He's worked as a bartender and cabdriver, personnel advisor and labor negotiator. Now retired from building databases about the endangered critters of the Northwest, he's looking forward to some fun reading and writing.

Mike lives in Vancouver, Washington, with his wife, Ellen, and close to his daughter and grandchildren. He enjoys reading, writing, dreaming, watching grandchildren for story ideas, and upgrading his computer—all are never-ending pursuits.

He's hard at work on Kris's next story: *Kris Longknife: Defender,* as well as several other books set in Kris's universe.

You can learn more about Mike and all his books at his website www.mikeshepherd.org, e-mail him at Mike_Shepherd@comcast.net, or follow Kris Longknife on Facebook.

An original military science fiction novella from

MIKE SHEPHERD

KRIS LONGKNIFE:
Welcome Home / Go Away

A Penguin Group eSpecial from Ace

Kris Longknife is back home from her galactic adventures, but her entire Fleet of Discovery has been annihilated. And the alien race that she fought has now declared war on humanity. Some people think Kris is to blame, and it may take more than the efforts of her war-hero great-grandfather to save her from the wrath of the angry—and frightened—citizens of her home planet!

• • •

Praise for the Kris Longknife series

"A rousing space opera that has extremely entertaining characters."   —*Night Owl Reviews*

"Kris can kick, shoot, and punch her way out of any dangerous situation, and she can do it while wearing stilettos and a tight cocktail dress."   —*Sci Fi Weekly*

Only available as an e-book!
Download it today!

facebook.com/AceRocBooks
mikeshepherd.org
penguin.com

M1140T0712